Southern Cross

Also by Patricia Cornwell

patricia cornwell

southern cross

DOUBLEDAY DIRECT LARGE PRINT EDITION

g. p. putnam's sons

new york

This Large Print Edition, prepared especially for Doubleday Direct, Inc., contains the complete unabridged text of the original Publisher's Edition.

g. p. putnam's sons
Publishers Since 1838
a member of
Penguin Putnam Inc.
375 Hudson Street
New York, NY 10014

Copyright © 1998 by Cornwell Enterprises, Inc.

All rights reserved. This book, or parts thereof, may not be reproduced in any form without permission. Published simultaneously in Canada.

ISBN 0-7394-0188-2

Printed in the United States of America

**This Large Print Book carries the
Seal of Approval of N.A.V.H.**

This is a work of fiction. The events
and characters portrayed are imaginary.
Their resemblance, if any, to real-life
counterparts is entirely coincidental.

To Marcia H. Morey
World champion in juvenile justice
reform and all you've ever done
For what you've taught me

chapter one

The last Monday morning of March began with promise in the historic city of Richmond, Virginia, where prominent family names had not changed since the war that was not forgotten. Traffic was scant on downtown streets and the Internet. Drug dealers were asleep, prostitutes tired, drunk drivers sober, pedophiles returning to work, burglar alarms silent, domestic fights on hold. Not much was going on at the morgue.

Richmond, built on seven or eight hills, depending on who counts, is a metropolitan center of unflagging pride that traces its roots back to 1607, when a small band of fortune-hunting English explorers got lost and laid claim to the region by planting a cross in the name of King James. The inevitable settlement at the fall line of the James River, predictably called "The Falls," suffered the expected tribulations of trading posts and forts, and anti-British sentiments, revolution, hardships, floggings, scalpings, treaties that didn't work and people dying young.

Local Indians discovered firewater and hangovers, and traded herbs, minerals and furs for hatchets, ammunition, cloth, kettles and more firewater. Slaves were shipped in from Africa. Thomas Jefferson designed Monticello, the Capitol and the state penitentiary. He founded the University of Virginia, drafted the Declaration of Independence and was accused of fathering mulatto children. Railroads were constructed. The tobacco industry flourished and nobody sued.

All in all, life in the genteel city ambled along reasonably well until 1861, when Virginia decided to secede from the Union and the Union wouldn't go along with it. Richmond did not fare well in the Civil War. Afterward, the former capital of the Confederacy went on as best it could with no slaves and bad money. It remained fiercely loyal to its defeated cause, still flaunting its battle flag, the Southern Cross, as Richmonders marched into the next century and survived other terrible wars that were not their problem because they were fought elsewhere.

By the late twentieth century, things were going rather poorly in the capital city. Its homicide rate had climbed as high as second in the nation. Tourism was suffering. Children were carrying guns and knives to school and fighting on the bus. Residents and department stores had abandoned downtown and fled to nearby counties. The tax base was shrinking. City officials and city council members didn't get along. The governor's antebellum mansion needed new plumbing and wiring.

General Assembly delegates continued slamming desktops and insulting one another when they came to town, and the chairman of the House Transportation Committee carried a concealed handgun onto the floor. Dishonest gypsies began dropping by on their migrations north and south, and Richmond became a home away from home for drug dealers traveling along I-95.

The timing was right for a woman to come along and clean house. Or perhaps it was simply that nobody was looking when the city hired its first female police chief, who this moment was out walking her dog. Daffodils and crocuses were blooming, the morning's first light spreading across the horizon, the temperature an unseasonable seventy degrees. Birds were chatty from the branches of budding trees, and Chief Judy Hammer was feeling uplifted and momentarily soothed.

"Good girl, Popeye," she encouraged her Boston terrier.

It wasn't an especially kind name for a dog whose huge eyes bulged and pointed at the walls. But when the SPCA had shown the puppy on TV and Hammer had rushed to the phone to adopt her, Popeye was already Popeye and answered only to that name.

Hammer and Popeye kept a good pace through their restored neighborhood of Church Hill, the city's original site, quite close to where the English planted their cross. Owner and dog moved briskly past antebellum homes with iron fences and porches, and slate and false mansard roofs, and turrets, stone lintels, chased wood, stained glass, scroll-sawn porches, gables, raised so-called English and picturesque basements, and thick chimneys.

They followed East Grace Street to where it ended at an overlook that was the most popular observation point in the city. On one side of the precipice was the radio station WRVA, and on the other was Hammer's nineteenth-century Greek Revival house, built by a man in the tobacco business about the time the Civil War ended. Hammer loved the old brick, the bracketed cornices and flat roof, and the granite porch. She craved places with a past and always chose to live in the heart of the jurisdiction she served.

She unlocked the front door, turned off the alarm system, freed Popeye from the leash and put her through a quick circuit of sitting, sitting pretty and getting down, in exchange for treats. Hammer walked into the kitchen for coffee, her ritual every morning the same. After her walk and Popeye's continuing behavioral modification, Hammer would sit in her living room, scan the paper and look out long windows at the vista of tall office buildings, the Capitol, the Medical College of Virginia and acres of Virginia Commonwealth University's Biotechnology

Research Park. It was said that Richmond was becoming the "City of Science," a place of enlightenment and thriving health.

But as its top law enforcer surveyed edifices and downtown streets, she was all too aware of crumbling brick smokestacks, rusting railroad tracks and viaducts, and abandoned factories and tobacco warehouses with windows painted over and boarded up. She knew that bordering downtown and not so far from where she lived were five federal housing projects, with two more on Southside. If one told the politically incorrect truth, all were breeding grounds for social chaos and violence and were clear evidence that the Civil War continued to be lost by the South.

Hammer gazed out at a city that had invited her to solve its seemingly hopeless problems. The morning was lighting up and she worried there would be one cruel cold snap left over from winter. Wouldn't that be just like everything else these days, the final petty act, the eradication of what little beauty was left in her horrendously stressful life? Doubts crowded her thoughts.

When she had forged the destiny that had brought her to Richmond, she had refused to entertain the possibility that she had become a fugitive from her own life. Her two sons were grown and had distanced themselves from her long before their father, Seth, had gotten ill and died last spring. Judy Hammer had bravely gone on, gathering her life's mission around her like a crusader's cape.

She resigned from the Charlotte P.D., where she had been resisted and celebrated for the miracles she wrought as its chief. She decided it was her calling to move on to other southern cities and occupy and raze and reconstruct. She made a proposal to the National Institute of Justice that would allow her to pick beleaguered police departments across the South, spend a year in each, and bring all of them into a union of one-for-all and all-for-one.

Hammer's philosophy was simple. She did not believe in cops' rights. She knew for a fact that when officers, the brass, precincts and even chiefs seceded from the department to do their own thing, the result was catastrophic. Crime rates went up. Clearance rates went down. Nobody got along. The citizens that law enforcement was there to protect and serve locked their doors, loaded their guns, cared not for their neighbors, gave cops the finger and blamed everything on them. Hammer's blueprint for enlightenment and change was the New York Crime Control Model of policing known as COMSTAT, or computer-driven statistics.

The acronym was an easy way to define a concept far more complicated than the notion of using technology to map crime patterns and hot spots in the city. COMSTAT held every cop accountable for everything. No longer could the rank and file and their leaders pass the buck, look the other way, not care, not know the answer, say they couldn't help it, were about to get around to it, hadn't been told, forgot, meant to, didn't feel well or were on the phone or off duty at the time, because on Mondays and Fridays Chief Hammer assembled representatives from all precincts and divisions and gave them hell.

Clearly, Hammer's battle plan was a northern one, but as fate would have it, when she presented her proposal to Richmond's city council, it was preoccupied with infighting, mutiny and usurpations. At the time, it didn't seem like such a bad thing to let someone else solve the city's problems.

So it was that Hammer was hired as interim chief for a year and allowed to bring along two talents she had worked with in Charlotte.

Hammer began her occupation of Richmond. Soon enough stubbornness set in. Hatred followed. The city patriarchs wanted Hammer and her NIJ team to go home. There was not a thing the city needed to learn from New York, and Richmonders would be damned before they followed any example set by the turncoat, carpetbagging city of Charlotte, which had a habit of stealing Richmond's banks and Fortune 500 companies.

Deputy Chief Virginia West complained bitterly through painful expressions and exasperated huffs as she jogged around the University of Richmond track. The slate roofs of handsome collegiate Gothic buildings were just beginning to materialize as the sun thought about getting up, and students had yet to venture out except for two young women who were running sprints.

"I can't go much farther," West blurted out to Officer Andy Brazil.

Brazil glanced at his watch. "Seven more minutes," he said. "Then you can walk."

It was the only time she took orders from him. Virginia West had been a deputy chief in Charlotte when Brazil was still going through the police academy and writing articles for the *Charlotte Observer.* Then Hammer had brought them with her to Richmond so West could head investigations and Brazil could do research, handle public information and start a website.

Although one might argue that, in actuality, West and Brazil were peers on Hammer's NIJ team, in West's mind she outranked Brazil and always would. She was more powerful. He would never have her experience. She was better on the firing range and in fights. She had killed a suspect once, although she wasn't proud of it. Her love affair with Brazil back in their Charlotte days had been due to the very normal intensity of mentoring. So he'd had a crush and she had gone along with it before he got over it. So what.

"You notice anybody else killing himself out here? Except those two girls, who are either on the track team or have an eating disorder," West continued to complain in gasps. "No! And guess why! Because this is stupid as shit! I should be drinking coffee, reading the paper right now."

"If you'd quit talking, you could get into a rhythm," said Brazil, who ran without effort in navy Charlotte P.D. sweats and Saucony shoes that whispered when they touched the red rubberized track.

"You really ought to quit wearing Charlotte shit," she went on talking anyway. "It's bad enough as is. Why make the cops here hate us more?"

"I don't think they hate us." Brazil tried to be positive about how unfriendly and unappreciative Richmond cops had been.

"Yes they do."

"Nobody likes change," Brazil reminded her.

"You seem to," she said.

It was a veiled reference to the rumor West had heard barely a week after they had moved here. Brazil had something going on with his landlady, a wealthy single woman who lived in Church Hill. West had asked for no further information. She had checked out nothing. She did not want to know. She had refused to drive past Brazil's house, much less drop by for a visit.

"I guess I like change when it's good," Brazil was saying.

"Exactly."

"Do you wish you'd stayed in Charlotte?"

"Absolutely."

Brazil picked up his pace just enough to give her his back. She would never forgive him for saying how much he wanted her to come with him to Richmond, for talking her into something yet one more time because he could, because he used words with clarity and conviction. He had carried her away on the rhythm of feelings he clearly no longer had. He had crafted his love into poetry and then fucking read it to someone else.

"There's nothing for me here," said West, who put words together the way she hung doors and shutters and built fences. "I mean let's be honest about it." She wasn't about to paint over anything without stripping it first. "It sucks." She sawed away. "Thank God it's only for a year." She pounded her point.

He replied by picking up his pace.

"Like we're some kind of MASH unit for police departments," she added. "Who were we kidding? What a waste of time. I don't remember when I've wasted so much time."

Brazil glanced at his watch. He didn't seem to be listening to her, and she wished she could get past his broad shoulders and handsome profile. The early sun rubbed gold into his hair. The two college women sprinted past, sweaty and fat-free, their muscular legs pumping as they showed off to Brazil. West felt depressed. She felt old. She halted and bent over, hands on her knees.

"That's it!" she exclaimed, heaving.

"Forty-six more seconds." Brazil ran in place like he was treading water, looking back at her.

"Go on."

"You sure?"

"Fly like the wind." She rudely waved him on. "Damn it," she bitched as her flip phone vibrated on the waistband of her running shorts.

She moved off the track, over to the bleachers, out of the way of hard-bodied people who made her insecure.

"West," she answered.

"Virginia? It's . . ." Hammer's voice pushed through static.

"Chief Hammer?" West loudly said. "Hello?"

"Virginia . . . You there?" Hammer's voice scattered more.

West pressed a hand over her other ear, trying to hear.

". . . That's bullshit . . ." a male voice suddenly broke in.

West started walking, trying to get into a better cell.

"Virginia . . . ?" Hammer's voice barely crackled through.

". . . can do it anytime . . . usual rules apply . . ." The male voice was back.

He had a southern drawl and was obviously a redneck. West felt instant hostility.

". . . time to . . . kill . . . Got to . . . or score . . ." The redneck spoke in distorted blurts.

". . . an ugly dog not worth . . . lead to shoot it . . ." A second redneck suddenly answered the first redneck. "How much . . . ?"

"Depends on . . . Maybe a couple hundred . . ."

". . . Just between us . . ."

". . . If . . . body . . . finds . . ."

". . . not invited . . ."

"What?" Hammer's voice surfaced and was gone.

". . . Use a . . . cold nose . . . Not your piece . . . shit . . . ! Blue . . ."

"Chief Hammer . . ." West started to say more, then caught herself, realizing the rednecks might be able to hear them, too.

". . . coons . . ." The first redneck came back. ". . . not one born too smart for . . . Dismal Swamp . . ."

". . . Got that right, Bubba . . . We covered . . . a blanket . . ."

"Okay, Smudge . . . buddy . . . early morning?"

West was silently shocked as she listened to two men plan a homicide that clearly was racially motivated, a hate crime, a score to settle that involved robbery. It sounded as if the murder would go down early in the morning. She wondered if a *cold nose* was slang for a snub-nosed revolver and if *blue* referred to a gun that was blue steel versus stainless steel or nickel-plated. Clearly, the psychos planned to wrap the body in a blanket and dump it in the Dismal Swamp.

Static.

". . . Loraine . . ." Bubba's fractured voice was back. ". . . At old pumps . . . cut engine . . . headlights off so don't wake . . ."

Static, and the cell cleared.

"Chief Hammer?" West said. "Chief Hammer? Are you still there?"

"Bubba . . ." the second stranger crackled again. "Somebody's on . . ."

Static, scratch, blare, blip.

"Goddamn it," West muttered when her phone went dead.

Bubba's real name was Butner Fluck IV. Unlike so many fearless men devoted to pickup trucks, guns, topless bars and the Southern Cross, he had not been born into the tribe of Bubbas, but rather had grown up the son of a theologian in the Northside neighborhood of Ginter Park, where old mansions were in disrepair and Civil War cannonballs on porches were popular. Butner came from a long line of Butners who always went by the nickname "But," and it was lost on his erudite father, Dr. But Fluck III, that calling his son But in this day and age set the child up for problems.

By the time little But had entered the first grade, the slurs, the slander and the derision were on every tongue. They were whispered in class, shouted on buses and playing fields, and drawn on sheets of notebook paper slipped from desk to desk or left inside little But's locker. When he wrote his name it was But Fluck. In the teacher's grade books he was Fluck, But.

Any way he looked at it, he was screwed, really, and of course his peers came up with any number of other renditions. *Mother-But-Flucker, Butter-Flucker, But-Flucking-Boy, Buttock-Fluck,* and so on. When he retreated into his studies and went to the head of the class, new pet names were added to the list. *But-Head, Fluck-Head, Mother-Flucking-But-Head, Head-But-Head,* et al.

For But's ninth birthday he requested camouflage and several toy guns. He became a compulsive eater. He spent a lot of time in the woods hunting imaginary prey. He immersed himself in a growing stash of magazines featuring mercenary soldiers, anarchists, trucks, assault weapons, Civil War battlefields and women in swimsuits. He collected manuals on simple car care and repair, automotive tools and wiring, wilderness survival, fishing, and hiking in bear country. He sneaked cigarettes and was rude. His tenth year he changed his name to Bubba and was feared by all.

This early Monday morning Bubba was driving home from third shift at Philip Morris, his CB and two-way radios turned on, his portable phone plugged into the cigarette lighter, Eric Clapton on the CD player. His stainless steel Colt Anaconda .44 with its eight-inch barrel and Bushnell Holo sight on a B-Square base was tucked under his seat within quick reach.

Multiple antennas bobbed on his red 1990 Jeep Cherokee, which Bubba did not realize had been listed in the *Used Car Buying Guide* as a used car to avoid, or that it had been wrecked and had a hundred thousand more miles on it than the odometer showed. Bubba had no reason to doubt his good buddy, Joe "Smudge" Bruffy, who last year had sold the Jeep to Bubba for only three thousand dollars more than the Blue Book value.

In fact, it was Smudge who Bubba had been talking to on the portable phone moments earlier when two other voices broke in. Bubba hadn't been able to make out what the two women were saying, but the name "Chief Hammer" had been unmistakable. He knew it meant something.

Bubba had been raised in a Presbyterian atmosphere of predestination, God's will, inclusive language, exegesis and colorful stoles. He had rebelled. In college he had studied Far Eastern religions to spite his father, but none of Bubba's acting out had eradicated the essence of his early indoctrination. Bubba believed there was purpose. Despite all setbacks and personal flaws, he had faith that if he accumulated enough good karma, or perhaps if yin and yang ever got along, he would discover the reason for his existence.

So when he heard Chief Hammer's name over the cell phone, he experienced a sudden release of gloominess and menacing persecution, a buoyant happiness and surge of power. He was transformed into the warrior on a mission he had always been destined to become as he followed Midlothian Turnpike to Muskrat's Auto Rescue, this time for another windshield leak. Bubba snapped up the mike of his two-way Kenwood radio and switched over to the security channel.

"Unit 1 to Unit 2." He tried to raise Honey, his wife, as he followed the four-lane artery of Southside out of Chesterfield County and into the city limits.

No answer. Bubba's eyes scanned his mirrors. A Richmond police cruiser pulled in behind him. Bubba slowed down.

"Unit 1 to Unit 2," Bubba tried again.

No answer. Some shithead kid in a white Ford Explorer was trying to cut in front of Bubba. Bubba sped up.

"Unit 1 to Unit 2!" Bubba hated it when his wife didn't respond to him immediately.

The cop remained on Bubba's tail, dark Oakleys staring straight into Bubba's rearview mirror. Bubba slowed again. The punk in the Explorer tried to ease in front of Bubba, right turn signal flashing. Bubba sped up. He deliberated over what form of communication to use next, and picked up his portable phone. He changed his mind. He thought about trying his wife again on the two-way and decided not to bother. She should have gotten back to him the first and second times. The hell with her. He snapped up the mike to his CB, eyeing the cop in his mirrors and keeping a check on the Explorer.

"Yo, Smudge," Bubba hailed his buddy over the CB. "You on track come back to yack."

"Unit 2," his wife's out-of-breath voice came over the two-way.

Bubba's portable phone rang.

"Sorry . . . oh my . . ." Honey sweetly said as she gasped. "I was . . . oh dear . . . let me catch my breath . . . whew . . . was chasing Half Shell . . . she wouldn't come . . . That dog."

Bubba ignored her. He answered the phone.

"Bubba?" said Gig Dan, Bubba's supervisor at Philip Morris.

"Trackin' and yackin', buddy," Smudge came back over the CB.

"Unit 2 to Unit 1?" Honey anxiously persisted over the two-way.

"Yo, Gig," Bubba said into the portable phone. "What's goin' on?"

"Need ya to come in and work the second half of second shift," Gig told him. "Tiller called in sick."

Shit, Bubba thought. Today of all days when there was so much to do and so little time. It depressed the hell out of him to think about showing up at eight o'clock tonight and working twelve straight hours.

"Ten-4," Bubba replied to Gig.

"When you wanna shine on yellow eyes?" Smudge hadn't given up.

Bubba didn't really like coon hunting all that much. His coon dog Half Shell had her problems, and Bubba worried about snakes. Besides, Smudge always got a higher score.

It seemed all Bubba did was lose money to him.

"Before slithers wake up, I guess." Bubba tried to sound sure of himself. "So go ahead and shake out a plan."

"Ten-fo, good buddy," Smudge came back. "Gotcha covered like a blanket."

chapter two

Smoke was a special needs child. This had become apparent in the second grade when he had stolen his teacher's wallet, punched a female classmate, carried a revolver to school, set several cats on fire and smashed up the principal's station wagon with a pipe.

Since those early misguided days in his hometown of Durham, North Carolina, Smoke had been written up fifty-two times for assault, cheating, plagiarism, extortion, harassment, gambling, truancy, dishonesty, larceny, disruptive dress, indecent literature and bus misconduct.

He had been arrested six times for crimes

ranging from sexual assault to murder, and had been on probation, on supervised probation with special conditions, in an Alternative to Detention Program, in detention, in a wilderness camp therapeutic program, in a community guidance clinic where he received psychological evaluation and in an anger-coping group.

Unlike most juveniles who are delinquent, Smoke had parents who showed up for all of his court appearances. They visited him in detention. They paid for attorneys and dismissed one right after the other when Smoke complained and found fault. Smoke's parents enrolled him in four different private schools and blamed each one when it didn't work out.

It was clear to Smoke's father, a hardworking banker, that his son was unusually bright and misunderstood. Smoke's mother was devoted to Smoke and always took his side. She never believed he was guilty. Both parents believed their son had been set up because the police were corrupt, didn't like Smoke and needed to clear cases. Both parents wrote scathing letters to the district attorney, the mayor, the attorney general, the governor and a U.S. senator when Smoke was finally locked up in C. A. Dillon Training School in Butner.

Of course, Smoke didn't stay there long because when he turned sixteen, he was no longer a minor according to North Carolina law and was released. His juvenile record was expunged. His fingerprints and mug shots were destroyed. He had no past. His parents thought it wise to relocate to a city where the police, whose memories were not expunged, would not know Smoke or harass him any more. So it was that Smoke moved to Richmond, Virginia, where this morning he was feeling especially mean-spirited and in a mood to cause trouble.

"We got twenty minutes," he said to Divinity.

She was leaning against him as he drove the Ford Escort his father had bought him when Smoke had gotten his Virginia driver's license. Divinity started kissing Smoke's jaw and rubbing her hand between his legs to see if anybody was home.

"We got all the time you want, baby," she breathed in his ear. "Fuck school. Fuck that little kid you pick up."

"We got a plan, remember?" Smoke said.

He was in running shoes, loose-fitting

sweats, a bandanna around his head, tinted glasses on. He wound his way through streets within a block of the Crestar Bank on Patterson Avenue, in the city's West End, and spotted a small brick house on Kensington where there was no car or newspaper— no one home, it seemed. He pulled into the driveway.

"Anybody answers, we're trying to find Community High School," Smoke reminded her.

"Lost in space, baby," Divinity said, getting out.

She rang the doorbell twice and was met with silence. Smoke got into the passenger's seat and Divinity drove him back to Crestar Bank. The sky was pale and clear, and traffic was picking up as people began a new work week and realized they needed cash for parking and lunch. The bank's ATM wasn't doing any business at the moment, and that was good. Smoke climbed out of the car.

"You know what to do," he said to Divinity.

He walked toward the bank as she drove off. He went around to the drive-thru where he could not be seen. It wasn't long before a young man in a Honda Civic hatchback parked in front of the ATM. Smoke came out from behind the bank, taking his time. The young man was busy making his transaction and didn't notice Smoke's angled approach out of range of the camera.

Smoke was so swift his victims were always too shocked to move. He slapped duct tape over the camera lens and the man's eyes. Smoke jabbed the barrel of his Glock pistol into the small of the man's back.

"Don't move," Smoke said quietly.

The man didn't.

"Hand the money behind you real slow."

The man did. Smoke looked around. Another car was pulling off Patterson, heading to the ATM. Smoke snatched the duct tape off the camera lens and ran behind the bank. He started jogging, turning on Libbie Avenue, then Kensington. He slowed to a walk in the driveway of the small brick house where Divinity was waiting in the Escort.

"How much you get, baby?" she asked as Smoke casually climbed in.

"Twenty, forty, sixty, eighty, a hundred," he counted. "Let's get the fuck outta here."

Judy Hammer couldn't believe it. This had to be one of the most bizarre things that had

ever happened to her. Two white suprema-
cists named Bubba and Smudge were going
to murder a black woman named Loraine.
She lived near some sort of old pumps
where the killers would park and wait with
engines and headlights off. Money was involved, perhaps several hundred dollars.
Hammer paced, Popeye anxiously at her
heels. The phone rang.

"Chief Hammer?" It was West.

"Virginia. What the hell was that?" Hammer asked. "Any way we can trace it?"

"No," West's voice returned. "I don't see
how."

"I'm assuming we both heard the same
thing."

"I'm still on a cell phone," West warned.
"Don't think I should go into it. But it sounds
like something we'd better take very seriously."

"I completely agree. We'll talk about it after the presentation. Thanks, Virginia." Hammer was about to hang up.

"Chief? What were you calling me about
when I was on the track?" West quickly reminded her.

"Oh. That's right."

Hammer searched her thoughts, trying to

bring up what she was calling West about when the rednecks broke into their conversation. She paced, Popeye with her every step.

"Oh, I remember. We're already getting responses to our new website," Hammer said, pleased. "Since Andy's op-ed piece."

"That worries me," West replied. "I think we should have done a little troubleshooting, Chief."

"It will all be fine."

"What are they saying?"

"Complaining," Hammer replied.

"I'm shocked."

"Don't be cynical, Virginia."

"Any reaction to what he said about escalating juvenile crime? And *Richmond's gang mentality* about not having gangs, or however he put it? About the country's *desperate need for radical juvenile justice reform*?"

It was not lost on Hammer that whenever West talked about Brazil, West's attitude was sharp to bump up against. Hammer knew when West was hurt. Hammer recognized a sadness in Brazil as well, a light not quite so bright in his eyes, a sluggishness in the creative energy that so profoundly singled him out. Hammer wished the two of them would get along again.

"The phones started ringing off the hook about that the minute the newspapers hit the driveways," Hammer replied. "We're shaking people up. And that's exactly what we're here to do."

Hammer got off the phone. She retrieved Brazil's op-ed piece from the coffee table and glanced through it again.

> . . . This past week our city's *children* committed at least seventeen cold-blooded felonies, including rape, armed robbery and malicious wounding. In eleven of these violent, seemingly random acts, the *child* hadn't even turned fifteen yet. Where do children learn to hate and harm? Not just from the movies and video games, but from each other. We do have a gang problem, and let's face it, kids who commit adult crimes aren't kids anymore . . .

"I expect my popularity just took another dip," Hammer said to Popeye. "You need a bath. A little of that good cream rinse?"

Popeye's black-and-white coat was handsomely reminiscent of a tuxedo, but her fur was very short, her freckled, pink skin very sensitive and prone to get dry and irritated.

Popeye loved it when every few weeks her owner would put her in a sink of warm water and lather her up with Nusalt antiseborrheic therapeutic shampoo, followed by the Relief antipruritic oatmeal and pramoxine cream rinse that her owner kneaded into Popeye's fur for exactly seven minutes, as the directions prescribed. Popeye loved her owner. Popeye stood on her hind legs and nuzzled her owner's knee.

"But a bath will have to wait, I guess, or I'll be late." Her owner sighed and got down to Popeye's level. "I shouldn't even have brought it up, should I?"

Popeye licked her owner's face and felt pity. Popeye knew her owner was denying the grief and the guilt she felt about her late husband's sudden death. Not that Popeye had known Seth, but she had overheard conversations about him and had seen photographs. Popeye could not imagine her owner being married to a lazy, independently wealthy, fat, whiny slob who did nothing but eat, work in his garden and watch television.

Popeye was glad Seth wasn't around.

Popeye adored her owner. Popeye wished there was more she could do to comfort this heroic, kind lady who had saved Popeye from being an orphan or being adopted by some unhappy family with cruel children.

"All right." Her owner got up. "I've got to get going."

Hammer showered quickly. She threw a robe around her and stood inside her cedar-lined closet, deliberating over what to wear. Hammer understood the subliminal power of clothing, cars, office decor, jewelry and what she ate at business lunches and dinners. Some days required pearls and skirts, other days called for unfriendly suits. Colors, styles, fabrics, collars or no collars, patterns or plain, pockets or pleats, watches, ear-rings and perfumes and fish or chicken all mattered.

She shoved hangers here and there, de-liberating, envisioning, intuiting and finally settling on a navy blue suit with trousers that had pockets and cuffs. She selected low-heel lace-up black leather shoes and match-ing belt, and a blue and white striped cotton shirt with French cuffs. She dug through her jewelry box for simple gold post earrings and her stainless steel Breitling watch.

She picked out a pair of gold and lapis cufflinks that had belonged to Seth. She fumbled with them as she put them on and remembered those times when Seth followed her around the house like Popeye, unable to manage buttons, lapels, matching socks or combinations, on those rare occasions when Seth dressed up.

It would have made sense to divide her late husband's jewelry, leather briefcases, wallets and other things male between their sons, but Hammer held on. When she wore something of Seth's, she had the eerie feeling that he wanted her to be the man he never was. He wanted her to be strong. Maybe he wanted to help her because now he could. Seth had always had a good heart. But he had spent his life at war with his compulsions and privileged past, spreading misery like the flu. He had left Hammer wealthy, relieved, pained, pissed off and as burdened with anxieties as he had been with his weight.

"Popeye, come here," Hammer called out.

Popeye was lazy in a bar of sunlight on the kitchen floor. She had no intention of changing venues.

"Let's get in our crate, Popeye."

Popeye regarded her owner through slitted eyes. She yawned and thought it silly that her owner always used the *we* word, as if Popeye wasn't smart enough to see through it. Popeye knew her owner had no intention of climbing inside that little plastic crate with Popeye any more than her owner was going to eat a heartworm pill or get a shot at the vet when the *we* word was used about those, either.

"Popeye." Her owner's tone firmed up. "I'm in a hurry. Come on. In the crate. Here's your squirrel."

She tossed Popeye's favorite stuffed squirrel inside the crate. Popeye couldn't care less.

"All right. Here's your fuzzle."

She tossed in the filthy lambs' wool chick that Popeye had chewed the eyes off and routinely flung into the toilet. Popeye was indifferent. Her owner walked with purpose across the kitchen and picked up Popeye. Popeye went into her Salvador Dalí limply-drape-over-everything-and-play-possum manifestation. Her owner tucked Popeye into the crate and fastened shut the wire grate door.

"We need to behave better than this," her

owner said, feeding Popeye several little pieces of lung treats. "I'll be back real soon."

Hammer set the burglar alarm and went out to her unmarked midnight-blue Crown Victoria. She drove down East Grace, passing the back of St. John's Church and turning on 25th where Tobacco Row was now upscale apartments and Pohlig Bros still manufactured "paper boxes of every design." A graffiti artist had spray-painted "Meat is Murder" and "Eat corn" and "Anita Hill started it" on an abandoned tobacco warehouse, and rusting fire escapes and dead vines held on to old brick shells. One could get a bargain on used tires at Cowboy Tire, and Strickland Foundry and Machine Company had refused to quit.

On the other side of Broad Street, past the coliseum, was the police department where Hammer now spent her days in an ugly precast building with a blue mosaic trim missing many of its tiles. The Richmond Police Department was dim and too small, with windowless corridors, asbestos and the stale smell of dirty people and dirty deeds.

She said good morning to cops she passed, and out of fear they returned her greeting. Hammer understood the trauma of change. She understood a distrust of any influence that came from the outside, especially if its sanction was federal. Resentment and hostility were nothing new, but never had she experienced it quite like this.

At precisely seven o'clock, she walked into the conference room. It was crowded with some thirty unenthusiastic commanders, captains, detectives and officers who followed her with stares. Computer mapping of the city projected onto a large screen showed statistics for murder, rape, robbery, aggravated assault, burglary, larceny and auto theft, or the big seven, during the most recent twenty-eight-day COMSTAT period and also year-to-date. Charts showed time frames and probability and days of the week when crimes occurred, and in what precincts and during what shifts.

Hammer took her seat at the head of the table between West and Brazil.

"Another ATM," West said in a low voice in Hammer's ear.

Hammer looked sharply at her.

"We just got the call, are still at the scene."

"Damn," Hammer said as anger stirred. "I want the details ASAP."

West got up and left the room. Hammer looked around the table.

"Nice to see all of you here," she began. "We've got a lot to discuss this morning." She didn't waste time as she looked around and smiled. "We'll start with first precinct. Major Hanger? I know it's early."

"Always is," Hanger grumbled. "But I know that's how they do things in New York."

He nodded at Officer Wally Fling, Hammer's administrative assistant, who was new at working the computer-mapping software that everyone hated. Fling hit several keys and a pie chart filled the screen.

"I don't want the pie chart yet, Fling," Hanger said.

Fling hit several more keys and another pie chart popped up, this one for fourth precinct.

"Sorry," Fling said as he nervously tried again. "I guess you want first precinct."

"That would be nice. And I don't want pies."

Hanger got one anyway, this time for second precinct. Flustered, Fling hit more keys and the department's shield flashed on screen, with its motto, *Courtesy, Profession-*

alism and Respect, or CPR, which Hammer also had borrowed from NYPD.

Several people groaned and booed. Brazil gave Hammer an *I've tried to warn you* look.

"Why can't we have our own logo?" asked Captain Cloud, who was a commander for the day and felt he had a right to speak.

"Yeah," other disgruntled voices joined in.

"It makes us look like second string."

"Maybe we can get their hand-me-down uniforms, too."

"That's one of the things that's griping us, Chief."

Two more pie charts flashed by on the screen.

"Officer Fling," Hammer said. "Put it back on the logo, please. Let's talk about this."

A pin map of handgun seizures filled the screen, little yellow revolvers pointed at the problem areas of the city.

"Go, Fling!"

"Check out *COMSTAT for Dummies.*"

"Shit," Fling said when he somehow ended up back at the main menu.

"Go back to your day job, Fling."

He banged the enter key four times and an error message told him to stop it.

"All right, all right," Hammer quieted the

room. "Captain Cloud? I want to hear what you have to say."

"Well," Cloud picked up where he'd left off, "it's like the city seal, George Washington on his horse. I gotta ask you, what's George Washington got to do with Richmond? I guess we what? Borrowed that from D.C., from another big city, in other words?"

"Amen."

"I agree totally."

"I bet he never even slept here."

"It's an embarrassment."

"D.C., and now we're swiping ideas from New York. How bad does that make us look?" Cloud said.

"Okay," Hammer raised her voice. "I'm afraid there's not a thing we can do about the city seal at this time. So let's get back to our motto. Captain Cloud, remember that part of accountability is to suggest a solution when you point out a problem. Do you have a new motto in mind?"

"Well, I played around with one a little bit last night."

Cloud had high blood pressure. His white uniform shirt was too tight around the neck, and his face was almost purple. He was center stage and sweating.

"I was thinking about what would be simple but direct, and, now don't get your hopes up that this is real creative or poetic or anything, but if you ask the question, what are we all about? I think the answer can be summed up in three words. *Tough On Crime.*" Cloud looked around the table. "TOC, in other words, which is real easy to remember and doesn't take up any more room than CPR if we're gonna paint it on things or add it to our patches."

"Doesn't do anything for me."

"Me either."

"Naw."

"Okay, okay," Cloud rushed forward. "I had a backup just in case. How about *Tough In Court and Tough On Crime*? TIC TOC."

"I don't like it."

"Ditto."

"Wait a minute," Cloud went on with conviction. "Everybody's always complaining how slow we are getting to scenes, to their house after their alarm's gone off, right? And how many times do we hear the public bitch about how long it takes to solve a case? I think TIC TOC sends a positive message about a new attitude, about us trying harder."

"It also makes it sound like we're watching the clock. Like we can't wait for shift change."

"Or something bad's about to happen."

"Besides, it would be TOC TIC because being *tough on crime* is gonna come before you get to court."

"It doesn't work, Cloud."

"Forget it."

Cloud was crushed. "Never mind," he said.

Hammer had been silent through all this because she wanted to give her troops a chance to be heard. But she could take no more.

"It's something for all of us to think about," she abruptly said. "I'm always open for something new. Thank you, Captain Cloud."

"Actually, I had a thought on the subject," Andy Brazil said.

No one spoke. Cops started shuffling through notes and shifting in chairs. They got up for more coffee. Cloud opened a little bag of Fisherman's Friend throat lozenges, paper tearing loudly. Fling rebooted the computer and it beeped and honked as it tried to come back.

Hammer felt sorry for Brazil. She was in-dignant that he was discriminated against for reasons beyond his control. It wasn't his fault that women and gay men of all ages could not take their eyes off him. He couldn't help that he was only twenty-five and talented and sensitive. Nor was there a thing he had done or intimated that gave credence to the vicious rumor that she had brought him with her to Richmond for sexual pleasure and then he had run off with his landlady.

"Go ahead, Officer Brazil." Hammer tended to be brusque with him. "But we need to move along."

"I really think we'd be better off without a motto," Brazil said.

Silence.

"CPR makes it sound like we need to be resuscitated," he added.

No one would look at him. Papers shuffled. Duty belts creaked.

"That we're in extremis," he said.

Silence.

Then Cloud spoke up, "I've always thought that. It's about time somebody said it before it got painted on all the cars."

"It's just one more thing for people to make fun of," Brazil pointed out. "Especially since the core of COMSTAT is *accountabil-*

ity. And what happens if somewhere down the road someone decides to add *accountability* to our motto?"

More silence as everyone puzzled. Some wrote words and letters on paper, rearranging acronyms, like Jumble. Hammer knew instantly where Brazil was going with this.

"CARP," Fling read from his notepad.

"PARC?" Captain Cloud volunteered.

"You get CRAP," Brazil told them.

"Interesting," Hammer said loudly, restoring order. "All of you have made me see this in a different light. Maybe we shouldn't have a motto. Those in favor, raise your hand."

All did except Cloud. He sipped his coffee, eyes cast down at his half-eaten glazed doughnut, a sour expression on his face.

"So I guess I can delete the motto from the computer," Fling said, tapping keys again.

"I don't want you deleting anything," Hammer told him.

chapter three

Puff Daddy & the Family were rapping on the CD player and air was blowing through a stuck back window of Smoke's Escort. He had changed clothes in the car and Divinity was gone, the scent of her cloying perfume lingering as Smoke and fourteen-year-old Weed Gardener headed west to Mills E. Godwin High School.

Smoke had money in his pocket. Tucked under the seat was the Glock nine-millimeter pistol he had traded twenty rocks of crack cocaine for on the street. He was high as he replayed the robbery again and again, a favorite scene in the movie that was his life. He was getting better. He was getting bolder.

He thought how cool it would be to walk into the band room and take out twelve, thirteen, maybe fifteen students and their fucking band director, Mr. Curry, who thought he knew so much and wouldn't let Smoke play in the marching band because Smoke was tone deaf and couldn't keep rhythm on the snare drum. But Weed got to play the cymbals when he didn't know them from garbage can lids, and why? Because Weed was good in art and never got into trouble. Well, all that was about to change.

". . . Who you know do it better . . ." Smoke rapped along, out of sync and off key, his blood heating up. *"Don't make an ass out of yourself . . . I'm gonna make you love me baby . . ."*

Weed joined in on percussion, playing his hands on his thighs and the dashboard and jumping in his seat as if he had a synthesizer for a central nervous system and a drumbeat for a pulse. Smoke hated it. He hated that Weed saw rainbow colors and pictures to draw everywhere he went. He was tired of Weed's art being put on display in the library. At least Weed was stupid. He was so stupid he had no clue that the only reason Smoke had befriended him and started giving him rides to school was that Smoke intended to use Weed up.

"*Ri-dicu-u-lous . . . you're in the danger zone you shouldn't be alone . . .*" Smoke's monotone got louder.

Smoke turned up the volume on the CD player and pumped up the bass as far as it would go. He kept working the switch for the left back window and swearing when the glass remained stuck open halfway. Air slapped and the music throbbed as Weed played on.

"Hey, retard, cut it out," Smoke said, grabbing one of Weed's hands to make him stop his solo.

Weed went still. Smoke imagined he could smell Weed's fear.

"Listen to me, retard," Smoke went on. "Maybe I'm coming around to giving you what you been dreaming about, the biggest offer in your puny nothing life."

"Oh." Weed dreaded what Smoke was about to say.

"You want to be cool, right? You want to be just like me, right?"

"I guess so."

"You *guess* so?" Smoke blurted.

He flicked Weed's nose so hard it started bleeding. Tears jumped into Weed's eyes.

"Now, what was that you said, retard?" Smoke's voice was flat with hate.

Blood trickled down Weed's face and dripped onto his Route 66 sand-blasted, re-laxed-leg jeans.

"You get blood in my car, and I'm gonna throw your ass out. How'd you like to be a skid mark on the road?" Smoke told him.

"I wouldn't," Weed quietly said.

"I know how much you want to be a Pike and been waiting for my answer," Smoke said. "And after a lot of consideration, I've decided to let you have a shot at it, even though you don't measure up to the stan-dards."

Weed didn't want to be a Pike. He didn't want to be part of Smoke's gang. They beat people up, stole things, broke into cars, cut holes in restaurant roofs and carried off cases of liquor. They did all kinds of things that Weed didn't even want to know about.

"So, what do you say?" Smoke had his hand up, fingers poised to flick Weed again.

"Yeah, man."

"First you say *thank you,* retard. You say,

I'm so honored I'm about to shit in my pants."

"It would be fucking cool, man." Weed dressed his fear in cocky words that started strutting off his tongue. "Think of the shit we could do, man. And I get to wear the colors?"

"Chicago Bulls, like you're fucking Michael Jordan. Maybe it will make you taller. Maybe it will pump up that flat inner tube between your legs and you can start juicing girls."

"Who says I don't juice 'em now?" Weed talked big.

"You ain't juiced anything in your puny little motherfucking life. Not even fruit."

"You don't know that."

Smoke laughed in his cruel, mocking way.

"You ain't got no idea," Weed went on, acting like a hardass, knowing what would happen if he didn't because weakness made Smoke meaner.

"You wouldn't know what to do with pussy if it rubbed up against your leg and purred." Smoke guffawed. "I've seen your tool. I've seen you whiz."

"Whizzing and juicing ain't the same thing," Weed let him know.

Smoke turned into the parking lot of Mills

E. Godwin High School, named after a former governor of Virginia and home of the Eagles. Smoke stopped and waited for Weed to get out.

"Ain't you coming?" Weed asked.

"I'm busy right now," Smoke said.

"But you'll be tardy."

"Oh, I'm scaaaarrrred." Smoke laughed. "Get out, *re-tardy.*"

Weed did. He opened the back door and gathered his cheap knapsack of books, papers and the bologna-and-mustard sandwich he had fixed before Smoke picked him up.

"After school, you get your ass right back here," Smoke said. "Right in this exact spot. I'm gonna take you over to the clubhouse so you can get initiated and make your dream come true."

Weed knew about the clubhouse. Smoke had told him all about it.

"I got band practice," Weed said as his spirit trembled inside him.

"No you don't."

"Yeah I do. Every Monday, Wednesday and Friday, we got marching practice, Smoke." Weed's blood lost its heat and his stomach made itself smaller.

"Today you're busy, re-tardy. Your ass better be right here at three."

Tears welled in Weed's eyes again as Smoke sped off. Weed loved band. He loved going outside on the practice baseball field and marching with his Sabian eighteen-inch bronze cymbals and dreaming of the red-and-white toy-soldier uniform with its black hat and plume that he'd get to wear in the Azalea Parade on Saturday. Mr. Curry said Sabians were the best made, and Weed was responsible for keeping them bright and shiny, the leather straps tied nice and tight in their special flat, braided knots.

Flags were waving in front of the tidy blond-brick school, where nineteen hundred boisterous upper-middle-class students were jostling and shuffling into classrooms. Weed's mood lifted. At least his father lived in the right school district. Weed kept clothes and other belongings in his father's house, pretending he lived there, too. If Weed couldn't go to Godwin, there would be no art or music in his life.

The 8:35 tardy bell was ringing as Weed slammed shut the door to his bright orange locker and ran through empty corridors of different colored walls, the classrooms he passed filled with chatter and laughter and the thud and flutter of books opening on desktops. Weed had a phobia of being late that preceded this moment by many years.

His mother worked all the time and was rarely home or awake to get Weed up for school. Sometimes he overslept, sending him flying down to the corner bus stop in a panic, without books or lunch, barely dressed. In his mind, *missing the bus* meant missing life and being left alone in an empty house that echoed with past fights between parents who had split and the loud, full-of-himself sounds of Weed's big brother, Twister, who was dead.

Weed galloped around a corner to the science department just as Mr. Pretty began hall duty from the table outside Mrs. Fan's biology class, where this second Weed was supposed to be getting ready to take a quiz.

"Whoa," Mr. Pretty called out as Weed ran past and the tardy bell stopped and doors up and down the halls shut.

"I'm going to Mrs. Fan's class," Weed gasped.

"Do you know where it is?"

"Yes, sir, Mr. Pretty. Right there." Weed pointed at the red door less than twenty steps away, and wondered what kind of stupid question was that.

"You're late," Mr. Pretty told him.

"The bell just quit," Weed said. "You can almost still hear it."

"Late is late, Weed."

"I didn't mean to be."

"And I don't guess you have a pass," said Mr. Pretty, who taught ninth-grade Western Civilization.

"I don't got a pass," Weed said as indignation gathered, "'cause I wasn't planning on being late. But my ride just got here and there wasn't nothing I could do about it and I ran all the way so I wouldn't be late. And now you're making me later, Mr. Pretty."

Mr. Pretty's compulsion was to pull kids but not ticket them. He was young and nice-looking and had an insatiable need for captive audiences. He was notorious for holding kids in the hall as long as possible while they fidgeted and stared at the rooms where they were supposed to be as classes and quizzes went on without them.

"Don't blame me or your ride for being tardy," said Mr. Pretty from behind his small table in the empty intersection of shiny, empty hallways.

"I'm not blaming. I'm just saying the way it is."

"If I were you, I'd watch my mouth, Weed."

"What you want me to do, walk around with a mirror?" Weed sassed him.

Mr. Pretty might have let Weed go on to class, but Mr. Pretty was pissed and decided to draw things out.

"Let's see, I believe you're in my third period," he said. "You remember what we talked about on Friday?"

Weed didn't remember anything about Friday except that he wasn't looking forward to spending the weekend with his father.

"Ah. Maybe this will jog your memory," Mr. Pretty said curtly. "What happened in 1556?"

Weed's nerves were tangling and popping. He could hear Mrs. Fan's voice through her shut door. She was passing out the quiz and going over instructions.

"Come on, I know you know it." Mr. Pretty picked on Weed some more. "What happened?"

"A war." Weed threw out the first thing that came to mind.

"A fairly safe guess since there were so many of them. But you're wrong. Fifteen fifty-six was when Akbar became emperor of India."

"Is it okay if I go in Mrs. Fan's class now?"

"And then what?" Mr. Pretty demanded. "What happened next?"

"What?"

"I asked you first."

"About what?" Weed was getting furious.

"About what happened next?" Mr. Pretty asked.

"Depends on what you mean by *next,*" Weed smarted off.

"*Next* as in what's *next* in the chronology of events that I handed out to every person in my class," Mr. Pretty answered with an edge. "Of course, you probably never looked at it."

"I did too. And it says right on it we don't have to memorize nothing unless it's in bold, and the India thing and what happened next ain't in bold."

"Oh really?" Mr. Pretty got haughty. "And how can you remember whether something was in bold or not if you don't remember anything in the first place?"

"I remember when something's in bold!" Weed raised his voice, as if he were suddenly talking in bold.

"No you don't!"

"Yes I do!"

Mr. Pretty angrily grabbed a ballpoint pen out of his shirt pocket. He began scribbling words on the Hall Duty *passes* and *no passes* sheet.

"All right, smarty pants," said Mr. Pretty as self-control slipped further out of reach. "I've written down ten words, some in bold, some not. You get one minute to look them over."

He handed the list to Weed: *forfend, effigy, pogrom, Versailles, mead, Fabergé, Fabian, Waterloo, edict, pact.* Not one word was familiar. Mr. Pretty snatched back the list.

"Which words were in bold?" Mr. Pretty demanded.

"I can't pronunciate them."

"Versailles," Mr. Pretty prodded him.

Weed looked at the list in his head and located the only word that began with a V.

"Fourth one, not in bold," he said.

"Pogrom!"

"Third, not in bold."

"Fabian!" Mr. Pretty fired back.

"He's four before last. Not in bold, either."

"Effigy!" Mr. Pretty blurted out, his attractive face distorted by anger.

"It's in bold," Weed said. "Just like five and ten are."

"Oh really?" Mr. Pretty was beside himself. "And just what are five and ten since you think you know so much?"

Weed saw *mead* and *pact* in his head and pronounced them his own special way. "Med and paced."

"What do they mean!"

Mr. Pretty was talking loudly and Mrs. Fan cracked open her door, out of concern, to check on things.

"Shhhhhhhhh!" she said.

"What do they mean, Weed?" Mr. Pretty lowered his scornful voice.

Weed did the best he could.

"*Med* is what you feel when someone disses you. And *paced* is what we use in art class," he guessed.

Officer Fling was guessing, too. He had gone to the *next layer control,* then hit function 3 for *thematic display,* and selected *remove* to get rid of the latest pie, and brought up *priority one, two and three calls* for fourth precinct, which was not what anyone was interested in at the moment.

Hammer flipped on the overhead lights. The presentation was never supposed to run over an hour and it was well past the limit. She was discouraged and frustrated and determined not to let it show.

"I realize we're all new at this," she said reasonably. "I understand that things don't happen overnight. We're going to leave computer mapping until Friday morning at seven hundred hours, by which time I'm sure we will be well versed in it?"

No one responded.

"Officer Fling?" she said.

His hands were lifeless on the keyboard. He looked dejected and defeated.

"Do you think you will be able to make this work by Friday's COMSTAT presentation?" Hammer persisted.

"No, ma'am." Fling was honest about it.

The door opened and West returned to the room and took her seat.

"Okay, Officer Fling, that's fair enough," Hammer said in a positive tone. "Is there anybody else who might want to learn how to work this program? It's really very user-friendly. The point was not to design it for programmers and engineers, but for police."

No one spoke.

"Officer Brazil, help me out here," Hammer said.

"Sure," he said dubiously.

"Maybe for now you'd better pitch in," Hammer said. "Deputy Chief West? You're also very familiar with the software. See if the two of you can't work to get this thing up and running. I expect smooth sailing by our next COMSTAT presentation."

"Who's willing to learn?" West asked, looking around the table. "Come on guys, show some guts."

Lieutenant Audrey Ponzi raised her hand. Captain Cloud's hand went up next, and Officer Fling decided to give it another try.

"Excellent," Hammer said. "Major Hanger? If you'll resume with your presentation. We'll proceed without the computer. And we really need to wind this up."

Hanger hastily looked through his notes and took a nervous sip of coffee.

"Nothing much has changed since our last meeting," he began. "We got the same rash of petit larcenies from autos, mostly Jeeps, broken into for their airbags."

"CABBAGES," Fling interjected.

All eyes turned toward Captain Cloud, who had come up with Car Air Bag Breaking

And Enterings and its acronym CABBAE, which the media had immediately mistaken for CABBAGE, or CABBAGES, and continued to do so, despite the police department's numerous corrections.

"Anyway," Hanger resumed, "we suspect most of the stolen airbags are ending up at two body shops recently opened by Russians. Possibly the same clan of Russians who opened the kiosk at the farmer's market last summer, on Seventeenth Street directly across from Havana '59. Selling cabbages, the kind you make slaw with, which has done nothing but add to the confusion." He glared at Cloud.

"But the CABBAGES might be related because the Russians possibly are," Fling figured.

"We're thinking that," Hanger said.

"Let's get back to the airbags," Hammer said.

"Well, the MO remains the same in these most recent petit larcenies." Hanger avoided using the term CABBAGE. "Owner returns to his vehicle, finds a window smashed, the airbags gone. These same cars go in to one of the Russian body shops to get the airbags replaced and ironically the stolen airbags installed to replace the ones stolen could be the very ones stolen out of the vehicle in question. So you're really paying for the same airbags twice, thinking you're getting new ones for three hundred bucks apiece, when in fact you're getting stolen ones. It's gotten to be a pretty big racket all over the world."

"But if you're getting your same airbags back, they're really not secondhand because they were never owned by a second person," said Fling. "Does that . . . ?"

"What are we doing about this situation?" Hammer raised her voice.

"We're coordinating with investigations to get an undercover guy in at least one of the body shops," Hanger replied.

"Are the airbags traceable?" Hammer asked.

"Not unless they start putting VINs on them," Hanger said, referring to the Vehicle Identification Numbers that were etched on the edge of all driver's doors. "I was thinking maybe we could get some kind of grant to help out. Maybe NIJ would be interested."

"To help out in what way?" Hammer frowned.

"To do a study on the usefulness of ABINs."

"ABINs?"

"That's what we could call them," Hanger explained. "Air Bag Identification Numbers. Thing is, if your same stolen airbags are put back in your vehicle, then for sure the ABINs are going to match."

"True."

"That would make it pretty easy."

Hanger nodded. "Not only could we start making cases here, but I'm pretty sure a lot of these stolen airbags are going overseas. So if we developed a system of ABINs, we could get Interpol involved, too. It might bring us some recognition."

"I see." Hammer fought a growing sense of hopelessness. "Anything else?"

"Two more stolen Saturns. We got a pattern going on."

"How many so far?"

"Twelve General Motors cars stolen in the past month."

"Any breaks?" Hammer asked.

"It appears several kids are involved. We think they bought master keys for Saturns from some kid named Beeper, supposedly in the area of Swansboro Elementary School on Midlothian Turnpike."

"Gang-related?" Hammer asked.

"Can't say for sure," Hanger answered.

"What does that mean?"

"Well, all we got to go on is this one snitch who's lied to us before."

Hammer jumped ahead. "We just had another ATM robbery, I'm sorry to say. I'm going to let Deputy Chief West give the details."

"Victim is an Asian male, age twenty-two." West looked at her notes. "Pulled up to the Crestar ATM at 5802 Patterson. Nobody else was there. Nothing seemed out of the ordinary, says duct tape was suddenly slapped over his eyes, a gun jammed into his back. A male, he couldn't tell race, demanded money. By the time the victim removed the tape, the perp was long gone."

"The duct tape is different," Hammer said.

"Absolutely," West said.

"That makes six ATM robberies," Hammer said. "Four on Southside, two in the West End. An average of one per week since early February."

"Let me just say that I'm extremely concerned about this latest one, assuming it's related," West spoke up. "Let's just go through it. We have the first four ATMs late night or early morning when it's dark. There's a male-female team. She diverts by asking the victim where the nearest post office, pay phone, whatever, is. The male appears, opens his jacket just enough to show the handle of a gun and says, *I want the money you took out of the machine.* Maybe the gun's real, maybe it's not. The perp takes the money and runs.

"Then we have a fifth ATM in Church Hill. Again, when it's dark out, but this time the male perp actually displays the gun. He gets into the victim's car, turns out the interior light so the victim can't see his face. Threatens if the victim ever tries to help cops ID him, he knows the guy's plate number and will find him and kill him. Then he forces the victim to drive several blocks. The perp jumps out with the money. Now we've got an ATM in the West End, and this time it's daylight. I'm seeing a possible pattern of escalation here. An escalation that could end in violence."

"We got anything more on these cases?" Cloud asked.

"Not anything helpful. Some of the victims

think the female perp's black, some think he is, and vice versa. Age unknown, assumed to be juveniles. No sign of a vehicle, if they use one," West replied. "Bottom line is we don't know."

"And bank tapes?"

"Of no use."

"Why not?" Hammer asked.

"In the first one, all you see is the back of her and it was dark," West said. "On the next four you don't see anything at all."

"And the cameras were functioning?"

"Nothing wrong with them."

"And the one this morning?"

"Seems fine."

"Anybody have anything even remotely similar going on in other parts of the city?" Hammer then asked.

No one did.

"What about third precinct? We haven't heard from you, Captain Webber," Hammer pushed ahead.

"Some Russians opened up an antique store on Chamberlayne, near Azalea Mall," Webber said. "They haven't done anything illegal yet."

"Any reason to think they will?" Hammer inquired.

"Well, it's just this Russian thing going on."

"How do we know they aren't gypsies?" burglary detective Linton Bean asked.

"Can gypsies be Russian?"

"Seems to me they can be anything as long as they drift around and con people."

"Yeah, but the ones we've had coming through here are mostly Romanian, Irish, English and Scotch. The Travelers. Well, that's what they call themselves. They get real pissed if we call them gypsies."

"How 'bout if we just call them tramps and thieves?"

"I've never heard of Russian gypsies."

"My sister went over to Italy last year and said they have gypsies over there."

"I know for a fact they got Hispanic ones in Florida."

"See, that's the whole thing," said Detective Bean. "There's no such country as 'Gypsy.' You can be from anywhere and be a gypsy, including Russia . . ."

"What are we doing about this problem?" Hammer interrupted.

"Stepping up patrols in neighborhoods like Windsor Farms, where you have mostly older people with money," said Bean. "Maybe forming a task force."

"Do it," Hammer said, glancing at her watch and conscious of the time. "Lieutenant Noble is commander for a day in second precinct. What do you have to report?"

"This week we arrested a domestic violence recidivist," said Noble, who spoke the proper police language and was resented by all.

"Very good," Hammer said.

"We're also doing warrant sweeps but so far haven't surfaced the suspect in the stairwell rapes," Noble added. "And if it's all right, Chief Hammer, I have a comment to make."

"Please," Hammer said.

"I'm not so sure it was a good idea to piss off all the citizens with this gang crap Brazil wrote about for the Sunday paper."

"It wasn't crap," Brazil said.

"Name one gang," Noble challenged him.

"It's all a matter of semantics," Brazil answered. "It depends on how you label *gangs.*"

Hammer agreed. "Juveniles are committing the worst crimes. They mentor each other, influence each other, form packs, gangs. We have them here and need to identify them."

"Most of the kids that go in schools and blow everybody away aren't in gangs. They're loners," Noble argued.

"Let's look at Jonesboro," West countered. "A fourteen-year-old recruits an eleven-year-old to pull the fire alarm, right? So what would happen if you had four, five, six kids involved? Maybe twenty kids and teachers would have died."

"She's got a point."

"Got to admit, it makes you think."

"You'd have to call in the damn National Guard."

"Kids are scary. They don't have any boundaries. They think killing's a game," West added.

"It's true. There's no concept of consequences."

"What happens if you get some charismatic gang leader and he really organizes? Imagine," Brazil said.

Insights and arguments were volleyed back and forth as Hammer deliberated over how to broach the next subject.

"Recent intelligence," she began, "indicates that two white males may be planning a hate crime, the robbery and murder of a black woman possibly named Loraine. The males may go by the names or aliases of Bubba and Smudge."

No one spoke for a moment, faces perplexed.

Then, "You don't mind my asking, Chief, where'd this come from?"

Hammer looked to West for help.

"We're really not at liberty to reveal the source at this time," West said. "You just need to be aware, keep your eyes and ears open."

"If there's nothing further?" Hammer said.

There wasn't.

"Then I do have two commendations to present and I believe both people are here." Hammer smiled. "Communications Officer Patty Passman and Officer Rhoad?"

They came forward. Hammer handed each a certificate and shook hands. Applause was weak.

"Communications Officer Passman, as you know, handled a nine-one-one last month that saved a man from choking on a hot dog," Hammer said. "And Officer Otis Rhoad issued three hundred and eighty-eight parking tickets last month. A department record."

"Booooo!"

"Yeah, a lot of 'em on our cars!"

Passman glared at Rhoad.

"He wins the prize for talking on the radio!"

"Rhoad Hog!"

Passman bit her lip, her face an angry red.

"*Rode*o!" Fling had to toss in, although the aspersion made no sense.

"That's enough," Hammer said. "I'll see all of you back here on Friday."

The Ford Explorer's turn signal was beating like a panicking heart as its driver, who had already missed his exit, tried once again to ease in front of Bubba. Bubba accelerated and the Explorer swerved back into its lane, where it belonged. The cop was still on Bubba's bumper and Bubba slowed to send the message that he wouldn't tolerate tailgaters no matter who they were. Bubba was a cowboy herding cattle on the open prairie of motoring life.

"Unit 2 to Unit 1." Honey was sounding increasingly concerned over the two-way.

Bubba was too busy to talk to his wife.

"Smudge," he got back to his good buddy, "Queen Bee's buzzing, got a city kitty tailwind, and a sixteener with a low seater's trying to wipe my nose." Bubba spoke in code, letting Smudge know that Bubba's wife was trying to get hold of Bubba, he had a city cop riding his ass and a 4x4 driven by a punk was trying to swipe in front of him.

"I'll leave ya lonely." Smudge signed off.

"Throwin' ya back. Catch ya later, good buddy." Bubba signed off, too.

By now, the kid in the Explorer seemed challenged and might have become violent but for the cop one lane over. The kid decided to default. He got in the last word by laying on his horn and giving Bubba the finger and mouthing *Fuckhead.* The Explorer disappeared in the current of other traffic. Bubba slowed to communicate to the cop one more time to get off his rear bumper. The cop communicated back by flashing his red-and-blue emergency lights and yelping his siren. Bubba pulled over into a Kmart parking lot.

chapter four

Officer Jack Budget took his time collecting his silver anodized aluminum Posse citation holder and dual clipboard. He climbed out of his gleaming blue-and-red-striped white cruiser, adjusted his duty gear and approached the red Jeep with the Confederate flag rear bumper sticker and BUB-AH vanity plate that he had been staring at for miles. Its redneck driver rolled down the window.

"Am I to assume you go by the name Bub-ah?" Budget asked.

"No, it's *Bubba,*" Bubba rudely said.

"Let me see your license and registration." Officer Budget was rude, too, although he might not have been had Bubba not started it.

Bubba pulled his nylon wallet out of his back pocket. Velcro ripped as he opened it and got out his driver's license. He fished around in the glove box for his registration, then handed both proofs of identification and ownership to the cop, who studied them for several long minutes.

"You have any idea why I stopped you, Mr. Fluck?"

"Probably because of my bumper sticker," Bubba stated.

Budget stepped back to look at the Jeep's rear bumper, as if just now noticing the Confederate flag on it.

"Well, well," he said as images of white pointed hoods and burning crosses violated his mind. "Still trying to win that war and round up Ne-groes to pick your cotton."

"The Southern Cross has nothing to do with that," Bubba indignantly said.

"The *what?*"

"The Southern Cross."

Budget's jaw muscles knotted. It had not been so long ago that he had been bused to one of the city's public high schools and had watched seats empty one by one as other black kids got locked up or killed on the street. He had been *Buckwheat, Sambo, drone, porch monkey, Uncle Tom.* He had grown up in the *niggerhood.* Even now on some calls, white complainants asked him to go around to the back door.

"I guess you know it as the Confederate flag," the white redneck asshole was explaining to him. "Although it was really the battle flag, versus the Stars and Bars or Stainless Banner or Naval Jack or Pennant."

Budget knew nothing of the various official Confederate flags that had gone in and out of vogue for various reasons during the war. He only knew that he hated the bumper stickers and tattoos, tee shirts and beach towels he saw everywhere in the South. He was enraged by Confederate flags waving from porches and graves.

"It's all about racism, Mr. Fluck," Budget coldly said.

"It's all about states' rights."

"Bullshit."

"You can count the stars. One for each state in the Confederacy plus Kentucky and Missouri. Eleven stars," Bubba informed him. "There's not a single slave on the Southern Cross. You look for yourself."

"The South wanted out because it wanted to keep its slaves."

"That's only part of it."

"So you admit that it's at least part of it."

"I'm not admitting anything," Bubba let him know.

"You were driving erratically," said Officer Budget, who wanted to grab Bubba out of the Jeep and smack him around.

"Was not." Bubba refused to admit it.

"Yes, you were."

"Not me."

"I was right behind you. I ought to know."

"That kid in the Explorer was trying to cut in front of me," Bubba said.

"He had his turn signal on."

"So what."

"Have you been drinking?" demanded Budget.

"Not yet."

"Are you on any kind of medications?"

"Not this minute."

"But you are sometimes?" Budget asked, for he knew that some drugs and poisons, such as marijuana and arsenic, stayed in the blood for a while.

"Not anything you need to know about," said Bubba.

"I'll be the judge of that, Mr. Fluck."

Officer Budget leaned closer to the open window, hoping he might smell alcohol. He didn't.

Bubba got out a cigarette. He smoked Merit Ultima instead of other brands because Merits, along with Marlboros and Virginia Slims, to name a few, were manufactured by Philip Morris. Bubba was very loyal to his employer and to all products made in America.

Bubba had no intention of telling Officer Budget that took Librax for cranky bowel syndrome and that now and then he needed Sudafed to control his allergic responses to dust mites, mold and cats. None of this was Officer Budget's business.

"Advil," Bubba answered the cop.

"That's all?" Officer Budget asked with severity.

"Maybe Tylenol."

"Mr. Fluck, you . . ."

"What did you say?" Bubba interrupted.

". . . certain you aren't on anything else?" Budget finished his sentence.

"I heard what you said and I'm going to report you to the chief!" Bubba exclaimed in rage.

"You do that, Mr. Fluck. In . . ."

"See!"

"In fact, I'll make the appointment. You can see her, Mr. Fluck, face . . ."

"That's it!"

An entire population of cruel schoolchildren stampeded through Bubba's brain. They chanted those awful names, shrieking with laughter. Bubba saw himself fat and in camouflage. Enough was enough, he could take no more.

"What's it?" Budget raised his voice, too.

"I don't have to listen to this!"

"You can tell the chief that face to face!" Budget exclaimed. "I don't give a flying . . ."

"Stop!"

"Man, you got a problem," Budget said.

Weed did, too. He made it to biology class in time to watch all completed quizzes passed up to the front and to hear Mrs. Fan go over homework he had not done.

His miserable eyes wandered around the room to worms, deer embryos, rhinoceros beetles, termite eggs and dog intestines suspended in formaldehyde, and butterflies and snakeskins pinned to boards. He felt trapped by Smoke.

Later, in Western Civilization, Mr. Pretty picked on Weed three times, and Weed knew the answer to nothing. Weed's fears gathered force.

His escape was Mrs. Grannis's class. She taught Art IV and V during fifth period, and was very young and pretty, with soft blond curls, and eyes as green as summer grass. She had told Weed more than once that he was the first freshman ever, in the history of the school, to attend her class. Ordinarily, only juniors could take Art IV, and only seniors and Advanced Placement students could take V. But Weed was special. He had a gift that was rare.

There had been much debate about pushing Weed so far ahead so fast, especially since he clearly lagged miles behind the troops on most other fronts. Questions about his maturity and social adjustment had been discussed at length among faculty and counselors. Even Mrs. Lilly, the principal, had been brought in at the end, and had proposed that Weed take a class at Virginia Commonwealth University or perhaps specialized classes at the Center for Arts. But the county did not provide transportation beyond the morning and afternoon buses Weed was afraid of missing. He had no way to get around in the middle of the day. Godwin decided to take a chance.

Weed had free period and lunch between 11:40 and 12:31 and he needed to hide. He did not want to run into Smoke somewhere. Weed was desperate and had come up with a secret, brazen, bizarre plan. At 11:39 he walked into Mrs. Grannis's classroom. His self-esteem was low. He was frightened about what lay ahead and could tell by the way Mrs. Grannis looked at him that she sensed he wasn't himself.

"How are you today, Weed?" she asked with an uncertain smile.

"I was wondering if it would be all right if I worked in here through free period," he said.

"Certainly. What would you like to work on?"

Weed stared at the computers on a back counter.

"Graphic art," he said. "I'm working on a project."

"I'm delighted to hear it. There are many, many job opportunities in that field. You know where the CDs are," she said. "And I'll see you back here fifth period."

"Yes, ma'am," Weed said as he pulled out a chair and sat in front of a computer.

He opened a drawer where graphic software was neatly arranged in stacks, and picked out what he wanted. He inserted CorelDRAW into the CD drive and waited until Mrs. Grannis left the room before logging onto America Online.

Lunch followed free period and Weed had no intention of eating. He hurried down the hallway to the band room, which was empty except for Jimbo "Sticks" Sleeth, who was doing his thing on the red Pearl drums.

"Hey, Sticks," Weed said.

Sticks was rolling on the snare, his feet keeping rhythm on the high hat and kick. He had his eyes squeezed shut, sweat running down his temples. Weed went over to a cabinet and retrieved the hard plastic Sabian case. He opened it and lovingly lifted out the heavy bronze crash cymbals. He checked the leather straps to make sure the knots were holding tight. He gripped the straps, index fingers and thumbs touching. He held the cymbals at an angle, the edge of the right one lower than the left.

Sticks opened his eyes and gave Weed the nod. Weed struck the left cymbal, glancing it off the right, punctuating toms and snare with his euphoric bright sound.

"Do it, baby!" Sticks yelled, and he started in.

It sounded like a musical war going on as Sticks beat and throbbed and boomed in a rhythm that made the blood wild, and Weed was march-dancing around the room, crashing and flipping up, flashing and spinning.

"Go! Go! Oh yeah!" Sticks was frenzied.

Weed was moonwalking, his bright sound rolling out from the edges, then crashing staccato, then crashing long. He didn't hear the bell ring but he finally noticed the clock on the wall. He packed up the cymbals and made it back to Mrs. Grannis's art room with two minutes to spare. He was the first one there. She was writing on a white board and turned around to see who had come in.

"Did you get a lot done during your free time?" she asked Weed.

"Yes, ma'am." Weed wouldn't meet her eyes.

"I wish everybody liked the computer as much as you do." She started writing again. "You have a favorite software so far?"

"Quark XPress and Adobe Illustrator and Photoshop."

"Well, you have a real knack for it," she said as he chose his place at one of the tables and tucked his knapsack under his chair.

"It's no big deal," Weed mumbled.

"Have you written your story of the power behind your fish?" Mrs. Grannis asked as she continued writing this week's project on the white board in long, looping letters.

"Yea, ma'am," Weed sullenly answered, opening his notebook.

"I can't wait to hear it," she continued to encourage him. "You're the only person in the class to pick a fish."

"I know," he said.

The assignment for the past two weeks had been to make a papier-mâché figure that was symbolic to the student. Most picked a symbol from mythology or folklore, such as a dragon or tiger or raven or snake. But Weed had constructed a cruel blue fish. Its gaping mouth bared rows of bloody teeth, and Weed had fashioned glittery eyes from

small compact mirrors that flashed at anyone walking past.

"I'm sure all of the students can't wait to
hear about your fish," Mrs. Grannis went on
as she wrote.

"We doing watercolor next?" Weed asked
with interest as he made out what she was
writing.

"Yes. A still-life composition that includes
reflective objects, texture." She wrote with
flourish. "And a 2-D object that gives the illu-
sion of a 3-D object."

"My fish is three-dimensional," Weed said,
"because it takes up real space."

"That's right. And what are the words we
use?"

"Over, under, through, behind and
around," he recited.

Weed could remember words in art, and
they didn't have to be in bold.

"Freestanding, or surrounded by negative
areas," he added.

Mrs. Grannis put down her Magic Marker.
"And how do you think you'd make your fish
three-dimensional if it was actually two-
dimensional?"

"Light and shadow," he said easily.

"Chiaroscuro."

"Except I can never pronunciate it," Weed told her. "It's what you do to make a drawing of a wineglass look three-dimensional instead of flat. Same for a lightbulb or an ice chicle or even clouds in the air."

Weed looked around at boxes of pastels and the 140-weight Grumbacher paper he only got to use on final sketches. There were shelves of Elmer's glue and colored pencils and carts of the Crayola tempera paints he had used on his fish. On a counter in the back of the room the computer terminals for graphics reminded him of the secret thing he had done.

By now, students were wandering into the room and scooting out chairs. They greeted Weed in their typically affectionate, smack-him-around fashion.

"Hey, *Weed Garden,* what's going on?"

"How come you're always in here before we are? Doing your homework early?"

"You finished the Mono Lisa yet?"

"You got paint on your jeans."

"Whoa, doesn't look like paint to me. You been bleeding, man?"

"Uh uh," Weed lied.

Mrs. Grannis's eyes got darker as she looked at him and his jeans. He could see a question mark in a little balloon over her head. Weed had nothing to say.

"Everybody ready to read what you wrote about your symbols?" She returned her attention to the class.

"Groan."

"I can't figure out what mine means."

"No one said we had to *write*."

"Let's take a minute to talk about symbols." Mrs. Grannis hushed them. "What is a symbol? Matthew?"

"Something that means something else."

"And where do we find them? Joan?"

"In pyramids. And jewelry."

"Annie?"

"In the catacombs, so the Christians could express themselves in secret."

"Weed? Where else might we find symbols?" Mrs. Grannis's face got soft with concern as she looked at him.

"Doodles and what I play in the band," Weed said.

Brazil was at his desk, drawing designs on a legal pad, trying to come up with a newsletter logotype as the chairman of the Governor's Blue Ribbon Crime Commission drove him crazy over the speakerphone.

"I think it is a dread-filled miscalculation," Lelia Ehrhart's emphatic, haughty voice sounded.

Brazil turned down the volume.

"To even suggest much less implicate we might have a gang here is to cause one," she proclaimed.

The logo was for the website and needed to attract attention, and since it was agreed that CPR was out the window, Brazil had to start over. He hated newsletters, but Hammer had been insistent.

"And not every children are little mobsters. Many of them are misguided and misled astray, mistreated and abusive and need our help, Officer Brazil. To dwell on those few bad, especially those to band together in little groups you call gangs, is to give the public a very wrong, untrue and false view. My committee is completely all about prevention and doing that first before the other. That's what the governor has mandated to tell us to do it."

"The last governor," Brazil politely reminded her.

"What is relevant about that and how does it matter?" retorted Ehrhart, who had been raised in Vienna and Yugoslavia and did not speak English well.

"It matters because Governor Feuer hasn't gotten around to appointing a new commission yet. I don't think it's a good idea for us to be making assumptions about his policies and mandates, Mrs. Ehrhart."

There was a high-pitched, outraged pause.

"Are you implicating that he might dissolute my commission and undo it? That he and I may be a problem in my relationship?" said Ehrhart.

Brazil knew that a good nameplate should attract attention without overdoing it. Perhaps because they were on the subject of gangs, Brazil suddenly scrawled *Richmond P.D.* graffiti-style.

"Wow," he muttered in excitement.

"Wow which?" Ehrhart's angry voice filled the office.

"I'm sorry." Brazil came to. "What were you saying?"

"I demand you tell me when you were saying *wow* about just there," she demanded.

Chief Hammer filled the doorway. Brazil rolled his eyes and put his finger to his lips.

"I think you were became impertinent!" Ehrhart went on.

"No, ma'am. I wasn't saying *wow* about anything that has to do with you," Brazil honestly answered.

"Oh really? And did *that* supposedly mean what?"

"I'm working on something here, and was saying *wow* about it."

"Oh, I see. Here I am taken my costly time to call your phone, and you're working on something else in addition to our conversing while I'm talking to you?"

"Yes, ma'am. But I'm listening." Brazil tried not to laugh as he looked at Hammer, who was never amused by Ehrhart.

West walked in.

"What . . . ?" she started to say.

Hammer motioned for her to be silent. Brazil clamped his pencil between his teeth and crossed his eyes.

"The upshoot, Officer Brazil, is I simple will not allow to permit you a commission quote for whatever your next column might be about in terms of so-called gangs. *You're hanging out by a thread on a limb all alone on this one!"*

Brazil snatched the pencil out of his mouth and wrote down the quote. West scowled. Hammer shook her head in disgust.

"We members on the Blue Ribbon Crime Commission are children pro-advocates, not bounty hunting," she preached on. "Even if children do formulate little groups, what by the when is perfect and normal, certainly all of us had our little clichés where we were in school and to start labels them as *gangs* is like all this millions of misspoken facts about well-meaning mens who play Santa Claus at Christmas all being children molesters, or that clowns are, or that the Internet becomes that. And this is how there things all get their inception. Because of the power of suggesting that the media has. Don't you view how you've opened a flooded gate? So I'm asking you reasonable to square a peg in that round hole right now."

Brazil was biting his hand. He cleared his throat several times.

"I understand what you're . . . " His voice went up an octave and cracked.

He cleared his throat again, tears in his

eyes, face bright red as he held back laughter that was fast becoming hysterical. Hammer looked like she wanted to break Lelia Ehrhart's neck, as usual. West's expression pretty much mirrored her boss's.

"Then am I to happily assumption that we won't hear no more about this gang paraphernalia?" said Ehrhart, who was famous for her creativity with self-expression.

Brazil simply could not speak.

"Are you where?"

Brazil mashed several buttons on the phone at the same time to give the impression there was trouble on the line. He quietly depressed the hang-up button and returned the receiver to its cradle.

"Gang paraphernalia!" He was weak with laughter.

"Oh great," West said. "Now she'll call us. Way to go, Andy. Every time you get with her on the fucking phone, this happens. Then she calls the chief or me. Thanks a hell of a lot."

"We have things to discuss," Hammer announced, coming inside the office. "We'll leave Lelia for later. She takes up far too much of our time as is."

"Why can't you say something to Governor Feuer," Brazil said as he took a deep breath and wiped his eyes.

"I will if he asks me," Hammer replied. "We need a very simple user's manual for COM-STAT. We've got to get this computer business straight. We're what? Three months into this? A fourth of our year is up. And they still can't use the computer? Both of you see how bad that is?"

"Yes." Brazil got serious. "I do. If we don't leave that much with them, I guess we've failed."

"I'm sorry to heap more on you." Hammer began pacing. "But we need the manual ASAP."

"How soon is *as soon as possible?*" West suspiciously asked.

"Two weeks from today, at the outside."

"Jeez." West sat down on the small couch. "I'm already working days and riding with patrol, detectives, inspectors, you name it."

"Me, too," Brazil said. "Plus I've got this website stuff."

"I know, I know." Hammer stopped to look out the window at the downtown skyline. "I have my computer at home. I'll add my thoughts, too. We're all in this together. I think the thing to do is give each of us our own responsibility. Andy, you're more into programming, commands and all that. You can handle the how-to technical part of it, and Virginia, you can help put it in very basic, black-and-white terms, nuts and bolts, that the cops will be able to follow."

West wasn't sure if she'd been insulted or not.

"I'll try to add the concepts, philosophies, put it all in context," Hammer said. "Then— Andy, you're the writer—you can compile the whole thing."

"I agree this has to be done," West said, "but if you ask me, the only thing that's going to really turn the guys on to COMSTAT is if they see it works."

"They aren't going to see if it works if they can't work it," Hammer logically replied.

Hammer walked out of the office. Brazil and West looked at each other.

"Shit," West said. "Look what you've gotten us into."

"Me!" Brazil exclaimed.

"Yes, you."

"She suggested the user's manual, not me."

"She wouldn't have suggested one if you weren't a writer." West saw the holes in her logic but would not back down.

"Oh, I see. So now everything's my fault just because I know how to do something in general that I've been told to do specifically and that you've been asked to help with, sort of."

West had to unravel this for a moment.

"What do you mean, *sort of?*" she asked. "It sounds to me like my involvement is more than a sort of."

Brazil's phone rang.

"Brazil. Oh, hi." His voice softened and he paused as the other person talked. "You're so thoughtful," Brazil said, listening again. "The usual place is fine," he said as the voice chattered on. "I'll look forward to it," Brazil said. "I've got to go.

"Sorry," he said to West.

"Do you have any idea how much I'm going to hate writing computer instructions?" she asked in an uneven, strained voice as she imagined Brazil's wealthy, beautiful landlady. "And you're not supposed to make personal calls at work!"

"I didn't make it. She called me. And you're not the one who has to do the writing. I am," Brazil replied.

"Well, writing, after all is said and done, is the easy part."

Brazil's anger mounted.

"You don't have any right to say it's easy," he said.

"I can say anything I want," she replied.

"No you can't."

"Yes I can," she asserted.

"Then you write it."

"Fuck no," she answered. "I've got enough to do."

"Excuse me," a voice behind them spoke up.

Fling was holding his schedule book, standing outside the door, afraid to walk in. West and Brazil stopped their bickering and stared
at him.

"I'm out of here." West left.

"Officer Brazil," Fling said, "I just wanted to remind you of your 1:56 appointment at Godwin High School. I believe you're speaking in the auditorium to all the students?"

"Dammit," Brazil muttered as he checked the time. "Do you know how to get there from here?"

"No," Fling said. "I didn't go there."

"Huh?" Brazil's mind was racing.

"I went to Hermitage," Fling said.

"Wait." Brazil popped up from his desk. "Virginia, come back here!"

"On Hungary Springs Road." Fling was warmed by the memories. "You know, Godwin isn't the only good school around."

West walked back into the office, defiant in a khaki suit that complemented the darkness of her eyes and deep red of her hair. Her body was far finer than she deserved for as little as she did to help it along.

"What?" she impatiently asked.

"You ought to go out to Hermitage, too. Talk with the students there, you know," Fling was going on and on. "That's the thing about doing one school. What about the others?"

"In case you've forgotten," Brazil said to West as he tightened the laces of his Rocky boots, "you're supposed to go with me to Godwin."

"Shit," she said.

chapter five

Muskrat's Auto Rescue was Bubba's home away from home, and today especially, he was grateful. It didn't matter that Officer Budget had let Bubba go with only a warning. Bubba was traumatized. The cop had called Bubba names. The cop had brought back old injuries and humiliations and then had been so unfair and ugly as to accuse Bubba of being the one with prejudices.

Muskrat's shop was behind his brick rancher on several junk-scattered acres off Clopton Street, between Midlothian and Hull. The fence bordering Muskrat's garage and its outbuildings was built of old railroad ties piled like Lincoln Logs. Transmissions littered the hard-packed dirt, tail housings covered with plastic quart oil bottles to keep out the rain. Cars, vans, pickups, a tractor trailer and an old fire truck used each year in the Azalea Parade were parked wherever Muskrat had left them last. Bubba pulled up to the shop's open bay door, cut the engine and climbed out.

He was momentarily cheered by Muskrat's automotive kingdom, which could very well have passed for a chop shop were most of the parts not rusty and from an earlier stage of vehicle evolution. Bubba stepped around an ancient air jack and a bearing press. He made his way through miscellaneous flower-pots, coils of garden hoses, fenders, head-lights, hoods, bumpers, car seats, stacks of split firewood and fifty-five-gallon drums overflowing with junk parts.

Bubba was convinced, although he spoke of it rarely, that there was a Bermuda Trian-gle for vehicles. He believed cars and trucks swept up in floods and tornadoes, or per-haps gone and believed stolen, ended up in places like Muskrat's shop, where they would be cared for and used to help humans continue their journeys through this life.

Bubba intended to write this insight to Click and Clack's Car Talk on the Internet or perhaps to his favorite, Miss Lonely Parts, a syndicated columnist who was really a man.

"Hey Scrat!" Bubba called out.

He walked inside the garage, where an old furnace burned a mixture of dirty motor oil and firewood.

"Scrat? Where the hell are ya?" Bubba tried again.

Muskrat wasn't always easy to locate within the jumbles of heater cores, batteries, oil pans, grease guns, chains, tow ropes, bungee straps, gas lines, vacuum hoses, homemade jumper cables, stands made of old Ford wheels, clutches. Pressure plates were stacked like doughnuts on sections of exhaust pipes. There were grinders, a chain horse to lift out engines, and hundreds of American and metric wrenches, ratchets, pliers, chisels, awls, vises, presses, springs, drill bits, spark plugs, dead blow mallets and brass hammers.

"How come you got the heat on, Scrat?"

"To keep my joints from aching. What'dya try to fix this time?" Muskrat's voice was muffled under a jacked-up 1996 Mercury Cougar.

"Who tried to fix?" Bubba accused.

Muskrat was flat on his back on a creeper. He rolled out from underneath the car, suddenly there, a wizard in a mechanic's blue work pants and shirt and a NAPA Auto Parts cap.

"What do you mean, I tried?" asked Muskrat, who was at least seventy, with hands rough and hard like horn.

"Windshield's leaking again," Bubba let him know. "You fixed it last, Scrat."

"Uh huh," Muskrat blandly said as he snatched toilet paper from an industrial roll overhead and began cleaning his glasses. "Well, drive her on in here, Bubba. I'll take a look but I keep telling you to get the boys at Harding Glass to put in a new windshield. Or dump the damn thing altogether and get something that don't break down every other minute."

Bubba walked out of the garage, not listening. He got into his Jeep and cranked the engine as anger pecked at him. He could not and would not believe that his buddy Smudge had cheated him. It couldn't be that Smudge had sold him a piece of shit. The possibility of it resurrected other injustices as Bubba parked inside the garage, in the bay next to the Cougar, and climbed out.

"I got to tell you right now, Scrat, there's police brutality in this city," Bubba announced.

"Oh yeah?" Muskrat mumbled as he started looking at the windshield.

"I think something's telling me to do something about it."

"Bubba, something's always telling you something."

"There're reasons too complicated to go into that the new chief, that new woman who just moved here, needs my help, Scrat."

"And you always got complicated reasons, Bubba. I'd stay out of it if I were you."

Bubba could not stop thinking about Chief Hammer. He had heard her name on his cell phone this morning. There was a reason for this; it was not random.

"It's time we mobilize, Scrat."

"Who's we?"

"Citizens like us," Bubba said. "We gotta get involved."

"I can't find your leak," Muskrat said.

"Right here." Bubba pointed to the top of the windshield, near the rearview mirror.

"The water drips in from this spot here. Want a cigarette?"

Bubba pulled out a pack.

"You need to cut back, boy," Muskrat said. "Chew gum. That's what I do to kill the craving when I'm around gasoline and what all."

"You forget I got TMJ. My jaws are killing me." Bubba clicked them side to side.

"I told you not to get all those damn crowns," Muskrat said as he retrieved a Windex spray bottle full of water and uncoiled an air hose. "You'd probably be better off if he just yanked all of 'em out and fixed you up with a pair of clackers like I got."

Muskrat grinned, showing off his dentures.

"I'll get on the inside with the hose, and when I tell you to, you start spraying," said Muskrat.

"Same thing we did last time," Bubba said. "And a lot of good it did."

"It's like fixing those crowns of yours," Muskrat wouldn't let up as he sat in the driver's seat. "All you do is go to the dentist. I'd get new ones that don't look like piano keys if I were you. And you sure as hell ought to replace this windshield. The car's been wrecked." Muskrat had told him this before. "That's why everything keeps going wrong with it, that and the fact that you're always trying to fix it yourself, Bubba."

"It ain't been wrecked, good buddy," Bubba said.

"It sure as hell has. Where you think all that Bondo came from, the factory?"

"I won't have you talking about Smudge that way," Bubba told him.

"I didn't say a word about Smudge."

"Smudge has been my good buddy since we were in Sunday school together, way back."

"Way back when you used to go to church and listen to your daddy," Muskrat reminded him. "Don't forget, you was the preacher's kid."

Bubba was shocked by another memory of name-calling. *The flucking preacher's kid.* He had forgotten all about it. For a moment, he couldn't speak. His bowels came alive.

"I'm just pointing out, for your own good, Bubba, that it didn't hurt Smudge one bit to be on the preacher's good side. Not everybody has as high opinion of Smudge as you do."

Muskrat had heard every tale there was about everybody in the city who had ever owned a car that needed fixing, including the Dodge Dart belonging to Miss Prum, who happened to be the director of Christian education at the historic downtown Second Presbyterian Church, where Dr. But Fluck had been the senior minister.

"Look, it's already six-thirty and I gotta start my shift early tonight, as if my day hasn't been bad enough. So I guess we'd better get this leak taken care of," Bubba said as an Escort drove up and parked outside the shop.

"I'm going as fast as I can," Muskrat said.

He peeled the Jeep's headliner and its cardboard away from the ceiling and examined the rubbery black polyurethane in the pitch well.

"Least you didn't try to fix this one yourself," Muskrat observed.

"Didn't have time," Bubba said.

"Good thing, since you're always screwing up things worse," Muskrat candidly said.

They did not see the clean-cut kid walk in until he was so close he startled them.

"Hi," the kid said. "Didn't mean to scare you."

"Don't go sneaking up on people like that, son," Muskrat said.

"I got a stuck window," the kid told him.

"Well, you just stand on back and hold your horses," Muskrat said. "I'll get with you as soon as I wind up here."

Bubba hadn't finished arguing yet.

"I did my own pigtail wiring on my trailer hitch," he said.

"And you got the turn signal lights backwards," Muskrat countered.

"So what, big deal."

"Well, I'll remind you of a *big deal.* Remember the serpentine belt?" Muskrat talked on.

"The directions weren't clear," Bubba answered.

"Well, you fought it out with that one for five hours and still put it on wrong—ribbed against smooth instead of ribbed against ribbed and smooth against smooth, and next thing you've lost the alternator, power steering, water pump. You're just lucky you didn't lock up the engine and have to get a new one. Bubba, you can start spraying."

"Excuse me?" the kid politely said. "You know how long you'll be?"

"You'll have to hold off for just a minute," Muskrat told him.

Bubba worked the Windex bottle along

the top of the windshield, spraying water near the rearview mirror while Muskrat blasted compressed air at the seal from the inside.

"Before that," Muskrat picked up where he'd left off, "you replaced the mercury switch in the trunk and did that wrong, too. So the trunk light stayed on all the time and your battery kept going dead. Before that it was replacing your brakes and putting the pad in backwards, and the time before that, you left out the antirattle spring, the horse-shoe clip in the emergency brake, and the lever fell into the drum."

Bubba winked at the kid as if to imply that Muskrat was exaggerating. Muskrat walked over to a workbench, where the heater box was warming up several tubes of SikaTack Ultrafast polyurethane. He picked up a caulking gun and dropped a tube inside it.

"Remember the time you forgot the cotter pin and the tire rod fell off and both wheels went out spread-eagle?" Muskrat kept on.

"He can tell a story," Bubba said to the kid.

Water trickled down the inside of the glass. Muskrat ran a thick bead of black polyurethane, licking his finger and pressing it flat. He stepped out of the car and ran a thin bead on the outside of the glass.

"We need to wait about fifteen minutes to test it again," he said. "Truth is, none of the seals in this thing are tight. Bet you get a lot of wind noise."

Bubba wasn't going to admit it. Muskrat walked over to the solvent bin and dipped his hands in the murky fluid.

"What'cha need?" Muskrat finally said to the kid.

"My left rear power window won't work." The young man was courteous, but his eyes were hard.

"The motor's probably gone bad," volunteered Bubba the ace mechanic. "But you're gonna have to wait. I was here first."

"We got a few minutes," Muskrat told Bubba. "Let me go on and take care of him."

Muskrat dried his hands and walked outside to the Escort. He opened the back door and popped the panel off as the young man scanned his surroundings.

"Bubba, how 'bout bringing me the wire strippers," Muskrat said. "You're lucky," he told his young customer. "It ain't the switch or the motor. You got a broke wire between the door and the jamb. All I gotta do is splice it. What's your name, by the way?"

"Smoke."

"Now that's a new one," Muskrat commented.

"What everybody calls me." Smoke shrugged. "Hope you get your problem taken care of," he then said to Bubba. "I'm new around here. People seem really nice."

"It's the South," Bubba bragged.

"I guess you're from here."

"Couldn't be from anyplace else. In fact, I'm even more southern than I used to be."

"How so?" Smoke asked with a smile that might have been interpreted as a faint sneer had Bubba paid attention.

"Born on Northside and moved to Southside."

"Oh yeah? Where 'bouts?"

"Forest Hills. Over on Clarence," said Bubba, who was flattered by the boy's interest and his respectful way of addressing him. "Can't miss my house. The one with the coon dog in the pen. Half Shell. She barks nonstop and wouldn't hurt a flea."

"Not much of a watchdog if she barks all the time," Smoke said.

"You got that right."

"You hunt with her?"

"Big into that," Bubba said.

"Seems all us southern guys are big on guns."

"You bet."

Muskrat twisted the wires he'd stripped and was done.

"When I was your age," Bubba said to Smoke, "I started fixing things like this myself."

"I'm not very mechanically inclined," Smoke said.

"You can work on it, son." Bubba beamed. "Go out and get the proper tools, some books, and it's trial and error. Same with things around the house. You build your own deck and fix your own roof—hell, just the other day I bought a new garage door at Sears. Installed it myself."

"No kidding," Smoke said. "Remote control and all?"

"You bet. Gives satisfaction money can't buy," Bubba said.

"You must have quite a shop," Smoke said.

"Had to add an addition to the garage. Everything from grove joint pliers to a DeVilbiss air compressor rated at 7.6 CFM at 40

PSI and 5.6 CFM at 90 to diagnostic tools like a Sunpro Sensor Probe so you can test manifold absolute pressure, mass air flow and vane air flow sensors."

"Don't need shit like that, and neither do you, Bubba," Muskrat let him know. "At least I know how to use what I got."

Muskrat replaced the door panel and got up. He climbed into the driver's seat, started the engine and tested the window. It hummed up.

"Smooth as silk," he proudly announced, wiping his hands on his pants.

"Gee, thanks," Smoke said. "How much do I owe you?"

"The first time's on the house," Muskrat said.

"Gee. Thanks a lot," Smoke said.

"Hey, the Gun and Knife Show's coming in two weeks," Bubba suddenly remembered. "Looking for a couple after-market clips, twenty rounds, for my new 92FS M9 Special Edition, finest military handgun in the world. Now that I gotta show you, Muskrat. Comes with pistol belt and holster, magazine pouch. Same thing used in Just Cause, Desert Storm, Desert Shield, Restore Hope, Joint Guard."

"Do tell," said Muskrat.

"I'm debating if I should've got the presentation case. Walnut, etched glass cover. And the walnut grips," Bubba agonized.

"Wouldn't be as practical if you ever plan to shoot it."

"I sure as hell do. Winchester 115-grain Silvertip high-power."

"How come you ain't in school?" Muskrat asked Smoke.

"Free period. In fact, I gotta get back."

Muskrat waited until Smoke was in his car, driving off.

"You notice that boy's eyes?" Muskrat said. "Looked like he'd been drinking."

"As if you and I didn't at that age," Bubba said. "So what d'ya think? This urethane hard enough yet?"

"Should be. But don't get your hopes up."

They used the air hose and spray bottle again. The leak was still there. Muskrat took his time studying the problem until he'd figured it out.

"You got a hairline crack in the roof line," he said.

chapter six

Weed refused to read his story, causing Mrs. Grannis to doubt that he had written one. This disappointed her greatly, and the other students in the class did not know what to think. Weed had always been so eager, the little boy-wonder in art class. Now, suddenly, he was uncommunicative and uncooperative, and the more Mrs. Grannis pressed him, the more obstinate he got. Finally, he was rude.

"Why I did the fish is my business," he said, reaching under his desk for his knapsack.

"You had an assignment, just like everyone else," Mrs. Grannis said firmly.

"No one else did a fish." Weed looked up at the clock.

"That's all the more reason we want to hear about yours," Mrs. Grannis answered.

"Come on, Weed."

"Read it to us."

"Hey, it's not fair. You heard ours."

It was 1:48. Fifth period ended in three minutes. Mrs. Grannis felt terrible. Weed was impossible, sitting rigidly in his chair, head bent, as if he were about to be beaten. His classmates shifted uncomfortably, waiting for the bell.

"Well," Mrs. Grannis broke the silence. "Tomorrow we start watercolors, and don't forget, we have a special program next period."

Henry Hamilton was the star pitcher of the baseball team, and he hated any activity that kept him sitting past two in the afternoon. He made a face, slumped in his seat and sighed loudly. Eva Grecci did the same because she had an aching crush on Hamilton. Randy Weispfenning wasn't happy, either.

"We have two very important police officers who have been sent to Richmond by the National Institute of Justice," Mrs. Grannis said. "They have generously agreed to come today and talk with us."

"About what?"

"Crime, I suppose," Mrs. Grannis said.

"I'm sick of hearing about it."

"Me, too. My mom won't even read the paper anymore."

"My dad thinks I should start wearing a bulletproof vest to class." Hamilton laughed, ducking when Weispfenning tried to cuff him.

"That's not funny," Mrs. Grannis said.

The bell rang. Everyone jumped up as if there was a fire.

"Off to see the wizzz-aarrrddd . . ." Hamilton sang and started skipping down an imagined Yellow Brick Road.

Eva Grecci laughed too hard.

"Weed," Mrs. Grannis said. "I need to see you for a minute."

He sullenly shuffled up to her desk. The room emptied, leaving the two of them alone.

"This is the first time you've not turned in an assignment," she softly said.

He shrugged.

"Do you want to tell me why?"

"Because." He shrugged again as tears smarted.

"That's not an answer, Weed."

He blinked, looking away from her. Feelings boiled up in him. In an hour he was supposed to meet Smoke in the parking lot.

"I just didn't get around to it," he said as he thought of the five-page story hiding inside his knapsack.

"I'm very surprised you didn't get around to it," she measured her words.

Weed said nothing. He had spent half of Saturday writing four drafts of it before painstakingly making the final copy in black felt-tip ink, letters perfectly formed in the calligraphy that he had learned from a kit and then modified to his bold, funky, completely unique style. The second bell rang.

"We need to go on to the auditorium," Mrs. Grannis said.

He felt her searching his face, looking for a clue. Weed knew she was hoping the faculty had not made a mistake advancing him to the outer limits of Godwin's art instruction.

"I don't want to listen to no cops," Weed told her.

"Weed?" It wasn't negotiable. "You're going to sit with me."

* * *

Brazil parked his marked patrol car on the circle outside the high school's front entrance, and despite his constant complaining during the drive, felt happy to be here as he climbed out of the car and students milling about stared. It did not occur to Brazil that his tall, chiseled, uniformed presence was striking, that this might have something to do with the attention he so often got.

He had never really accepted his physical self. In part this was because he was an only child left to the mercy of a mother who had always been too miserable and eventually too drunk to see him as someone separate from herself. When she looked at him, she saw a bleary projection of her husband, who had been killed when Brazil was ten. In her rages, it was Brazil's dead father she ranted to and struck and begged not to leave her.

"You got any idea where the hell we're going?" West asked as she pushed shut the car door.

Brazil scanned the notes Fling had given him.

" 'Go in, take a left,' " he read.

"Go in where?"

"Uh," Brazil scanned some more. "Doesn't say. We 'go through doors ahead to green hallway through more doors to a blue one until see a bulletin board with photographs.' "

"Fuck," West said as they walked.

"After that," Brazil said, "we 'can't miss it.' "

"It's a conspiracy. I'm telling you, Andy. They deliberately had Hammer inherit Fling to fuck her."

"I don't know," Brazil said as he opened one of the front doors for her and they entered the commons. "The former chief had him for three years."

"The former chief also got fired for incompetence."

"Ah." Brazil spied a pretty young teacher walking with one of her students. "Excuse me," Brazil said to her with a smile. "We're trying to find the auditorium. I'm Officer Brazil and this is Deputy Chief West."

"Of course," Mrs. Grannis answered with enthusiasm. "You're exactly who we're on our way to see. I'm Mrs. Grannis and this is Weed. You can just follow us. It's just straight ahead. I'm sure everybody else is already seated and waiting with great anticipation."

"What'cha say?" Brazil said to Weed.

"Nothing," Weed said.

"Ah come on," West said. "I hear they teach a lot more than nothing here."

"Weed's our star artist," Mrs. Grannis proudly said, patting Weed's shoulder.

He moved away from her, his lower lip protruding in a combination of hostility and near-tears.

"That's cool," Brazil said, shortening his long strides. "What kind of art, man?"

"Whatever kind I want," Weed said.

"Oh yeah?" Brazil said. "You do sculpture?"

"Yeah."

"How about pen and ink?"

"Yeah."

"Watercolors?"

"Going to."

"Papier-mâché?"

"Easy."

"Impressionism. You like Cézanne? 'Le Château Noir'?"

"Huh?" Weed looked up at Brazil. "Say what?"

"Cézanne. He's one of my favorites. Go look him up."

"Where's he live?"

"He doesn't anymore."

Weed frowned, following the two cops and

Mrs. Grannis into the auditorium. It was full, students turning around in their seats, wondering what Mrs. Grannis and Weed were doing with the two important guests. Weed held his head up, walking cool in his baggy look of the day. He and Mrs. Grannis slipped into the second row, near other teachers. Brazil and West made their way onto the stage and sat in chairs on the dais, spotlights on them. West tapped her microphone and it thudded loudly.

"Can everybody hear?" she asked.

"Yes," voices returned.

"All the way in the back?"

"Yes."

"Where's your gun?"

Laughter started rolling through the rows.

"We'll start with that," West said, her voice booming. "What's all this crap about guns? Yeah, sure, I've got one on."

"What kind?"

"The kind I don't like," she answered. "Because I don't like any gun. I don't even like being a cop, and you know why? Because I wish we didn't need guns or cops."

She and Brazil talked for about twenty minutes. Afterward the principal, Mrs. Lilly, made her way up to the front of the auditorium as the applause continued. Brazil bent down and handed Mrs. Lilly the microphone. She squinted in the glaring lights and announced there was time to take a few questions.

Smoke had returned to school after a quick stop at Sears, where he had shoplifted ten garage remote controls. He stood up from an aisle seat on the tenth row.

"I was wondering," he spoke loudly and sincerely, "if you think some kids are born bad."

"I think some are," the lady cop bluntly answered.

"I'd like to believe that's not true," Mrs. Lilly piped up.

"We'd all like to believe it's not true," the blond uniformed cop said. "But I think what's important is that at the end of the day, people make choices. Nobody makes you cheat on that test or steal that car or beat somebody up."

Smoke continued to stand in the darkness, listening attentively, his expression innocent and thoughtful. He wasn't finished yet.

"But what do you do if someone's really bad and nothing's going to change him?" he asked in a loud, sure voice.

"Lock him up." The lady cop meant it.

Laughter.

"About all you can do is protect society from people like that," the blond cop added.

"Isn't it true though that genetically bad people are usually smarter and harder to catch?" Smoke asked.

"Depends on who's trying to catch them." The blond cop was a little cocky.

Laughter swelled as the bell rang. Smoke slipped out of the auditorium first, through a side door, heading straight for the parking lot. A cold smile played on his lips as he envisioned the blond cop and his sidekick with the big tits and imagined himself in direct combat with them. The thought aroused him.

Power lifted him and pumped through his blood as he trotted to his Escort and unlocked it. He sat behind the wheel, working himself into intense excitement as he stared at the circle of yellow school buses and the hundreds of kids suddenly streaming out of doorways, cheerful, playful and in a hurry.

Smoke started the car and drove to the

appointed spot in the parking lot, forcing other students to go around him or turn and head out the other way. He wasn't going to move for anyone. Traffic and voices were loud as he sat watching for Weed, who was about to hurt like hell and make Smoke famous.

Smoke wanted to touch himself again, but resisted. When he deprived himself, he couldn't be stopped. He could do anything. He would get a faint metallic taste in his mouth as energy rushed up from between his legs and lifted the top of his head. He could work himself into anything.

All he had to do was play the same fantasy over and over again in his mind. He was sweaty and dirty on a downtown rooftop with an AR-15, taking out half the fucking cops in the city, slapping magazine after magazine into his assault rifle, shooting down helicopters and slaughtering the National Guard.

Smoke never carried the fantasy much beyond that point. A rational part of his brain realized that the last scenario most likely would be his death or imprisonment, but neither was enough to get his attention when he was consumed by lust so intense and seething that these days he did little beyond playing with plans.

It was five past three when Weed walked up to the car, knapsack limp in his hand. Smoke was silent as Weed climbed in, shut the door and fastened his shoulder harness. Smoke drove off, slowly making his way out of the parking lot. He turned onto Pump Road and followed it south to Patterson Avenue while Weed got increasingly nervous, licking his lips, staring out his side window.

"So how come you asked the cops all those questions?" Weed finally mustered up the courage to ask.

Smoke said nothing.

"I thought they was good questions."

Smoke was silent as he turned east on Patterson Avenue. He started driving faster. He felt Weed's fear, and the heat of rage pressed against Smoke like a wall of fire.

"I thought the cops were fuckin' stupid." Weed tried to sound big. "Hey. You hungry, Smoke? I didn't eat my sandwich at lunch. You want it?"

A long silence followed. Smoke turned south on Parham Road.

"Hey, Smoke, how come you ain't talking

to me?" Weed's voice jumped. "I do something?"

Smoke's right hand flew out as if it were alive on its own. It chopped Weed hard between the legs.

"What time I tell you to meet me in the parking lot?" Smoke yelled as Weed shrieked, doubled over, arms locked under his crossed legs, head practically in his lap. "What time, you fuckin' little shit!"

"Three!" Weed cried, tears running down his face in little rivers. "Why'd you do that? I didn't do nothing." He hiccuped. "Smoke, I didn't!"

"And what time was it when you walked up to my car, you little fuck!" Smoke grabbed the back of Weed's woolly cornrows. "It was *five after three!*"

He yanked. Weed screamed again.

"When I say three, what does that mean, retard?"

"I couldn't get away from Mrs. Grannis!" Weed choked, gasping and making awful faces as Smoke gripped Weed's hair, tearing some of it out by the roots. "I'm sorry, Smoke! I'm sorry! Oh please don't hurt me no more."

Smoke shoved him away and started

laughing. He turned up 2 Pac on the CD player, every other word *fuck* and *nigger*. Smoke reached under his seat and snatched out the Glock. He shoved it between Weed's ribs, getting off on how bad the little shit was shaking. Weed put his hands over his face. He farted and burped.

"You pee or shit in here, and I'll blow your dick off," Smoke told him.

"Please, Smoke," Weed begged in a tiny, pitiful voice. "Please don't, Smoke."

"You gonna do what I say from now on?"

"Yes. I'll do anything you want me to, Smoke. I promise."

Smoke tucked the pistol back under his seat. He turned up 2 Pac and started rapping along. There was no further conversation as Smoke headed across the river toward Huguenot Road, winding here and there, cutting over to Forest Hill, avoiding tolls whenever he could. Weed had gotten very quiet. He dried his eyes and kept his legs tightly crossed. The kid was so puny his Nikes barely touched the floor. Smoke knew all about timing. He knew exactly how to make people do what he wanted.

"Feeling better?" Smoke asked, turning down 2 Pac.

"Yes," Weed politely answered.

They were on Midlothian Turnpike now, passing German School Road.

"You know what an oath is?" Smoke asked.

He was nice now, relaxed and taking his time, as if they were going out for a hamburger or just cruising.

"No," Weed softly answered.

"You need to speak up," Smoke said. "I can hardly hear you."

"I don't know what it is," Weed said more loudly.

"You ever been a Boy Scout?"

"No."

"Well, to be one you got to take an oath. On my honor I promise to do my best and on and on, whatever. That's an oath. Something you swear to, and if you break it, something really bad happens."

Businesses along this stretch of Midlothian Turnpike were all about cars and trucks and everything that went with them. A Cheers restaurant had gone out of business, and an adult bookstore had only one car in the lot. Smoke cut up an unpaved side street and drove through the middle of a trailer park, where balding, muddy yards were littered with metal chairs, flowerpots and ceramic lawn ornaments. Scrawny cats darted out of the way. Wind chimes tinkled, and parked trucks reflected the sun.

They turned into the cracked, weed-infested parking lot of the Southside Motel, which had been out of business and boarded up for years. A chain was strung across either end of the drive leading into it, air conditioning units outside the rooms rusted, a breeze sucking dingy white curtains in and out of broken windows. Junipers had grown out of control in clumps, shielding entire blocks of rooms, and grass was dead and treacherous with broken glass. Smoke drove around to the back of the motel and parked next to a Dumpster.

"Remember when I drove you through here last week?" Smoke said. "Remember, the first rule is, nobody parks back here. You see all the No Trespassing signs?"

"Yeah," Weed answered, looking around and scared.

"Well, the cops don't come here, but I can't take the chance. They see your car, and you're fucked."

He put the Escort in gear and drove back around to the front. Weed was quiet as

Smoke backtracked and parked on the side of a rutted, muddy road on the outskirts of the trailer park.

"This is how I go in," Smoke said, cutting the engine and reaching down for his Glock. "You gonna have to come in another way because they don't have nothing in here but white trash and you'll attract attention. They might even call the cops."

"Then what do I do?" Weed asked, climbing out and casting furtively about.

"Cut in through Fast Track, Jiffy Tune, Turnpike Auto Parts, one of those other places on the strip, and just come through the woods behind the motel," Smoke said, sticking the pistol down the front of his jeans and pulling his Chicago Bulls sweatshirt over it.

He kept a good pace along the unpaved road, Weed limping along as fast as he could, obviously hurting. Smoke knew his latest recruit was wondering if he was going to get his brains blown out behind an abandoned motel in the middle of nothing, and Smoke let him worry. Smoke understood fear. The gratification was instant when he made something suffer. He had learned this as a little boy when he could see panic in the eyes, when he could feel terror in the rapidly beating heart of the weaker creature he tortured to death.

Smoke came from a better home than most, one of comfortable, open-minded parents who had never gotten in his way or tried to hold him back or believed their son could be bad. They preferred to give permission rather than force the child into clandestine behavior. They believed if they were trusting and fair-minded, their three children would make the right choices. Smoke's older brother and sister had seemed to prove the philosophy right. They were making good grades in college and associated with nice people and had normal ambitions.

Smoke had always been different. During the interminable evaluations and counseling sessions in Durham and training school at Butner, he had not complained about his family or a single event that had or hadn't happened to him. He had blamed no one for who he was, and in fact, took full credit. He had diagnosed himself as a psychopath. He worked hard to be a good one. Smoke had no doubt that one day the world would know his name.

Smoke wasn't giving Weed a hard time

right now, and Weed was grateful and appropriately cooperative. Their feet clinked bits of broken bottles and dislodged rocks, and acres of dense woods shielded the back of the motel from busy highways and streets just blocks away. Smoke headed straight for a large sheet of plywood propped against a wall behind a clump of junipers. His eyes narrowed as he looked around and listened. He slid the plywood to one side and stepped through the empty bent aluminum frame of what was left of sliding glass doors.

"Who's bartending?" Smoke announced to the girl and three boys inside the boggy, musty-smelling suite. "We got something to celebrate. Weed, meet your new family. That's Divinity, and the three assholes there are Dog, Sick and Beeper."

"That's their real names?" Weed couldn't help but ask.

"Their slave names," Smoke replied.

chapter seven

The Pikes were sipping vodka out of Dixie cups and smoking cigarettes. They looked at Weed and seemed amused, their eyes laughing at him as they lounged on stained, sour-smelling mattresses.

Divinity was dark-skinned, but Weed didn't think she was black, maybe Hispanic or a little bit of everything. She wasn't wearing a bra, and her tight sheer black undershirt showed more than Weed had ever seen in person. Her slender legs in their worn-out jeans were spread wide. She was really pretty.

Dog was big and looked mean and stupid,

and Sick had acne and a dark buzz cut and five loops in his right ear. Beeper seemed a little nicer, or maybe it was just that he was small like Weed. Each of them had a number tattooed on the right index finger and seemed oblivious to the nasty mattresses and the rotting wall-to-wall brown carpet beneath them.

Strewn about were plain oak chairs that Weed associated with school, and TV trays, and boxes of paper napkins and Dixie cups. Candles of all description sat in puddles of hardened wax on windowsills, and the motel furniture was so warped the Formica lamination was curling up. Piled in corners were boxes of chalk, erasers, a slide projector, library books, a corkboard, throw pillows, and at least a dozen empty wallets and ladies' purses and just as many pairs of leather tennis shoes of different sizes. Cases of liquor were stacked up to the water-stained ceiling. Smoke lit one of the candles while Divinity poured Smirnoff into a Dixie cup and handed it to him.

"Are you gonna change my name?" Weed asked.

"Give him some," Smoke ordered Divinity.

She poured a cup of vodka for Weed and laughed when he hesitantly took it from her.

"Go on." Smoke jerked his head at Weed.

Weed's daddy drank straight liquor all the time, but Weed never had. He knew it made his daddy mean and sent him out running around and not coming back, sometimes the entire weekend Weed was visiting. The vodka burned and almost gagged Weed. Instantly his face heated up and his brain got lighter.

"Naw," Smoke said as he held out his cup for more and gestured for Divinity to refill Weed's as well. "You got such a fucking stupid name, I'm just gonna leave it. We couldn't do much better than *Weed* if we tried, could we?" he said to his gang.

"No, baby." Divinity sighed as she lay back on her mattress, hands beneath her head, breasts pointed up at the ceiling.

Smoke caught Weed staring.

"You never seen tits before, retard?" he asked.

Weed downed his second cup of vodka and thought he might be sick.

"Sure I seen 'em," he stuttered.

"Bet you haven't either, retard." Smoke

laughed. "Except maybe in pictures when you try to jerk off that little golden rod of yours."

Everybody laughed with him, including Weed. Weed tried to get cocky and show no fear.

"Fuck," Weed strutted. "I seen tits bigger 'an hers."

"Show him." Smoke snapped his fingers at Divinity.

She pulled up her shirt and smiled at Weed. He stared, his mouth falling open, his face so hot he thought he had a bad fever. She had tattoos of targets and flower petals in places he could not believe.

"You can look, but you touch and I shoot your balls off," Smoke said in a menacing tone. "Everybody knows the rule, right?"

Beeper, Sick and Dog nodded blearily. They didn't seem the least bit interested in Divinity or her equipment. Smoke dropped down next to her on the mattress. He started feeling her and kissing her, his tongue about to get dislocated from his mouth. Weed had never seen anybody act like that in front of other people. It didn't make any sense to him, and he wanted to run as fast as he could and wake up in another city.

"All right, baby, you ready to cook?" Smoke asked, his tongue in her ear.

"Yeah, sugar."

She languidly reached behind her and got hold of a box of syringes and a Bic ballpoint pen. Weed watched with growing terror as Smoke started heating a needle in the candle flame while Divinity smashed the pen with the butt of the vodka bottle. She pulled out the slender ink tube and dabbed a dot of black ink on her wrist, as if she were testing the warmth of baby's milk.

"We got it, sugar," she said.

"Get your ass over here," Smoke ordered Weed.

Weed was paralyzed.

"What'cha gonna do, Smoke?" His voice got small again.

"You gotta get your slave number, retard."

"I don't need one. Really I don't."

"Yeah you do. And you don't get your puny ass right here right now"—he patted the mattress where he and Divinity sat—"then I'm gonna have to get the boys here to convince you."

Weed walked over and sat on the mattress, a musty, yeasty smell assaulting his nostrils. He held his legs close together and wrapped his arms around his knees, his fists clenched to hide his fingers as best he could. Smoke slowly turned the needle in the flame.

"Hold out your right hand," he commanded.

"I don't need no number." Weed tried not to sound like he was begging, but knew he did.

"You don't hold it out now, I'm gonna chop it off."

Divinity poured another cup of vodka and handed it to Weed.

"Here, honey, this will help. I know it don't feel good, but we all had it done, you know?" she said, holding out her delicate finger with its homemade 2 tattoo.

Weed drank the vodka and caught on fire. His mind went somewhere and when he put out his hand, he was surprised that he could tolerate the sticks and deep scratches of the red-hot needle. He didn't cry. He threw a switch that turned off pain. He didn't look as Divinity dripped ink into the wounds and rubbed it in good. Weed swayed and Smoke had to tell him twice to sit still.

"Your slave number's five, little shit," Smoke was saying. "Pretty good, huh. That makes you in the top ten—hell, it makes you in the top five, right? That makes you a first-string Pike. And a fucking lot is expected of a first-string Pike, right, everybody?"

"Sure as fuck is."

"Fucking got it fucking straight."

"Honey, don't you fret. You're gonna be just great," Divinity reassured Weed.

"We're going to initiate you, retard," Smoke said as again he stuck the needle in Weed's right index finger, above the first knuckle. "You're gonna do a little paint job for us."

Weed almost fell over and Divinity had to hold him up. She was laughing and rubbing his back.

"We're gonna show this city who we are once and for all," Smoke went on, full of liquor and himself. "You got paints, don't you, little art fag?"

Smoke's words whirled inside Weed's head like the Milky Way.

"He's gone, man," Beeper said. "Whatta we do with him?"

"Nothing right now," Smoke said. "I got an errand to run."

* * *

It was almost eight P.M., and Virginia West was glad. Working long hours meant she didn't have the energy to get emotional about the dishes in the sink, the dirty clothes on the floor, the clean ones draped over chairs and falling off hangers.

She didn't have to wait for Brazil to ring her up and suggest a pizza or just a walk like he used to back in Charlotte. She knew from her InLog of calls that he never tried, but why should he? She made sure he knew she was never home. If it even crossed his mind to call, he wouldn't because it was pointless. She was busy, out, not thinking of him, not interested.

In fact, eight P.M. was earlier than usual. West preferred to roll in around ten or eleven, when it was too late to even call her family on the farm, where she rarely visited anymore because she now lived so far away. Time had become West's enemy. A pause in it echoed with an unbearable emptiness and loneliness that sent her fleeing from the nineteenth-century town house she rented on Park Avenue, once known as Scuffletown Road, in Richmond's Fan District.

Although the name "Fan" meant nothing to outsiders or even the majority of Richmond residents who were not interested in the history of their city, a quick look at a map brought much clarity to the matter. The neighborhood *fanned out* several miles west of downtown, spreading fingers of quaint streets with names like Strawberry, Plum and Grove. Homes and town houses of distinctive designs were brick and stone with slate and shingle roofs, stained glass transoms, elaborate porches and parapets, finials and even medallions and domes. Styles ranged from Queen Anne to Neo-Georgian and Italian Villa.

West's town house was three stories with a gray and brown granite front on the first floor and red brick on the two above. There were stained glass bands around the sashes on the second-floor windows and a white frame sitting porch in front. Although Park Avenue had once been one of the most prominent addresses in the city, much of the area had become more affordable as Virginia Commonwealth University continued to expand. Quite frankly, West was growing to hate the Fan, finding its unrelenting noises were causing her mood swings, which in turn seemed to be causing the same in Niles, her Abyssinian cat.

The problem was that West had unwittingly picked a location several houses down from Governor Jim Gilmore's birthplace, which had become increasingly overrun by tourists. She was across the street from the crowded Robin Inn, a popular hangout for students and cops who liked big servings of lasagne and spaghetti and baskets full of garlic bread. As for finding parking on the street, it was a chronic lottery with chances always slim to none, and West had grown to despise students and cars. She even hated their bicycles.

She dropped her briefcase in the foyer, and Niles slinked out of the office and regarded his owner with crossed blue eyes. West threw her suit jacket on the living-room couch and stepped out of her shoes.

"What were you doing in my office?" West asked Niles. "You know not to go in there. How did you anyway? I know I locked the door, you little fleabag."

Niles was not insulted. He knew as well as his owner did that he didn't have fleas.

"My office is the worst room in the house," his owner said as she walked into the kitchen and Niles followed. "What is it about going in there, huh?"

She opened the refrigerator, grabbed a Miller Genuine Draft and screwed off the cap. Niles jumped on the windowsill and stared at her. His owner was always in such a hurry that she just thought she closed doors, cabinets, windows and drawers, and put away things Niles might enjoy in her absence, such as loose nails and screws, balls of string, half-and-half or part of an egg and sausage sandwich left in the sink.

His owner took a big swallow of beer and stared at her Personal Information Center, an expensive gray phone with a video screen, two lines, caller ID and as many stored telephone numbers as Niles's owner decided to program into memory. She checked for messages, but there were none. She scrolled through the Caller ID InLog to see if anyone had called and not left a message. No one had. She took a big swallow of beer and sighed.

Niles stayed on the windowsill and stared down at his empty food bowl.

"I get the hint," his owner said, taking another swig of beer.

She walked into the pantry and carried out the bag of Iams Less Active.

"I'm gonna tell you this right now," his owner said as she filled Niles's handmade ceramic food bowl, "if you walked on my keyboard again or screwed around under my desk and unplugged anything, you've had it."

Niles silently jumped down and crunched on his boring, fat-free, meatless food.

West left the kitchen for her office, dreading what she might find. Abyssinians were unusually intelligent cats, and Niles certainly went beyond the norm, which was a problem since he was curious by nature and didn't have enough to do.

"Goddammit," West exclaimed. "How the fuck did you do that?"

Glowing on her computer screen was a crime map of the city. That simply could not be possible. She was certain the computer had been turned off when she left the house that morning.

"Holy shit," she muttered as she seated herself in front of the terminal. "Niles! Get your butt in here right now!"

Nor did she remember the map's colors being orange, blue, green and purple. What happened to the pale yellow and white spaces? What were all these small, bright blue fish icons clustered in second precinct's beat 219? West looked at the icons one could click on at the bottom of the screen. Homicides were plus signs, robberies were dots, aggravated assaults were stars, burglaries were triangles, vehicle thefts were little cars. But there were no fish, blue or otherwise.

In fact, there was no such thing as a fish icon in COMSTAT's computer network, absolutely not, and she could think of no explanation whatsoever for why beat 219 was filled with fish, or why the beat was outlined in flashing blood red. West reached for the phone.

chapter eight

Andy Brazil also lived in the Fan, but on Plum Street in a fifteen-foot-wide row house with a flat roof and cornices of plain brick, and old plumbing and appliances, and creaking hardwood floors scattered with worn-out braided rugs.

The house was furnished and owned by the old spinster Ruby Sink, a shrewd businesswoman and busybody, one of the first who heard the NIJ team was coming to town and might need a place to stay. As it so happened, she had one vacant rental property she had been trying to fill for months. Brazil had taken it sight unseen.

Like West, he regretted his choice in living accommodations. The trap he had fallen into was plain to see. Miss Sink was rich, lonely, cranky and a compulsive talker. She popped over whenever she wished, ostensibly to check on the small patch of landscaping in front, or to make sure no repair work or touch-ups were needed, or to bring Brazil homemade banana bread or cookies and to inquire about his job and personal life.

Brazil climbed the steps to the front porch, where a package was propped against the front screen door. He recognized Miss Sink's fussy cursive penmanship on the brown wrapping paper and got depressed. It was late. He was exhausted. He hadn't eaten. He hadn't gone to the store in days. The last thing he wanted was another one of Miss Sink's cakes or tins of cookies, which was sure to be followed by yet another visit or a phone call.

"I'm home," he irritably and sarcastically announced to nobody as he tossed his keys on a chair. "What's for dinner?"

He was answered by a dripping faucet in the guest bath down the dark paneled hall. Brazil began unbuttoning his uniform shirt as he walked in the direction of the master bedroom, on the first floor and barely big enough for the double bed and two chests of drawers.

He unsnapped his holster and slipped out the Sig Sauer nine-millimeter pistol, setting it on a bedside table. He unbuckled his duty belt, took off his boots, pants and lightweight body armor. He rubbed his lower back as he headed to the kitchen in his socks, briefs and sweaty undershirt. His office was set up in the dining room, and as he passed by it, he was shocked by what was on his computer screen.

"My God," he exclaimed as he pulled out a chair and placed his hands on the keyboard.

Glowing on his computer screen was the city crime map. Beat 219 was filled with little blue fish and outlined in flashing red. That particular area of second precinct was bordered by Chippenham Parkway to the west, Jahnke Road to the north, railroad tracks to the east and Midlothian Turnpike to the south. Brazil's first thought was that some terrible disaster had happened within those boundaries since he had marked End Of Tour twenty minutes ago. Perhaps there had been a riot, a bomb threat, an overturned chemical truck, a hurricane watch.

He got on the phone and called the radio room. Communications Officer Patty Passman answered.

"This is unit 11," Brazil abruptly announced. "Is something big going down on Southside, specifically in beat 219?"

"You marked EOT at 1924 hours," Passman came back.

"I know," Brazil ten-foured.

"Then why are you asking about 219? Are you monitoring the scanner?"

"Ten-10," Brazil let her know he wasn't. "Is something on it about 219?"

"Ten-10," Passman said as radio chatter sounded in the background.

"Oh. I thought when you asked if I was monitoring 219 maybe you meant that something was going on," Brazil said, realizing that ten-codes were not necessary over the phone.

"Ten-10, unit 11," said Passman, who no longer knew how to talk in anything but. "Ten-12, unit 11," she told him to stand by. "Ten-10," she came back. "Nothing 10-18," she let him know nothing urgent was afoot.

"What about anything at all?" Brazil couldn't let it go.

"How many times do I have to 10-9 myself?" She was getting increasingly impatient as she let him know she wasn't going to repeat herself again.

"What about a fish truck overturning, for example?"

"What?"

"Anything that might have to do with fish? Blue ones, maybe?"

"Ten-12," she told him to stand by again. "Hey, Mabie!"

Passman inadvertently keyed the mike. Brazil and all on the radio, including felons and hobbyists with scanners, could hear every word.

"Anything come in about fish?" Passman was saying in a loud voice to dispatcher Johnnie Mabie.

"Fish? Who wants to know?"

"Eleven."

"What kind of fish?"

"Blue fish. Maybe a truck overturning or a problem with one of the fish markets or something."

"I'll have to get hold of an inspector. Unit 709."

Horrified, Brazil snapped on his scanner.

"Seven-oh-nine," the inspector's voice blurted into Brazil's dining room.

"Anything going on with fish in second, specifically in 219?" dispatcher Mabie came back.

"Who's Fish?" 709 responded.

"Anybody's."

"I meant is Fish a subject?" 709 qualified. "Or are you referencing fish?"

"Fish," Passman bullied Mabie out of the way. "A fish spill, for example."

"Ten-10," 709 replied after a long pause. "Possible fish could be an a.k.a.?"

Passman got back on the phone without ever having gotten off it, really. She posed the question to Brazil. He could think of no wanted subject with the alias *Fish* or *Blue Fish*. Brazil thanked her and hung up as other units began calling in with insincere questions and mocking tips about *fish* and *fishy* people, incidents, situations, false alarms, mental subjects, prostitutes and pimps named one or the other, and vanity plates. Brazil snapped off the scanner, furious that the Richmond cops now had one more thing to ridicule him about.

Reporters and camera crews were out in force this night, stalking La Petite France, waiting for Governor Mike Feuer and his wife, Ginny, to emerge from a power dinner of fine French food and warm chats with the chef.

The media wasn't necessarily interested in the Virginia Economic Development Section of the *Forbes* magazine CEO kickoff banquet going on inside. But Governor Feuer had appeared on *Meet the Press* over the weekend. He had made controversial statements about crime and tobacco, and *Richmond Times-Dispatch* police reporter Artis Roop felt dissed because the governor had not given the quotes to him first.

For weeks Roop had been working on a significant series about the impact of black-market cigarettes on crime and life in general. Roop believed if the price of Marlboros, for example, climbed as high as thirteen dollars and twenty-six cents a pack, as predicted by financial analysts as recently as the end of trading today, citizens would start growing tobacco in hidden places, such as cornfields, wooded backyards, backyards enclosed by high walls, greenhouses, logging roads, private gardens, private clubs and anywhere that ATF might not look. Citizens would begin illegally manufacturing their own cigarettes, and who could blame them.

The country would revert to the days of stills, or *smokes,* as Roop called the imagined contraption necessary to make bootleg tobacco products. He further theorized that in Virginia, especially, people would get away with operating smokes, since not a day went by when there wasn't controlled burning, a forest fire, a fire in a landfill or on a hearth somewhere. Smoke drifting from acres of trees or refuse or out of the chimneys of historic homes would not necessarily raise suspicions.

Roop was smart enough to know that if he was one of the twenty or thirty aggressive members of the media perched outside the restaurant door, he would not get special treatment. He had wisely chosen to sit in his car, monitoring the scanner as usual. He had been perplexed and excited when he picked up something about a fish spill in second precinct's beat 219. Roop was a streetwise investigator. He was certain *fish spill* was a code for big trouble, and he would get the scoop as soon as he finished with the governor.

* * *

Even as he was thinking *Shit,* and staring at the computer screen, it suddenly came to Brazil that what he was seeing was not COMSTAT computer mapping at all, but a clever, creative screen saver that someone had downloaded into the police department's new website.

"I'll be damned." He was incredulous.

He noticed the light flashing on his answering machine. He played his messages. There were three. The first was from his mother, who was almost too drunk to talk and demanding to know why he never called. The second was Miss Sink making sure he had gotten the sweet potato pie she'd delivered, and the third was from West, wanting him to call right away.

Brazil knew her number, even though he never dialed it. He switched to speakerphone, his pulse running harder, hands busy on the keyboard to no avail. He could not get rid of the screen saver or alter it in any way.

"Virginia?" He ran his fingers through his hair and strangled his nervousness before it could speak. "I'm returning your call," he easily said.

"There's something bizarre going on with the computer." She was all business.

"Yours too?" He couldn't believe it. "Fish?"

"Yes! And get this. I leave home this morning and my computer's off, right. Then I come home and not only is it on now, but there's this map of 219 with all these little blue fish swimming around in it."

"Has anyone been inside your house today?"

"No."

"Your alarm was set?"

"Always."

"You sure you didn't just *think* you turned your computer off?"

"Well, I don't know. It doesn't matter. What are all these fucking fish? Maybe you should come over."

"I guess you're right," Brazil hesitated to say as his heart beat harder to make itself heard.

"We've got to get to the bottom of this," West said.

Chief Hammer had been fighting with her computer for the past hour, trying to figure out how the city crime map had gotten on her screen and why there were fish in it. She tapped keys and rebooted twice while Popeye restlessly paced about, in and out of her toybox, scratching, standing on her hind legs, and jumping on furniture and finally into Hammer's lap.

"How am I supposed to concentrate?" Hammer asked for the tenth time.

Popeye stared up at Hammer as she pointed the mouse at an X and tried again to exit the map on her screen. This was crazy. The computer was locked. Maybe Fling had screwed up the software. That was the risk when all PCs had to log into the micro-processor downtown. If Fling put a bug in the system, everybody on the Richmond network was infected. Popeye stared at the screen and touched it with her paw.

"Stop it!" Hammer said.

Popeye stepped on several keys that somehow jumped Hammer off the map and landed her on an unfamiliar screen with the heading RPD PIKE PUNT. Under it were strings of programming that made no sense: *IM to $im__on* and *available* and *AOL% findwindow("AOL Frame2.5" , 0&),* and so on.

"Popeye! Now look what you've done. I'm in the operating system where I absolutely don't belong. Let me tell you something, I'm not a neurosurgeon. I don't belong here. I touch one thing and I could brain-damage the entire network. What the hell did you hit and how am I supposed to get out?"

Popeye stepped on several keys again, and the map and fish returned. She jumped to the floor, stretched and trotted out of the room. She came back with her stuffed squirrel and started slinging it. Hammer swiveled her chair around and looked at her dog.

"Listen to me, Popeye," Hammer said. "You've been home all day. When I left the house this morning, my computer was on the main menu. So how could it be that when I walked in just a little while ago I find this map with all those little fish? Did you see anything? Maybe the computer made noises and things started happening on it? We don't have fish in any of our COMSTAT applications that I am aware of."

She reached for the phone and called Brazil, catching him just before he was out the door.

"Andy? We've got trouble," she instantly said.

"Fish?" he asked.

"Oh God. You too," she said.

"And Virginia. Same thing."

"This is awful."

"I'm on my way to her house right now."

"I'm coming," Hammer said.

chapter nine

The adult bookstore was enjoying a steady business at twenty minutes past eight, when Smoke parked between a Chevrolet Blazer with eight-inch superlift and 39x18.5 custom tires, and a granny-low Silverado 2500. He turned the engine off, waiting for a break in spent, dazed, afraid-the-wife-or-mother-would-find-out male traffic exiting the small sex shop.

A gimpy old man in overalls emerged from the door, looking this way and that, Viagra worn off, face wan, exhausted and paranoid in the sick glow of neon lights. He stuffed a bandanna into his back pocket and checked his fly and touched the side of his neck to see what his pulse was doing. He was unsteady as he made a dash for his El Camino. Smoke waited until it was spitting gravel and lurching onto Midlothian Turnpike. He knew his way through the woods so well he didn't turn on the flashlight until he reached the plywood entrance of his clubhouse.

Candles had long since been snuffed out, the gang gone except for its newest member. Weed was sitting in his own vomit on a mattress, hands and ankles bound with belts. He was shaking and whimpering.

"Shut up," Smoke said, shining the light in Weed's terrorized face.

"I didn't do nothing," Weed repeatedly muttered.

Smoke quickly undid the belts, keeping his distance and not breathing.

"Maybe I ought to dump your ass," he said in disgust. "You're nothing but a puny little pussy. Throwing up all over the place and crying like a queer. Well, I'll tell you one thing, Mr. Picasso. You're cleaning up this place before you go anywhere."

* * *

West was running around her house, picking up, straightening up, throwing out pizza and fried chicken boxes, stuffing dishes into the dishwasher while Niles stuck with her feet like a soccer ball.

"Get out of my way," West told Niles. "Where's your mouse? Go get your mouse."

Niles wouldn't. West trotted into the bedroom. She sat on the left side, where she didn't sleep, and bounced up and down. She punched the pillow and rumpled the spread. She ran back into the kitchen and got two wineglasses out of a cupboard. She dusted them, swirled a small amount of Mountain Dew in each, raced back to the bedroom and placed them on the bedside tables. She dropped a pair of athletic socks that could have passed for a man's.

She was out of breath when she hurried inside her office and began digging in drawers for a greeting card, maybe a letter that looked suspiciously personal from someone besides Brazil, who had written her often back in days that meant nothing to her anymore. She came across a florist's card still in its envelope, her name typed on it. She walked quickly into the foyer and dropped the card on a table, in plain view of anyone who came through the front door.

Bubba was late, the night without a moon or stars or possibility of redemption. He had no choice but to exceed the speed limit on Commerce Road. He had no time to indulge in nostalgia as he sped by the Spaghetti Warehouse, where he had taken Honey last Mother's Day, despite their not having children. Bubba did not want them, because Bubba believed the Flucks, especially those named Butner, were overbred and had reached the end of the line.

Bubba smoked and rode hard past Sieberts Towing, and Fire Station # 13, Cardinal Rubber & Seal, Estes Express, Crenshaw Truck Equipment Specialists, Gene's Supermarket, John's Seafood & Chicken, and all the other businesses paralleling I-95. It had begun to rain, limber drops diving through the crack in the Jeep's roof and kicking below the rearview mirror and over polyurethane before touching the dashboard in record time. The Lucky Strike water tower and tip of the Marlboro sign loomed on the horizon no matter which way Bubba turned, reminding him that cigarette making, like life, went on.

Bubba felt hateful toward Muskrat because he had refused to do anything further to Bubba's leaky Jeep. Bubba was angry with Honey, who had not lived up to her name when he had finally gotten home. She had not apologized for gummy Kraft macaroni and cheese and charred Tombstone pizza, both dashed with too much Parm Plus! Seasonal Blend. Honey cared not that Bubba's ritual glass of Capri Sun was tepid, the Jell-O cheesecake warm, or that the Maxwell House left over from breakfast could have blacktopped the driveway.

Honey had gone from ridiculing the Cheez Whiz and Miracle Whip that Philip Morris had spread over the earth, to launching into a weepy litany that Bubba could not escape because she had hidden his car keys. He did not know what had gotten into her. Before this night, she had never caused him to be late for work, even though she had no way of knowing that he wasn't really late because he was going in early to cover the second half of Tiller's shift.

Philip Morris sparkled like a jewel and was as perfectly pitched as a tuning fork amid

the depressing tarnish and unbearable dis-
cord of the awful traffic and endless road
repairs of I-95. The grounds of the 1.6-
square-mile administrative offices and manufacturing plant were immaculate, the
expansive green often used as a helipad by
those of a higher order that Bubba revered
and rarely saw. Shrubs were perfectly
sculpted. Japanese maple, crabapple, Brad-
ford pear and oak trees were lush and precisely placed.

Over the years, Bubba had become increasingly convinced that Philip Morris had
been sent to earth on a mission that, like
God's will, wasn't entirely revealed but
merely hinted at, even to its well-paid chosen employees. Bubba had never been inside a building with so much varnished
parquet and sparkling glass surrounded by
gardens so splendid they had been dedi-
cated by Lady Bird Johnson.

Big video screens communicated to workers from all corners, the industry's technology so secret that not even Bubba
understood half of what he did every day.
Bubba knew it was all too enlightened to be
of this world. He had come up with a theory
that he discussed only with those who had,

over time, been drawn into the secret society of Alien Ship Helpers, or ASH.

ASHlings believed the fourteen thousand cigarettes produced per minute, twenty-four hours a day, seven days a week, were really fuel rods needed by the massive throbbing engine room that propelled the spacecraft through dimensions one could accept only on faith. These fuel rods were inert unless burned, and this required millions of humans to help out by lighting up and causing the collective combustion needed to keep the spacecraft moving at warp speed through its secret dimension.

It made perfect sense to Bubba that the good and loving Consciousness had figured out long ago the planet wasn't going to make it unless IT intervened. It followed logically, according to Newton's Third Law, that if all actions cause an equal and opposite reaction, there would have to be an Evil Force who liked things exactly the way they were and wanted them to get worse.

Thus it was, as more combustible fuel rods were produced and ignited around the planet, the Evil Force got increasingly desperate and irritable. It studied history to figure out what had worked in the past. It came up with a destructive and divisive campaign of nonsmokers' rights that instantly resulted in discrimination, hate groups, censorship and fame for the surgeon general. Sweeping anti-smoking campaigns, lawsuits, horrendous taxes and bloody skirmishes on the Senate floor unfurled like the Southern Cross and sent litigious and greedy troops into a senseless war that could be watched by all on CSPAN and CNN.

The ASHlings alone knew that if the campaign of evil aggression caused people to quit lighting up, soon there would be no more combustion, except by cars, which didn't count. The production of fuel rods would cease. The engine room would be silenced. The alien spacecraft would have no choice but to change course lest it be powerless and adrift.

Bubba was thinking about all this and was in quite a state by the time he stopped at the guard booth and Fred, the guard, opened his window.

"How ya doing, Bubba?" Fred asked.

"I'm late," Bubba said.

"Seems to me you're early. You don't look like you're in a good mood."

"I didn't read the paper today, Fred. Didn't have time. How're we doing?"

Fred's face darkened. He was a closet ASHling and often conspired with Bubba when Bubba rolled up in his piece-of-shit Jeep and displayed his parking permit.

"You saw the video board downtown, that Dow Jones display in front of Scott and Stringfellow?"

"Didn't get there."

"Bubba, it's getting worse," Fred told the truth in a hushed voice. "It's up to eleven ninety-three a pack. Help us, Lord."

"No, it can't be right," Bubba said.

"Oh yeah it is. Let me tell ya, they're talking about taxes and settlements pushing up the price even higher, as much as twelve dollars a pack, Bubba."

"And then what?" Bubba angrily blurted out. "Black market. Bootlegging. Layoffs. And what about the cause?"

"Won't help the cause, no sir," Fred agreed, shaking his head as Bubba held up traffic.

"You got that straight. Most of the rods, especially Marlboros, will end up overseas. Meaning the ship will head that way, following the smoke to the Far East. And where does that leave America?"

"Farther down the drain, Bubba. I'm glad I'm past sixty-five, can retire tomorrow if I want, have a drawer in the new mausoleum at Hollywood Cemetery and know if I pass on tonight, I spent my life in the right camp."

Fred lit a Parliament and shook his head again as the line of cars behind Bubba got longer.

"People these days don't see beyond their damn hood ornaments, which are a helluvalot nicer than yours and mine, Bubba, because of all these people suing and getting rich for faking coughs and blaming ailments on deep pockets. And I ask you, Bubba. Did we stick the goddamn things in their mouths and tell 'em to inhale? Did we blindfold 'em and line 'em up against the wall and say we're gonna shoot 'em if they didn't light up? Did we force 'em off the highway into Seven-Elevens at all hours of the night? Did we make Bogart smoke in the movies?"

The unfairness and downright criminality of it all sent Fred into a fury. The line of cars was almost out to Commerce Road, dozens of other Philip Morris employees about to be late as Bubba was no longer early.

"Tell it, brother." Bubba couldn't agree more. "Why don't we just sue waste treatment plants because it's their fault we shit."

"Amen."

"Why don't we just drag KFC to court because we're gonna drop dead of a stroke." Bubba was inspired.

"How's your cholesterol doing, by the way, Bubba?"

"Honey keeps bugging me to get a check-up. Who the hell has time?"

"Well, I have a new attitude about it," Fred said. "I've decided if your body says 'Eat eggs' or 'Sprinkle a little salt,' it's talking to you, telling you what it needs." Fred crushed out the cigarette. "Course, if I get high blood pressure, I'll just sue the umbrella right out of that little Morton Salt girl's hands!"

Bubba guffawed. Fred laughed so hard his eyes watered. He began waving cars around them. Drivers were panicked as they sped past the guard booth, competing for parking.

Brazil was panicking, too. It occurred to him that neither he nor anyone else would be able to fix the new website he had begged Hammer to delay until the department had someone other than Fling banging away on the keys every day.

Brazil was computer literate and actually quite good at understanding instructions and help files, unlike West, who had no patience for any sort of tool or material she couldn't grip in her hand or saw in two. But Brazil could not cure computer viruses, and he was convinced the blue fish were a fulminating eruption caused by a fatal new strain that had slipped in unnoticed, perhaps because it was widely assumed if one abstained from practicing unsafe disks, there was nothing to worry about. How could he have been so naive? How could he have been so careless when he knew damn well that viruses could be transmitted over the Internet, and therefore his website had put all of COMSTAT in jeopardy?

Brazil's heart battered his ribs as he drove his cosmos V6 BMW Z3. The leather still smelled new, the paint was without a flaw, yet he didn't love the car the way he did the vintage BMW 2002 that had belonged to his father. When Brazil had covered it and left it at his childhood home in Davidson, he had thought it was the thing to do. It was time to start over. It was time to leave his past.

Maybe it was time to finally get away from his alcoholic mother.

He passed through the endless intersections and one-way streets of the Fan, avoiding bicycles and pedestrians and the crowds trying to get in and out of Helen's, Joe's Inn, Soble's, Konsta's, Commercial Tap House, Southern Culture and various markets and Laundromats. Brazil was terrified of telling Hammer the truth about COMSTAT, and worse, parking wasn't possible in West's part of town. Brazil had no luck, and groaned when he saw Hammer turning up and down narrow streets, impatient and picking up speed, for whenever she could not get somewhere, she did it in a hurry.

Brazil parked in front of a fire hydrant as a Mercedes V12 roared away from a curb and a Jeep Cherokee tried to bulldoze its way into the space. Brazil jumped out of his car, trotted over to the Jeep and held up his hand to halt. Shari Moody was at the wheel. She scowled as she rolled down her window.

"Look, I was here first," she said.

"That's not the issue," Brazil told her.

"It sure as hell is."

"I'm Richmond Police."

"The whole department?" she scoffed.

"An officer."

"An officer? Just one?" she said sarcastically.

"There's no point in being rude, ma'am."

"Police officers don't drive BMWs and you're in jeans," she retorted. "I'm so sick and tired of people trying to cheat me out of parking just because I'm a woman."

Brazil got out his creds and displayed them as he noted Hammer racing by again.

"We drive all kinds of cars and aren't always in uniform," Brazil explained to Shari Moody, whose parking place he was going to appropriate. "Depends on what we're doing, ma'am, and gender has nothing to do with it."

"Bullshit," she said, popping gum as she argued. "If I was a guy, you wouldn't be standing here."

"Yes, I would."

"What are you going to do, anyway? Give me a ticket for something I didn't do, as usual. You know how many tickets I get just because I'm a woman in a four-by-four?"

Brazil had no idea.

"Lots," she said. "If I had a Suburban or, God forbid, a Ford F-350 Crew Cab with a four-hundred-and-sixty-cubic-inch engine, a brush guard and tow package, I'd probably be on fucking death row."

"I'm not giving you a ticket," Brazil told her. "But I'm afraid you're in a U.Z. and I'm going to have to ask you to leave for your own protection."

"An Uzi?" She was suddenly frightened and locked her doors. "You mean drug dealers with machine guns are in this neighborhood, too?"

"This is an Unsafe Zone," Brazil explained in his best police tone. "We've been having an epidemic of Jeeps broken into around here."

"Ohhhhh," she said as it dimly came to her. "I've read about that. The cabbage thing."

"You definitely don't want to park your Jeep here, ma'am," Brazil told her as Hammer flew by again, going faster the other way.

"Well, gee," Ms. Moody said, finally easing up and appreciating how good-looking and helpful the cop was. "I sure am glad you told me. You new around here? Some way I can get hold of you if I need further information about U.Z.s and the cabbage problem?"

Brazil gave Ms. Moody his card and moved her along. He managed to flag down Hammer as she was racing through the intersection again. He motioned her into the space at the curb, got back into his car and had to park five blocks away, close to a run-down section of West Cary where citizens stared at him from porches and calculated how much a chop shop would pay for his car.

chapter ten

Bubba hurried along in his blue uniform and safety shoes and earplugs, already getting sweaty as he race-walked through two filter rooms. He trotted under the observation deck that had not been used since Philip Morris had started giving scheduled tours on small trains.

He ran and walked and ran and walked over shiny floors filled with spotless beige Hauni Protos II and G.D. Balogna making machines, computers and OSCAR units in bays where the roar and rat-a-tatting of production never ceased and there was no such thing as dirt or killing time.

Driverless, bright yellow robotic cars loaded with cases of cigarettes hummed back and forth, pausing to recharge at computerized magnets, never tiring or loitering or forming unions. Gray-uniformed maintenance workers zipped back and forth in supply carts and were careful turning corners and passing through busy intersections.

Huge spools spun cellulose too fast to see while thousands of pristine white cigarettes flowed down tracks and were fed into veins that configured them in rows of 7-6-7 for soft packs and 6-7-7 for flip-top boxes before a plunger kicked them into a pocket where they were wrapped in double-wide foil which was married to blanks that were labeled and glued on the sides and fed into big wheel drying drums and finished in cellophane and tear tape and marched single file into stacker towers where ten-packs were pushed into cartons that were carried by elevators up to exit stations with conveyor belts that eventually carried cases out of the building to awaiting trucks.

Bubba was breathless when he reached Bay 8, where he was a maker operator, or more formally, a tech 3, the highest pay grade. His responsibility was huge. He was the sole captain of a module that had been predicted to produce exactly 12,842,508 cigarettes by the end of this day's twenty-four-hour period, or 4,280,836 cigarettes during Bubba's eight-hour shift.

No module was ever unattended at Philip Morris, and Bubba's supervisor, Gig Dan, had been forced to fill in for the last half of second shift and the first sixteen minutes of third. Dan was relieved but unhappy when Bubba appeared, dripping sweat and panting.

"What in the hell has gotten into you, Bubba?" Dan said loud enough for both of them to hear through their earplugs.

"I got pulled by the cops," Bubba bent the truth.

"And getting a ticket took four and a half hours?" Dan didn't buy it.

"He spent a long time warning me and then the radio was down or something. I'm telling you, I was pissed. There's a lot of police bullying going on out there, Gig. It's time some of us got involved and . . ."

"Right now, I just want you to get involved in your module, Bubba!" Gig Dan yelled above machines. "Our goal today was fifteen million and we were some 719,164 below that even before you decided to take your time smelling the roses!"

"I wasn't . . ." Bubba tried to protest.

"So guess what? The latest readout has us at 3,822,563.11 this shift, which is exactly 458,272.0 below what we were gonna make when we were already below what we were damn supposed to make. And why? The tipping paper's already broke twice, rejects is three times the usual because the circumference dropped below 24.5 and the weight didn't hit even close to nine hundred and the dilution was minus eight percent, and then the glue got a bubble because there was air in the line, and why?

"Because you weren't here to hand-feed five lousy cigarettes into the Sodimat. You didn't inspect the quality. You didn't check out the machines because you were too goddamn busy getting stopped by the police or whatever the hell it was you were supposedly doing!"

"Don't worry," Bubba loudly told him. "I'll make up the slack."

Brazil was late, too, through no fault of his own. He had jogged in the dark from his endangered car, back to Park Avenue, and when he reached West's apartment he took a moment to settle down. He rang the bell and she wasn't the least bit warm as she let him in.

"Where have you been?" she asked, standing in front of the foyer table.

"Trying to find a deli," Brazil dryly said.

"What for?"

"A deli, a restaurant, a bank. Anyplace I could maybe park."

"Obviously you succeeded," she said.

"Depends on if my car's still there after we're done."

She oddly continued to stand in front of the table, and he sensed there was something on it she didn't want him to see.

"We're in my office. On the left, just past the bedroom." She waited for him to go first as she continued to stand in front of the table.

Brazil was already getting a sick feeling. He didn't want to see what was on the table. He walked past the bedroom and refused to look inside. He entered West's office and didn't look around. Hammer was sitting close to the desk, reading glasses on, eyes fixed on the strange map on the computer screen.

"What were you saying to that woman in the Jeep?" Hammer asked him right off. "The one whose parking place I took."

"I told her she was in a garbage zone."

"A what?" West said as she walked in.

"Where trucks pull in and out all night as they make their rounds to restaurant Dumpsters. I showed her my badge and she complied."

"You probably shouldn't have done that," Hammer told him. "You got anything to drink in this house, Virginia?"

"Good stuff?"

"I'm driving my police car."

Brazil found a chair and set it down near Hammer.

"Water and Sprite," West said.

"What about Perrier?" Hammer asked.

"Not since the benzene scare."

"That's ridiculous, Virginia. When chickens get avian flu, do you never eat them again?"

"Has that happened recently? I got Diet Coke."

"Tap water is fine," Hammer said. "Andy, we've been sitting here talking and not getting anywhere at all. Do you have a clue as to what this is about? Please explain how fish got into COMSTAT."

"Well, they didn't, not directly, Chief Hammer," Brazil said. "And I'd love some water, too," he said to West. "But I can get it. I can get Chief Hammer's, too, if you want. I'd be happy to."

"I'll do it. And don't be so polite, it makes me sick."

"I'm sorry." Brazil was polite again.

It was awful being inside West's home and reminded that she had never invited him over, not even once since they had moved to Richmond. It was the first time he had seen her in anything but business suits or running clothes, and she was wearing the worn-out jeans that had always driven him crazy. Her gray tee shirt was made out of really soft cotton that clung to every contour of full breasts he was no longer allowed to see, much less touch. He ached all over.

"If you look at the top of the screen here." He ran his finger across the monitor, addressing Hammer as if West had been caught up in the rapture, never to be seen again. "This tells you what we're looking at is our website, because that's its address."

"No," Hammer said in disbelief.

" 'Fraid so," Brazil said.

Hammer and West bent close to the screen and stared in shock at:

```
http://www.sen__orrin__hatch__r__utah.g
ov/sen__bill__10/sen__judic__com-
mit/dept__justice/nij/nypd__1__pol__plaz
a/comstat/comp__map__center  __dc/in-
terpol/scot__yrd/fbi/atf/ss/dea/cia/va__nat
__guard/va__state__pol/va__corr__dept/
va__crim__just__serv/juv__just__serv/va
__att__gen/va__gov__off/va__dept__heal
th/va__dept__safety/city__mang/gsa/city__
hall/city__counc//rich__pol__dept/off__
pub__info/qa/rich__times__disp/ap/upi/link
__ntwk/all__rights__resrv/classfyd/as-
need/othrwyz/pub__domain.html
```

"Andy, I've never seen such shit as this," Hammer exclaimed. "Please don't tell me this is how the public accesses our web-site."

"I'm afraid that's it," Brazil told her anyway.

"How the hell do you expect anyone to re-member something like that?" West asked, scowling at the screen.

Brazil ignored her. "At least it works," he said. "We know that much since we've got-ten some responses."

"But why the hell is ours so goddamn complicated?" Hammer wanted to know. "How many responses are we going to get with an address like that?" She paused for a minute, a shadow falling over her face. "Don't tell me Fling had something to do with this."

Silence.

"Oh God," Hammer muttered.

"Well," Brazil answered her, "you wanted this ASAP, Chief Hammer. It was a matter of finding gateways to pass through en route to our website, sort of the way mail is routed here and there before it finally gets to you, or the way you may have to change planes at four different airports before you get where you need to go . . ."

"Oh great," West said. "So Fling has people going to fifty different airports just to get from one end of the city to the other. He has the post office routing a letter through twenty different states just to travel two blocks."

"To give Fling a little credit, the more gateways, the more secure your system is," Brazil said objectively.

"Ha!" West really snorted this time. "We're safe, all right! The damn website's been up and running for a few days and we have fucking fish all over the place and are locked out of COMSTAT!"

"It would also seem to me," Hammer followed the bread crumbs of what little logic there seemed to be in this dark forest, "that the security situation is rather much the opposite of what you said, Andy. It would seem to me that the more gateways, the more possibility of outsiders getting in. Like doors in your house. The fewer the better."

"There's that side of it, too," Brazil agreed. "Look, to be honest, I had no idea Fling put together an address like that until it was too late."

Hammer peered at the screen some more. Her disgust grew.

"Let me make sure I've got this straight," she said. "The first gateway to our small Richmond website is Senator Orrin Hatch, the chairman of the judiciary committee, the patron of Senate Bill 10?"

"Yes," Brazil calmly replied as he imagined pepper-spraying Fling and throwing him off an overpass.

"What does the Violent and Repeat Juvenile Offender Act of 1997 have to do with our website, Andy?" Hammer demanded.

Brazil didn't have a clue.

"And from that we go through Interpol and

Scotland Yard? And FBI, ATF, DEA, Secret Service and CIA gateways?"

Hammer abruptly got up and began pacing.

"And NYPD at One Police Plaza? And the Virginia governor's office? And goddamn city hall, yada, yada, yada?"

She threw up her hands in despair.

"Is there any fucking place on the earth where inquiries from the Richmond public won't land before they get to our website?" Hammer's voice rose dangerously.

Niles fled out from under the table, where he had been asleep on top of West's foot.

"Look!" Brazil could take no more. "I had nothing to do with the Internet address, okay? All the important programming was done by NIJ's Computer Mapping Center. Fling was just supposed to come up with a very simple address."

"And now we have fish!" Hammer exclaimed.

"We don't know that the address has anything to do with the fish getting in." Brazil didn't believe what he was saying. "They might have gotten in anyway, no matter how short the address."

West got up for another Miller.

"Let's forget the address shit for a minute," she called out from the kitchen. "This web thing is new."

"As new as slick-soled shoes," Brazil said to Hammer instead of answering West.

West glared at him as she returned to the table. She hated it when he made analogies. She hated it more when he pretended she was a lamp, a chair, some mundane object he didn't notice.

"Yes, it's exactly like that," said Hammer, who had slipped across marble and hardwood quite enough in life whenever new shoes had all-leather soles that needed to be roughed up by bricks, pavement or perhaps a serrated knife.

"So how does somebody know enough about our brand-new website to download fish?" West asked. "I mean, come on. We all know damn well the fucking Fling address is how the fish got in."

"That's a very good point," said Hammer.

"The op-ed that ran Sunday a week ago. Remember? I said we were starting a web page so citizens could write in their questions, concerns, complaints, whatever. They were told the new address would be ready in a couple days and they could call HQ for it. Obviously Fling gave it out."

"That's how the fish swam in then," West said again, gulping Miller. "Got to be unless someone inside the department did this."

"Sabotage. A virus," Brazil thought out loud.

"I'm afraid that's also possible," Hammer said. "But saying it's not a virus or a deliberate attempt to crash the system, then there is the other thought that the fish might be a symbol, perhaps a code of some sort."

"Probably making a joke of us, as usual," West said. "First we're the *Ninjas,* then the *Ni-Jays,* then the *Nee-gees.* Now we're fish. Maybe *fish out of water,* implying that everyone wants us to go home."

"I don't think this is about us being fish out of water or fish, period," Hammer stated.

"Maybe we're *fishing* for something, then." West wouldn't let it go.

"Like what?" Brazil asked. "And you know, if you don't mind, Chief, I think I'd like a beer."

"I don't care."

Brazil got up and went into the kitchen.

"Fishing for clues? For crime patterns? For hot spots?" West kept on.

"This is nonsense." Hammer was pacing.

Niles slinked back into the dining room. Brazil was right behind him, sipping a Heineken.

"Took the good stuff," he politely said to West. "Hope you don't mind."

"That's Jim's good stuff, not mine."

Brazil sat down and drained half the bottle in one swallow.

"Andy," Hammer was thinking. "Is there any way to trace this fish-thing?"

He cleared his throat, his cheeks burning, his heart pounding irregularly and dully.

"I doubt it," he said.

"Let's break it down for just a minute." Hammer stopped pacing and leaned closer to the brilliantly colored map on the screen. "Sector 219 is outlined in flashing bold red and there are one, two, three, four . . . , eleven bright blue fish inside it. Everywhere else we find just the usual icons."

She looked at both of them.

"Possible this could be a warning of some sort?" she suggested.

"Fish?" Brazil thought about it. "There are only a few fish markets in 219. No lakes or reservoirs or even many seafood restaurants except Red Lobster and Captain D's."

"What possible illegal use could there be for fish?" Hammer explored. "I can't imagine a black market in them, not unless there's a proposed fish bill we don't know about yet, a huge fish tax in the works and the lawsuits that would inevitably follow."

"Hmmmm." Brazil was willing to consider anything at this point. "Let's just go down that path for a minute. Let's say this is going on in the Senate and no one knows about it yet. Well, since one of the primary gateways is the Senate Judiciary Committee, and saying fish is a big issue, then could it be we somehow picked up some of their coding as our data passed through?"

"I'm getting a headache," Hammer said. "And Virginia, would you please get your cat off my foot. He won't move. Is he dead?"

"Niles, come here."

chapter eleven

Weed tried to get to his feet and fell back on his butt. He crawled across the floor, his new tattoo throbbing. Smoke lit half a dozen fat candles and carried over several gallon jugs of water and a roll of paper towels. Weed started cleaning up his mess and would have thrown up again had anything been left.

"Now, go outside and take your shirt and pants off," Smoke said.

"What for?" Weed barely asked as his stomach heaved like a small boat on an upset ocean.

"You're not getting in my car stinking like

that, retard. So go dump water over yourself until you're clean, unless you want to walk from here."

Weed carefully made his way in wavering candlelight, stepping through the sliding glass door frames. He peeled off his shirt and jeans. It wasn't as warm out as it had been, and he shivered uncontrollably as he dumped three gallons of water over himself, his slight body clad in nothing but soaked boxer shorts and Nikes that sloshed when he walked.

"You got something for me to wear?" Weed asked Smoke, who was throwing down vodka again.

"What's wrong with what you got on?"

"I can't go anywhere like this!" Weed begged. "Oh, man, my head hurts so bad. I feel real sick and I'm freezing, Smoke."

Smoke handed him a Dixie cup of vodka. Weed just stared at it.

"Drink it. You'll feel better," Smoke said.

He went behind cases of liquor and returned with a pair of folded Gottcha jeans, a black tee shirt, and Chicago Bulls jersey, windbreaker and cap.

"Your colors," Smoke proudly said.

For an instant, Weed was happy and forgot his head throbbed. He felt important as he worked the relaxed-leg jeans over his soaked hightops and pulled the tee shirt and jersey over his head. He didn't want any more vodka but Smoke forced it on him.

Weed had very little awareness as he struggled and tripped after Smoke through dark woods and ended up at the adult bookstore, hiding behind cars until the coast was clear, then jumping inside the Escort and speeding away. Weed was beginning to think that things weren't too bad when Smoke stopped on a dark street corner in Westover Hills. He reached in back and pulled out two dark blue pillowcases. One was empty, the other filled with things that clanked and clacked together.

"Get out and keep your fucking mouth shut," Smoke said. "Don't make a fucking sound."

Weed barely breathed as he followed Smoke along Clarence Street to a simple white frame house surrounded by a picket fence that leaned this way and that and had uneven spaces between the boards. The redwood deck listed as if sailing into a stiff wind, and the big add-on garage was out of proportion to the rest of the house. An old Chevy Cavalier wagon was in the drive, lights were on in several rooms of the house and a dog was baying in its pen.

"Do exactly what I do," Smoke whispered.

"What about the dog?" Weed said.

"Shut up."

Smoke scanned the empty street, bent close to the ground and darted across the yard, ducking behind trees and finally crouching around the corner from the shut garage door. Weed was right behind him, his heart hammering as Smoke reached inside the pillowcase and pulled out a handful of remote controls. He tried one after another.

"Fuck," he whispered as nothing happened.

On the eighth try, he got his reward. The Sears home-installed garage door cranked up slowly and sounded ill. No other lights went on inside, the dog barking and barking. Weed thought of running and Smoke seemed to know it because he grabbed him by the collar.

"Don't fuck with me," he snarled in Weed's ear.

Smoke slid a small Mag-Lite out of a pocket. He looked around. The same windows in the house were lit up. There was no sign of motion.

"Follow me," Smoke whispered.

Weed's brain was sliding around inside his skull like an egg yolk. His vision was blurred. He grabbed Smoke's shirttail and crept along behind him, catching his toe on concrete, lurching inside the garage. Smoke stopped. He scanned, breathing hard, listening. He turned on the flashlight and the bright finger probed hundreds of shiny saws, drills, hammers and other tools Weed didn't recognize.

"Fucking unbelievable," Smoke whispered. "The asshole can't even hammer a nail straight and look at all this shit."

He shone the light on a tall cabinet with a padlock that promised treasure inside. He didn't bother with the bolt cutters in the pillowcase because there was a better pair hanging on the peg rack. Smoke lifted it off the hooks and opened and closed the cruel steel beaks. He seemed pleased. He snapped through the lock as if it were soft lead and it pinged into the darkness, clanking against the floor.

Smoke quietly opened the doors. He ran the light over shelves of camouflage, targets, boxes of ammunition, revolvers, pistols, rifles and shotguns. His hands flew as he stuffed everything he could into the pillowcases Weed held open for him. Smoke filled the pockets of his relaxed-leg jeans, tucked handguns into his waistband. He snapped open a black plastic thirty-gallon bag and stuffed it and handed it to Weed. Smoke slung the bulging pillowcases over his shoulder like Santa Claus making the rounds for the NRA.

"Run!" Smoke whispered to Weed.

They clanked and banged across the yard and along the street, not going anywhere fast. They were sweating and miserable. They were slowing down when Smoke spotted a thick boxwood hedge and stashed the bags out of sight. Light of foot, they ran back to the Escort.

They jumped in and drove back to Clarence Street and parked by the hedge. The loot was where they'd left it. Smoke emptied his pockets and shut everything he had stolen inside the trunk. Not a single car passed. Nothing stirred. Bubba's dog barked the way it always did.

Smoke started laughing hysterically as he drove off. Weed had no idea where they were going. He had never broken the law in his life except for the time he drew a disrespectful picture of a teacher he didn't like and was sent to in-school suspension for two days.

"I just held the bag, so I didn't really steal anything, did I, Smoke?" Weed asked. "I mean, I'm not keeping any of it, either. It's all yours, right?"

Smoke laughed harder.

"Where we going?" Weed dared to ask.

Smoke started digging through CDs.

"Can I go home now?" Weed asked.

"Sure," Smoke said.

He started rapping to Master P.

"It don't look like we're going the right way." Weed raised his voice.

Smoke told him to shut up. Somehow they ended up on West Cary Street, which was nowhere near Weed's neighborhood. Smoke stopped the car in the middle of the road.

"Get out," he said.

"What for?" Weed protested. "I can't get out here!"

"You're walking for a while. To make sure you're wide awake when we pick you up later."

Weed didn't know a thing about later. He

didn't dare ask. Smoke's meanness was coiling and about to strike.

"Get out, retard," Smoke warned.

"I don't know where I am."

"Keep walking that way and you'll get to your street in a couple miles."

Weed didn't move as he stared wide-eyed into the night, his head pounding. Smoke was checking his mirrors.

"Meet you two blocks from your house at three A.M. At Schaaf and Broadmoor," Smoke said.

Weed didn't understand. His stomach was pushing everything the wrong way again.

"Bring your paints, retard. Whatever will work on a life-size metal statue in a grave-yard."

Weed opened his door and spat up bile on the pavement. He got out and almost fell again.

"Remember what happened last time when you were late," Smoke reminded him. "And anybody finds out what you're doing, I'm going to hurt you real bad."

Weed stumbled to the side of the road and grabbed a speed-limit sign to steady himself. He watched Smoke's taillights van-ish down the dark road. Weed sat down hard and begged God to help him. He got up and couldn't remember which way to go or where he was. He ducked behind walls and trees whenever headlights appeared, sometimes lying flat on his face and playing dead.

Niles was playing dead, too. He had given up trying to hint that he had been sitting right on top of his owner's desk the instant the fish appeared on the computer screen, which had been at exactly 12:47 this afternoon.

Niles had done nothing to cause this unusual event, and frankly had assumed his owner had loaded a new screen saver for Niles's benefit, since he was very fond of fish and his owner was always looking for ways to please him and occupy his attention so he'd stay out of trouble.

Hammer moved her feet again under the table. Niles held on, paws snugly around her ankles, claws tucked in so he didn't run her hose.

"What about using fish to body-pack co-caine," West said.

"Virginia, that's brilliant," Hammer said, shaking her feet again.

"Drugs could get in undetected from Maine, Miami, from almost anywhere," West went on.

"I want narcotics on it right away," Hammer said. "And Andy, call NIJ's Crime Mapping Center first thing in the morning and see what they can tell us. We'll hope the fish problem's not pervasive, not an indication of a virus."

"With an address like that," Brazil was frank, "I'm worried about how many sites on the network might have been affected."

"Tell NIJ our situation is urgent, that we're locked out of COMSTAT until we can resolve this," Hammer said. "I've really got to head on and let Popeye out. Virginia, please get your cat so I can move."

"Niles, enough!"

Niles draped over Brazil's shoe. Brazil leaned over and played Niles's ribs like piano keys. Niles purred. Niles was very fond of Brazil and had nicknamed him Piano Man when all of them lived in Charlotte and Piano Man and Niles's owner used to get along and play tennis and go shooting and watch movies and talk about Piano Man's eventually leaving the *Charlotte Observer* and becoming a cop so he could write stories about crime that would change the way people thought.

Niles wanted his owner and Piano Man to get along again, even if it meant being thrown off the bed every night. Niles was irritated with his owner. She wasn't being the least bit friendly to Piano Man and was annoyed that Niles was purring for him. Niles jumped in Piano Man's lap.

"Sorry. Gotta go," Piano Man said to Niles.

"Thanks for the beer," Brazil politely said to West as he scooted back from the table. "Chief Hammer, I'll get you safely to your car."

West showed them out. She stood in front of the foyer table again, but not in time. Brazil saw the florist's card with West's name typed on it.

"Good night," West said to them.

chapter twelve

Brazil was jittery and angry as he trotted under streetlights along Mulberry, worrying that he would find his BMW gone or vandalized. He was tempted to turn around and show up at West's house, demanding an explanation.

It was true that their relationship in Charlotte had been somewhat complicated by their differences. She was older and accomplished. She had power. Her personality was the opposite of his. But she had been his mentor when he worked the police beat for the paper and rode the streets at night as a volunteer cop. Those had been the best stories Brazil had ever written. They had won prizes and changed the way people thought. They had changed the way he thought, too.

He had decided to become a real cop, as his father had been, and West had given Brazil the courage. She had helped him and loved him even through fights that were violent storms. When they made up it was always unbelievable. Brazil could not think of her without reliving every taste and touch. He did not know why she had changed so abruptly, and when he had asked, she would not say. It was as if they had never been lovers or even close friends. He did not push because maybe his primal fear was true. He just wasn't worth it. No one in his life had ever made him feel he was. His father had died when Brazil was a boy and Brazil's mother did not love herself and wasn't capable of loving anyone. For a while, West had filled a terrible space in Brazil's life. He hated Jim. How dare Jim send her flowers.

Smoke ordered Sick, Beeper, Dog and Divinity to keep an eye on Weed and make sure he didn't try taking a detour that might screw up their plans for the night.

So the Pikes set out in Dog's '69 Pontiac Lemans, cruising dark stretches of West Cary looking unsuccessfully for any sign of the drunk little motherfucker.

"I'm thirsty," Divinity said.

"Fucking yeah," said Beeper.

"Come on, Dog. Let's see you do your trick," Divinity said.

Dog didn't like being thought of as a dog that did tricks. He never said anything, though. He pretty much just went along and did what he was told.

"What flavor you want this time?" Dog asked.

"Lemme see," Divinity considered. "How about something *ice,* baby? Maybe Michelob Ice? I'm fucking sick of Bud and all that other shit you're always getting that tastes like piss. 'Sides, baby, ice got more spin in it. You know, makes your head go round and around."

She thought she was very funny and just loved laughing with herself. Dog pulled into a 7-Eleven and used his fake ID to buy a second six-pack of Michelob Ice while Beeper and Sick caused a diversion by Beeper's pretending to slip on the floor and Sick's having to help him up as Divinity browsed shelves and tucked whatever she wanted inside her denim bag.

"I think we find him we have some fun," Dog said as he peeled out of the parking lot and started thinking about Weed again. "I don't like him."

"That's 'cause he paints, baby, and you can't do a fucking thing," Divinity said.

Dog felt himself get meaner. "He needs to learn about life," Dog said. " 'Bout showing respect."

"You go about making him show respect and Smoke's gonna tear your ass off and feed it to a pit bull," Divinity said as she sipped her beer.

"Fuck Smoke." Dog turned back onto West Cary Street. "I'm not fucking afraid of him."

It wasn't true. Dog hadn't been Dog until last Christmas when he'd just turned fifteen and was shopping around for a little crack and ran into Divinity and Smoke at the mall on Chimborazo Boulevard. Smoke sold Dog a couple rocks and then pulled a pistol and stole the rocks back and kept Dog's money.

"Hey, gimme my money if you ain't giving me the rocks," Dog told him.

"Not unless you earn it," Smoke said.

Smoke talked Dog into robbing some

woman at gunpoint downtown near the Monroe Building. Dog turned over forty-seven dollars to Smoke. Dog would never forget what Smoke said to him next.

"Now you're mine. I own you." He pointed his Glock between Dog's eyes. "You're my slave. Know why?"

Dog said he didn't.

"Because you ain't got shit in life. You go home to shit. You've got shit for brains. You're so fucking shitting stupid you came out here buying crack and robbed some poor old lady, probably gave her a heart attack. That could be murder if she dies. I might just have to tell the po-lice."

"You can't." Dog was so confused. "But you can't do that."

Smoke started laughing at Dog and Divinity joined in. Dog was named Dog and became a Pike. He started cutting school so much he got suspended all the time, which gave him permission to keep cutting school, which was kind of confusing, to him. So much was confusing, and whenever Dog questioned and maybe said he didn't want to rob nobody else or break into another car or restaurant, Smoke got in his bad way.

He knew how to hurt Dog and make Dog

scared for his life. Smoke didn't mind killing. Dog had seen Smoke run over animals on purpose, like a cat the other day, and a puppy that was all the way off the road on someone's driveway. Smoke had a game he called "Squash the Squirrel," which was just what it sounded like. Smoke would swerve all the hell over the place to run over a squirrel and he kept count. Smoke bragged he had killed somebody before in the city in North Carolina where he used to live.

He said he walked right into a crippled lady's house and stabbed her fifty times just so he could take her handicap van for a drive. He said he came back after ditching the van and stole whatever he wanted and fixed a sandwich and ate it, staring at her dead, bloody body and then opening up her clothes. He said she was so ugly he cut on her a little more in places he wasn't even supposed to look at. He said his grandmother used to live with his family until he punched her in the face and she decided to move. He said she had nagged him one last time and that was that.

Smoke said he got locked up for killing the crippled lady and was let loose free as a bird the minute he turned sixteen, and no one except his family knew what he had done and never would, because that was the way the law worked. Dog knew it wouldn't be long before Smoke killed somebody again. He had that need. Dog didn't want to be the one who filled it.

"Baby, oh baby," Divinity suddenly said as she twisted the top off another beer. "Look at that ride. Ummmm ummmm."

"We gotta keep looking for Weed," Beeper reminded her.

"Oh no," Divinity told him. "Uh uh, baby. Stop right here 'cause I'm getting out."

At West Cary Street, the alarm sounding inside Brazil's head seemed as audible as a fire truck moving traffic out of the way. Three teenage boys and a girl who looked like a hooker were fondling Brazil's car as if they wanted to gang-rape it.

The boys were laughing, making their cool moves in wide-legged jeans half falling off, one leg rolled up, one down, big high-tops, Chicago Bulls jerseys and stocking caps. The girl was dressed in a short tight black skirt and low-cut black tee shirt. They stared defiantly at Brazil and he stared back.

Brazil walked directly to his car, keys in hand, a Colt Mustang strapped around his right ankle under the leg of his worn-out jeans. His mood had been bad before he got here. Now it was dangerous.

"This your car, baby?" the girl asked.

"Yup," Brazil replied.

"Where you get it?"

"Crown BMW on West Broad," Brazil said with a smart-ass smile. "They got a good selection."

"Oh yeah?" the girl said. "Well, Pretty Boy, that don't matter 'cause I just picked this one."

Divinity decided she was the spokesperson for the gang. For one thing, she wasn't as drunk as the others. For another, the car man was as fine-looking as hell and she might just enjoy herself a little.

"Listen, baby." Divinity stepped closer to him. "Why don't you take little Divinity here on a little ride in that bad car of yours?"

She stepped closer. Pretty Boy moved back. The other three closed in. Pretty Boy was standing by the driver's door, street punks all around him.

"What's the matter, sugar?" Divinity brushed her fingers over Pretty Boy's chest. "Euuuuu. What a man! Ummm-ummm."

She pressed both of her hands against his muscular chest and liked what she was feeling.

"Don't touch me," Pretty Boy said.

Beeper got in Pretty Boy's face.

"What'd you say to her, motherfucker?"

"I told her not to touch me. And get out of my face, asshole," Pretty Boy said without raising his voice.

"Get outta my way," Divinity told Beeper. "He's mine."

Beeper stepped aside. Divinity wanted to touch Pretty Boy again. She was getting interested in him touching her back. She leaned her breast against Brazil's arm.

"How's that feel, baby?" she cooed. "It sure do feel good to me."

"What the fuck you doing?" Dog exclaimed, grabbing her elbow and pulling her away.

"Man!" Sick started walking in cocky circles. "Smoke see you, he kill all our asses!" he almost screamed.

Only Beeper kept his thoughts to himself. He seemed tired of Divinity showing off her parts as if she was some kind of V10 Viper that everybody wanted to drive.

"Let go of the white-meat boy," Beeper suggested to her.

"Let's just take his car and get the fuck outta here," Dog nervously said, looking around and wetting his lips.

"I'm not giving you the car," Pretty Boy told them. "It's not paid for."

Divinity laughed and got close to him again.

"It's not paid for!" she hollered. "It's not paid for! Oh baby, well it's good to know that 'cause we sure wouldn't want to steal no car that wasn't paid for!"

Sick, Dog and Beeper got into it. They started laughing and sneering, strutting around like badass chickens in a barnyard, pants hanging lower, boxer shorts riding higher.

Divinity put her hands on Brazil again, and she smelled like incense and her breath was bad. Her fingers trailed over his chest, and when she pressed up against him, grinding her pelvis into his, he shoved her away.

"You don't touch me unless I give permission," Brazil told her in a tone that was four-star general.

"Motherfucker," she hissed. "Nobody pushes away Divinity."

She reached under her short skirt and slipped out a thin switchblade. It zipped open, the long steel blade glinting in the uneven light of the street.

"Man, it's time to go," the little mean kid with the buzz cut said.

"Put the fucking knife away," the dumb one told Divinity.

"Get outta my face!" Divinity spat. "You fuckheads leave, now. I got business to do and a nice new car to ride."

"We leave you, Smoke will kill us," the dumb one matter-of-factly stated.

"You don't and I'll kill you," Divinity promised.

The three guys ran off. They disappeared around the corner toward Robinson Street. Divinity pointed the knife at Brazil's throat, moving in.

"I thought you wanted to be alone with me," Brazil said as if nothing had ever scared him or ever could. "What kind of way is that to start?"

"Don't fuck with me," Divinity said in a soft, menacing voice.

"I thought that's what you wanted me to do. Fuck with you."

"When I'm finished with you, baby, you won't be fucking nothing no more."

Brazil pointed the remote key at the BMW's door and the lock clicked free.

"You ever been in one of these?" he asked her as the knife caught light.

He knew he could grab her faster than she could stab, but he would get cut, probably badly. He had something else in mind. He opened the car door.

"What do you think?" he said.

Divinity couldn't keep her eyes from wandering inside, taking in the dark, soft leather upholstery and thick carpet.

"Climb in," Brazil said.

She looked uncertain.

"What's the matter? You afraid to be seen with me?" Brazil asked. "You afraid your boyfriend will do something?"

"I'm not afraid of nothing," she snapped.

"Maybe I just need to look the part, huh?"

Brazil said. "Maybe I'm not dressed right, huh?"

He sat sidesaddle in the driver's seat. He pulled his Polo shirt over his head and tossed it in back. Divinity stared at his bare chest. Sweat was rolling down it. He picked a Braves baseball cap off the dashboard and put it on backward.

Divinity grinned. She lowered the knife.

"I got Nikes on already." Brazil held up his right foot. "So all I gotta do is roll up the pants leg and then you climb in with me, baby. And we'll drive the night away."

Divinity started giggling. She started laughing harder when Brazil reached down and started rolling up his right pants leg. She gasped when Brazil was suddenly pointing the Colt Mustang between her eyes. The switchblade clattered to the pavement. Divinity started running. An old shark-gray Lemans roared around the corner and slammed on the brakes. The back door flew open and Divinity dove in. Brazil stood in the middle of West Cary Street, the gun by his side, his heart pounding.

He thought about chasing them, but his better judgment told him to leave well enough alone. The Lemans was gone so fast, Brazil got only a glimpse of a Virginia plate. He got back in his BMW and drove along West Cary toward home.

The first time the Lemans slowly rolled by, its muffler was dragging the pavement and making a terrible noise, sparks flying as if the car were a match trying to light the street.

The bass was up so high the night throbbed worse than Weed's head, and he had scraped both palms when he dove into a ditch just in time. He had peeked through weeds and made out four people jumping around to the rap inside the car. One of them turned to look back as she drank out of a bottle. Weed had realized with horror that Divinity, Beeper, Sick and Dog were in that car and probably looking for him.

It was past ten the second time Weed heard the awful rumble of the souped-up engine and the clanging of the muffler and the boom-boom of the bass coming from a distance. He vaulted over a wall and crouched behind a spruce on the property of some rich person who lived in a brick mansion with big white pillars.

The Pikes disappeared down the road. Weed waited a good five minutes before he came out of hiding. He climbed back over the wall at the precise moment a small sports car purred around the bend, its high beams on and pinning Weed against the night like a moth against a window.

chapter thirteen

Bubba was too busy to take so much as one sip of Tang, which had been room temperature when Honey had spitefully filled his thermos, and therefore would still be room temperature if he ever had time to drink it. There wasn't the slightest chance Bubba would make it to the break room to microwave his Taco Bell Lunchable, which Honey had not ruined because she couldn't.

Bubba had not a moment to think about the Icehouse or Molson Golden or Foster's Lager filling the refrigerator in the mud room, waiting for him when he finally rolled in, exhausted, around half past seven every morning except Tuesday and Wednesday, his days off. Bubba did not eat, drink or smoke anything that wasn't Philip Morris. He would have bought nothing but Philip Morris stock if he didn't spend so much on its products and his Jeep and tools.

Bubba Fluck's feelings were lacerated to the point of rage. He was being treated like shit as he tried like hell to speed things along in Bay 8. Sure, there had been a lot of rejects flying into the bins on the floor, destined for the ripper room, where they would be fed into a machine, the precious tobacco separated from the paper and reclaimed. Bubba refused to accept defeat. He figured if three shifts could crank out thirty million packs of cigarettes every twenty-four hours, then he, by God, could whip out an extra half a million cigarettes or twenty-five thousand packs before shift change.

Bubba worked like one possessed, dashing back and forth between the computer and the maker. When the resistance to draw got a little too close to the red line, Bubba was right there making the adjustment. He intuitively knew when he was going to run out of glue and made sure the attendant pulled up the cart early. When the tipping paper broke again, Bubba spooled it back through the air channel, up into the feed rollers, threaded it into the garnisher and hit reset in a record thirty-one seconds.

When the paper broke another time, he realized he had dull knives in the cutting head and summoned a fixer to take care of the problem. Bubba sweated through more lost minutes and worked even faster to make up the time. He ran three hours without another mishap, without stopping, and by four A.M., the production report on the computer screen showed Bubba was only 21,350 dual rods, or less than two minutes, behind Bay 5.

Production supervisor Betty Council monitored quality and oversaw fixers and electricians, and coordinated shifts. She had been keeping her eye on Bubba for weeks because he seemed to have more technical problems than any of the other operators. Gig Dan had told her he was getting fed up with him.

"How are we doing?" she called out to Bubba as the vacuum in the maker sucked blended tobacco down, and rods formed almost faster than the eye could follow.

Bubba was too busy to answer.

"You don't have to kill yourself," said Council, who was on her way to being promoted again because she was smart, hardworking, and several months ago had increased production three percent by encouraging competition among the bays.

"I'm fine," Bubba said as rods were glued, cut, plucked into the transfer drum, carried to another knife and flipper, then to another drum. Plugs from the plug hopper were cut and married to the rods.

"I'm absolutely amazed," she yelled above the roar and strike of machines. "You and Smudge are almost neck and neck."

Brazil stepped on the gas in pursuit of the kid half-falling and zigzagging on the side of the road. It was commonly accepted in policing that if a subject was running, usually there was a reason. Brazil rolled down his window.

"What's going on?" he called out as he drove and the kid continued to dash about.

"Nothing," the kid gasped, the whites of his eyes showing all the way around as fear propelled his Nikes.

"Something is, or you wouldn't be running," Brazil called back. "Stop so I can talk to you!"

"Can't."

"Yes, you can."

"Uh-uh."

Brazil pulled off the road ahead of him and jumped out. The kid was exhausted and intoxicated. He was wearing a Bulls jersey and looked vaguely familiar, even in the dark.

"Leave me alone!" he screamed as Brazil grabbed him by the back of his jersey. "I didn't do nothing!"

"Whoa," Brazil said. "Calm down. Wait a minute. I've met you before. You're that kid at Godwin, the artist. A different sort of name. What was it . . . ? *Week? Wheeze?*"

"I'm not telling you nothing!" The kid was heaving, sweat shining on his face and dripping off his chin.

Brazil looked around, wondering, listening. He didn't see anyone else. There was no burglar alarm hammering anywhere, the road dark, the night silent.

"Weed," he suddenly remembered. "Yeah, that's it."

"No it ain't," Weed said.

"Yeah, it is. I'm sure of it. I'm Andy Brazil."

"You're that cop who came to school," Weed accused him.

"Something wrong with that?" Brazil asked.

"So how come you're out here in a BMW?" Weed demanded to know.

"A better question is how come you're drunk and running like a maniac?"

Weed looked up to where the moon would be, were it not covered in clouds.

"I'm taking you home," Brazil said.

"You can't make me," Weed defied him, his words slurring and knocking one another down.

"Sure I can." Brazil laughed. "You're drunk in public. You're a juvenile. You can either come downtown or I'm taking you to your house, and if I were you, I'd choose the latter and take some aspirin and go to bed."

Weed was thinking. A U-Haul truck rumbled past, then a station wagon. Weed was still thinking, wiping his face on his sleeve. A VW Rabbit buzzed by, then a Jeep that reminded Brazil of CABBAGES. Brazil shrugged and walked over to his car. He opened his door.

"I'll call a unit to come take you downtown," he said. "I'm not hauling prisoners in my personal car."

"You said you'd drive me home in it," Weed countered. "Now you saying you ain't."

"I said I'm not hauling your butt downtown."

Brazil shut his door.

Weed yanked open the passenger's door and slid onto the leather seat. He fastened his shoulder harness and didn't say a word. Brazil pulled back onto West Cary.

"What's your real name?" Brazil asked him.

"Weed."

"How'd you end up with a name like that, huh?"

"I dunno." Weed stared down at his untied hightops.

"Sure you do."

"My daddy works for the city."

"And?" Brazil encouraged him.

"Cuttin' grass and stuff. Pullin' weeds. Called me Weed 'cause he said I'd grow like one."

Instantly he was humiliated and alarmed. It was obvious he had never grown like a weed, and he had told the cop way too much. He watched the cop write down

Weed on a little notepad. Shit! If the cop figured out Weed was a Pike, Weed would die. Smoke would see to that.

"What's your last name?" Brazil then asked.

"Jones," Weed lied.

Brazil wrote this down, too.

"What's the five for?"

"Huh?"

"The five tattooed on your finger."

Fear turned to panic. Weed's mind went blank.

"I don't got no tattoo," he stupidly said.

"Yeah? Then what am I looking at?"

Weed examined one hand, then the other as if he had never taken a good look at himself before this moment. He stared at the 5 and rubbed it with his thumb.

"It don't mean nothing," he said. "I just did it, you know?"

"But why the number five?" Brazil persisted. "You picked it for a reason."

Weed was beginning to shake. If the cop figured out that 5 was Weed's slave number, one thing might lead to another.

"It's my lucky number," Weed said as sweat trickled from his armpits, down his sides, beneath his Bulls colors.

Brazil fiddled with the CD player, jumping around from Mike & The Mechanics to Elton John before deciding on Enya.

"Man, how you listen to that?" Weed finally said.

"What about it?"

"It ain't got nothing to it. No good drums or cymbals or words that mean something."

"Maybe the words mean something to me," Brazil answered him. "Maybe I don't care about drums or cymbals."

"Oh yeah?" Weed got mad. "You're just saying that because I play cymbals and pretty soon gonna learn drums."

"You mind telling me where we're going?" Brazil said. "Or is it a secret."

"I bet you don't know nothing about cymbals." Weed's logic was fading in and out, the dark smooth ride sedating him further. "We're in the Azalea Parade, too."

"I know you have to live somewhere near Godwin or you couldn't go to school there." Brazil was getting increasingly frustrated.

Weed was falling asleep. He smelled bad and Brazil still didn't know why the kid had been out on the street drunk and running as if Jack the Ripper were after him. Brazil reached over and gently shook him. Weed practically jumped through the roof.

"No!" he screamed.

Brazil turned on the light above the visor and took a long hard look at Weed. Brazil noticed that the number 5 on his right index finger was crude and puffy.

"Tell me where you live," Brazil said firmly. "Wake up, Weed, and tell me."

"Henrico Doctor."

"The hospital?"

"Uh huh."

"You live near Henrico Doctors' Hospital?"

"Uh huh. My head hurts so bad."

"That's not in Godwin's district."

"My daddy live in the district. My mama don't."

"Well, who are you going home to, Weed? Your mother or your dad?"

"I don't hardly ever go near him. Just now and then, maybe a weekend every two months so he can go out and leave me alone, which is all right by me."

"What street does your mother live on?"

"Forest and Skipwith. I can show you." Weed's tongue was sticking to the roof of his mouth.

Brazil plucked Weed's right hand out of his lap.

"What'd you go and get a tattoo for?" he said again. "Somebody talk you into that?"

"A lotta people get 'em." Weed pulled his hand away.

"Looks to me like you just got it," Brazil said. "Maybe even today."

chapter fourteen

Apparently Governor Feuer and his party had gone on to other courses and conversations. They had yet to emerge from La Petite France, and Roop was tired of waiting. He decided he might as well gather a little intelligence on the fish problem and dialed Hammer's home number, thanks to Fling, who had stupidly given it to Roop.

"Hammer," she answered.

"Artis Roop here."

"How are you doing, Artis?"

"I guess you're wondering how I got your home number . . ."

"It's in the phone book," Hammer said.

"Right. Listen, Chief Hammer, I'm looking into this fish spill business . . ."

"Fish spill?" she sounded alarmed. "Who told you about a fish spill?"

"I can't reveal my sources. But if there's a fish spill, I do think the public needs to know for its own protection, or if for no other reason, so they can choose alternate routes for work in the morning."

"There is no fish spill that I know of," Hammer answered firmly.

"Then what are people talking about?"

"This is simply a housekeeping matter you're referring to, Artis."

"I don't understand."

Roop was getting anxious as the door to the restaurant remained closed with no sign of activity. It suddenly occurred to him that the governor might try escaping through the service entrance. Maybe he had already gone. Roop unplugged the phone from the cigarette lighter and scrambled out of the car, still talking.

"How can fish or a fish spill be an internal matter?" he persisted.

"A computer glitch," she replied.

"Oh," he said, baffled. "I still don't get it. Is fish some sort of virus?"

"We hope not," said Hammer, who was always straightforward unless she refused to comment.

"So the COMSTAT telecommunications system is down?" Roop got to the raw nerve of the matter.

Hammer hesitated, then said, "At the moment."

"Everywhere?"

"I have nothing more to say," Hammer flatly replied.

Roop was certain the fish problem was big. But he also had other fish to fry. Executive Protection Unit state police officers were coming out of La Petite France, the governor not far behind. Camera lights and flash guns fired from all sides, the governor gracious and unflappable, as was his wife, because they were used to this shit. Roop listened to *governor this* and *governor that* and was pleased that Feuer had no comment. Roop casually strolled over to Jed, the governor's EPU driver.

"I don't want to bother him," Roop said. "I feel sort of sorry for him being bothered like this all the time. Can't even eat dinner without everyone stalking him."

"I wish everybody else felt like that," Jed said.

"How the hell do you park that thing?" said Roop as he looked over every curve and inch of the gleaming black stretch Lincoln limousine.

Jed laughed as if it were nothing.

"I mean, really," Roop went on as the governor and his wife were briskly escorted to the car. "I couldn't be a driver to begin with. I get lost everywhere. You know how hard it is to roll up on a crime scene when you don't know where the hell you are?"

Roop had gathered intelligence on Jed, who was known by all, except the governor, to be directionally compromised and deceitful about it.

"You're kidding?" said Jed as he opened the back door for the first family and they climbed inside.

"Good evening, Governor and Mrs. Feuer," Roop bent over to politely say.

"And to you," replied the governor, who was a very gracious man if you could get to him.

"I saw you on *Meet the Press*," Roop said.

"Oh, did you?"

"Yes, governor. You were great. Thank God someone's sticking up for the tobacco industry," Roop gushed.

"It's common sense," said Feuer. "Person-ally, I don't smoke. But I believe it's a choice. Nobody forces it on anybody, and unemploy-ment and black market cigarettes are not a happy prospect."

"Next it will be alcohol," Roop said with righteous indignation.

"Not if I have a say about it."

"There'll be smokes instead of stills, gov-ernor," Roop pitched the line that he be-lieved would win him a Pulitzer Prize.

"I like that," Feuer said.

"So do I," said the first lady.

"Smokes." Governor Feuer smiled wryly. "As if ATF doesn't have enough to do. By the way," he said to Roop, "I don't believe we've met."

The small house around the corner from Henrico Doctors' Hospital was brick with freshly painted blue shutters, and a well-cared-for yard. The driveway was gravel. There was no car. Brazil pulled in, small white rocks pinging under the BMW. He de-liberated over what to do.

"When does your mom come home?" he asked Weed.

"She's home." Weed was a little more alert.

"She doesn't own a car?"

"Yes she does."

"It's not here," Brazil said. "It doesn't look to me like she's home."

"Oh." Weed sat up straighter and stared out the windshield, his fingers on the door handle. "I want to go to bed. I'm tired. Just let me out now, okay?"

"Weed, where does your mother work?" Brazil persisted.

He was eager to go home and call it a day, too, but he felt very uneasy about leaving this evasive little kid alone.

"She works at the hospital," Weed said, opening the door. "She does stuff in the operating room."

"She a nurse?"

"I don't think so. But she could be here about midnight."

"Could?"

"Sometimes she's gone longer. She works real hard 'cause what she makes is all we got, and my daddy gambles a lot and got us bad in debt. I wanna go to bed. Thanks for the ride. I never been in a car this nice."

* * *

Officer Brazil drove off the minute Weed locked the front door. He looked around the empty living room, wishing his mother was home and glad she wasn't. There was left-over meat loaf and cold cuts, and Weed wasn't sure if eating would make things better or worse. He gave it a try, grilling a ham and cheese sandwich, which helped calm down his stomach.

He went down the hall, pausing to open the door to Twister's bedroom. Weed stared at all the basketball trophies and posters, the bed unmade, throw rug rumpled, University of Richmond tee shirt on the floor, the computer on the desk with its Bad Dog screen saver. Everything was exactly the way Twister had left it the last time he had been in his room, August 23, a Sunday, the last time Weed had ever seen him alive.

Weed wandered inside and imagined he could smell Twister's Obsession cologne and hear his laughter and teasing talk. He envisioned Twister sitting in the middle of the floor, long muscular legs folded up as he put on his shoes and called Weed his "little minute."

"See, it takes sixty of those to make an hour," he would say. "Now I know you can't add worth shit, but trust me on this one. Soon you'll be an hour, then a day, then a week, then a month. And you'll be big like me."

"No I won't," said Weed. "You was twice as big as me when you was my age."

Then Twister would unfold himself and start dribbling an invisible basketball. He would take on Weed, faking left and right, keeping the ball tight against him, elbows going this way and that.

"Time's running out on the clock and I got just one *little minute!*" Twister would laugh as he snatched up Weed and dunked him on the bed, bouncing him up and down until Weed was dizzy with delight.

Weed walked over to the desk and sat down. He turned on the computer, the only thing he ever touched inside his brother's room, because Twister had taught Weed how to use the computer and Weed knew Twister would want him to keep using it. Weed logged onto AOL. He sent e-mail to Twister's mailbox and checked to see if anybody else had.

Other than the notes Twister got daily from Weed, there was nothing else.

Hi Twister

You reading my letters? They ain't been opened, but I bet you don't have to open them the way other people do. I ain't changed nothing in your room. Mama don't come in it. She always keeps the door shut.

Weed waited for an instant message. He somehow believed that one of these days Twister was going to contact Weed through the computer. He was going to say, *What's ticking, little minute? I sure am glad you're writing me. I see everything you're doing so you better be keeping your ass straight.*

Weed waited and waited. He logged off and turned out the light. He stood in the doorway for a while, too depressed to move. He wandered into his bedroom and set the alarm clock for 2:45 A.M.

"Why you not here?" he said to Twister.

The dark had no answer.

"Why you not here, Twister! I don't know what to do no more, Twister. Mama quit coming home, works so much it's like she got hit on the head or something. Just sleeps and gets up and goes. She hardly talks no more ever since you went on. Daddy gives her a real hard time and now I got Smoke. He might kill me, Twister. He wouldn't if you was here."

Weed went to sleep talking to Twister. Weed slept hard, his head full of cruel dreams. He was being chased by a garbage truck that made horrible scraping sounds as it rumbled down a dark road looking for him. It was on his tail no matter which way he went. He was sweating, his heart hammering when the alarm clock buzzed. He snatched it from the bedside table and turned it off. He listened, hardly breathing, hoping his mother was still asleep.

He turned on the light and quickly dressed. He went over to the small card table beneath the window and sat down to think about what he would need to paint the metal statue, and wishing he could have come right out and told Officer Brazil what was going on and why he had the tattoo. But Weed knew Smoke would get him. Somehow he would.

The big question was whether Weed should use oils or acrylics. He rummaged through shelves of his precious art supplies, lovingly looking through the Bob Ross master paint set his mother had worked over-time to buy for him last Christmas. It had cost almost eighty dollars, and included eight tubes of oil paint, four brushes and a Getting Started videotape which Mrs. Grannis had let Weed watch at school since he didn't have a VCR.

Weed opened the caps of sap green, cadmium yellow and alizarin crimson. He looked through his Demco Collegiate set and thought about how long it took oil paints to dry and how much cleaning up he'd have to do. He didn't want to smell like turpentine.

He studied his tubes of Apple Barrel acrylic gloss enamel paints. He had forty-six colors to choose from, but to really get a good effect he needed to sand the statue first and apply two coats. That would take forever, and in truth, the last thing Weed wanted was to do something to a statue. If nothing else, God would do something to Weed. Messing with the statue of someone famous would be as bad as painting graffiti on a church or putting a mustache on Jesus.

Weed came up with a daring plan. Maybe he could use poster paints. He had bags full of them. They were inexpensive and didn't make a mess. In fact, they could be washed off with soap and water, but there was no way Smoke could know that when Weed was painting away.

Weed had never used water-based tempera on metal, and tried a little green on the metal trash basket in his room. He was thrilled and a little surprised when the paint went on smooth and stuck. He gathered every jar he had and stuffed them inside his knapsack and a grocery bag. He dug through his box of perfectly clean paint-brushes and decided on two aquarelle for thin lines and two wash/mops for broad washes. He threw in one Academy size 14 round style just in case.

chapter fifteen

The New York City Police Department was beyond Artis Roop's usual scope of things. He had started with directory assistance and been bounced from Midtown North Precinct to the Rape Hotline to the Crack Hotline to the College Point Auto Pound and finally to a property clerk in Queens who gave him a number for the radio room. From there, Roop was able, by lying, to get Sergeant Mazzonelli to talk to him.

"Yeah, I know what COMSTAT is. Who you think started it?" Mazzonelli was saying.

"Of course, I know you guys did," said

Roop from his cluttered desk inside the *Richmond Times-Dispatch* newsroom.

"You're damn right we did."

"We're having a problem in the mapping center," Roop said.

"What mapping center? I ain't heard nothing about no mapping center."

"At NIJ."

"In New Jersey?"

"NIJ. Not NJ," Roop corrected Mazzonelli.

"So where the hell are you calling from?" Mazzonelli asked. He put his hand over the phone. "Yo! Landsberger! You going out to Hop Shing's?"

"Who wants to know?"

"Your mother."

"Yeah? What's she want? *Fish?*"

Roop got excited.

"Hey! That ain't even funny," another cop said.

"Stromboli. Provolone, extra onions. The usual," Mazzonelli said.

He took his hand off the mouthpiece and was back. "So you was saying?" he said to Roop.

"We're showing a problem with the COM-STAT computer network."

"Who's *we?*"

"Look, this is Washington, we've got a problem." Roop said it the way he'd heard it in the movies. "A possible virus has infected the network and we want to know how extensive it is."

Silence.

"It may show up as fish," Roop added.

"Shit," Mazzonelli barely said. "So youze guys got it in D.C., too, the same thing? All these goddamn little blue fish swimming around in 219, wherever the hell that is?"

"Richmond, Virginia," Roop informed him. "We believe that's the wormhole the virus entered through. The carrier, in other words."

"Richmond is?"

"We think so, sergeant. This is worse than I feared. If your COMSTAT telecommunications system is locked out as well," Roop went on, writing furiously, "then everybody's down."

"Shit. It's the weirdest friggin' thing I ever seen. We got three experts up here right now trying to get the damn thing off the screen, but we're totally down. Now, I don't do the computer shit myself, you know? But I got eyes and ears and know when something's real bad. From what they're saying, we can't find hot spots or patterns at all."

"Exactly." Roop flipped a page. "Apparently no one can."

Roop's editor Clara Outlaw stopped by his desk to see what was going on and if he planned on making the last edition deadline. He gave her a big thumbs-up. She started to say something. He scowled and put his finger to his lips. She tapped her watch. He nodded and gave her an okay sign. She didn't believe him. She tapped her watch again. He shook his head and motioned her to hold on a minute.

"It was early afternoon, so I hear, and all a sudden this fish map flashed on the screen and we can't get it off. It just came outta friggin' nowhere," Mazzonelli went on and on.

Roop scrawled *Fishsteria* on a piece of notepaper. He ripped it off and handed it to Outlaw. She frowned and wrote *Pfiesteria?* Roop shook his head. This was not to be confused with the microbe responsible for massive fish kills on the East Coast, or was it? What did anybody know right now? Roop grabbed the piece of paper back from her and underlined *Fishsteria* four times.

* * *

At ten minutes to three in the morning, Weed crept out of his bedroom, pausing before his mother's shut door, hoping she was snoring. She was, as loud as ever. Weed left the house and waited on the street corner where Smoke had told him to be.

Minutes later, the Lemans sounded in the distance and Weed was reminded of his nightmare about the garbage truck. His hands started shaking so badly he worried he wouldn't be able to paint. He started feeling sick again, and he was tempted to run back inside the house and call the police or at least grab his acrylics, just in case Smoke figured he'd been tricked.

The back door of the Lemans was pushed open. Weed climbed in and protectively set the knapsack and bag of paints in his lap as he stared at the back of Smoke's head. Divinity was in the front seat, against Smoke's shoulder.

"I guess the others aren't coming," Weed said, doing his best to keep his voice steady.

"Don't need 'em," Smoke said.

"How come you're not driving your own car?" Weed asked as his terror swelled like a wave about to crash.

"Because I don't want my own car parked

out where someone might find it," Smoke said.

"Dog don't care if someone sees his car?" Weed asked.

"Don't matter if he cares," Smoke coldly said. "And you can shut the fuck up, retard. When it comes to questions, I do the asking. You got that straight?"

Divinity laughed and stuck her tongue in Smoke's ear.

"Yes," Weed barely said as tears flooded his eyes and he wiped them away so fast they didn't have time to go anywhere.

He said not another word as Smoke headed downtown and through the row houses of Oregon Hills where they left the car in a small park on the river. The cemetery fence was thick with ivy and about ten feet high. Weed saw no easy way to climb it, but Smoke did. Weed had never heard of a business advertising on a cemetery fence, but apparently Victory Rug Cleaning thought the idea was a good one. Its large metal sign was fastened to the fence at the intersection of South Cherry and Spring Street.

Smoke showed Weed and Divinity how simple it was to grip the edges of the sign and boost themselves up far enough to grab the thick overhanging branch of an ancient oak tree on the other side of the fence. In no time, the three of them had dropped to the ground and were inside the dark, silent cemetery. To Weed it was a ghost city with narrow lanes winding everywhere and headstones and spooky monuments as far as he could see. It suddenly occurred to him that Smoke and Divinity might think it was funny to leave him here.

Maybe that was their real plan. It caused shivers right up his bones and through his teeth. Weed had heard stories of pimps punishing hookers by tying them to trees inside graveyards and leaving them overnight. Some of the ladies lost their minds. Some died when their hearts attacked and beat themselves to death, trying to get out. One hooker chewed her hand off to escape while another committed suicide by holding her breath. Weed willed his teeth not to chatter. He knew he could not show fear.

"Cool," he said, looking around. "Man, I could paint in here for weeks."

He and Divinity were following Smoke, who seemed to know where he was going.

"You know, all these gravestones, like clean canvases and sketching paper.

Ummm um. I could paint my ass off in here,"
Weed went on. "After the statue, can I do a
few more?"

"Shut up," Smoke told him.

Weed got quiet. It felt like little bugs were
crawling on him, and he was sweating and
cold at the same time. He wondered how
many dead people were in here. More than
he could count, that was for sure, especially
since Weed usually got an F in math. It
amazed him how many of them were
PAXes. No one in his school was a PAX, although there were quite a few Paxtons, and
one Paxinos who had moved down from
New York and thought he was the only one
who knew how to talk.

But it was the dead rich people who bothered Weed most, all of them inside little marble houses with all kinds of carvings and
names chiseled above huge heavy metal
doors. There were windows, too, and the
thought of looking through them raised
every hair on Weed's body. Images jumped
in his mind and started messing with him
bad. A moldy face with sunken eyes and
green rotting hands held a white Bible and
any minute was going to turn to a page with
a curse on it saying Weed was going to hell.

A grinning skeleton in a long satin dress, bony hands folded around a dried-up rose, was about to sit up and fly after him, rattling and rustling.

Weed's legs almost collapsed. He dropped his knapsack and the straps grabbed his feet. He stumbled and got more entangled and crashed through a sculpted boxwood and almost regained his balance before tripping over an urn and landing flat on his face, his head just missing an Indiana limestone marker shaped like a tree. Weed didn't know who Lt. Col. Peachy Boswell was, but Weed had just stepped all over his grave.

Smoke and Divinity were laughing their asses off, hands over their mouths, trying not to make any noise, choking, bent over and hopping around like the ground was hot. Weed took his time getting up, taking an inventory of his parts to make sure nothing was missing or damaged, but his elbow stung a little and he realized blood was running down his arm. He knelt in the grass and replaced clods he had kicked up. He collected his knapsack and bag of paints. He shrugged as if it didn't bother him in the least that he had just desecrated a grave, for which there was usually a curse like the one he'd imagined in the white Bible.

Divinity dug inside her denim bag and pulled out a pint of Wild Turkey. She and Smoke started swigging. Smoke handed Weed the bottle. Weed refused. Smoke shoved it at him. Weed wouldn't budge.

"It'll mess me up," Weed whispered. "You want me to paint, don't you?"

"Sure fucking do." Smoke started to laugh. "The statue's right over there, retard. And guess what? You're on your own. We ain't hanging around."

Weed tried to keep cool.

"Okay," he said. "But how do I get home?"

"Any way you can!" Smoke grabbed Divinity's hand and they ran away, laughing and drinking and not caring where they stepped.

Weed looked around, trying to figure out where he was. It was a part of the cemetery that was very close to the river and populated with a lot of rich people, many of them so important they had their own squares of grass big enough for the entire family. Weed saw the silhouette of the statue two streets and one circle away, and his heart swelled with awe. It was tall and erect against the night, a man standing proud, his profile handsome and sharp.

As Weed got closer, he could see there were six walkways leading to the statue, meaning the man must have been some kind of hero, maybe the most famous person alive when he was. He wore a long coat and knee-high boots, hat in one hand, the other on his hip. He stood on a marble base surrounded by azaleas and ivy. Two redneck flags were planted at his feet.

Weed did not recognize the name Jefferson Davis. Weed knew nothing about the man whose statue he was about to paint, except that Davis was "an American soldier and defender of the constitution" who had been born in 1808 and died in 1889. The math took Weed a few minutes to figure out. He opened his knapsack and began pulling out paints and brushes and bottles of water.

Eighty-nine minus oh-eight, he moved his lips as he calculated. He drew a blank and tried again. *Nine minus eight was one. And eight minus zero was still eight.* So Jefferson Davis was only eighteen when he died. Weed was overwhelmed by sadness.

He looked around at the marble sculpture

of a mournful woman holding an open Bible. An angel with big wings was sitting nearby. They seemed to be watching him and waiting. Weed suddenly knew why he had been brought here. It had nothing to do with Smoke, not in the big scheme of things. There was no curse but an unexpected gift. Joy filled his heart. Weed knew what he was supposed to do. He didn't feel lonely and he wasn't afraid.

chapter sixteen

Sleep was a stranger that would have no part of Brazil's life at the moment. He kicked the sheets off again, got up for water, walked around in the dark for a few minutes, sat down in front of the computer screen and stared at the map and its blue fish. He drank more water and imagined that West was tormented, too.

He hoped she was fitful and full of bad dreams, her heart aching as she thought of him. Then his fantasy was shattered by a face he did not know, someone named Jim. Brazil thought hard of every cop he knew West was acquainted with, and he could think of no one named Jim she would be remotely interested in. West liked tall, well-built men who were intelligent, funny and sensitive, men she could watch movies and go drinking and shooting with. She was tired of being hit on. She required patience and a gentle touch. Indifference sometimes worked, too.

Brazil stalked back into his bedroom. It was almost five. West had made it clear she didn't intend to run with him this morning because she hated running and needed a day off. Brazil put on sweats and went out by himself. He ran fast through the Fan, picking up speed as he obsessed about Jim. All Brazil knew about him was that he drank Heineken, or at least had brought a six-pack to West's house, so it was also possible that he simply thought she liked Heineken. Jim might not drink beer at all. He might be into Scotch or fine wine, although Brazil had noticed neither in West's kitchen. Of course, he hadn't looked in her cabinets.

He hadn't looked in her bedroom as he had walked past because he knew he couldn't bear seeing men's clothing in a pile on the floor, the bed a mess. Brazil clipped off five miles. He worked with free weights and did ab crunches until his upper body was on fire. He took a long, hot shower, miserable and furious.

Brazil shaved and brushed his teeth in the shower and decided he couldn't let West get away with this any longer. Damn her. He played and rewound and played again and again the last time they had touched, on Christmas Eve, when he'd gone to her house to deliver her Christmas present. He'd saved money for months to buy her a gold and platinum bracelet that she had stopped wearing days after they moved to Richmond.

Brazil felt used. He felt lied to and trivialized. If she really loved him as much as she used to say she did, then how could she suddenly get involved with someone named Jim and how long had it been going on? Maybe she'd been cheating on Brazil from the start, was seeing some other Jim back in Charlotte, had Jims all over the world. Brazil was going to call her and demand an explanation. He toweled his hair dry as he rehearsed what he would say. He put on his uniform, taking his time as he debated.

* * *

Hollywood Cemetery usually came alive around dawn. Clay Kitchen worked maintenance and took his job very seriously. He also liked overtime and found that if he showed up around seven each morning, he could add a good ten hours, or two hundred eighty-five dollars and eighty cents, to his twice-monthly paycheck.

Kitchen drove his blue Ford Ranger slowly through the Confederate soldiers section where eighteen thousand brave men and General Pickett's wife were buried, their simple marble markers closely spaced in perfect rows that were hard to mow around. Kitchen parked by the ninety-foot-high Confederate Monument pyramid, built of granite quarried from the James River in 1868 when the only machinery was strong bodies and fearlessness and a derrick.

Kitchen had heard the stories. There had been accidents. The workers had gotten very nervous. The project's timetable had stretched into a year and everyone was getting tired. When all that was left was to climb to the top and guide the capstone into place, the crew balked. Forget it. You got to be kidding. No one would do it, so an inmate at the nearby state penitentiary allegedly volunteered and performed the perilous task without incident, on November 6, 1869, while a happy crowd cheered.

The grass was getting a little high about the pyramid's base and in need of string trimming. But that would have to wait until Kitchen finished his inspection of the one hundred and thirty-five acres that kept him so busy. He moved on, cruising along Confederate Avenue, then Eastvale and onto Riverside, which took him to Hillside and on the Presidents Circle, to Jeter and Ginter, eventually approaching Davis Circle where he saw the problem immediately and from a distance.

Jefferson Davis was wearing a red-and-white basketball uniform. The hat he held in his left hand had been turned into a basketball, although an oddly shaped one. His skin had been painted black. The marble base he stood on had been turned into a gym floor.

Kitchen sped ahead, shocked, crazed, almost out of control. He slammed on the brakes to get a closer look. The number on the jersey was 12. Kitchen was a sports fan and knew without a doubt the University of Richmond Spiders uniform. The number 12 on the jersey was that of Bobby Feeley, who was one of the most pathetic recruits Kitchen had ever seen. Kitchen yanked the portable radio off his belt and raised his supervisor on the air.

"Someone's turned Jeff Davis into a colored basketball player!" Kitchen declared.

chapter seventeen

Niles would not leave West alone. The cat had never been easy, but there was one sin he wasn't allowed to commit. No cat or anyone else kept West awake unless she chose to be awake, and she had chosen no such thing.

"What the hell's wrong with you?" West complained, turning over and punching the pillow under her head.

Niles wasn't asleep, but he wasn't moving, either. He'd been in the same position since midnight when his owner had finally decided to toss aside that silly *Chicken Soup for the Soul* book that promised a hundred and one happy heartwarming stories that meant nothing to Niles.

"Shut up!" his owner said, kicking the sheets.

Niles's ribs silently rose and fell as he breathed. He wondered when his owner would figure out that she always got cranky whenever Piano Man had been sighted in the area.

"I can't take this anymore," his owner announced.

She sat up. She picked up Niles and dropped him on the floor. He had put up with quite a lot in the past few hours, but enough was enough. He jumped back up on the bed and batted her chin with his paw, keeping his claws tucked in.

"You little shit!" She popped Niles's head.

Niles jumped on her abdomen as hard as he could, knowing how much she hated that in the morning when she had to pee. His owner threw him off the bed again, and he jumped back and hissed and nipped her little finger and leaped back off the bed and ran like hell. She jumped out of bed in pursuit.

"Come back here, you little fuckhead!" she yelled.

Niles ran faster, taking the corner into his owner's office and springing on the top shelf of her bookcase, where he waited with swishing tail, crossed eyes staring. His owner made the turn not quite as gracefully, hitting her hip on the door frame and swearing some more. She pointed her finger at Niles. Niles wasn't intimidated. He wasn't even tired. She came closer and reached up, trying to grab him.

Niles sprang over her head, landing on her desk. He hit InLog on her Personal Information Center phone until he found the number he wanted. Then he hit Speaker and Dial. He waited until his owner almost had her hand on the back of his neck. He bopped her nose and was gone again as a phone loudly rang and rang over the speaker.

"Hello?" Piano Man answered.

West froze.

"Hello?" Brazil asked again.

She snatched up the phone.

"How'd I call you when I didn't?" she demanded to know as she read Brazil's number on the video screen.

"Who is this?" Brazil asked.

"Niles did it, not me," West said.

"Virginia?"

"I didn't do it," she said, glaring at Niles, who was stretching one leg after another from a safe distance.

"It's not like it's a crime if you called me," Brazil said.

"That's not the point."

"You want to have breakfast or are you tied up?" Brazil said haltingly, as if he was just being nice and had no interest whatsoever in seeing her.

"God, I don't know," she replied as she ran through a list of other fabricated options. "What time is it? Niles kept me up all night."

"It's almost seven."

"I'm not running with you if that's what you're really asking," West shot back as her heart forgot its rhythm.

"I've already done that," Brazil said. "River City Diner? You been there?"

"I can't remember the names of everything around here."

"It's really good. You mind picking me up since you get to take home a car and I don't?"

"So I guess you know all the places around here," West said.

Popeye would not give Hammer a moment's peace this morning, either. She jumped all over Hammer. She brazenly ran into Hammer's office and jumped into the desk chair and stared at the computer screen and the fish on it. She would not let Hammer sit and drink a first cup of coffee or glance at the paper. Popeye was stubborn on her walk. Treats were of no interest. She wouldn't sit, lie down, come or stay.

"What good does it do for me to read all those books and consult with an animal behaviorist?" Hammer asked in exasperation. "I don't need this, Popeye. I have tried reasoning with you. I've talked with you at great length about how important it is to cooperate and be a pleasure to have around. I've asked you many times if something traumatic might have happened to you before I got you from the SPCA, something that has caused you to start nipping at people and jumping in their faces.

"But whatever it is, you won't let me know, and it's not fair, Popeye. You know how much

I care. You know my life is hard and I need no more stress. You know I will be sued if you bite someone and they fake emotional distress, disfigurement and sexual dysfunction because they know I have money and don't need bad publicity. Now sit, and I mean it."

Hammer squatted, holding a treat in her fist.

Popeye assumed her defiant stance and just stared at her.

"Sit."

Popeye wouldn't.

"Lie down."

Popeye didn't.

"What's gotten into you?" Hammer asked.

The shockwaves traveled quickly and with alarming repercussions. Hollywood Cemetery's maintenance supervisor immediately alerted the cemetery association president, Lelia Ehrhart, who instantly called every member of the board, including Ruby Sink, the association secretary and the most likely person to spread the news.

Miss Sink decided to go out and get her newspaper at the precise moment Chief

Hammer was walking by with Popeye. Hammer quickly moved past the two-story brick town house with its Doric front porch and original cornices and windows. Miss Sink picked up speed, shuffling down steps and over cobblestones.

"Come back here," Miss Sink called out.

Hammer did not appreciate being ordered about.

"Good morning, Miss Sink," she politely said without slowing down.

"I need to speak to you."

Hammer stopped while Popeye did her best to continue on course.

"It's just a darn good thing you showed up," Miss Sink answered.

"Be good, Popeye." Hammer pulled the leash.

Popeye pulled back.

"Popeye," Hammer warned.

"What an awful name for a dog," said Miss Sink. "What's wrong with her eyes?"

"It's normal for the breed."

"Did you have her tail chopped off?"

"No," Hammer replied.

Miss Sink leaned over to get a better look at the stumpy, cock-eyed tail that covered nothing important. Popeye began to lick herself in a naughty place and suddenly sprang straight up into the air, her tongue darting into Miss Sink's mouth. Miss Sink jumped back and screamed. She rubbed her lips and looked sick as she thought about where that tongue had just been. Popeye grabbed the hem of Miss Sink's pink robe and almost pulled the frail old woman off her feet.

"Now Popeye, you behave. Sit," Hammer emphatically said.

Popeye sat. Hammer fed her a Lung Chop. Miss Sink was mortified and momentarily speechless. She rubbed her mouth and checked the hem of her robe, looking for damage.

"What was it you wanted to talk to me about?" Hammer asked.

"You mean you don't know?" Miss Sink raised her voice. She glared hatefully at Popeye as she bent over to pick up the paper.

"Know what?" Hammer asked, irked that there might be something Miss Sink might know before Hammer did.

"Someone vandalized Hollywood Cemetery!" Miss Sink's fury gathered. "Graffiti all over the statue of Jefferson Davis!"

"When did you find this out?" asked Ham-

mer as Confederate troops rose up and began marching through her mind.

"I want to know what the police are doing,"
Miss Sink demanded.

"Have we been called?" Hammer asked.

Miss Sink thought for a moment.

"This is the first I've heard of it," Hammer
went on as Popeye got interested in Miss
Sink's ankles.

"I don't know if anyone called," Miss Sink
said. "That's not my responsibility. I just assumed whoever happened upon the crime
would have called the police. Of course, I
just got the call myself a few minutes ago.
They think some U of R basketball player
did it."

"Who's *they?*"

"You can ask Lelia Ehrhart that. She's the
one who called me."

Hammer's resentment blossomed and
flourished.

"And how did Lelia find out?" Hammer
asked.

"She's the president of Hollywood," Miss
Sink replied as if there was only one Hollywood. "The city's being ruined. And if we had
more police out doing their jobs, this sort of
thing wouldn't happen. Not to mention the

continuing deterioration of this neighborhood. *Here* of all places."

Hammer feared that one of these days
she was going to tell the nagging, horse-
faced woman to go to hell.

"The people coming in here," Miss Sink
railed on. "As if this is some sort of subdivi-
sion with McDonald's and aluminum sid-
ing!"

Miss Sink used to feel perfectly safe and se-
questered on her famous tree-lined street,
where in 1775 Patrick Henry had stood inside St. John's Episcopal Church, in the
third pew from the left, and declared ". . .
Give me liberty or give me death!" It was
here, just several houses down, that Elmira
Royster Shelton and Edgar Allan Poe had
been reunited and began a second
courtship not long before he died.

Although Miss Sink was not Episcopalian
and had never been engaged and did not
read frightening stories, she revered history
and the famous people in it. More to the
point, Miss Sink had an inspired indignation
when any outsider violated the sanctity of
her restored neighborhood, and that in-

cluded Judy Hammer, who was not from Richmond, but from Arkansas, which as far as Miss Sink was concerned was not the true South.

Popeye emptied her bladder on a blooming yellow forsythia bush. She began sniffing tulips and the lamppost, ready to claim other territory.

"Actually, crime is down six percent in our neighborhood, Miss Sink," Hammer reminded her without adding that it was soaring everywhere else. "Thanks in part to the community effort here, thanks to our crimewatch people like you, the eyes and ears of the street."

"Six percent my foot." Miss Sink stamped her pink slipper and yanked the plastic wrapper off the newspaper. "Tell me why someone stole the fountain from Libby Hill Park?"

"It was recovered and is back right where it always was, Miss Sink."

"Doesn't matter. It was stolen. Right out from under us like a rug. An entire iron fountain, and nobody saw a thing. So much for eyes and ears." She dug in a pocket and pulled out a tissue. "Not to mention rocks thrown at gas lamps and cars. Most of my friends and family are in Hollywood Cemetery."

Miss Sink dabbed her nose and gave Hammer's ugly little dog the fish eye. She opened the newspaper to see what else was going on in the city. The headline above the fold stood up in huge black type:

FISHSTERIA HYSTERIA!
mysterious virus crashes police computer network

Hammer snatched the paper out of Miss Sink's hands.

"Excuse me," Miss Sink said indignantly. "That was rude."

Hammer didn't give a shit. She read the story, incredulous. It even included an artist's rendition of the little blue fish that were suspected, according to the article, to be the carrier of the virus.

"Oh God. So it's hit New York, too," Hammer said as she read. "It's everywhere. That goddamn Roop. The media doesn't care. This is only going to make matters worse, rewarding some hacker with front-page news. Oh great, great, great. Whatever happened to people trying to work together? When I was getting started, you could plant a story with the local media and they would run things that would actually help the police.

"But can you imagine such a thing happening now?" Hammer went on. "Does it ever occur to self-serving people like Roop that when we can't do our jobs, he suffers too? What happens when his airbag is stolen?"

"I've read about that. Why do you call it CABBAGES?"

"What happens when he's robbed at gunpoint at an ATM?" Hammer went on.

"Those are awful," Miss Sink said with a shudder. "I see they had another one yesterday. Of course, look how early it was. People have no business getting money out of machines at night when nobody's around."

Popeye lunged again. She got up on her hind legs, dancing about, front paws held out as if she wanted to hug Miss Sink. It made no sense.

"What's wrong with that dog?" Miss Sink said. "It's like she's trying to tell me something."

"Popeye is very intelligent. She's intuitive. Frankly, she knows so much it scares me," Hammer confessed.

"And for the record," Miss Sink went on, "I think ATMs and the Internet are the 666 in Revelation. The beast leading up to Armageddon."

Popeye jumped at Miss Sink again. Popeye growled. She hopped over to Miss Sink and tried to hug the old woman. Miss Sink smacked the newspaper against her hand as a warning. Popeye darted behind her owner's legs, wrapping her leash around them. She was shaking.

"It's all right, little baby." Hammer was distressed and furious.

She squatted and put her arms around her dog and held her close. She gave Popeye another treat.

"Please don't do that again," she sternly said to Miss Sink.

"Next time I'm going to smack her little bottom," Miss Sink promised.

"Actually, you won't," Hammer said in her dry *don't fuck with me* tone of voice.

"That dog's going to bite someone," Miss Sink chastised Hammer. "You wait. And then won't you be in Dutch? These days people sue just like that." She tried to snap her fingers and missed.

Popeye growled.

"Well, I've got to go in and call all the other board members. I guess telling you is the same thing as calling the police," Miss Sink said.

She headed back down her walk, her feet loud on her Doric porch, her cat darting out from behind a hedge.

chapter eighteen

Despite Bubba's incredible efforts, no matter his eight straight hours of relentless work in Bay 8, his productivity had fallen short by 3,901 cigarettes. He was devastated. It was the last night of the competition of the month, and the second month in a row that Bay 5 had claimed victory.

"Don't take it so hard," Smudge said.

"I can't help it," Bubba despondently replied.

They stopped outside the cafeteria and Bubba inserted his ID card into the cigarette machine, selecting the free pack all workers got daily. Bubba chose his usual Merit Ultima. Smudge did, too, and sold his pack to Bubba at the slightly discounted price of eight dollars and twenty-five cents. Smudge smoked Winstons, which were not made by Philip Morris. For the first time it bothered Bubba that Smudge didn't offer his daily allotted pack to Bubba for nothing, since it cost Smudge nothing. It bothered Bubba that it just so happened that Smudge and Gig Dan played golf together.

"I guess Gig had a long day," Bubba commented as he and Smudge headed out of the building.

"He looked pretty tired when he left," Smudge agreed. "Too bad you were so late."

"Wouldn't've been if that asshole Tiller wasn't supposedly sick again."

Smudge made no comment.

"Funny how he always gets sick on the night the competition ends," Bubba made another casual remark.

"Maybe losing is something he can't face," Smudge suggested.

"Also funny how nothing in my module works worth a shit the last night of the competition. Know how many times the tipping paper broke? Or how many glue bubbles I got? Had a dull knife, too. So I clean up right before shift change, and find dust in the machine and glue balled up on the glue roller," Bubba said.

Smudge stopped at his gleaming red Suburban. He got out his keys.

"See, I think someone gets to Kennedy on first shift and sucks him into the conspiracy. So Kennedy works the first half of second shift because Tiller's called in sick, because he's been told to. Then Kennedy fucks up everything he can so when I'm supposed to come in and work one and a half shifts, I've got all this dust, glue balls and shit waiting for me."

"Sounds rather elaborate, like a spy thriller. Don't be paranoid, Bubba." Smudge patted Bubba's shoulder.

But it wasn't just paranoia. Bubba wasn't stupid. He knew Gig Dan was involved in the plot as well or he would have said something to somebody about how dirty the machine was. He had to have known, since he inadvertently had to fill in for Bubba because Bubba was late being early and then ended up late for being on time because Fred held him to a conversation. Bubba kept his conviction to himself as he began to see just what Smudge was

really made of. Whatever it was, it was beginning to stink.

"You owe me and everyone else in Bay 5
two cases of beer, good buddy," Smudge
said as he cranked the Suburban.

"Yeah, I know," Bubba said. "What will it
be?"

"Hmmmm. Let me think," Smudge jerked
Bubba around. "I guess Corona." He added
insult to injury.

Corona was not a Philip Morris product,
and Smudge knew Bubba would rather eat
poison than spend a nickel on anything not
Philip Morris.

"Okay, but you gotta give me a chance to
get you back," Bubba said.

Smudge laughed. "Lay it on me."

"Tomorrow night. Highest score. Let's
raise the stakes higher, more than two hundred dollars," Bubba said.

Smudge's face lit up as he lit up a Win-
ston.

"You're on. Rain or shine," Smudge said.

Bubba thought of the leak in his Jeep and
everything else Muskrat had to say about it.
Bubba tested Smudge one more time this
morning.

"You want me to drive?" Bubba said.

"We'll be better off in my hunting truck." Smudge said exactly what Bubba antici- pated. "I'll drive, you can pay for gas. Meet me at my house."

Brazil was watching out the window for West's unmarked Caprice, and every other minute, he ran back to the bathroom and wet his fingers and ran them through his slightly gelled hair, giving it that wet look, making sure one strand fell down the middle of his forehead. He had brushed his teeth four times and couldn't stand still.

When West parked in front of his house, he took his time. He waited for her to come to the door. He waited until she had knocked five times.

"Andy? Are you in there?" she loudly said.

He ran to the door and opened it, tucking in his uniform shirt, adjusting his duty belt as if he was busy with many things and running behind.

"Gosh, I'm sorry," he politely said. "I was on the phone."

It wasn't quite a lie because Brazil had been on the phone. He just didn't say *when* he'd been on it.

"I don't have much time," West smacked the volley back. "We'd better go. This was probably a bad idea," she continued as she went down the steps. "I've got the day from hell. I'm not even hungry."

Brazil locked the door and followed her to the car, his feelings stung again.

"It doesn't matter to me," he said. "If you need to get to HQ, you can go on. You don't even have to give me a ride. It's not a problem."

"I'm already here," she retorted.

"I'm not that hungry either," Brazil announced.

West put the car in gear and pulled away from the curb.

"You should fasten your seatbelt," Brazil told her.

"Forget it."

"Look, I want to be able to get out of the car fast, too, if something goes down. But I don't want to be thrown out, like through the windshield. Besides, how long does it take you to unbuckle a seatbelt, if you're really honest?"

"You work the streets as long as I have, you don't have to be really honest." She reminded him of his inexperience and her high rank.

"Have you ever been to The Forest?" Brazil asked.

"What forest?"

"The neighborhood hangout on Forest Hill."

"That's the other side of the river."

"There's more parking there than down-town where the River City Diner is."

"Since when are we eating breakfast again? I thought we'd decided that issue," West said.

She turned on the radio, tuning in to WRVA. Adrenaline was shorting out Brazil's central nervous system as he groped for just the right words. He had a right to know why she treated him the way she did. He had a right to know about Jim.

"I guess I'm realizing if I don't eat some-thing now, I don't know when I will," Brazil said, making sure she understood how busy he was, too.

"River City is closer to HQ."

"Try parking on Main Street during rush hour."

West decided to head Southside.

"How did you find out about The Forest?" she asked as the radio broke the news of Fishsteria.

"I've been there a couple times." Brazil's thoughts were tangled like fishing line.

". . . believed to be a new strain of computer virus that cannot be detected by the standard antivirus software most of us have," Johnny, of the popular *Johnny in the Morning Show,* went on.

"I pretty much stick to the Fan," West said. "There are so many good restaurants, bars, like Strawberry Street Vineyard. Why go anywhere else?"

"Strawberry Street Vineyard is a wine shop," Brazil corrected her.

"I didn't say it wasn't," she fired back.

"Best wine in the city. They can get anything. I picked up a Ken Wright Cellars Pinot Noir the other week. Outstanding." Brazil had to rub it in.

". . . hibernates in bottom sediments," explained *Johnny in the Morning*'s special guest, Dr. Edith Sandal-Viverette, a biologist with the Virginia Institute of Marine Science. "And releases toxins that are stunning and killing all these fish. Crabs are falling victim, as well. What's curious, Johnny, is the microbes like the temperature of the water to be eightyish. It's a little early for that."

"But Fishsteria isn't related to Pfiesteria, right?" Johnny worried.

"I'm not sure we can say that at this moment."

Brazil felt stubborn again. He didn't care enough to ask West anything. She didn't matter.

"I've really gotten into French burgundies, too," Brazil rubbed it in some more.

"I get tired of red wine," West said.

"Then you ought to try a white burgundy."

"What makes you think I haven't?" West fired back.

"Well, it's really scary," Johnny said as Brazil and West continued not to listen.

Bubba knew what had happened when he was half a block away from his house. The garage door was wide open. His heart was seized by fear. He pulled into the driveway and jumped out of his car, screaming his wife's name.

"Honey!" he yelled as he ran up the front steps. "Honey! Oh my God! Honey! Are you all right!"

Bubba dropped his keys three times before he managed to unlock the front door.

He burst into the living room as Honey's slippers swished along the hallway. He ran to her and hugged her hard.

"Why, what on earth is the matter?" Honey said, rubbing his back.

Bubba started sobbing.

"I was so scared something happened to you," he cried into her permed, honey-blond hair.

"Of course nothing's happened to me, sweetie," she said. "I just this minute got up."

Bubba stepped back from her, his mood suddenly skipping discs. He was enraged.

"How the hell could you sleep through someone breaking into the workshop?" he yelled.

"What?" Honey was dazed. "The workshop?"

"The garage door's wide open! You leave it open for some reason, like the awful Jell-O and room temperature Tang? Is this the final blow to hurt me? Is that how they got in?"

"I don't go near that door," said Honey, who knew better than to ever set foot inside his workshop. "Would rather take the Lord's name in vain and be a Mormon or a queer or a feminist than dare to get near your shop!" exclaimed Honey, who was Southern

Baptist and knew the party line by heart. "I don't want to go near your tools, much less touch them. I never ask anything about them even if I can see them plain as day when you're working on some project that never turns out quite right."

Bubba ran back out the door. Honey held her robe together and followed. Bubba walked into the garage. He held his breath, hands clenched as he took in what had to be the biggest disaster of his life. Tools were scattered everywhere, and all of his hand-guns were gone. Someone had pissed all over Bubba's electronic caliper and it would convert inches into metric dimensions no more. The dual sander and air hammer had been cruelly dropped into the ten-gallon drum of dirty oil that Bubba saved for Muskrat's heater.

Bubba staggered back out into the sun-light. Honey grabbed his arm to steady him.

"Maybe I should call the police," she said.

West and Brazil were close to The Forest when several things happened at once.

Brazil's flip phone trilled. The police radio broadcast a possible B&E on Clarence

Street, and WRVA played an ad for Hollywood Cemetery's new Chapel Mausoleum,
located in one of the oldest sections of the
cemetery, adjacent to a convenient roadway
and with no additional expenses for a vault
or monument, one price covering everything
including the inscription.

"Hello?" Brazil said into his phone.

". . . Any unit in the area," the police radio
was repeating, ". . . possible B and E at
10946 Clarence Street."

". . . the Hollywood Cemetery Chapel
Mausoleum reflects a combination of both
beauty and dignity . . ." the ad continued,
jazz playing in the background.

"Andy? It's Hammer," Chief Hammer said
over the phone.

"Three," West answered the radio.

"Our computer problem's hit the national
news. I guess you saw this morning's paper,"
Hammer said to Brazil.

"Go ahead, 3," said Communications Officer Patty Passman, who was surprised that
the head of investigations was answering
the call.

"Actually, I didn't know," Brazil honestly
replied to Hammer.

"Front page," Hammer said. "They're making fun of us, fun of COMSTAT, saying we've crashed around the world because of a virus called *Fishsteria.*"

"*Fish* versus *Pfiesh?*" Brazil asked.

"Figure it out, Andy."

". . . . designed to reflect the classic elements found with Hollywood's hills . . ." said the ad.

"We're just a couple blocks from there," West told Communications Officer Passman. "We'll take the call."

"And a vandal or vandals hit Hollywood Cemetery last night," Hammer went on.

"Ten-4, 3. Complainant's a Mr. Butner Fluck."

"Appears a Spiders basketball uniform was painted on the statue of Jefferson Davis," Hammer explained.

Brazil was stunned. He started laughing and could not stop.

"And I'm afraid his race was altered," she went on.

"You mean, he got Michael Jordanized?" Brazil choked.

"This isn't funny, Andy."

"I think I'm gonna be sick." Brazil was doubled over, hardly able to talk.

West made a U turn on Forest Hill and accelerated.

"Lelia Ehrhart's called an emergency meeting of city leaders tomorrow morning at eight," Hammer told Brazil.

"I hope she's not going to speak!" Brazil's voice went up an octave. He couldn't help himself.

"What's wrong with you?" West glanced over at him as she drove fast out of habit, taking every shortcut she could to get to the scene.

"Look into it," Hammer said to Brazil.

"Fishsteria or *Magic Jeff?"* Brazil's stomach hurt, his eyes watering.

"All of it," she said to him.

The house on Clarence Street was very peculiar, but not for obvious reasons at a glance. Rather it was the sort of phenomenon that caused an unsettled, odd feeling of disharmony and something just not quite right that was discarded, like a lost file, the instant the person drove or walked past or delivered the newspaper and moved on.

But to someone with a trained eye who took a hard look, the problem was clear.

"Good God," West said, stopping the car in the middle of the road as she stared in wonder.

"Wow," Brazil chimed in. "I think he home improved when he was drunk."

Dark green shutters were askew, the paint not quite as white to the left of the red front door as it was to the right. The white picket fence was the worst West had ever seen. Clearly the soil was unstable and the builder had not driven the 4x4 posts far enough into the ground or set them in cement, nor had he bothered with a plumb line, it didn't appear, or chamfered the tops of the posts, meaning rainwater did not run off and the wood was beginning to rot. The rails sloped uphill on one side of the ill-fitting gate and downhill on the other. The pickets were unevenly spaced like bad teeth.

Apparently this same well-intentioned but misguided builder had expanded his garage by adding on a homemade shed that leaned north, suggesting the pressure-treated posts had not been sunk below the frost line and the new addition had shifted during the winter. Nothing was right. Shingles were not aligned, window boxes were different sizes, the stone garden fountain in front was dry, the herringbone pattern of the outdoor bench near the slumping brick barbecue was chaos. A long dog pen of torqued and drooping chain link was near the woods, and a blanket-back coon hound was perched on top of a barrel, bawling.

West turned into the driveway and a gas-station bell announced Mr. Fluck had company. A curtain in a window moved, and immediately a man emerged from the house. He was fat and didn't have much hair, his round head and small eyes bringing to mind a smiley face that wasn't. Mr. Fluck looked depressed and bereft, as if his wife had just walked out or come back, depending on how he felt about her.

"Uh oh," Brazil said, unfastening his seat belt.

"No kidding," said West.

Bubba followed his uneven brick walk to the driveway, where the unmarked white Chevrolet Caprice had pulled in. His mind was dark with ruined dreams, cruel predestination and bad karma.

His father, Reverend Fluck, had always disapproved of Bubba's fondness for guns, and Bubba was suspicious that his father had prayed for such a thing to happen. It was just too coincidental that, for the most part, only guns had been stolen. His expensive tools had been left. The burglar had not tried to break into Bubba's house or Honey's station wagon.

A tall, well-built blond man in uniform climbed out of the Caprice. The driver was a woman in plain clothes, a detective, Bubba assumed. They walked up to him, radios chattering.

"Are you Mr. Fluck?" the woman asked.

"Yes," he said. "Thank God you came. This is the worst thing that's ever happened to me."

"I'm Deputy Chief Virginia West, and this is Officer Andy Brazil," West said.

Bubba felt better. He sighed. The police had sent a deputy chief. This had to be Chief Hammer's doing. She was looking after Bubba. Somehow she had been touched as had he, their destinies entwined. Chief Hammer knew that a terrible injustice had been perpetrated against Bubba.

"I sure appreciate Chief Hammer contacting you," Bubba said.

Both cops looked mystified.

"She did, didn't she?" Bubba's faith wavered. "Just now, when I called nine-one-one?"

"Actually," Brazil faltered. "Well, yes. How did you know she just called me?"

Bubba looked heavenward and smiled, despite his pain.

West started walking toward the workshop. Brazil followed. Both of them stood on the driveway, looking at the mess. Brazil recorded the month, day, year and victim's name and address on the offense report attached to his clipboard.

"What a disaster," Brazil said.

"It's unspeakable," Bubba said.

"Do you have any idea when the B and E occurred?" West asked.

"Sometime between eight o'clock last night and seven-thirty this morning."

"I need your home and business phone numbers." Brazil was writing.

Bubba gave them to him.

"I got home from work and found this," Bubba said, almost in tears. "Exactly like this. I didn't touch anything. I didn't move anything, so I'm not a hundred percent sure what's missing."

West's expert eye skimmed over stand-alone tools such as a drill press, a drum sander, bench grinder, jointer, thickness planer, shaper, and all the expected chisels, Forstner bits, wire-brush wheels, brad-point bits, plug cutter, countersink set. There was protective gear of every description, and more hand tools than Bob Vila probably had in his workshop.

"It's interesting that you have so many expensive tools, yet the burglar or burglars didn't take them," West observed.

"He was after guns," Bubba said. "I know they're missing."

He pointed to the cabinet and its severed padlock on the floor.

"You got bolt cutters?" West asked.

"Toolsmith, eighteen-inchers."

"Still have them?" Brazil said.

"I can see them from here," answered Bubba.

"What kind of lock was on the gun cabinet?" West asked.

"Just a plain Master lock."

"Case hard?"

Bubba looked ashamed.

"I was meaning to get around to it," he said.

"So it *wasn't* case hard," Brazil wanted to make sure as he took the report.

Bubba shook his head.

"That's too bad," West said with feeling. "I've never seen a pair of bolt cutters that can go through a case hard Master lock. And considering what you had in your cabinet, you should have had the best."

"I know, I know," Bubba said as his shame deepened. "I know how foolish I was."

West walked in to inspect more closely, noting that Bubba had painted his initials in white on all tools and equipment. She stepped over dozens of step-by-step books on plumbing, deck and patio upgrades, painting and wallpapering, pruning, and home repair problem solving.

She picked her way around a Stanley thirty-foot heavy-duty tape measure and its Nicholas leather holder, a Makita tool holster, a McGuire-Nicholas wide saddle-leather belt, a top-grade cowhide Longhorn hammer holder, red Nicholas heavy-duty suspenders, and a foam rubber knee pad with double straps that had become separated from its mate.

West recognized top quality. She knew all the brands and how much they cost. She was curious. She was envious.

"And you have no alarm system," Brazil said.

"The 'No Trespassing' sign and the bell in the driveway. I can hear anybody drive in."

"I didn't know they used those anymore," Brazil said.

"Muskrat's Auto Rescue has a bunch of them," Bubba said.

"What about your dog?" West asked.

"Half Shell bawls all day and night. Nobody listens to her anymore."

"So Half Shell and the gas-station bell were your only alarm system?" West gave him a skeptical look.

Bubba could tell she wasn't impressed with him. He was suddenly conscious of how pretty she was. Bubba felt fat, dirty, unattractive and inferior. He felt the way he had most of his life. Deputy Chief West saw through his guns and tools and home repairs. She saw Bubba as a persecuted little boy with an awful name and a world that ridiculed him. Bubba could see it in her eyes. It suddenly occurred to him that she might have gone to school with him.

"Are you from around here?" he asked her.

"No," she said.

"You sure?"

"What do you mean, *am I sure?*"

He was paranoid and obsessed. He had to be convinced.

"So you're not from Richmond," he said.

"No." She was getting curt with him.

"It's just that you look like someone I went to school with whose name was Virginia," Bubba lied.

"We didn't go to school together," West told him.

"Did the burglar or burglars urinate in here?" Brazil asked.

"Yes." Bubba pointed. "Does that mean something?"

"Oftentimes burglars urinate or defecate in the place they've broken into," West explained. "It's part of an MO, and may or may not matter."

Brazil made a note of it.

"The sort of thing your police computer might have picked up on if it didn't have the fish virus," Bubba said. "I heard about it on the news when I was driving home. So you won't be able to check for a pattern."

"Don't you even worry about it." Brazil avoided the subject. "You got a list of the guns and their serial numbers?"

"I got them all at Green Top," Bubba said. "Never buy guns anywhere else."

"That helps," Brazil said. "But I want to list on the report what's missing so the detective can follow up."

"I guess you won't be able to use the computer to see if someone else got broken into like this," Bubba said, disappointed. "Because of the fish problem."

"Don't worry about how we do our jobs," Brazil told him. "Now, about the list."

"One Browning Buck Mark Bullseye .22," Bubba recalled, "a Taurus eight-shot M608 .357, Smith and Wesson Model 457 alloy frame .45 ACP and its Bianchi Avenger holster, a Pachmayr pocket cleaning kit, a mini-Glock G26 nine-millimeter with night sights, Sig P226 nine by nineteen millimeter, same thing used by Navy SEALs. Let's see. What else?"

"Jesus," West said.

Brazil was writing at top speed.

"A Daisy Model 91 Match pistol, air gun, in other words. Ruger Blackhawk .357 revolver, and a couple Ruger competition handguns."

"Are you a competition shooter?" West asked.

"Haven't had time," Bubba said.

"Is that it?" Brazil asked.

"I just got a M9 Special Edition nine mil, fifteen-round clips, still in the box. It makes me sick. I never even got to try it out. And I had a bunch of speed loaders and about twenty boxes of cartridges. Most of them Winchester Silvertips."

"What about anything else?" West asked.

"It's hard to tell," Bubba said. "But the only other thing I'm not seeing anywhere is my Stanley tool belt. It's really nice. Black nylon with a padded yellow belt, lightweight and not as hot as leather. Can fit everything but the kitchen sink."

"I've always wanted one of those," West confessed. "They cost about sixty bucks."

"That's if you get a discount," Bubba said.

"What about suspects?" Brazil had gotten to that part of the report. "Anybody you think might have done this?"

"It had to be somebody who knew what I had inside my shop," Bubba said. "And the

door wasn't forced, so the person had a remote, too."

"That's interesting," Brazil commented.

"You can buy them at Sears," West said,
looking up at the retracted Sears garage
door. "Mr. Fluck, I'm going to see to it that a
detective comes by before the day's out to
look for any possible evidence, prints, tool
marks, whatever."

"My prints will be in here," Bubba worried.

"We'll have to print you, now that you
mention it, to know what's yours and what's
not," West said.

They walked out of the workshop, careful
where they stepped. Half Shell was bawling
and jumping in circles.

"Thank Chief Hammer again for me,"
Bubba said, following West and Brazil to
their car.

"*Again?*" Brazil looked baffled. "Have you
spoken to her?"

"Not directly," Bubba said.

chapter nineteen

Hammer was extremely sensitive to racial issues and had studied the Richmond metropolitan area's thoroughly. She knew it wasn't so long ago that blacks couldn't join various clubs or live in certain neighborhoods. They couldn't use golf courses or tennis courts or public pools. Change had been slow and in many ways was deceptive.

Memberships and neighborhood associations began to accept blacks, and in some cases women, but making it off the waiting list or feeling comfortable was another matter. When the future first black governor of

Virginia tried to move into an exclusive neighborhood, he was turned down. When a statue of Arthur Ashe was erected on Monument Avenue, it almost caused another war.

Chief Hammer was worried as she and administrative assistant Fling drove through Hollywood Cemetery to inspect the damage and find out if the descriptions of it were exaggerated. They weren't. Hammer parked on Davis Circle, where the painted bronze statue was clearly visible in the distance, rising amid a background of magnolias and evergreens, small Confederate flags fluttering at the marble base, the perimeter secured with yellow crime-scene tape.

"Looks like he's hogging the basketball and won't pass it to anyone," Fling observed. "He looks kind of stuck-up, too."

"He was," Hammer commented.

She stifled laughter, her blood fluttering with peals of it that were almost impossible to suppress. The statue of Davis had always been described as having a proud and haughty air. He had worn the southern gentleman's dress typical of his day, before the graffiti artist, remarkably, had transformed the long coat into a baggy jersey and voluminous shorts to the knees. Trousers had become muscular legs and athletic socks. Boots had been turned into hightop Nikes.

Hammer and Fling got out of the Crown Victoria as the throaty roar of a black Mercedes 420E came up from behind. The sedan, with its sunroof and saddle interior, swerved around Hammer's car and parked in front of it.

"Shit," Hammer said as Lelia Ehrhart gathered something off the Mercedes's front seat and opened her door. "Where's the interpreter?"

Although Ehrhart had been born in Richmond, she had spent most of her growing-up years in Vienna, Austria, where her father, Dr. Howell, a wealthy, prominent music historian, had labored for years on an unauthorized psychological biography of the very gentle, sensitive Mozart and his fear of the trumpet. Later the family had moved to Yugoslavia where Dr. Howell explored the subliminal influence of music on the Nemanjic dynasty. German was Lelia Ehrhart's first language, Serbo-Croatian followed, then English. She spoke nothing well and had combined the three, stirring and folding, as if making a cake.

For a moment, Ehrhart stood, transfixed by the statue, her lips slightly parted in shock. She wore yellow Escada jeans, a full yellow-striped blouse with an E on the breast pocket, a black belt studded with brass butterflies and shoes to match. Although Hammer mostly wore Ralph Lauren and Donna Karan, she knew other designers and recognized that the butterflies were several seasons old. This gave Hammer a little satisfaction, but not enough.

"This will excite a riot," Ehrhart exclaimed, moving in closer to the crime scene, a Canon Sure Shot in hand. "Nothing like this has even happened before this."

"I'm not sure I'd go so far as to say that," Hammer replied. "Not so long ago someone painted graffiti on the statue of Robert E. Lee."

"That was different."

"He wasn't changed into a black basketball player," Fling agreed. "Not saying he wouldn't have been, but he's on a horse with a sword, and right there on Monument Avenue where if you spent a lot of time, someone's bound to notice. So I really don't see how you could easily do him. Or doing anybody on Monument Avenue. Arthur Ashe's holding a tennis racket and the other guys are on horses. Unless you did polo, I guess."

"I want to know how you're doing about this?" Ehrhart said to Hammer as a sudden gust of wind stirred trees and whipped the Southern Cross at Davis's feet. "And where were your officers when some vandal came in here like Michelangelo in the Sistine Chapel?"

"The cemetery is private property," Fling reminded her.

"If a serial killing shows up on my private property, is that a *so-what* also?" Ehrhart indignantly replied.

"Not if we know he's a serial killer," Fling retorted.

"The truth is," said Hammer, "we do patrol the cemetery."

"That's even worst," Ehrhart said. "You certainly must have somewhere been elsewhere last night."

"The beat car is very busy in that area, Lelia. We've got VCU, Oregon Hills. We get many, many calls," Hammer said. "When calls involve living people, they take priority."

"As if I would know this!" Ehrhart indignantly answered.

"It's confusing what's city and what isn't."

Fling tried to gloss over his misinformation. "And Mrs. Ehrhart, my earlier point that I wanted to emphasize was you shouldn't take this so hard when it may simply be a random choice because of how remote being in a place like this is if you're up to no good."

"That's easier to say," said Ehrhart.

Hammer felt as if she were listening to aliens.

"When about Bobby Feeley?" Ehrhart was becoming more accusatory.

"We're working hard on this, Lelia," Hammer replied.

"He's twelve," she persisted. "That ought to add up for something."

"We are investigating this with great seriousness," said Hammer, who frankly thought the statue was much improved by the new outfit.

"He probably alibied his way from there to here and you take it at fact value." Ehrhart wouldn't let it rest.

"I think he wasn't feeling good last night and didn't go out," Fling offered. "There are witnesses."

Hammer glared at Fling, who had just divulged sensitive information about the case.

"Well, we'll put this up at my meeting. And by the way, I've had to move it earlier to seven A.M. in the morning, Judy." Ehrhart started taking photographs of the crime scene. "The Commonwealth Club private boarding room. If you don't know where it is, they'll ask you at the door when you cash your coat."

"It's a little warm for a coat," Fling said.

For the past century, Lelia Howell Ehrhart's alleged ancestors had been laid to rest in stately family plots and tombs, and remembered by obelisks and urns, and blessed by crosses, and guarded by Carrara marble angels of grief and a cast-iron dog, and embellished with ornamental metalwork.

It was well known that her family tree included Jefferson Davis's wife, Varina Howell, although genealogists had thus far been unsuccessful in tracing Ehrhart's bloodline back to any geographic region even close to Mississippi, where Mrs. Davis was from.

Ehrhart was traumatized and personally outraged. She took the vandalism personally and couldn't help but think it was directed at her, and therefore gave her the right to find the monster who had done it and lock him up for the rest of his life. Ehrhart didn't need the police. What good were they anyway?

What mattered most and got things done was connections, and Ehrhart had more than the Internet. She was married to Dr. Carter "Bull" Ehrhart, a millionaire dentist and alleged descendant of Confederate General Franklin "Bull" Paxton. Bull Ehrhart was a University of Richmond alumnus. He was on the Board of Visitors. He had donated hundreds of thousands of dollars to U of R and rarely missed a basketball game.

It had been no great matter for Lelia Ehrhart to call Spiders head coach Bo Raval and find out exactly where she might get her hands on Bobby Feeley. Probably the gym, she had been told. She turned off Three Chopt Road onto Boatwright and followed it to the U of R campus. She turned into the private lot, where members of the Spiders Club parked during the games. She tucked her Mercedes at an angle, taking two spaces, far away from those less expensive cars that might hit her doors. She walked with purpose up the Robins Center's front steps.

The lobby was empty and echoed with the

memory of many games won and lost that Ehrhart had not enjoyed. Eventually, she had refused to attend them with her husband, nor would she subject herself to football. She simply would not watch sports on TV anymore. Bull could get his own beer and make his own microwave popcorn. He could point the remote as often as he wanted, playing God, controlling, master designing, making things happen, and she didn't care.

A basketball bouncing beyond shut doors sounded lonely and determined. Ehrhart entered Milhouser Gym, where Bobby Feeley was shooting foul shots. He was tall, as expected, with long sculpted muscles and a shaved head and a gold loop earring, like all basketball players. His skin glistened with sweat, gray tee shirt soaked in back and front, shorts baggy down to his knees and swirling as he moved. Feeley paid no attention to Ehrhart as he tried again and hit the rim.

"Shit," he said.

She said nothing as he dribbled and faked, rushed, elbows flying, turning, faking again, fast breaking, leaping and slam-dunking, hitting the rim again.

"Fuck," he said.

"Excuse me," Ehrhart announced herself.

Feeley slowly dribbled the ball, looking at her.

"Are you Bobby Feeley?"

She stepped onto the gym floor in high-heeled shoes with brass butterflies.

"That's not a good idea," he said.

"Excuse me?"

"Your shoes."

"Who's not right with them?"

"They aren't tennis shoes."

"Yours aren't wearing tennis shoes," she said.

He dribbled some more, frowning.

"What do you call these?" he asked.

"Basketballs shoes," she said.

"Ah. A purist. Okay," said Feeley, an honors English student. "But you still can't walk on the floor in those shoes. So you can take them off or go somewhere else, I guess."

Ehrhart slipped out of her shoes and drew closer to him in knee-high hose.

"So, what can I do for you?" Feeley asked as he pulled the ball away, elbows out and dangerous, eluding an imaginary adversary.

"You're number twelve," Ehrhart said.

"Not that again," Feeley exclaimed as he dribbled. "What is this anyway? You people think I have nothing better to do? That I would do something as sophomoric as painting graffiti in a cemetery?"

He dribbled between his legs and missed a jump shot.

"This is not just graffiti as you watch on subway trains. It's not 'The Screech' and schmucks you watch on buildings."

Feeley stopped dribbling and wiped sweat off his brow, trying to interpret.

"I think you mean *scream,*" he tried to help her out. "As in Edvard Munch's 'The Scream.' And maybe you mean *schmoe?* Schmuck's not a nice word, although those unfamiliar with Yiddish usually don't get it."

"Spray-painting Mountain Rushmore, how about then?" she indignantly said.

"Who did?" Feeley asked.

"So you can go paint your basketball uniform, number twelve included, on my ancestor!"

"You're related to Jeff Davis?"

Feeley ran and dunked. The ball bounced off the backboard.

"I'm related to Vinny," Ehrhart stated.

"As in Pooh?"

"Varina."

"I thought that was a place or maybe something else we shouldn't allude to."

"You are vulgarly rude, Mr. Feeler."

"Feeley."

"It disdains me that people from your generation respect not a thing that's gone before in the past. And the point is, it isn't gone even if it started before you in. I'm standing here, as evident."

Feeley frowned. "How 'bout ringing me up again. I think we have a bad connection."

"I wouldn't," she flatly said.

He cradled the ball under his arm. "What did I do?"

"We know both what you did."

He dribbled into a hook shot that swished below the net.

"Sorry," Feeley said, "but I didn't do a job on Mr. Davis's statue, although I must say that it was about time somebody put him in his place."

"How dare can you!"

Feeley flashed his big smile. He dribbled back and forth from one hand to the other and hit his foot.

"Indicted for treason but never tried. First and last president of the Confederacy. Ha!"

He missed another foul shot. "Got to feel sorry for him, when you think about it. Inferior railroad, no navy, no powder mills or shipyard and forget arms and equipment." A jump shot sailed over the backboard. "Congress fighting like cats and dogs." Feeley walked and hit his toe again. "Lee surrenders without asking Davis if it's all right." He trotted after the ball. "Jeff Davis finds himself in leg irons and ends up an insurance salesman in Memphis."

"Not truth." Ehrhart was incensed.

"Sure as hell is, ma'am."

"Where were you last night?" she demanded to know.

"Right here, practicing." A last-second shot from half court hit the stands. "I didn't go to the cemetery and have never been inside that cemetery."

He trotted after the ball again and started spinning it on his middle finger.

Ehrhart misinterpreted. "Are you giving to me an obscenity gesture?"

The ball wobbled off. Feeley tried again. He tossed it around his back and missed.

"Rats," he said.

"I fine you most lacking in respect," Ehrhart said loudly and with emotion. "And you can alibi from then on and in the end, what comes and goes around!"

"Look, ma'am." Feeley tucked the ball under his arm. "I had nothing to do with the statue. But I sure do intend to go take a peek."

Many people in the Richmond area had decided the same thing. Clay Kitchen had never seen such a solid line of cars without headlights on. He had never in his twenty-seven years of faithful service observed such unbecoming behavior.

People were cheerful. They had rolled windows down and were enjoying the premature spring weather. They were playing rock & roll, jazz and rap.

Kitchen and West zipped along in the truck, avoiding the flow of traffic by entering the crime scene from Lee Avenue. West looked out the window, rather amazed by the interest. When the statue came in view she almost lost her proper police decorum. She almost said *fucking unbelievable.*

"Stop right here," she said to Kitchen. "I don't want people seeing me getting out of your truck."

Kitchen completely understood. West was here in plain clothes and would not tell him why, but he was quite a reader. He knew what was going on. Criminals often returned to the scene of the crime, especially if they were pyromaniacs or wanted to apologize or had forgotten to take a souvenir. Kitchen had talked to police when they patrolled the cemetery on slow days. Kitchen had heard the stories.

He remembered the man who stabbed his wife almost a thousand times and slept with her body for days, bringing her breakfast in bed, watching TV with her, talking about the good times. Of course, that really wasn't the same thing as returning to the scene since he'd never left it, Kitchen supposed. He did know for a fact that up north a few years back, a woman ground up her husband in a wood chipper and came back several days later to burn up his pieces in the backyard. A neighbor apparently got suspicious.

The crowd was pressing too close to the statue and threatened any moment to duck under or even break the crime-scene tape. West got on her radio and requested backups. There was a near riot situation at the cemetery, hundreds of people. Many of them had been drinking and probably still were.

"Three," Communications Officer Patty Passman came back. "Is this 10-18?"

West checked her annoyance. People pushed against her. Passman was always questioning West's calls, and now she had the nerve to ask if the situation was urgent. *No, why don't you get around to it when you can,* West felt like saying. *After I've been stampeded.*

"Three, 10-10. At the moment."

"Three, what's your exact 10-20?"

"I'm exactly at the statue," West tersely answered.

"Hey! Who's the chick with the radio?" some man yelled.

"We got undercover cops here!"

"FBI."

"CIA."

"Yay!"

"You want my fingerprints, baby?"

The smell of alcohol was strong as bodies pressed closer and jeering people got in West's face. Her body space wasn't there. People were jostling her, touching her, laughing. She got back on the radio and suddenly noticed the small blue fish painted on the statue's base, just below Jefferson Davis's left Nike. A kid came up behind her and pretended to go for her gun. She lifted him off the ground by his belt and tossed him like a small bag of garbage. He laughed, running off.

"Three, 10-18!" West exclaimed over the air as she stared at the fish, her thoughts crashing into each other.

"Any unit in the area of Hollywood Cemetery, an officer needs assistance," Passman calmly broadcast.

"Step back!" West shouted to the crowd. "Step back now!"

She was against the crime-scene tape, the crowd getting frenzied and moving in.

West whipped out her red pepper spray and pointed it. People paused to reflect.

"What the hell's gotten into you?" West yelled. "Step back now!"

The crowd inched back a little, faces twitching with indecision, fists balled, sweat rolling, the air throbbing with the heat of violence about to erupt.

"Someone want to tell me what this is all about!" West yelled again.

A youth wearing a Tommy Hilfiger shirt and stocking cap, one relaxed pants leg rolled up, one down, spoke for the group.

"Nobody wants us in here," he explained. "Maybe it gets to you, you know? And then one day something happens and you snap."

"Well, there'll be no snapping here," West sternly told all. "What's your name?"

"Jerome."

"Seems like these people listen to you, Jerome."

"I don't know any of them, but I guess so."

"I want you to help me keep them calm," West said.

"Okay."

Jerome turned around and faced the mob.

"CHILL!" he shouted. "EVERYBODY FUCKING BACK OFF AND GIVE THIS LADY SOME FUCKING SPACE!"

Everybody did.

"Now listen up." Jerome stepped into his new role and had no problem with it. "The deal is you people don't know what it's like," he told West.

"Tell it!" a woman yelled.

"You think anybody wants us in here?" he whipped up the crowd.

"Fuck no!" they screamed.

"You think anybody wants us dropping by?"

"Fuck no!" the crowd chanted.

"You-think-you-go-Hollywood-who's-gonna-let-you-they're-gonna-get-you-throw-your-ass-in-the-grass-cemetery-in-the-hood?" Jerome started rapping.

"Never!"

"The-mon-u-ment-like-the-mom-u-meant-is-cold-I'm-told-how-many-times-I-gotta-tell-it." Jerome was strutting before the crowd. "What's-it-take-to-taste-and-smell-it-when-you-got-no-chance-to-sell-it-'cause-every-thing's-for-sale-except-for-me-and-you-no-matter-what-we-do-we're-the-boys-in-the-hood-ain't-no-fuck-in-Holly-wood."

"AND-THE-*GIRLS*-IN-THE-HOOD!"

"Boys-and-*girls*-in-the-hood-ain't-no fuck-in-Holly-wood," Jerome politically corrected himself.

"AIN'T-NO-FUCK-IN-HOLLY-WOOD!" the crowd rapped back.

"Thanks, Jerome," West said.

"AIN'T-NO-FUCK-IN-HOLLY-WOOD!" The crowd was out of control.

"Jerome, that's enough!"

"Say it again, brothers!" Jerome was spin-

ning and kick-boxing. "AIN'T-NO-FUCK-IN-
HOLLY-WOOD!"

"AIN'T-NO-FUCK-IN-HOLLY-WOOD!"

Sirens sounded in the distance.

chapter twenty

The Robins Center, where the Spiders played basketball before great crowds, was between the private lot where Ehrhart had tucked her Mercedes, and the X lot where commoners parked, no more than two rows of parking spaces or approximately fifty yards from the track, where this moment Brazil was running hard for the second time this day.

It was late afternoon. He had spent hours working on the COMSTAT computer crisis while the media continued to kick around mean-spirited stories about Fishsteria and the vandalism of Jefferson Davis's statue.

Comments of low intelligence and terribly poor taste streaked through e-mail and were passed word-of-mouth through offices, restaurants, bars and health clubs before at last finding their way to the ears of the police.

Cops finally *catch* something, no longer let crooks *off the hook.*

Knock knock. Who's there? Police. Police who? Plice get rid of the fish.

Jeff Davis *coloredized.*

What's black and white and red all over? (Jeff Davis.)

Brazil had been desperate for a break. He needed to clear his head and work off stress. What he did not need was to see Lelia Ehrhart walking out of the Robins Center, heading toward her black Mercedes parked in the Spiders Club lot. He instantly knew what she was up to and was furious.

Brazil sprinted off the track and through the gate. He got to her as she was backing up. He tapped on her window as the car continued to move. She braked, made sure her doors were locked and the window down an inch.

"I'm Officer Brazil," he said, wiping his face with the hem of his tank top.

"I didn't recognize you," Ehrhart said, appraising him as if thinking about a purchase.

"I don't mean to be rude," Brazil said, "but what were you doing in the gym?"

"Fact finishing."

"Did you talk to Bobby Feeley?"

"Yes."

"I wish you hadn't done that, Mrs. Ehrhart," Brazil said.

"Someone had to, and I have a personal interested in this that has to do with me. Aren't you visiting outsiders from Charlotte always telling us to community police? Well, here I am. How old are you?"

"Community policing does not include interfering with an investigation," Brazil told her.

She stared at his legs.

"You are quite the athletic," she flirted. "I have a trainer. If ever you want to work in together, the both of us, wouldn't that be nice?"

"It's generous of you to offer." Brazil was courteous, professional and respectful.

"Which gym do you work in out of?" She rolled the window down the rest of the way, caressing every part of him with eyes that had huge purchasing power.

"I've gotta go," Brazil said as she stared at his crotch.

"How often do you hang yourself out here?" she inquired, continuing her physical examination of him. "You are very sweating. It's running all down you in little rivets and you look very hots. You should take your shirts off and drinks some Gatorades." She patted the passenger's seat. "Come sits, Andy. Out of the heats. I have a swimmer pool at my house. We could go and jump on it. Think how good that would feeling when you are so hots."

"Thank you, Mrs. Ehrhart." Brazil couldn't get away fast enough. "But I've got to head out."

He ran off. Her window hummed up. Her tires sounded angry when she sped away.

Brazil took two steps at a time and ran in-side the Robins Center, dashing into the gym, where Bobby Feeley was working on defense and fouling imaginary Cavaliers.

"Mr. Feeley?" Brazil said from the side-lines.

Feeley dribbled the ball over to him. He started laughing.

"What is this? The inquisition? Or are you just looking for the track, man?"

"I'm with the Richmond Police Department, investigating the vandalism that occurred in Hollywood Cemetery last night," Brazil explained.

"You always go to work dressed like that?" Feeley tried another jump shot and the ball didn't even come close.

"I just happened to be out running when I saw Lelia Ehrhart drive off," Brazil said.

"Now that's a piece of work." Feeley retrieved the ball. "How long's she been on this planet?"

"Look, Mr. Feeley . . ."

"It's Bobby."

"Bobby, do you have any idea why someone would paint a statue to look like you?" Brazil said. "Assuming you didn't do it."

"I didn't do it." Feeley faked passes. "And although it's very flattering to think there's a statue of me in a historic white cemetery, I don't think so." He missed a layup. "I'm a pretty sorry basketball player and not likely to be anybody's hero."

"How'd you get on the team?" Brazil had to ask as he watched Feeley miss another layup.

"I used to be better than this," Feeley said. "I pretty much ripped up the court in high school, got recruited a million places and decided on Richmond. So I get here and something goes haywire. I'm telling you, man, I started worrying that maybe I had lupus, muscular dystrophy, Parkinson's."

Feeley sat on the basketball, resting his chin in his hand, depressed.

"Doesn't help that I'm wearing Twister Gardener's jersey," Feeley said despondently. "I've wondered if that's part of it. Getting psyched out, you know, because everybody looks at my number twelve and remembers him."

"I'm not from here." Brazil sat beside him. "More into tennis than basketball."

"Well, let me tell you," Feeley said, "Twister was the best player this school's ever seen. I got no doubt he'd be playing for the Bulls right now if he hadn't got killed."

"What happened?" Brazil asked as something started stirring deep in his mind.

"Car wreck. Some fucking drunk driver on the fucking wrong side of the road. Last August, right before his sophomore year."

The story pained Brazil. It enraged him that an extraordinary talent could be completely annihilated in a second by someone who had decided to throw back a few more beers at the bar.

"I'm just glad I got to see him play. I guess you could say he was my hero." Feeley got up and stretched his limber seven-foot frame.

"Pretty tough to wear your hero's jersey," Brazil commented as he got up, too.

Feeley shrugged. "It's part of running with the big dogs."

"Maybe you should get your number changed," Brazil suggested.

Feeley was startled. His face got hard, eyes flashing.

"What did you say?" he asked.

"Maybe you should retire the number, let someone else have it," Brazil explained.

Feeley's eyes snapped. His jaw muscles bunched.

"Fuck no."

"Just a suggestion," Brazil said. "But I don't understand why you'd want to keep it if you get psyched. Give it up, Bobby."

"No fucking way!"

"Just do it."

"Fuck you!"

"It really makes sense," Brazil reasonably went on.

"Motherfucking never!"

"Why not?"

"Because nobody would fucking care about it as much as I do!"

"How do you know?"

Feeley threw the basketball as hard as he could and it swished in without touching the rim.

"Because nobody would respect Twister, treat him right, spread the word about him like I would!"

Feeley ran full speed for the ball, dribbled with his right hand and left and slam-dunked.

"And I'll tell you what, too, you'll never see that jersey dirty or tossed in a corner some-where!" He dunked the ball over the back of his head, the rim vibrating. "Some little spoiled piece of shit coming in here and wearing Twister's number!"

He hooked it in, rebounded, slam-dunked, snapped it up, thundered to the top of the key and banked it in, wrestled it away from grabbing hands and jumped a good two feet off the floor, sinking it.

"Does Twister have family around here?" Brazil asked.

"I remember going to the home games

and seeing him with some little kid. Twister would sit the little guy right behind the bench," Feeley said, hitting free throws and talking at the same time. "I got the impression it might be his little brother."

At James River Monuments, Ruby Sink was doing a little investigating on her own. The noise of air hammers and pneumatic tools was awful, and someone was bouncing a four-point bumper on Southern Georgia granite. The sandblaster was going and an overhead crane was lifting a thirteen-hundred-pound monument that was chipped and stained green along the top from moss.

White Vermont marble was very difficult and not used anymore and Floyd Rumble had a chore on his hands. He was a bit overwhelmed, anyway. It had been one of those days. His back hurt and his son was stuck at the desk inside the office because the secretary was on vacation.

Then Colonel Bailey, who had Alzheimer's, had come in for the fourth time in a week to say that he was to be buried in uniform and wanted something very patriotic engraved on his Saint Cloud Gray marble monument. Each time, Rumble made out a new order because the last thing he'd ever do was humiliate anyone.

Rumble picked up a knife and resumed cutting a leaf on Nero Black marble, thinking how bad he'd felt when stockbroker Ben Neaton had suddenly dropped dead of a heart attack and the wife had to come in here, too distraught to think, much less pick out something.

So Rumble had suggested the elegant black stone because Mr. Neaton had always driven shiny black Lincolns and worn dark suits. The inscription, *Not Gone, Just Reinvested,* had been stenciled into a sheet of rubber which was placed over the face of the stone. The sandblaster had etched the letters in a matter of minutes, but Rumble always cut the detail work, such as ivy or flowers, by hand.

It was common for bereft, shocked people to ask Rumble to make all decisions and unfold the story of their lost loved one's life, and what the person had last said or eaten or worn, or had intended to do the next day. Always there was that *one little thing* that gave the person a bad feeling.

Rumble would hear endless renditions of

how the husband didn't go out and get the paper like he always did while his wife was fixing breakfast and school lunches and getting the kids up and ready for school and making sure they didn't miss the bus before she fixed his eggs the way he liked them and asked what he might like for supper and what time he'd be home.

Ruby Sink had worn out Rumble's patience. She had been planning her monument ever since her sister died eleven years ago, and it wasn't uncommon for Miss Sink to wander in once a month just to see what sorts of things Rumble was working on. First she wanted an angel, then a tree, then a plain African granite headstone with raised lilies, then she got into marbles and went through them like a woman rifling through her closet trying to figure out what color dress to wear. She had to have Lake Superior Green, then Rainbow, then Wausau, then Carnelian, then Mountain Red, and so on.

Rumble's business had been in the family for three generations. He had dealt with all sorts and was smart enough to quit placing orders for Miss Sink after the third time she had changed her mind.

"Good afternoon, Floyd." Miss Sink walked right in talking loudly above the chop chop chop and rat-a-tats of machines and blasting of carbon sand and whirring of the exhaust fan and roaring of compressors.

"I guess so," he said.

"I don't know how you stand all the dust in here." She always said that.

"It's good for you," he always replied. "Same thing they use in toothpaste. All day long your teeth get cleaned. You ever see a Rumble with bad teeth?"

In part, he went down this path to distract Miss Sink. Sometimes it worked. Today it didn't.

"I guess you heard." She moved close to confide in him.

The thirteen-hundred-pound monument hung perilously midair and Rumble thought about what a chore restoring it was going to be. All duplications of old work like that had to be chiseled by hand, and there was no way he was going to start on it while Miss Sink was within a mile of his shop. She'd decide she had finally found what she wanted. She'd know without a spark of doubt that she had to have soft white Vermont marble chiseled by hand.

He started looking through trays of stencil types, preparing to etch a Hebrew inscription on Sierra White marble while his crew lowered the damaged monument into a cart.

"You heard what they did to Jefferson Davis," Miss Sink told him.

"I heard something about it."

Rumble started laying out stencil types. They had to be plastic so one could see through them, but they broke all the time.

"As you know, Floyd, I'm on the board."

"Yes, ma'am."

"The overwhelming matter that must be taken care of is how badly is the statue damaged, how do we go about restoring it and how much will it cost."

Rumble hadn't gone into the cemetery to look yet. Nor would he bother at all unless he was offered the job.

"He paint any of the marble base or just the bronze?" Rumble inquired.

"Mostly the bronze." Just the thought of it made her sick. "But he did paint the top of the base to look like a basketball floor. So yes, some of the marble was involved."

"I see. So he's standing on a basketball floor. What else?"

"Well, the worst part. He painted a basketball uniform on him, tennis shoes and the whole bit, and changed his race."

"Sounds like we got two problems here," Rumble said as he tossed out another broken letter and the diamond saw in a corner started cutting through stone. "To fix the marble, I'm going to have to chisel it down and put on a new surface. As for the bronze, if we're talking about oil-based paints . . ."

"Oh we are," she said. "I could tell. Nothing spray-painted here. This was all done in thick coats with a brush."

"We'll have to strip that down, maybe with turpentine, then refinish with a polyurethane coating so we don't get oxidation."

"We'll study this, then," Miss Sink announced.

"We should," Rumble said. "Eventually we'll have to get Jeff Davis in my shop. I can't be doing all this work on him in the middle of a public cemetery with people all over the place. Means we'll have to hoist him up with a crane and a sling, lower him in a truck."

"I 'spect we should close the cemetery while you're doing all this," Miss Sink said.

"During the removal, for sure. But I'd do it now anyway in case other people get ideas about other monuments. And I suggest you get security patrolling around there."

"I'll get Lelia to take care of it."

"In the meantime, I don't want anyone touching that statue. Now that's saying you're asking me to fix it."

"Of course you're the one, Floyd."

"It will take me a day or so to get it out of the cemetery, and then I don't know how long after that."

"I guess all this is going to cost a pretty penny," the parsimonious Miss Sink said.

"I'll be as fair as I can be," Rumble said.

Bubba had no intention of being fair. There had been too much trauma and disruption for him to even think about sleep, and as soon as the detective had left with lifted prints and other evidence, Bubba had returned to his shop. He had cleaned up fast and hard, anger giving him boundless energy while Half Shell bawled and bawled and ran around in circles and jumped up and down from the overturned barrel.

Bubba's karma had not been favorably inclined so far this day. He had bought a bag of large white marbles and a bottle of iridescent yellow paint. His attempts at drilling holes through the marbles were disastrous. They kept slipping out of the vise, and when he tightened the vise more, the marbles cracked. The drill bit kept sliding off, then broke. This went on and got no better until he came up with a clever idea.

At several minutes past three P.M., Honey poked her head inside the shop, a concerned expression on her face.

"Sweetie, you haven't eaten a thing all day," she worried.

"Don't have time."

"Sweetie, you always have time."

"Not now."

She spotted what was left of her favorite large pearl necklace on the workbench.

"Sweetie, what are you doing?"

She dared to venture several inches inside his shop. The pearls were loose and Bubba was widening the holes through them with a 5/64th-inch drill bit.

"Bubba? What are you doing to my pearls? My father gave me those pearls."

"They're fake, Honey."

Bubba threaded black string through one of the pearls and tied a tight knot. He did the same thing with another pearl and took the two lengths of string and tied them together maybe four inches below the pearls. He slowly whirled this above his head like a lasso. He liked the way it felt, and proceeded to make several more.

"Honey, you go on back inside the house," Bubba said. "This is something you don't need to see or tell anybody about."

She wavered in the doorway, her eyes uneasy.

"You're not doing something sneaky, are you?" she dared to ask.

Bubba didn't reply.

"Precious, I've never known you to do anything sneaky. You've always been the most honest man I've ever met, so honest everybody's always taking advantage of you."

"I'm meeting Smudge at his house around six and we're heading out to Suffolk."

She knew what that meant. "Dismal Swamp? Please don't tell me you're going there, Bubba."

"May or may not."

"Think of all the snakes." She shivered.

"There's snakes everywhere, Honey," said Bubba, who was acutely phobic of snakes and believed no one knew it. "A man can't spend his life worrying about snakes."

* * *

Smudge had his own workshop, which was much better organized than Bubba's and equipped with only the essentials. He had the expected table, power miter, radial-arm and band saws, a thickness planer, wood lathe, workbench and shop vacuum. Smudge wasn't fond of snakes, either, but he used common sense.

The weather had been unseasonably warm. Water moccasins might be stirring in the Dismal Swamp, meaning Smudge had no intention of hunting coons down there. Southampton County would be better, although probably not for Bubba. Smudge was at his workbench Super-Gluing a real rattlesnake rattle to the tail of a long rubber snake. He snagged the snake with a simple eagle-claw hook threaded with twenty feet of monofilament.

chapter twenty-one

Smudge loaded the portable dog pen on the back of his coon-hunting fully loaded V10 Dodge Ram.

"Get in, Tree Buster," Smudge commanded.

The open-spotted male coon hound eagerly jumped into the truck and got inside his pen. Tree Buster was born to tree coons and that's all he lived to do, that and eat. Tree Buster was a Grand Show Champ. He had a horn bawl with a lot of volume, which was the best voice a coon dog could have, unless one was hunting in the mountains, and then a higher pitch would carry better.

Smudge was proud of Tree Buster and fed him Sexton dry food ordered out of Kentucky. Tree Buster had tight cat feet, strong legs and good muscles, his ears reached the end of his nose, his bite was good and he could carry his tail up like a saber. This was not quite the quality of hound Smudge had encouraged Bubba to order from an ad in *American Cooner.*

Bubba was certain he'd gotten a great deal. The dog was already broken in and was sired by Thunder Clap, who had placed high in a number of world hunts. Bubba had bought the dog for three thousand dollars sight unseen, not knowing she'd been raised tracking coyotes, deer, bear, bobcats. She was especially good at sniffing out armadillo, or *possum on the half shell* as the good ole boys called them, thus explaining the dog's name.

Bubba parked his Cherokee in Smudge's driveway. Bubba slid his portable dog pen out the back and loaded it into Smudge's truck. Half Shell stopped bawling. Her tail was wagging furiously.

"Kennel up," Bubba told his dog.

Bubba tossed in his knee-high waders, headlamp, flashlight, gloves and oilcloth

Barbour coat, a portable phone, a compass, a Bucktool and a lock-blade Spyderco knife. He set his knapsack on the floor in front of his seat. It was packed with many things, including Cheez Whiz sandwiches, Kool-Aid, his Colt Anaconda and tricks.

"Looks like you packed for a snowstorm," Smudge commented as he backed out of the driveway.

"Never know what the weather might do this time of year," Bubba replied.

"It's pretty warm, Bubba. I don't know about the Dismal Swamp. Snakes might be squirming."

Bubba acted as if he didn't care while the hair stood up all over his body.

"We can talk about it at Loraine's," Bubba said.

They drove through peanut country, mulch plants and bleak stretches of newly plowed farmland. Nothing much had changed in Wakefield over the years, except for the new National Weather Service WSR-88-D Doppler radar installation. It looked like a huge high-tech water tower and had stirred up superstitions among neighbors who didn't particularly want the thing even close to their yards.

Bubba, for one, always got an eerie feeling when the radar dome appeared over the tops of trees. Sure, he had no doubt that it was used to track towering storm clouds, wind direction and provide county-level coverage of tornado threats. But he also believed there was more to it than that. Aliens were involved. Perhaps they used the radar installations to communicate to the mother ship, in whatever wrinkle of time or plane of reality that might be. After all, the aliens had been sent here by someone. They needed a way to call home.

There had been a time when Bubba might have confided such a theory with Smudge, but no more. He glanced at his good buddy and felt resentment. When they passed the Shrine of the Infant Jesus in Prague church, Bubba did not feel like turning the other cheek. When they cruised by Purviance Funeral Home, Bubba experienced dark feelings about Smudge's longevity. When they entered Southampton County, where buzzards on the road were looking for snacks, Bubba thought about how Smudge had picked Bubba's bones clean ever since they'd been friends in church.

Just beyond wetlands, Loraine's Restaurant offered Fast, Friendly Service, a neon sign out front advertising FR ED SHR P OYST & CRA LE S $13.25 with a blinking arrow pointing to the small cream building with red trim. The parking lot was an old truck stop with piles of gravel, and islands where there used to be gas and diesel pumps. A Norfolk-Southern train rumbled behind the building as Bubba and Smudge parked and walked past front windows hung with Smithfield hams.

Loraine's was a favorite hangout for coon hunters, although not as busy in chasing season as it was in killing season, which was fine with Myrtle, the cashier. She supposed she could understand killing coons years back when pelts were going for twenty dollars apiece. But no one bothered once the price dropped to eight dollars. Whatever the boys shot usually stayed in the woods.

Myrtle was always happy to see Smudge and Bubba. They hunted for the joy of putting their dogs through their paces, it seemed. They only killed coons when it was important to rev up the dogs again, make them believe if they treed a coon, maybe they'd get to kill it. Myrtle couldn't count all the times coon hunters came into the restaurant dressed in Delta Wings camouflage covered with blood. The guys smoked and chewed. They ordered lots of hot coffee and All-U-Can-Eat fried oysters and shrimp, Captain's Platters and meat loaf.

Tables were plastic-covered and designated with bingo numbers. Bubba and Smudge chose B4, with its cheery message, "Come Back Real Soon." Bubba started digging in the little wicker basket of A-1, Worcestershire, sugar, Tabasco, and packets of jellies to see if there were any captain's wafers hiding in there. A ceiling fan turned slowly. Smudge and Bubba looked at the specials on the board, next to a sign that read "We reserve the right to refuse service to anyone."

"Let's put it all out on the table, Bubba," Smudge said, taking off his Ducks Unlimited cap. "How much?"

"How much you want?" Bubba tried to sound macho and confident, but inside he was Jell-O.

"Five hundred," Smudge said, studying Bubba carefully to see his reaction.

"I'll raise it to a thousand," Bubba said as his gut turned to ice.

"You on the map, good buddy? Or just mud flapping."

"I got it in my pocket," Bubba said.

Smudge shook his head. "That old hound of yours has treed a chicken on top of a chicken pen and a goat on top of a stump. Closest it got to a coon was treeing one on top of a telephone pole. She won't go across water, just barks at it when she's not hanging around your feet. Half Shell ain't worth the lead to shoot her, Bubba."

"We'll see," Bubba said as Myrtle came up to the table, notepad in hand.

"You boys decided yet?"

"Iced tea, fried shrimp and oysters," Bubba said.

"One-time plate or all-u-can-eat?"

"Lay it on me," Bubba said.

Myrtle laughed, chewing gum. "And Smudge?"

"The same."

"You boys sure are easy," she said, brushing crumbs off their table and walking back to the kitchen.

"Where we headed?" Bubba asked.

"Gonna start out at the intersection of 620 and 460 right over there." Smudge pointed. "And head left way up in the middle of nowhere. Just muddy roads, forest and creeks. I did some checking into the Dismal Swamp and you definitely don't want that right now. Apparently when it's warm during the day, snakes are balled up like earthworms, there's so many of 'em. When it cools off at night, you run over 'em like sticks on the road."

Bubba was having a hard time breathing.

"You all right, good buddy?" Smudge said.

"Allergies. I forgot to bring my Sudafed."

"Chances are where we're going the snakes aren't going to be near that bad," Smudge went on. "And if we see a snake, just let it be. They're more scared of us than we are of them."

"Who says?" Bubba blurted out. "Did a snake actually tell someone that? It's like saying dogs have no sense of time. Did someone ask Half Shell if it's true? I've heard tales of a snake going up somebody's pants leg. So how scared is that?"

"Good point," Smudge thoughtfully replied. "I've heard the same thing. I must admit I've also heard of snakes chasing people and cobras spitting you in the eye, although I can't say whether it's true."

* * *

Divinity tried to calm Smoke and get him out of his dangerous mood. But when he got like this, there was no point ranting and raving about something unless she wanted to get the treatment.

"Baby, it's just I don't want nothing bad to happen to you," she tried one more time as he sped along Midlothian Turnpike, away from the slum he called a clubhouse where he now had enough of an arsenal to take out an entire police precinct.

"I find him, he's dead," Smoke said.

Wu-Tang was playing "Severe Punishment." Smoke turned it up louder.

"What'd I tell him to do?" Smoke glared at Divinity.

"You told him to paint up the statue," she quietly said, watching his hands to make sure he didn't head them her way.

"I told him to *paint up,* as in *fuck up,* as in *ruin.*" Smoke gripped the wheel hard. "I knew I shoulda stayed there and watched. God-damn it. Shit! Then he paints that little fuck-ing blue fish and the whole fucking world thinks that fish virus has got something to do with it! Where's our credit, huh? Where does it say the *Pikes?*"

"Don't look like we got credit, baby." She was freezing up inside, waiting for that beast in him to jump out.

"Well, I'm gonna fucking fix that, and you know how?"

"No, baby," Divinity said, rubbing his neck.

"Don't touch me!" Smoke shoved her away. "My mind's working."

The newsroom at this hour was left to a certain breed, the cave fish of journalism, those who slept through the sun and monitored life at its darkest hours. Artis Roop did not keep to a schedule.

He was energized and almost crazed as he hammered on about "Smokes," Fishsteria and the same blue fish painted ever so subtly on the base of Basketball Jeff. There had been no real breaks. Roop was rearranging old information, and he knew it. There was nothing else going on except the same old drug shootouts and fights in city council.

"Shit."

He leaned back in his chair and stretched, cracking his neck to the right and left.

"Got anything for last edition?" night editor Outlaw called out.

"Working on it," Roop called back.

"How big?"

"How much space I got?" Roop asked.

"Depends on what comes in over the wire," Outlaw said.

Roop was about to confess that he had nothing worth shit when his phone rang.

"Roop," he answered.

"How do I know for sure?"

"Huh?" Roop asked.

"How do I know I'm talking to Roop," the tough male voice came back.

"What is this, some kind of crank call?" Roop was about to hang up.

"I'm the blue fish guy."

Roop was silent. He flipped open his notepad.

"You ever heard of the Pikes, man?"

"No," Roop confessed.

"Who the fuck you think painted that fucking statue? What the hell do you think the fucking fish is?"

"A pike?" Roop was fascinated. "The fish is a pike?"

"You fucking got it."

"There've been suggestions the fish is actually the state fish, a trout," Roop let him know.

"It ain't no trout and you better pay attention 'cause there's a lot going down in this city that the Pikes are taking charge of."

"So is it fair to say that the Pikes are a gang?" Roop asked.

"No, fuckhead, we're a Girl Scout troop."

"Then it's all right if I refer to the Pikes as a gang in my article. Who are you?" Roop cautiously asked.

"Your worst nightmare."

"I mean, really."

"The leader. I'm whatever I decide to be and I do whatever I want. Your fucking city ain't seen nothing yet. And you can print that in red. Remember the Pikes. You're going to hear from us again."

"But why a basketball player, and does the fish tag have anything to do with the computer crash . . . ?"

Roop was answered by a dial tone. He called the police.

At this point, tables B3, B6, B2 and B1 had gotten caught up in Bubba and Smudge's conversation.

"Let me tell you what happened to me one time," said an old man in overalls. "Found one in my toilet. Lifted the lid and there it was, all curled up, its tongue sliding in and out."

"Oh my!" exclaimed a woman at the other table. "How could that have happened?"

"Can only figure it was a hot summer and he wanted to cool off."

"Snakes are cold-blooded. They don't have to cool off."

"Might've come up from the sewer."

"I was out in my johnboat one early morning before it was light, looking for duck when a damn water moccasin dropped into my boat, right on top of my foot, I kid you not. He must've been that big around." He made a huge circle with his fingers.

"Every time you tell that story, Ansel, the darn thing gets bigger."

"What'dya do?" Smudge asked as Bubba sat in silence, his face ashen.

"Kicked the damn thing as hard as I could. It sailed right over my head, all wriggly, and I could feel it brush my hair as it went past before splashing in the water."

"We had one right here in the cooler." Myrtle came over to join in. She pulled out a chair as if dinner no longer mattered.

"It was the worse scare of my life, fellas.

Apparently he was out back sunning his-self on the loading dock when Beane went into the walk-in cooler to get a barrel of pickles. Must've walked right by that God-awful rattlesnake and neither noticed the other. All we could figure after the fact is while Beane had the cooler door open, the snake went on in and got locked up. So lit-tle ole me goes in there the next morning for bacon and the minute I opened that door and step inside, I hear something rat-tling."

She paused, shivering, shutting her eyes. Everyone was silent and horror-struck as they hung on to every word.

"Well," Myrtle went on, "I didn't move. I looked around and couldn't see nothing at first and then I heard the rattle again. By then I pretty much knew what it was. I mean a rattlesnake's rattle has a rattle all its own and that's what I was hearing sort of in the direction of the ten-gallon buckets of potato salad and coleslaw." She paused again.

"Where was it?" The man in overalls could wait no longer.

"I'll bet it was eating a rat back there."

"We don't got rats in the cooler," Myrtle was quick to defend.

"Then where the hell was it, Myrtle?" Smudge said.

"That far from me." She held her index fingers six inches apart.

Everybody gasped.

"It was coiled up right next to the mop, its tail sticking up and rattling to beat the band."

"What'cha do!" Voices chimed in.

"Why, I got bit," Myrtle said. "Right there on my left calf. Happened so fast I hardly felt a thing and then that snake was gone like a streak of grease. I was in the hospital a week, and let me tell you, my leg swole up so big they thought they might have to cut it off."

No one spoke. Myrtle got up.

"Your food ought to be ready," she said, heading back to the kitchen.

Ruby Sink tried for hours to get Lelia Ehrhart on the phone, but when call waiting kicked in, whoever was on the line simply ignored it.

Agitation and loneliness usually sent Miss Sink into the kitchen, where she had no one to cook for these days except that sweet young police officer renting one of her many properties. She had often thought about inviting him in for dinner, but she didn't have time to cook a big meal.

Making shortbread cookies was one thing. But pot roast and fried chicken were another. Her various boards and associations consumed her, really. It was a wonder she could ever get around to fixing that boy anything. She dialed his pager and left her number, assuming he was probably busy at a crime scene.

The page landed in Brazil's beeper as he was knocking on Weed's front door. It hadn't taken much investigation to check the city directory and see that the Gardeners, not the Joneses, lived in the small house behind Henrico Doctors' Hospital where Brazil had dropped off Weed last night.

When Roop tipped off the police that a gang called the Pikes had claimed responsibility for the cemetery vandalism, Brazil knew Weed quite possibly was into something deep and dangerous.

Brazil knocked again and no one answered. It was dark out with no moon. There were no sounds coming from inside the house and no car in the driveway.

"Anybody home?" Brazil loudly tapped the door with his Mag-Lite.

West covered the back door, and after several minutes of silence she came around to the front.

"He knows we're looking for him," West said, slipping her nine-millimeter Sig back into the shoulder holster.

"Maybe," Brazil said. "But we can't assume he's figured out we know who his brother was."

They were walking back to the unmarked car. Brazil shone the flashlight on his pager and read the number. He got out his phone and dialed. Miss Sink answered immediately.

"Andy?"

"Hi," Brazil sweetly said as he thought of the florist's card on the table in West's hallway.

"We're closing the cemetery to the public," she told him right off.

West took her time unlocking her door. Brazil was certain she wanted to know who he was talking to.

"I think that's a great idea," Brazil said.

"The statue's going to have to go into the shop, which is no easy thing when you think how much it weighs. So until we can get it out of the cemetery, the association has decided to keep everybody out except funeral parties, of course."

"What time?" Brazil said in a hushed voice.

"What?" Miss Sink said. "I can't hear you."

"Right now?"

"Oh." Miss Sink sounded confused. "You mean is it closed right this minute?"

"Yes."

"It is. Do you like pot roast?"

"Don't tease me," Brazil whispered as West jerked open her door.

"I'm not wheezing," Miss Sink said. "But this time of year, the pollens are awful, especially if you're in the garden very much. Well, I guess pot roast isn't what young people eat these days. Not fried chicken either."

"Oh yes I do," Brazil said as he went around to his door and got in.

"You know what the secret is?" Miss Sink's mood was considerably uplifted.

"Let me guess. Honey."

West abruptly pulled out onto the street and gunned the engine.

"Exactly right," Miss Sink exclaimed. "How did you know that?"

"Had it before. About time I had it again."

"Now that's talking," Miss Sink said. "I'll get back with you and we'll do something about it."

"I sure hope so," Brazil said. "Gotta go."

West was driving as if she hated the car and was determined to punish it.

"At least I don't make personal calls on the job," she exclaimed.

Brazil was silent. He stared out his window. He took a deep breath and sighed. He glanced over at her, his feelings a volatile mixture of euphoria and heartache. She was jealous. She must still care. But he couldn't stand to hurt her. He almost told her the truth about Miss Sink. But when he remembered the florist's card, he thought, *forget it.*

Bubba was not in good spirits as Smudge drove through the tar-black night, rocking over ruts and splashing. Stars were out and stingy with their light. Bubba wished he'd never come. He felt awful. He thought he might throw up.

"We really haven't gone over the rules," Smudge cheerfully said.

"I thought we said they'd be the same as always," Bubba despondently replied.

"No, I think we ought to add a default clause," Smudge proposed. "Since so much is at stake and this is a one-on-one competition."

"I don't understand," Bubba commented as suspicions gathered.

"Let's say Half Shell's being her typical loudmouth cold nose and starts treeing about two or three trees away from the tree where the coon is. And Half Shell's doing it every time. You might just want to bag it instead of staying out in the woods all night. Same thing goes for me."

"So if I default, you get the thousand dollars. If you default I get it. If both of us default, neither of us get a thing," Bubba deduced.

"You got it, good buddy. We'll go one hundred and twenty minutes, five minutes' rest between each segment, regular competition rules."

Bubba had no idea where he was when

Smudge finally parked the truck on a muddy road and climbed out, leaving the headlights on so they could see. They sat on the tailgate and put on their boots and coats.

"Left my Bucktool inside," Bubba mumbled.

He crawled into the front seat, far out of Smudge's view, and dug inside his knapsack for the pearls on black string. He stuffed them into a pocket. He slipped out his Colt Anaconda .44. It was not his gun of choice for the night. But Bubba had nothing left. The rest had been stolen. He slid the monster revolver into a Bianchi on-belt HuSH nylon holster beneath his long, full coat.

"We all set?" Smudge asked.

"Let's get on with it," Bubba bravely replied.

They let their dogs out of the pens and both began howling and baying, tails wagging as Bubba and Smudge restrained them with heavy nylon leashes.

"Good girl," Bubba said as he kneaded Half Shell behind her long silky ears.

Bubba loved his dog, no matter her deficits. She looked like a long-legged, sleek Beagle with surprisingly soft fur. She loved to lick Bubba's hand and face. Bubba was reluctant to let her go crashing through those woods. If she got snake-bit or a coon tore her up, Bubba couldn't live with it.

Smudge had out the stopwatch. Bubba was petting Half Shell and encouraging her to find a coon this time.

"Go!" he said before Bubba was ready.

Weed ran through the dark along Cumberland Street until he neared I-195's Cherry Street overpass. Banking either side of it were thick growths of trees and shrubs closed in by a high chain-link fence.

He walked over a grassy bank, furtively looking left and right as he reached the fence, which he could not see through because the foliage was too dense. He almost didn't care what was on the other side. So what if he fell fifteen feet into rushing traffic? What was left in life but for Smoke to find him?

Weed climbed the fence and pushed branches away from his face as he worked his way down the other side. He held his breath as his feet touched ground and blindly pushed his way through tall grass and shrubs, holding his arm in front of his face to protect his eyes. He found himself in a clearing where he could just make out a small camp and a figure sitting in the middle of it, the tip of a cigarette glowing. Weed's heart flipped.

"Who's there?" an unfriendly voice sounded. "Don't try anything. I can see in the dark and I know you're puny and don't got a gun."

Weed didn't know what to say. He had no place to run unless he tried to get back over the fence or decided to jump the wall and land on the expressway.

"What's the matter, kitty got your tongue?" the man asked.

"No, sir," Weed politely said. "I didn't know nobody was here. I'll be glad to leave."

"No place to go. That's why you're here, now ain't it?"

"Yes, sir."

"You can stop all that yes sir shit. My name's Pigeon."

"That ain't your real name." Weed ventured a little closer.

"I don't remember my real one anymore."

"How come they call you that?"

"Because I eat 'em. When I can, that is."

Weed's stomach flopped.

"What's your name, and why don't you come a little closer so I can get a good look at you."

"Weed."

"That ain't your real name," Pigeon mimicked him.

"Yes, it is, too."

Weed was hungry and thirsty, and the constant thunder of traffic frightened him. A chill had settled over the night and he was cold in his baggy jeans and Bulls jersey. Pigeon lit another cigarette and Weed caught a glimpse of Pigeon's face in the spurt of flame.

"You're pretty old," Weed said.

"Older than you, that's for damn sure." He inhaled deeply and held it.

Weed stepped closer. Pigeon smelled as if he were rotting alive.

"Once you been in here awhile, your eyes start seeing again. Notice? I think all those lights from the cars below us have something to do with it," Pigeon said. "You don't look like you're much older than ten."

"Fourteen," Weed indignantly replied.

Pigeon dug in a trash bag and pulled out part of a submarine sandwich. Weed's mouth watered but he felt kind of sick, too. Pigeon dug in the bag again and set down a two-liter bottle of Pepsi that was half empty. He flicked the cigarette butt into the night.

"Want some?" Pigeon asked.

"I ain't eating or drinking nothing that came out of the garbage," Weed said.

"How you know it came out of the garbage?"

"'Cause I seen people like you digging things outta the garbage. You go around with shopping carts and don't live anywhere."

"I live here," Pigeon said. "That's somewhere, isn't it? Get your butt closer. I'll show you something."

Weed tried to block out the smell as he walked all the way to the blanket Pigeon sat on. Pigeon reached into a pocket of his ragged Army jacket and showed Weed a Baggie filled with something.

"Peanut butter crackers," Pigeon confided in his rough, raspy voice. "Didn't come outta the trash. The soup kitchen downtown is where."

"You swear?" Weed said as his stomach begged him to help out a little.

Pigeon nodded.

"I gotta bottle of water that's never been

opened. Soup kitchen again. I guess I can share with a little lost boy."

"I'm not lost," Weed said.

Bubba was. The minute the dogs had been cut loose, Half Shell had taken off through the woods in one direction while Smudge and Tree Buster had gone in another. The dogs crashed through underbrush for a good ten minutes before Half Shell barked three times.

"STRIKE, HALF SHELL!" Bubba hollered.

The crashing in Smudge's direction stopped. Bubba started running as best he could, breaking branches so he could find his way back, stepping over logs and wading through creeks, his headlamp clearing the way. He stamped and crackled, hoping if there was a snake in the area, it would think twice about getting near all that noise. Bubba's heart was pounding and he was gasping for breath as he followed the sound of his dog.

Half Shell's front paws were up an old pine tree and she was barking and bawling, her tail wagging, when Bubba appeared. Bubba had no doubt that Half Shell had either backtracked and followed the scent of where the coon had been instead of where the coon was going, or Half Shell had found yet one more slick tree that no more had a coon in it than an iceberg had sugarcane. Bubba shone his submersible Super Sabre-Lite up into the branches, sweeping the beam from high to low, disappointed but not surprised.

He dug out two iridescently painted pearls on a string and whirled them over his head. He flung them as high as they would go and was relieved when they snagged halfway up the pine tree. He shone his light on them and they glowed yellow, two perfect coon eyes. Bubba's heart swelled with euphoria as Half Shell continued barking at nothing and Tree Buster crashed in on them, Smudge right behind him.

"TREE, HALF SHELL!" Bubba yelled.

"No way," Smudge said, trying to catch his breath and sweating.

"Look for yourself."

Bubba shone the light on the bright yellow eyes high up in the black branches of the tree.

"If there's a coon up there, then how come Tree Buster's just sitting here and isn't trying to tree it, too," Smudge declared as Tree Buster panted and stared.

"That's your problem, good buddy," Bubba said. "And you can't tell me you don't see it."

"I see it," Smudge had to admit. "Damn thing sure is crouched up there at a funny angle. Looks like he's sideways."

Bubba got out his score card.

"A hundred points for the strike and another hundred and twenty-five for the tree," he said, jotting the numbers in the Tree column.

Smudge was sullen. They put the dogs back on the leashes and walked through the woods for five minutes. Smudge started the timer and again they let the dogs loose. Tree Buster bolted off as if he knew something. Half Shell disappeared no more than a hundred feet into the woods before she hit a creek and barked three times.

"STRIKE, HALF SHELL!" Bubba let loose his battle cry.

Tree Buster barked three times much farther away.

"STRIKE, TREE BUSTER!" Smudge yelled.

The two men went after their dogs. Bubba almost tripped over a root and stepped into a hole as he tried not to think about snakes. It was on his mind that if Smudge caught on to what Bubba was doing, Smudge might just leave Bubba out here. Hunters would find Bubba's skeleton years later.

Half Shell continued barking at the shallow creek and Bubba picked her up and carried her across it, setting her under another thick, winter-bare oak tree.

"Bark at that," Bubba told her.

Half Shell wasn't interested.

"Come on, girl," Bubba begged.

Half Shell sat, tongue hanging out. Bubba sighed. He reached inside a pocket and pulled out another pair of marbles and a Cheez Whiz sandwich on white bread. Half Shell started barking and drooling as Bubba waved the sandwich in front of her nose. The dog went crazy. Bubba reached up and stuffed the sandwich in a knothole. Half Shell started jumping up at it, barking and baying as Bubba flung another set of eyes high up in the branches of another slick tree.

This went on until there were only twenty minutes left of the two-hour competition. Bubba had amassed nine hundred points. Smudge had nothing. He had stopped talk-

ing forty-five minutes ago. He no longer pet-
ted his dog.

"We may as well call it a day," Bubba proposed. "There's no way you can catch up,
Smudge."

"It ain't over 'til it's over," Smudge let him
know.

The last chance was for Bubba to default, to
quit before the competition was over.
Smudge knew he had no choice as they
walked deeper into the woods during their
five-minute break between segments.

Smudge quietly reached inside his knapsack and grabbed hold of the rubber snake,
closing his hand around the rattle to silence
it as he withdrew the rattler and uncoiled the
monofilament attached to it. Smudge cast
the snake over Bubba's head. It landed
about six yards in front of Bubba's feet.

"What the hell was that?" Bubba asked
with fear in his voice.

"What was what?" Smudge asked as he
started jerking the line and the rattle
sounded.

"Oh God!" Bubba exclaimed, standing
perfectly still and shining his light on a huge

rattlesnake wriggling toward him at great speed.

"AHHHHHHHHH!!" Bubba screamed, crashing this way and that, tearing open his coat as the snake jumped and tumbled and rattled after him.

"Run! Run!" Smudge yelled, darting wherever necessary to keep the snake where he wanted it.

Bubba suddenly wheeled around, his .44 Anaconda revolver with its eight-inch barrel and scope gripped in both shaking hands. He fired again and again and again as pieces of the snake flew straight up into the air and Smudge dove over a dead tree and rolled through bushes and over a bank and into the creek.

chapter twenty-two

Weed was chilled and achy as he stared out at the city from the dark, stinking camp he shared with Pigeon, who had fallen asleep after drinking a quart of Colt 45.

Weed wondered what Officer Brazil was doing and if everybody was out looking for him. Weed wondered if the cops had found anything that might cause him a problem. Maybe they could make him doodle on some kind of lie detector and figure out he was the one who painted the statue.

Pigeon had shared two peanut butter crackers with Weed. He had given Weed four sips of water, saying it had to last.

Weed decided his hideaway stunk worse than the Pikes' clubhouse, and he thought of his nice home and good food and clean bed.

Weed would never go back to his mama again. He'd probably never see her again. He'd never spend another weekend with his father, not that he really wanted to, anyway. Weed would have to live like Pigeon because the Pikes would always be looking for him. He could never be free again. He had a slave number to remind him in case he forgot.

Pigeon rolled over and came to about the time his beer wore off. He fluffed the mound of dirty clothes that served as his pillow. His yawn was an open garbage can Weed could smell two yards away.

"You awake?" Weed said.

"Not by choice."

"How come you live the way you do, Pigeon?" Weed asked. "You always lived this way?"

"I was a little kid like you once," Pigeon said. "Grew up and fought in Vietnam, came home and didn't want to be part of nothing."

"How come?"

"Way I felt. Still do."

"Me, too," Weed said. "Maybe I'll just hang out with you from now on."

"The hell you will!" Pigeon said in a voice that startled Weed. "You ever been shipped off to war, had your foot shot off, part of your hand, too? Ever been in mental hospitals 'til they can't keep you no more so they dump your ass out on the street? Ever slept on the sidewalk in the dead of winter, nothing but a newspaper for a blanket? You ever eaten rats?"

Weed was horrified. "Did you really get your foot shot off?"

Pigeon raised his right leg and showed his stump. Weed couldn't see it in detail because it was covered with a sock and the morning was still pretty dark.

"How come you were in mental hospitals?" Weed got around to the most important question as he had second thoughts about staying with Pigeon.

"Crazzzzzzy." Pigeon shook his body and rolled his eyes.

"No you ain't."

Weed thought of the fence again and if he could get back over it fast.

"Well, I am. Sometimes I see things that aren't there. Especially at night. People coming at me with knives, guns. Cut off arms, legs, blood flying everywhere. They got all kinds of names for it, but it don't matter in the long run, Weed. No matter what you call something, it's still the same thing."

Pigeon fished another cigarette butt out of his pocket, and when he lit it, Weed saw his mangled hand. All that was left was part of the index finger and thumb.

"What you running from?" Pigeon asked.

"Who says I am?"

"I do."

"So what."

"Cops after you for something?" Pigeon asked. "Don't be shy, boy. They been after me a time or two."

"So what if they is?" Weed said.

"Huh." Pigeon blew out smoke, wheezing in the dark. "Someone's after you for sure. I bet it's some other kid out there. Maybe you stole his drugs or something."

"No, I didn't! I never even seen drugs! He's just mad 'cause I didn't do what he told me to!"

"How mad? Like maybe he's gonna really get you?"

Tears filled Weed's eyes. He wiped them away, hoping Pigeon couldn't see.

"Huh, one of those *bad* kids. Shoot people for the hell of it," Pigeon went on. "Whole new breed. And they get away with it too, for the most part."

Weed's fury burned hot like the cigarette filter burning Pigeon's lips. Pigeon tossed it and seemed disappointed.

"Kids worse than what I saw in 'Nam. All strapped up with bombs. *Hi, nice to meet ya. KABOOM!*" Pigeon went on. "Least over there we had a reason. Sure as hell wasn't no goddamn sport, tell you what."

"He already hurt me more 'an once," Weed blurted out. "Made me join his gang and tattooed my finger when I didn't want to and now I'm not in school and ain't been to art class or the last two band practices! And he knows where I live and if I go anywhere he'll find me and blow my head off. He's worse than the devil!"

"Sounds like only one thing to do." Pigeon pondered the situation. "You said the cops might be looking for you?"

"Maybe."

"What'd you do?"

"Painted a statue in the cement-tary."

"Let them catch you."

Weed was shocked.

"Why would I want to do that?" he asked.

" 'Cause you get locked up, the devil can't get you."

"I don't want to go to no jail!"

"They put you in a home for kids, right across the street from the jail. You get clothes, three meals a day, your own little room, play basketball, watch TV, go to class. You want a doctor, a shrink, they give it to you. How bad's that? Oughta hear the kids on the street. *Vacation. Where you been, man? Man, I been on vacation.* Rotten little bastards.

"Now kids, I'm afraid of. Been beat up, robbed, rolled, cut on, kicked in the nuts. One time they set me on fire for the helluvit. And what happens to 'em? They go away on fucking *vacation* for two, three weeks. Come right back out, laughing, strutting under streetlights, big wads of cash in their pockets."

"I don't want to go on vacation," Weed said.

"You want to die?"

"No. Uh uh, Pigeon. I don't."

"Then get locked up somewhere 'fore the devil gets you," Pigeon said. "Maybe by the time you get out, someone will've got him first. People like him don't live too old."

* * *

Three blocks south on Spring Street, Brazil and West were inspecting a section of fence encircling the final resting place of presidents, governors, Civil War heroes, Richmond's first and finest families, and more recently, citizens of all sorts who wished to be interred there, realizing, of course, that all lots with river views were taken.

Early morning sunlight was touched by cool fingers of shade in a remote section of Hollywood Cemetery where low-lying ground gave way to brambles and the river. West and Brazil had discovered a hole in the fence that was big enough to allow unlawful passage to an average-size adult. But there was too much rust to suggest the chain links had been cut in recent months or possibly years.

"He didn't come in this way," Brazil decided as he looked around.

West was irritated by the deduction, mainly because she had not made it first.

"Didn't realize you were a detective. Thought you were flack," she said.

"I'm not flack."

"All right, P.R., a reporter, a novelist."

Brazil was reminded of the op-ed piece due pretty soon and he hadn't even started it. He couldn't do anything about the newsletter for the website, either, because the computer system was still frozen on the same fish map. Nor had Brazil given even a moment's thought to the computer manual he was supposed to help write, as if it mattered right now, anyway.

"My obvious point is he certainly could have gotten in easily," West said.

Brazil stepped through the hole, careful not to snag his uniform or cut himself.

"You're right," he said. "You coming in?"

"No. This is your hunch, not mine. I, for one, don't think he's going to return to the scene of the crime, as you put it. What makes you so sure of that?"

"Because what he did was very personal and emotional," Brazil said. "I think he won't be able to resist taking another look. To him the statue's not Jeff Davis. It's a monument to Twister. There's got to be a lot of stuff going on inside Weed's head, and I intend to get to him before the Pikes find him first."

"Maybe they've already found him," West said.

Brazil thought about that as he scanned leaning headstones so old the inscriptions were ghosts of words no longer readable.

Trees that had been around before the Civil War cast thick shadows, and leaves rustled with breaths of wind.

"Look, Virginia, I'm going to hang out here for a while," Brazil said. "I'll radio someone to come get me when I'm done."

She hesitated. Brazil sensed she was bothered that he would stay, that he didn't seem to care if she went on without him.

"Well, anyway." West hesitated again, then was disagreeable. "All I can say is it's amazing the problems in this fucking city and what? They'll spend a fucking fortune on a fucking cemetery."

"Actually," said Brazil, who had done much research on Richmond and its surroundings, "Hollywood's a nonprofit, nonstock corporation owned by its lot owners, not the city."

"Huh," retorted West as she stalked off. "Who cares."

Lelia Ehrhart did. She was serving her eighth term as chairman of Hollywood Cemetery's board of directors, which required very little of her time, really. The majority of lot owners were dead, the annual meeting with the board always poorly attended, suggestions and complaints few.

Ehrhart had never needed anyone at meetings. She had never needed the opinions or suggestions of others. It had been her idea, and her idea alone, to ban picnics, snacks, alcoholic beverages, bicycles, jogging, motorcycles, skateboards, Rollerblades, recreational vehicles, vehicles pulling trailers and boom boxes from the grounds. Ehrhart was passionately devoted to the cemetery and its importance as a tourist attraction and celebration of lives faded but not forgotten, especially those Ehrhart claimed as her relations.

"This is far more than vandals," Ehrhart declared in the private boardroom of the Commonwealth Club, where she had called the meeting and then changed the time of it. "This is a front to our unalien rights, to their liberty and happiness, to our very civilization. These vandals, these unrepentent, cold-bloody juvenile delinquents that call themselfs Pikes have descegraded everyone sitting in their room."

* * *

This did not include Chief Judy Hammer, since she was originally from Arkansas. She ran through the ivy-framed entrance and up the old brick front steps of the historic and aristocratic club where women could not be members, but as guests of husbands or male friends were welcome to enjoy all amenities except the Victorian bar, Men's Grill, swimming pool, gym, steam and sauna rooms, squash and racquetball courts and reading rooms.

Such restrictions were of little concern to public-service minded women busy with forming various committees for the Bal du Bois and its debutantes, or supporting the arts with auctions of wine, vacations, fine jewelry and other luxury items, or planning wedding receptions or exhibits for the Maymont Flower & Garden Show, or lunching with the Virginia Federation of Garden Clubs, Daughters of the American Revolution or Daughters of the Confederacy, and with the Junior League, and of course, first families of Virginia and wives of legislators.

Hammer was twenty minutes late. She rushed into the marble foyer, impervious to the splendid Oriental rug, the antique crystal chandelier, the velvet love seat and gilt mirrors and wall-size portrait of George Washington. She did not pause to check her coat or to admire the stunning paintings of Robert E. Lee and Lighthorse Harry. Judy Hammer had little interest in a hundred-and-eight-year-old club founded by former Confederate officers who, according to the original charter, wished to promote social intercourse and maintain a library.

The door to the board room on the first floor was shut. She opened it slowly and quietly as Lelia Ehrhart held forth. Hammer scanned the faces of City Councilman Reverend Solomon Jackson, Mayor Stuart Lamb, Lieutenant Governor June Miller, NationsBank president Dick Albright, *Richmond-Times Dispatch* publisher James Eaton, and Metropolitan Richmond Convention & Visitors Bureau president Fred Ross.

The men glanced at Hammer. Several of them nodded. All of them looked restless and ready to tell Ehrhart to commit suicide. Hammer found a seat.

". . . It's so much and more than the city of the deads," Ehrhart was saying with authority. "It is the Valhalla of we brave mens who carried the Southern Cross into their bosom of deadly, waving it for the because of states' right, to at last be buried, many we don't know who, in Hollywood."

Ehrhart would have been a stunning blond were it not for several physical flaws that caused her to be more unpleasant and driven than she otherwise might have been. Her hair wasn't really as blond as she let on, and as she got older it was getting darker, requiring frequent trips to the Simon & Gregory hair salon. Nor did arduous hours with her personal trainer remedy her genetically coded long neck, narrow shoulders, tiny breasts and broad hips.

Ehrhart covered up as best she could, exclusively in Escada. This morning she was dazzling in a blaze orange skirt and blouse with matching earrings, pumps and purse. Hammer, out of breath and perspiring beneath her gray pinstripe suit, thought Ehrhart looked like a traffic cone.

"Two presidents and five governors are restful there," she preached. "Not to forget, also, Brigadier Generals Armistead, Gracie, Gregg, Morgan, Paxton, Stafford and Hill."

"Hill was a *major* general," Lieutenant Governor Miller blandly remarked. "And all the generals you just mentioned were interred in Hollywood only for a time. Aren't still there, in other words."

Ehrhart had found the seven names in the back of a booklet listing Confederate States of America generals, and had not noticed nor comprehended the parenthetical phrase *interred for a time.* Indeed, it wasn't until this moment she realized her husband's alleged ancestor, General Bull Paxton, was among the seven war heroes whose remains she was now being told had been moved out of the cemetery. Ehrhart refused to stand corrected.

"I believe I'm in the right." She smiled coolly at the lieutenant governor.

"You're not," he matter-of-factly replied in a voice that rarely rose or showed strain. "There are twenty-five generals in Hollywood, but not those seven. You might want to go back and check your booklet."

"What booklet?"

"The one you didn't read very carefully," he said.

chapter twenty-three

Bubba, Smudge, Half Shell and Tree Buster had spent the night in the woods. This was not by choice. When Bubba had blasted the rubber rattlesnake and Smudge had taken a flying leap, Smudge had ended up with a bump on his head.

Smudge was confused and disoriented and bleeding a little. This left navigation entirely in Bubba's hands. It meant he alone had to restrain two dogs on leashes to make sure that one or both of them didn't go after a coon.

"Watch the root there," Bubba said to Smudge as they trudged through brush and trees so thick they could have been in a rain forest for all Bubba knew.

"How far?" Smudge slurred.

"Can't be much farther." Bubba said what he had been saying for the past eight hours.

Smudge wasn't going to be able to walk much longer. It was a good thing Bubba had brought food, although it was a shame he had stuffed half of his Cheez Whiz sandwich in a knothole. Boy, what he wouldn't give for that now. At least water wasn't a problem. The fucking stuff was everywhere, and each time they happened upon it, Half Shell would dig in her feet and bark, and Bubba would have to carry her over another creek, some of which were very swift and deep. The only thing that kept Bubba going was anger.

"I still can't get over what a rotten thing that was to do," he said to Smudge yet once again.

Smudge was too exhausted and disoriented to answer.

"I could've had a heart attack. You're just lucky I'm a nice guy."

They reached another creek, this one a trickle, but Half Shell didn't care.

"I've had it," Bubba said to the dogs. "I

can't drag your asses another step." He un-hooked their leashes. "You're on your own."

Tree Buster shot off like a rubber band, crashing through brush and barking three times for a strike that no one gave a god-damn about. Half Shell went off to the left. She kept looking back at Bubba every cou-ple of steps, her eyes intense and caring.

"What is it?" Bubba asked her.

Half Shell ran ahead ten feet and looked back again.

"We supposed to follow you?" Bubba asked his dog.

Half Shell barked. Bubba and Smudge fol-lowed her for another forty-five minutes while Tree Buster treed coons and won-dered why nobody showed up. Mist was ris-ing, the world silent, sunlight breaking through the canopy of trees. It seemed a miracle when suddenly they were in a clear-ing, Smudge's truck straight ahead on the muddy road.

It was important that Pigeon venture out at dawn to avoid the thunder of rush hour, and more important, to forage before Dumpsters were emptied behind restaurants that would not open for hours.

Often he discovered unexpected treasures such as money, jewelry and doggie bags that drunk people dropped on their way back to their cars. Once he found a Rolex watch and got enough money from the pawn shop to keep him happy for months. He had found a number of portable phones, calculators and pagers, and an occasional gun.

"You can stay here if you want," Pigeon said to Weed.

Weed was sitting on the blanket and didn't know what to do. In daylight, his predicament seemed even worse, maybe because it was harder to hide when the sun was looking him in the eye.

"There's got to be places the devil won't go," Pigeon said.

Weed gave it some thought.

"I guess he wouldn't go back to the cement-tary," Weed decided.

Pigeon got an idea.

"People ever leave good stuff on the graves? Like the dead person's favorite food, whiskey, wine, cigars, sort of like they used to do in the Pyramids?"

"It was dark when I was in there," Weed told him. "I didn't see nothing 'cept those little flags you see everywhere. But it's a big place."

The world was no longer big enough to accommodate traffic, and this was fortunate for Officer Otis Rhoad. It was almost seventhirty and rush hour was out of the gate.

Soon there would be thousands of personal cars driven by solitary commuters indifferent to the wear and tear of the ozone and jealous of their right to come and go when and how they pleased in whatever they could afford to drive, using their own flight plans.

He steered his cruiser with a bony knee as he lit a Carlton Menthol, one eye in the rearview mirror, the other on a traffic light that was about to turn red and the guy in the Camaro next to him who thought he was going to make it. He did. Rhoad was disappointed.

Rhoad was tall, skinny, slightly cross-eyed and close to sixty. When he had been growing up south of the river, he had dreamed of being a radio disc jockey or perhaps a singer.

This had gone nowhere, and after high school he signed on with the Richmond Police Department. His first week in the academy he learned the assigned radio frequencies and areas, the proper operation of the radio, the correct procedures for relaying confidential information, the disposition of codes, the phonetic alphabet and, most important, ten signals.

When he was finally let loose on city streets, he was relentless, fluent, precise and omnipresent on the mike. He rode radio waves like the DJ he had never become, and cops, dispatchers and 911 operators dreaded his unit number and resonating voice.

They resented and loathed his habit of running his colleagues off the airways and into one another, and hogging the communication system in general. He was "Rhoad Hog." He was "Talk in a Box," and all wished the brass would transfer him out of traffic, into the silence of the property room, information desk, maintenance division or tow lot.

But the chiefs preceding Hammer were

zealous about quotas, and Rhoad was a relentless one-person posse pursuing citizens who exceeded the speed limit, went the wrong way, ran red lights and stop signs, made U turns where not allowed, drag raced, drove drunk and ignored Rhoad's lights and siren.

As time passed and maturity waved Otis Rhoad through new intersections of his life, he realized that more important than his war against moving violations was an insidious disease that clearly was becoming the epidemic of modern times. The world was running out of parking spaces.

He began punishing those who left their cars at expired meters, in handicap spaces or in more selfish and ruder appropriations such as lawns, shoulders, driveways that did not belong to them, businesses or churches they did not visit, and bicycle paths. He started carrying his ticket book off duty, especially after the city changed to twenty-four-hour meters.

Rhoad tapped an ash and gripped the mike. In exactly six minutes and forty seconds it would be eight-forty A.M., and Communications Officer Patty Passman's meter would expire.

* * *

It was possible that Smudge had a slight concussion, but he refused to be taken to the
hospital, and Bubba refused to let Smudge
drive. Bubba had to admit that he'd never driven a truck quite as nice as Smudge's and he
felt the bitterness once again, a resentment
that had pickled a part of Bubba since the beginning of time. In his own way, Smudge was
no different from all who had mocked and
wounded Bubba throughout his life.

"Some good buddy you are," Bubba muttered because Smudge seemed asleep.
"Sell me that piece-of-shit Jeep. Sabotage
Bay 8 so you can win the competition every
month. Get your free packs of cigarettes and
sell 'em to me."

"You say something?" Smudge mumbled
as Bubba turned into Smudge's driveway,
where Bubba had left his crappy Jeep last
night.

"I guess you owe me a thousand dollars,"
Bubba told him.

Smudge suddenly became alert. He sat
up straight in his seat and blinked several
times, taking in his surroundings.

"Where are we?" he asked.

"In your driveway," said Bubba. "Don't be changing the subject on me, Smudge. I won."

He started to say *fair and square* but saw his manufactured coon eyes glowing in trees.

"Won?" Smudge acted drugged. "Won what?"

"Our bet, Smudge."

"What bet?"

"You know what bet!"

"Huh?" Smudge slurred. "Think I have amnesia. Don't even know where we are. Don't recognize a thing. Where are we?"

"Your expensive house in Brandermill!" Bubba wanted to give Smudge a more serious concussion. "The one with the swimming pool and the brand-new Range Rover in front. Because you don't give a shit about buying American or being loyal to Philip Morris who doesn't pay you enough to live like this! So you're cheating, lying, stealing all over the world!"

Smudge grappled with the door handle and almost fell getting out of the truck. Bubba got Half Shell out and she jumped into the back of his Jeep. Smudge's wife boiled out the front door to assist Smudge. She threw Bubba a menacing look as he backed out of the driveway. He didn't care. He didn't stop to explain. He sped through Smudge's rich neighborhood with its big homes and wooded lots. He darted out on Midlothian Turnpike and passed everyone.

Bubba was having a hard time staying awake, but this didn't stop him from driving aggressively. He wouldn't let anyone into his lane. If someone got too close to his rear bumper, he slowed down more abruptly than he usually did.

He turned off his CB because there was no good buddy to talk to anymore. He didn't raise Honey on the two-way because he would be seeing her soon enough. He un-plugged his phone so it wouldn't ring.

At Cloverleaf Mall, misfortune, or perhaps bad karma, began to swarm in. It started with a tattooed woman on a Harley-Davidson. She thundered around Bubba, flying between two lanes, dyed blond hair streaming out from her bright red helmet.

"Hey!" Bubba yelled as if anyone could hear. "What the fuck you think you're doing?"

The woman rode on. Bubba sped up. He wove through traffic and floor-boarded it af-ter her, squealing off on Oak Glen after she did and backtracking to Carnation and

Hioaks, past the Virginia Department of Corrections Headquarters, and down Wyck Street and over to Everglades Drive.

Bubba was too exhausted, his mood too foul, to realize the woman was having a good time with him. When she shot back onto Midlothian Turnpike, Bubba took the turn too wide and didn't bother checking for cars. Horns blared. People cursed. An old woman in a Toyota Corolla pointed her finger at him like a gun and fired.

A city police cruiser darted in behind Bubba, blue-and-red lights flashing in Bubba's rearview mirror. This time Officer Budget yelped his siren as he pulled Bubba into the same Kmart where they had met before.

chapter twenty-four

Communications Officer Patty Passman was overweight, with prematurely gray hair and bad skin. She was single, antisocial, and suffered from hypoglycemia, but she was no fool. She, too, knew that her parking meter on 10th Street was about to expire.

If she didn't get to her car before Otis Rhoad, he would anchor yet one more ticket beneath her wiper blade. What was it now? An average of two a week at sixteen dollars each? Of course she would be better off parking in the nice new safe parking deck one street over, but there were no spaces left today. Whenever this happened she was forced out on the street, where Rhoad was always chalking tires and stalking expired meters.

Officer Budget recognized the red Jeep Cherokee immediately and couldn't believe he was pulling it again in the same damn parking lot. What was wrong with this guy? Was he doing it on purpose? Did he have some kind of dysfunction like those people who were always getting sick so they could go to the doctor?

The Jeep pulled into the Kmart parking lot, in front of First Union Bank, same as last time. Budget got out and approached the driver's door. Bubba was wearing camouflage. He was glassy-eyed and filthy. A dog was in a pen in the back. Budget rapped on the glass with his portable radio. Bubba rolled down his window.

"Step out of the car," Budget said.

"If you don't mind, I'll just give you my license and registration like last time, Officer Budget. I've been up all night lost in the woods coon hunting."

The racial slur was astonishing.

"Not a good time to say something like

that, Mr. Fluck," Budget said in an icy voice. "How many you catch, huh? You hang 'em from trees or shoot 'em?"

"We get 'em in trees if we can," Bubba said. "It's not legal to shoot 'em right now."

Budget jerked open the door and looked down at Bubba. He wanted to beat him up. It occurred to him that he might be able to get away with it since this was Rodney King in reverse. But they weren't in California.

"Once we get 'em up in the trees," Bubba was talking too much because his nerves were frayed, "we shine a light in their eyes. Course, it's the dogs that get them first, really. The dogs track 'em down."

Budget looked back at Half Shell. The dog seemed docile enough.

"And just what kind of dog? Pit bulls? Dobermans?" Budget hatefully said.

"No, no. Coon dogs."

"That's a *coon dog* in the back?"

"One of the best."

Budget continued to stare at Half Shell. She stared back. She started barking and tried to break out of her pen.

"You sit right here and don't you move." Budget backed away from the Jeep. "And that dog gets out, you're in a lot of trouble."

* * *

Passman was about to dash out to her car when 218 sounded in her headphones.

"Unit 218. Traffic stop," Budget let her know.

"Go ahead, Unit 218." Passman was stressed as she looked up at the clock.

"Sixty-eight hundred block Midlothian Turnpike with Boy-Union-Boy-hyphen-Adam-Henry."

"Ten-4, 218 at 0748 hours," Passman said, getting desperate.

Bubba punched in the cigarette lighter and noticed the tip of his .44 Magnum Colt Anaconda protruding from underneath his seat. Fear seized him. He broke into a cold sweat. He had a concealed weapon and no permit for such.

He kicked at the revolver, trying to shove it out of sight. It resisted his efforts, stainless steel glinting in plain view. Bubba slowly sneaked his right hand down to the floor, but his arm wasn't long enough to reach the gun unless he bent over or got on the floor. He knew it would not be a good idea to give the impression he was hiding something or had hidden something under his seat.

Bubba shoved some more and realized that his monster revolver was hung up on something. He envisioned the release lever or a bolt or maybe an exposed spring pushing against the trigger. He imagined rotted fabric caught in the hammer. With the slightest motion the gun would go off.

Brazil had gotten off to a miserable start. He was hot. Gnats had begun to pay attention to him. His urge to use the bathroom overrode decorum and he'd finally relieved himself behind azalea bushes near a plot of realistic tree-shaped markers that had something to do with the Woodmen of the World.

Brazil was tired of waiting for Weed to show up. Brazil couldn't bear to admit that West had been right. Worse, he had to tell the radio room he needed a ride. The thought was awful.

All cops on the air and people with scanners would know Brazil was alone on foot in Hollywood Cemetery. He could hear the jokes. He could imagine the sniggers. *The pretty boy's been reassigned to the dead beat.*

"Unit 11," Brazil got on the air.

"Go ahead, 11," Patty Passman quickly came back.

"At Hollywood Cemetery. Need a unit to 10-25 me here."

"Ten-4, 11, 0749 hours. 562."

"Unit 562," Rhoad came back.

Brazil recognized Talk in a Box's unit number and cringed. *Oh please don't ask him to pick me up.*

"Five-six-two. Need you to 10-25 a party at Hollywood Cemetery ASAP." Passman's voice was strained as it came back.

Passman had fabricated calls in the past to divert Rhoad from her illegally parked car, and he wasn't about to fall for it this time.

"What's your 10-20?" Passman asked Rhoad over the air.

"Unit 562. Broad and Fourteenth," he answered.

"Ten-4, 562, 0750 hours."

"Unit 562," he got back to her.

"Five-six-two."

"Unit 562," he said. "Got to make one stop first. Can 10-30 11 with an estimated 10-26 of 0830 hours."

"Eleven," Brazil shoved his way on the air. "Radio, can you send another unit? Need to get out of here long before then."

Passman was in a panic as she glanced up at the clock. She frantically stuffed the other half of a chocolate eclair into her mouth.

"Eleven, that's 10-10," she informed Brazil. "All other units are 10-6."

"Can you 10-9 that?"

"All other units are 10-6," she repeated.

It was a lie. Everyone on the air knew radio traffic had been light so far, with no indication whatsoever that all other units, or even half of them, were tied up.

"Ten-12." She told Brazil to stand by.

"Eleven." Brazil's voice was getting irritated. "Ten-5 562 and ask his 10-20."

"Five-six-two." Rhoad didn't wait for the message to be relayed, since he clearly heard what unit 11 asked and was capable of being direct. "Ten-20's Broad and Ninth."

"Well, can you 10-25 me now or not?"

"Ten-10. Got to make a stop first."

"Radio, can you please get me another ride?" Brazil asked again.

"Ten-10, 11. Five-six-two's en route."

"Five-six-two. No I'm not. I got to make a stop first."

Passman finished the eclair.

"I need someone to 10-25 me ASAP," Brazil answered back.

"Five-six-two. Can't do it, 11."

Mikes began clicking as other cops on the air voiced their amusement and encouraged Rhoad and Brazil to keep it up.

"Units 562 and 11," Passman snapped into her microphone. "Ten-3."

"All other units are 10-6," she repeated.

It was a lie. Everybody on the air knew that even half of them were tied up.

Passman's order to *stop transmitting* brought about complete silence, but only temporarily.

"Five-six-two." Rhoad could not stop. He was addicted. "Could you 10-9 that?" he said.

"Ten-3." Passman ordered him for the last time, in the secret language of cops, to shut up.

"Eleven?" Rhoad could not.

There was no response.

"Eleven?" Rhoad repeated, talking faster, doing his best to outrun Communications Officer Passman, whose habit it was to cut him off and speak unkindly whenever she could. "Everything 10-4?"

"No!" Passman blurted into her mike. "Everything's not 10-4, unit 562! It's *10-10!*" she exclaimed.

Her hands were shaking. She felt faint. Patty Passman was furious at a damn city that had no parking for loyal employees like her who worked eight-hour shifts in the windowless, dimly lit radio room, talking to lumpheads like Otis Rhoad. Her blood sugar spiked. Insulin dumped.

Her blood sugar went crashing lower than before. Her vision blacked out and she almost fainted when she jumped to her feet, turning over her coffee. Other dispatchers answered other calls as she ran out of the radio room.

Officer Budget had been waiting ten minutes for Communications Officer Passman to get back to him. Budget finally got another dispatcher to run a 10-27 and 10-28 on Bubba's red Jeep.

Budget was disappointed but not surprised to learn that Butner U. Fluck IV's driver's license was still valid through 2003 with no restrictions, and that the Jeep continued to be registered to the same party with an address on Clarence Street in the city.

"Shit," Budget said.

He climbed out of his cruiser and approached the Jeep again, pleased to find Bubba seemed appropriately scared for once.

"I'm charging you with reckless driving," Officer Budget said severely, doing his best to make the asshole feel even worse. "But you're lucky it's not a lot worse. So Mr. Fluck, head . . ."

"Please," Bubba interrupted, holding up an arm as if he were about to be struck.

"About time you showed some manners," Budget said, returning Bubba's identification and registration.

Passman's stubby feet rang loudly on worn metal steps as she raced up to the street, her heart startled like a deer or a duck fired upon. Her chest heaved as she shoved through double glass doors.

Rhoad was parking his patrol car next to her 1989 white Fleetwood Cadillac. The toe of her left New Balance jogging shoe caught on a crack in the sidewalk. She stumbled but caught herself, flailing and out of alignment.

"Stop!" she yelled at Rhoad as he approached her car, ticket book in hand, pen out. "*No!*" she screamed.

The digital reading clearly showed the time on the meter had expired.

"Sorry," Rhoad told her.

"You're not sorry, you son of a bitch!" Passman jabbed her finger at him as she fought to catch her breath.

Rhoad was unflappable as he filled in the meter number, the vehicle make and license plate number, and the mode, which in this case was an *A* for automobile. Rhoad slipped the ticket inside its envelope. He tucked it under the wiper blade. Passman moved closer to him, glaring, panting, sweating, her blood roaring. She drilled small dark homicidal eyes into him.

"I would have gotten here sooner and moved my car if you could shut the fuck up on the air!" she bellowed. "It's your goddamn fault! It's always your goddamn fault, you stupid, cow-brained loser, cross-eyed, dickless, son-of-a-mother-fucking-bitch-dumb-fuck!"

She marched to her Cadillac and snatched the summons off the windshield. She violently wadded it in his face and stuffed it down the front of his neatly pressed uniform shirt, knocking loose his clip-on tie.

"Now you've done it," Rhoad indignantly told her.

She flipped him a double bird.

"You're under arrest!" he exclaimed.

Traffic slowed, people ready for a good fight on an otherwise meaningless Wednesday morning.

"Stuff it up your ass!" Passman screamed.

"Go, girlfriend!" a woman called out from her Acura.

Rhoad fumbled with the handcuffs on the back of his Sam Browne belt as Passman yelled more obscenities, her blood sugar dipping lower into its dark crevice of irrationality and violence as an audience gathered and encouraged her.

Rhoad grabbed Passman's wrists. She kicked him in both shins and spat. He sputtered, wrenching her left arm behind her back as her right fist knuckle-punched him in the neck. Rhoad had not handcuffed anyone in many years, and steel cracked against Passman's wrist bone as he snapped and missed. Passman howled in pain as he jerked and smacked and steel jaws finally locked around her wrist and bit hard.

"Do it! Do it!" someone yelled from a black Corvette.

Passman's free hand grabbed Rhoad between his legs and twisted.

chapter twenty-five

Ruby Sink's one-year-old grandniece, Loraine, was running a fever and had kept her mother awake all night.

"Poor baby," Miss Sink said over the phone. "Are you rocking her? Did you give her a baby aspirin?"

"Yes, yes," Miss Sink's niece, Frances, said. "I don't know what else to do. If I miss another day of work, well, there're plenty of people out there wanting my job."

Miss Sink could hear Loraine squalling and imagined the child's bright red face. Day care was out of the question. Miss Sink simply would not allow the sick child to stay with strangers, nor did she want Loraine to pass on whatever she had to others.

"I'll be pleased as punch to keep her while you're at work," Miss Sink said. "And I bet you're frantically trying to get ready even as we speak."

"Yes," Frances said in despair. "I haven't even showered yet."

"I'm on my way right now," Miss Sink said. "I'll pick up Loraine and we'll have a grand day."

"And if her fever doesn't break you'll call Dr. Samson? Just to make sure she's all right?"

"Of course, dear."

"Oh, thank you, Aunt Ruby."

"I was going to get out anyway at some point," Miss Sink said. "I've got only two dollars in my billfold and I owe the yard man and probably half of everybody else in this town."

"You always say that, Aunt Ruby. The most broken record I ever heard. Mother said you were the richest poor person she ever knew."

Miss Sink was saddened by the thought of her dead sister. Miss Sink had no one left except Frances and Loraine. Her spirit settled in that low place she could not tolerate.

"Why don't you have supper with me after work," Miss Sink said. "When you pick up our little angel child."

"Depends on what you're cooking," Frances said.

"I might just invite this lovely police officer I know," Miss Sink said. "The handsomest young man you ever saw, and so sweet. The one who writes editorial pieces for the paper. He rents my little place on Plum Street."

"Him? Lord have mercy, I've seen his picture. He's too young for me, Aunt Ruby."

"Why, that's nonsense," Miss Sink said. "Things aren't like they used to be."

"He wouldn't be interested in me. He's so good-looking and all."

"And you're pretty as a rosebud."

"I'm older than him and have a child, Aunt Ruby. Reality, you know?"

"I'm going to make my sesame-honey fried chicken. Cheese grits and fresh tomatoes with balsamic vinegar," Miss Sink said.

"And just where are you going to get fresh tomatoes this time of year?"

"You forget I can them," Miss Sink said. "Now quit talking so I can be on my way."

* * *

Smoke's girlfriend, Divinity, was the first to notice the red Jeep Cherokee abandoned in the Kmart parking lot, no more than a hundred feet from the First Union Bank.

"Well, look at that," Divinity said to Smoke. "That Jeep just sitting there, nobody in it and engine running, waiting for us, baby."

"No it's not 'cause we don't want it," Smoke told her.

Smoke's mind was going through its routine, his concentration focused. He had turned off Puff Daddy when he'd picked up Divinity at the McDonald's on West Broad Street, where she'd let him know by pager that she was waiting for him. She had her hand on his thigh, but at the moment, he was aroused by other things as he watched an ancient Chevy Celebrity driven by an old woman park in front of the twenty-four-hour money stop.

"Oh, now don't be telling me you're into that one," Divinity complained. "Some old bitch driving that piece of shit?"

"It's the people with new cars that don't have money," Smoke said as he watched the old woman rummage in her purse.

He drove past her and tucked his Escort out of sight behind the bank.

"Get in line behind her," Smoke ordered Divinity.

"For what? She probably only gonna get twenty, thirty dollars. I'd rather do the Jeep."

She looked longingly back at it, wondering why someone would be so stupid to leave it like that in times like these days. Smoke rubbed his hand between her legs. Divinity laughed and grabbed him back.

"All right, all right," she said. "Whatever you say, baby."

Miss Sink felt perfectly safe as she continued digging in her purse. She had no reason to worry about withdrawing cash from this particular location because it was just across from the Kmart parking lot, and Kmart opened at eight. Already there were quite a number of cars pulling in for bargains.

Loraine was awfully quiet in the back. She was strapped in and warmly dressed, and at the moment, not crying. Miss Sink got out of the car, still digging for her wallet. Her heart got tight as she tried to remember where she had shopped last, and if she might have left her billfold there. Her memory wasn't as good as it used to be and she was always making up all kinds of excuses to deny it.

At first, she didn't pay much attention to the young woman who stepped up behind her and started grabbing things out of a faded denim bag.

"I can't find nothing inside this thing, either," the young woman said, loudly rummaging. "Drives me crazy!"

Miss Sink turned around and was rather taken aback. The young woman was hard-looking in a very short skirt, tight black tank top and red Chicago Bulls windbreaker. She had rings in her ears, nose and one eyebrow, the style of the day, which in Miss Sink's opinion was no different from the mutilation she used to see in *National Geographic.*

"I don't know where I put it," Miss Sink muttered in irritation.

She glanced back at her car, hoping the baby aspirin had helped and Loraine was asleep. The young woman stepped a little closer and something inside Miss Sink suddenly woke up. She got uneasy. She was relieved when a nice-looking young man came around from the back of the bank.

"Save any for me?" he said in a friendly voice.

He was well groomed and neatly dressed in the baggy, sand-blasted, Chicago Bulls fashion of the day. Miss Sink gave him an uncertain smile.

"Morning, ma'am," he said to her.

Miss Sink didn't like his eyes. They were so intense, more like a stare, and there was something in them that spoke to her but she didn't want to listen. The young woman was standing oddly to one side of the machine, as if avoiding the camera. Miss Sink was beginning to feel frightened. She wanted to believe the young man would protect her.

"Worst thing ever invented. Spits out money like it's Monopoly," the young man said as he also stayed out of range of the camera.

"Tell me about it," the young woman said. "I go through it like candy these days. Or would if some people'd hurry on up."

He seemed like the sort of boy who might live in Miss Sink's part of town. He was probably getting money on his way to school, and she bet he went to one of the private schools like Saint Christopher's or Collegiate.

"You know, some of us gotta be some-where," the young woman said loudly. She was making faces, sighing, looking around and rolling her eyes. "I can't be standing here all day!" She glared at Miss Sink.

"I'm sorry," Miss Sink stammered, her ner-vous hands fluttering through her purse. "I just hope I haven't lost it. Oh dear, oh dear."

"You can't find it, old woman, then just get outta the way!"

"Hey, cool it," the young man suddenly said.

He stepped closer to Miss Sink, but still off to the side.

"She was here first," the young man told the little tramp.

"Well, I got my Visa card out, ready to go. Nobody tells Divinity what to do. Why you think they call me that? Because I am as di-vine as Jesus, that's why."

"A terrible way to talk!" Miss Sink ex-claimed. "You better pray for forgiveness."

"You better pray I don't take that tongue of yours and tie it around your old-ass neck."

"That's enough!" the young man said to her.

"Fuck you, pretty boy."

Miss Sink was trembling when she finally found her credit card. She promptly dropped it on the sidewalk. She almost lost her balance as she snatched it up, her heart drilling. She fumbled and dropped it again while the nasty young woman named Divinity made exaggerated sighs and swore.

Miss Sink managed to insert her Master-Card into the machine, and typed in her PIN and answered all questions. She could smell Divinity's cloying perfume and feel her evil spirit as ten twenty-dollar bills were ejected from the machine.

"That's a lot of bus money," Divinity sarcastically said to her.

"Please leave me alone," Miss Sink said in a shaky voice.

"Don't you tell me what to do, old bitch," Divinity said in a tone mean enough to break the skin.

"Come on," the young man said to Miss Sink. "I'll walk you to your car, ma'am."

"Oh thank you." Miss Sink almost grabbed his hand. "Oh you're so nice. I can't thank you enough."

Miss Sink caught a glimpse of Divinity tearing off a strip of duct tape and slapping it over the money machine's camera.

"We should call the police!" Miss Sink whispered to her escort as he opened the driver's door for her.

She didn't understand why he went around and opened the passenger's door, too.

"I want to ride with you maybe half a block just to make sure you're okay," he explained as Divinity hung around the money machine, waiting to cause trouble for the next poor person who showed up, Miss Sink assumed.

She turned around to check on Loraine. Thank goodness she was sleeping. Miss Sink started the engine and locked the doors.

"I don't like the looks of that girl," the young man said. "Sometimes people like that work in pairs, like snakes. I'm worried there might be someone else around. You know, there's just something about all this that doesn't feel right. And I guess you've heard about these ATM robberies."

"Oh, yes!" Miss Sink exclaimed. "Thank God you came along when you did! You must be my guardian angel. I don't believe I know your name."

"People call me Smoke."

"Well, I hope you don't. Once upon a time I did. Can't tell you how hard it was to quit."

"That's not why they call me that."

Miss Sink backed up as the camera's blind eye observed nothing.

"They call me Smoke because I used to burn up things when I was a kid," he said between clenched teeth as he snatched a gun out of the back of his pants and rammed it hard into her ribs.

"Oh dear God!" Miss Sink exclaimed. "Oh no!"

"Keep driving," Smoke snapped. "That way. Around the back of Kmart."

"Oh please, for God's sake," Miss Sink begged. "There's a child in the car. Just take what you want and leave us be."

"Shut up, bitch!" he said.

Smoke watched Divinity drive the Escort from behind the bank, where it had been hidden. She inserted herself into the solid line of traffic creeping toward downtown, early morning light winking off windshields. He smelled shit and pee and at first thought it was the kid in the back seat.

"Fuck," he said when he realized his victim

had lost control of her bowels and bladder. "I wish you hadn't done that."

"I'm sorry. Please don't . . ."

"Shut the fuck up, bitch. You're going to drive real normal and you try anything I'm gonna blow your sweet little baby's brains all over the back of the car while you watch."

"Take anything," she cried. "Just don't hurt her. Anything you want. Oh please! Anything . . . !"

"Shut up!" Smoke hissed.

Miss Sink was crying so hard her teeth were chattering. They drove behind Kmart and parked where asphalt gave way to acres of woods. Smoke grabbed her wallet out of her purse. He took the ten crisp twenties she had gotten from the money stop.

He robbed her of an additional two dollars and sixty-two cents, and quarters and tokens for tolls. Her watch and necklace weren't worth the trouble, and pawn shops were risky. She stunk so bad he was about to gag, and the fucking kid was waking up and beginning to cry.

"Loraine, it's all right, sweetie. Please be quiet, honey. My name's Miss Sink and this

is my grandniece, Loraine," Miss Sink prattled on. "You don't want to hurt us. For God's
sake, you must have a mother, a grandmother . . ."

"SHUT UP! QUIT NAGGING ME, YOU
UGLY OLD BITCH!"

Smoke turned the radio up loud. The kid
began to howl.

"SHUT THE FUCK UP!" Smoke yelled at
the baby.

"Oh God in heaven! Please don't hurt us!
Dear God! Think about what you're doing!
You look like a smart young man. You don't
want trouble like this!"

"I hate ugly old women like you. So
you better shut the fuck up and consider
yourself lucky I don't do other things to
you. But you stink too bad," he said in a
low, cold voice. "So now you're gonna
bend over. So you don't see me when I get
out. Okay?"

"Okay," Miss Sink whimpered.

She pressed her face against the steering
wheel. She squeezed her eyes shut and
tightly covered them with her hands. She
didn't move. She barely breathed. Annie
Lennox was stepping on broken glass on
the radio as Smoke dug through the glove

box and the kid screamed. Smoke emptied the purse on the floor mat and helped himself to a pack of spearmint Freedent gum, fingernail clippers and a prescription bottle of Atavan.

"Thanks, *Miss Sink,*" he said. "Grow up to be a good girl, *Loraine.* Y'all don't forget me, promise?" He laughed.

He popped a stick of Freedent into his mouth and scanned the area. No one was around.

"You know what I look like, bitch?" he said. "I mean, you gonna recognize me on the street?"

"No. No. I didn't see you! Please," Miss Sink begged.

"What 'bout that ugly little motherfucker of yours in her little seat back there. She know what I look like?"

"No! She's just a baby! You don't want to hurt us!"

Miss Sink was shaking as if she was having a seizure.

"Let me think about this. What's a guy to do?"

Smoke smacked his gum. He pulled back the slide of his Glock and it snapped forward with a loud clack.

He felt the power. Smoke was high and hard with it as he pumped three Winchester hollowpoints into the back of Miss Sink's head.

chapter twenty-six

Brazil stood with his hands in his pockets, impatiently staring out at sloped, loamy land sutured by railroad tracks and tangled with brambles and trees. Steam billowed from the Fort James Paper Company, and the river was soft music played with fingers of wind and bright notes of sun.

The portable radio on Brazil's belt was a staccato of dispatchers and cops cutting in and out in spurts and codes. Nothing was going on. A handicap van was abandoned on a roadside, traffic was tied up because a light wouldn't flash, a driver had been stopped at a Kmart.

Unit numbers and military time peppered the air, but Passman and Rhoad were strangely silent. Passman dispatched no calls. Rhoad answered no one. Brazil was furious. He was certain the cops were messing with him.

"Eleven," Brazil tried again.

"Go ahead, 11," answered a communications officer whose name Brazil did not know.

"Radio, I'm still at the cemetery," Brazil said, trying to keep the anger out of his voice. "Need someone to 10-25 me right away."

"That's Hollywood."

"Ten-4."

"Any unit in the area of Hollywood Cemetery, need someone to 10-25 unit 11 there."

"Unit 199."

"Go ahead, 199."

"Just two blocks away, I'll swing by the cemetery, 10-25 11."

"Ten-5, 199, 0812 hours."

Brazil turned away from the river as he heard a rustle. He caught a flash of red on the other side of the cemetery fence where Spring and South Cherry streets intersected. The chain link was dense with ivy.

Through it Brazil could just make out the back of the large metal sign advertising Victory Rug Cleaning, an arrow pointing to the business a block away. He turned off his radio and didn't move.

The fence began to shake as someone gripped the edge of the sign and hoisted himself up. Brazil was hidden by the thick shadows of holly trees as he watched Weed reach for a tree branch and pull himself up with ease, swing over the fence and drop branch by branch to the ground. Brazil took cover behind a monument.

"Come on, it's easy," Weed said to someone on the other side.

The fence shook harder. Brazil was baffled when a scraggly, bearded face was followed by a filthy, raggedly dressed body missing part of a hand and an entire foot. The street person grabbed a branch, got snagged a couple times, but somehow made it over.

"Can't believe I did that," the street person said. "Haven't done anything that agile in years."

He looked around at the mute stony tongues of the dead speaking from the grass, as if searching for something.

"Shit," he said. "It ain't all too promising so far unless I plan on a steady diet of flowers."

Weed nervously wiped sweat off his face with the tail of his extra-extra-large Bulls jersey and rubbed his hands on his relaxed-leg jeans.

"Go on," the street person said to Weed. "I'll scrounge around and catch you later."

Weed trotted off in untied Nikes as if he knew exactly where he was going. Brazil ducked behind more monuments, boxwoods and trees as he tailed Weed and kept an eye on the street person Weed had brought with him.

Weed jogged past the Presidents Circle and the graves of Jeb Stuart and John Tyler, on to Jeter Avenue and Bellvue, directly to Davis Circle where the vandalized statue of the first and last president of the Confederacy was still dressed for the game, lumpy basketball in hand. Weed stood in front of it and stared in reverence. Every now and then he cast about, his furtive gaze sweeping over the marble sarcophagus where Brazil this moment was hiding.

* * *

A swarm of histamines rushed forth to combat the dust mites storming into Bubba's sinuses and lungs as he probed with a flashlight on the floor of his Jeep. He began to sneeze. His throat and eyes itched and his nose started to run.

"Goddamn!" he said.

The Anaconda's Holo sight was hung on the position spring wire running from one seat to the other. The exposed CB antenna wires Bubba had installed himself and covered with a mat and his work rag were snagged on the trigger.

Smudge's voice came over the CB because Bubba had not been able to stand the silence and had turned radios and the phone back on. Smudge must be feeling better, Bubba snidely thought. Bubba had nothing to say.

"Shit!" Bubba cried when he bumped his funny bone on the door handle and numbness shot up his arm.

He sneezed three more times as he carefully groped under the seat, the engine running.

"Smudge to Bubba. You stealthing on me, good buddy? Called Queen Bee, says you're no show."

Bubba's eyes were on fire and streaming. He couldn't breathe out of his nose. The stick shift kept grabbing his shirt. Smudge wouldn't shut up and Bubba's portable phone rang. He answered no one. He lay his head against old carpet, straining to see what was required to free his Colt revolver with its eight-inch barrel. He sneezed so hard his nose began to bleed.

Something hard tapped loudly and with authority on his driver's window, startling Bubba. He jumped and yelled and his shoulder banged the gear shift and knocked the Jeep into reverse. Bubba jammed down the brake with his right hand. He shoved the Jeep back into park and crawled up into his seat, in pain and gasping for breath. He was dazed when Officer Budget jerked open the door.

"You almost ran me over, you son of a bitch!" Budget's eyes were wild, his pistol pulled. "Get out with your hands up. Now!"

"What did I do?" Bubba cried, mopping his face with his sleeve and sneezing.

"Get out!"

Bubba did. He was dazzled by sunlight. He was bloody and congested and filthy.

"Legs spread, hands against the car!" Budget meant it.

He frisked Bubba, finding nothing useful.

"What were you doing hiding on the floor?" Budget demanded as he holstered his pistol.

"Nothing," Bubba lied.

"Bullshit!"

"Queen Bee's gonna sting your butt," Smudge was back. "Buzz is you ain't touched down since we faced last. Where you truckin', buddy?"

"You mind if I tell him I can't talk right now?" Bubba asked Budget.

"Don't you move!"

Budget peered through the window at a mat bunched on the floor. Bubba could tell by his reaction that he saw the revolver protruding from under the seat. Bubba froze, despair and terror rocking him like an earthquake while he watched, as if in slow motion, Budget snatch handcuffs off the back of his belt and snap them hard on Bubba's wrists and tensely radio for a backup unit and a detective.

Brazil didn't hear the call because his radio was still turned off, and Weed was staring at the statue, as if in a trance.

Brazil's legs were cramping. His expandable tactical baton and Mag-Lite were digging into his ribs. He was sweltering in his Progressive Technologies body armor, and his knees had seen too many years of hard tennis to take squatting or kneeling for very long.

He was about to make his move when Weed touched the statue. He traced the number on the uniform. He hung his head, his narrow shoulders shaking as he quietly sobbed.

Weed wiped his eyes on the sleeve on the back of his hand and was glad no one was around to see him cry. He never got weak like that, not even when his daddy smacked him or when Smoke was mean.

Weed didn't feel anything when people forgot his birthday or other kids ignored him and didn't invite him to parties or when basketball started up and he didn't get to go anymore. The last time Weed Gardener remembered crying hard out of sadness was in August when Twister was jogging and got hit by a car that kept on going.

So why Weed was crying that way now

made no sense to him, unless it was being alone in a graveyard and reminded of Twister, who was buried in Forest Lawn Cemetery on the north side of the city. It was Twister who had always encouraged Weed's art, laughing and making a big fuss over Weed's wild designs and cartoons, because Twister was famous and made good grades, but he couldn't draw. He couldn't match colors when he fixed up his dorm room or got dressed.

He used to tell Weed all the time that Weed was a *fucking genius.* Those were his exact words. Weed wanted Twister to admire what Weed had done to the statue. He wanted Twister to be flattered. He wanted Twister to beat up Smoke or maybe even kill him so Weed wouldn't have to hide anymore, so he could go back to art class and practice with the band.

Tears streamed down Weed's face and he swallowed hard as he remembered TV people and the newspapers calling Twister *a tornado on the basketball court.* Twister was tall like a tree, good-looking, and girls taped posters of him up in their bedrooms. He could have been a model or a movie star if he wanted.

He and Twister had no one but each other, and Twister used to take Weed swimming in the quarry, and to Regency Mall, and to Bullets for burgers and of course to the games, where he sat right behind Twister, who now and then turned around to wink at him in front of all those thousands of people. Weed missed Twister so much, he refused to believe Twister was gone for good.

"You lookin'?" Weed sobbed as he talked to his dead big brother. "See what I done? I worked real hard all alone in the dark. How come you ain't here, Twister?"

A loud voice suddenly sounded behind him, and Weed almost came out of his shoes and screamed, his eyes huge.

"Don't move!" Officer Brazil exclaimed.

Brazil was standing so close he could tackle Weed.

"What, what, what?" Weed stammered.

"What are you doing here?" Brazil demanded in that tone cops use to remind people that the law rules.

"Looking," Weed said. "Nothing wrong with looking," he added, hoping it was true.

"Looking at what?"

"The paint job. I heard about it," Weed said. "So I came to look."

"Who were you talking to?"

"I wasn't talking."

"I heard you," Brazil said.

Weed had to revise. It took him a minute.

"I was praying to Jesus," he said.

"About what?"

Brazil was trying to be mean, but Weed didn't think he really was.

"About all these dead people," Weed said.

"How did you get here. You walk?"

Weed nodded.

"Nobody gave you a ride? You're by yourself?"

Weed shook his head.

"*No* to which?"

"Being here by myself," Weed answered.

"Meaning you are here by yourself or you're not?"

"Yeah."

"Yeah?" Brazil had to get it straight. "You're here by yourself?"

Weed nodded.

"And you got in by climbing over the fence."

"Huh?"

"I saw you. You grabbed the Victory Rug Cleaning sign and climbed over."

"Why you think they advertise on a

cement-tary fence? Who they think gonna get their rugs done? Dead people?" Weed tried to divert the conversation.

"Why did you climb over the fence?" Brazil asked him.

"It was quicker." Weed was trying to act cool but his heart was attacking him.

"Why aren't you in school?"

"It's a holiday."

"Oh really?" Brazil asked. "Which one?"

"Can't remember."

"I'm pretty sure today isn't a holiday," Brazil said.

"Then how come there's no school?" Weed said.

Brazil didn't find Weed threatening in the least, but Brazil looked him over to make sure he wasn't carrying anything Brazil ought to know about.

"Then what are you doing way over here?" Brazil asked.

Brazil stepped closer to the statue to get a better look at Magic Jeff. He couldn't help but smile.

"I think it was one of those teacher work

days," Weed lamely offered. "All I know is it was something, you know, something they was doing and we didn't have to go. And my mama had to go to work. So I'm just hanging, you know?"

"It would only take me a minute to find out whether you're telling me the truth," said Brazil, who was distracted and upset that West had left him and 199 hadn't shown up yet. "What I ought to do is haul your tiny butt back to Godwin and let them deal with you. But guess what? All they'd do is suspend you and that would only keep you out of school longer, right? So that'd just give you what you want, right?"

"I don't want to be out of school!" Weed fired back. "I'd be there now if . . ."

"I thought you said it was a holiday," Brazil said.

Weed was horrified that he'd just tripped over his lie and landed flat on his ass. There was no going back. His eyes danced around, looking for some place to run.

"All right, Weed," Brazil said. "Let's get down to business."

"What kind of business?"

"It's time for the truth," Brazil said as Pigeon suddenly appeared, heading toward them, his gait listing and awkward.

"For one thing, your last name isn't Jones, now is it?" said Brazil, who could not see Pigeon at his back.

"No," Weed said.

"It's Gardener, and your brother was Twister."

Weed was speechless.

"Weed, tell me what the five's for?"

"Huh?"

"The five tattooed on your finger. Let's try that story again and see if it comes out better this time."

Fear turned to panic. Weed's mind went blank.

"I told you before it don't mean nothing," Weed said.

"I know it does," Brazil persisted. "The Pikes. The gang taking credit for painting the statue, right?"

Weed was beginning to shake, Pigeon right behind them. Brazil probably smelled him and suddenly spun around, hand on his gun.

"Don't go shooting me, I ain't worth it," Pigeon calmly said as he eyed the statue. "Now that's special."

"Who are you?" Brazil asked Pigeon, relaxing his shooting hand a little.

"Pigeon. I've seen you before," Pigeon said. "Usually with some hot-looking lady cop. Can't be on the street as much as I am and not see everybody eventually."

Pigeon studied the statue again. Weed wasn't sure, but he thought he saw admiration shining in Pigeon's eyes. For an instant, Weed felt joy.

"So," Brazil said, "either one of you got any idea who painted this statue to look like Weed's brother?"

Weed tensed.

Pigeon waited.

"Well," Weed said in a tight voice, "they was both eighteen. Maybe that's why somebody did it."

Pigeon squinted at the inscription on the statue's base.

"What?" Brazil frowned.

"It says right there." Weed pointed. "The man in the statue was eighteen just like Twister was."

"You need to recheck your math," Pigeon

said to Weed. "Jeff Davis was eighty-one when he died."

"What'd he do anyway?" Weed asked.

"Went to jail for a while," Pigeon said. "About two years, leg irons and the whole bit, as I recollect."

Weed stared at the statue and got a frightened expression on his face. He wondered if leg irons were like big handcuffs and if he'd have to wear them, too. He didn't want to go to jail for two years. He tried to console himself by hoping Mr. Davis had done something worse than paint a statue.

"What you do to him if you catch him?" Weed said.

"Catch who?" Brazil asked.

"The one who did the paint job."

"Can't say for sure. I'd have to talk to him first and find out why he did it," Brazil thoughtfully replied. "Whoever it is, your brother must be very special to him."

"Lock him up right this minute," Pigeon was quick to volunteer. "That's what I'd do with him."

"Naw," Brazil replied. "If all he did was paint this statue, what good would it do to

lock him up? Better to get him to do something helpful to the community."

"Like what?" Weed asked.

"Like cleaning up what he's done."

"You mean getting rid of it? Even if it's
good?" Weed said.

It didn't matter that his artwork wouldn't
survive the first rain or spray of a hose.
Weed couldn't stand the thought of cleaning
it up himself. It would just kill him to wash
Twister away.

"Doesn't matter if it's good," Brazil was
saying.

But it did to Weed, and he couldn't resist
asking, "You think it is?"

"I sure as hell think so," Pigeon said. "I
think the artist ought to open a gallery in
goddamn New York."

"That's not the issue," Brazil said to Pigeon. "There's someone running around out
there who's unusually gifted, I'll admit that.
But this isn't the way to show it."

"What does gifted mean?" Weed said.

"Special. Really good at something. You
sure you don't know who might be doing
this?" Brazil asked.

Brazil knew. Weed could tell.

"Come on, Weed, fess up," Pigeon ratted on him. "Remember what we talked about, huh? Remember the devil out there?"

Weed ran like hell, his knapsack flapping on his back. Two paintbrushes flew out and landed on Varina Davis's grave.

chapter twenty-seven

At the Commonwealth Club, Hammer was losing her polish and becoming argumentative. She had not eaten breakfast and unwisely had washed down a Multi-Max 1 sustained release multivitamin, two Advils, two BuSpars and three tropical-fruit-flavored Tums calcium supplements with black coffee. Her stomach burned.

"I think we need to put things in perspective," Hammer announced.

"I think there's exactly why we're doing it," Ehrhart answered her.

"The point is not our reverence of monuments and a historic cemetery," Hammer said, knowing she was venturing into an Indian burial ground.

"It's not a matter of reverence but of a far-stretching perception," Ehrhart butted in. "Hollywood Cemetery is a symbolism of the prospering advancement of culture that midway in the middle of the nineteenth century catapulted our marveling city into the twenty-fifth bigger of the others in America."

"Anybody know how many big cities there were back then?" challenged Reverend Jackson.

"Anybody know what she just said?" Mayor Lamb whispered in Hammer's ear.

"At least thirty-five," offered publisher Eaton.

"Closer to forty. South Dakota entered the union in 1859," Lieutenant Governor Miller quietly corrected the mayor.

"I'd like to finish what I was saying," Hammer pushed forward. "The important point is that a painted statue is not the worst crime that's ever happened here." She looked pointedly at Ehrhart. "It might be a better idea to focus on gangs and escalating juvenile crime, and on the community's refusal to participate in protecting and taking care of itself. Which is what brought me here to begin with."

"Why did you thinking were in here there morning if not to *participate?*" Ehrhart said with emotion. "And for the records, it's never been my believe we needed Charlotte to telling us how to ruin our police department and our city."

"Well, they're sure as hell running things a whole lot better than we are," commented NationsBank president Albright, who had worked out of the headquarters in Charlotte before transferring to Richmond.

"We're not here today to talk about Charlotte," the mayor irritably said.

"Nothing wrong with learning from somebody else," said the lieutenant governor.

"I suggest the Blue Ribbon Crime Commission pave the way, Lelia," Hammer said to Ehrhart, who was looking at her gold and diamond Rolex watch and getting anxious. "You're in a strong position to mobilize citizens and state and city officials. You have a voice."

"It's the responsible *police,* not the *citizens* what do away with crime. You already know the commission's subscription. We need to hire another additional more one hundred officers. We need more patrols on feet. Police officers should be forced even if they don't want to, to live with the city and carry there police cars home so there's more in our neighborhoods to be visible."

"Who's going to pay for all that?" the mayor wanted to know. "You never have explained that part, Lelia."

Hammer's flip phone vibrated. She absented herself from the gathering umbrage at the conference table and went out the door.

"Chief?" West's voice came over the cell.

"Now's not a good time," Hammer said.

"I'm at 6807 Midlothian Turnpike," West said. "I think you'd better come."

The handcuffs around Bubba's wrists had been snapped on with contempt and no nonsense. Steel teeth bit into his soft flesh. The air conditioning inside the patrol car was up too high and Bubba's cranky bowel syndrome had rumbled out of remission.

Bubba had always known it was risky to tuck his Anaconda .44 under the seat, but he had never imagined he might get into this much trouble. Police were everywhere, some of them detectives. Moments ago, two fire trucks and an ambulance had screamed past, heading around to the back of Kmart. The media was rolling in and a helicopter was circling the area.

Officer Budget was standing outside the car talking to the woman deputy chief who had come to Bubba's house after the break-in. He recalled her name was West. She kept glancing in at Bubba, her face hard, eyes sharp with anger that Bubba was certain was directed at him, although he didn't know why. He didn't understand why the cops had wanted his filthy tee shirt.

No one would tell him anything except that he had committed a class one misdemeanor by concealing a weapon from common view, a weapon that Budget had freed from beneath the seat and checked to see how many cartridges were inside the cylinder. With growing panic Bubba watched a tow truck turn off Midlothian Turnpike and park beside his Jeep.

Bubba tapped his manacled hands against his window. Budget glared in at him. West stopped talking. Bubba tapped again. Budget opened the front passenger's door and leaned inside the car.

"What?" Budget asked in a most unfriendly way.

"I need to use the bathroom," Bubba lowered his voice because he didn't want West to hear.

"Yeah, yeah," Budget said with no compassion.

"I can't wait," Bubba quietly told him.

"You're gonna have to."

"Can't." Bubba gritted his teeth, pressing his buttocks tightly together.

"Too bad." Budget shut the door.

Hammer rolled up in her midnight-blue Crown Victoria as a detective and two crime-scene technicians searched for evidence. The twenty-four-hour money stop had been cordoned off with yellow tape, and two more officers were standing sentry around a red Jeep Cherokee. West and another officer were talking by a patrol car, a suspect in back.

Hammer parked and got out as a blue medical examiner's van turned off Midlothian Turnpike and drove slowly through the Kmart parking lot, heading to the crime scene.

"Chief." Budget greeted Hammer.

"What's going on?" Hammer asked West.

"We've got a white female shot in the head behind the Kmart, found at 0832 hours inside her vehicle, a baby in the back seat, strapped in a car seat."

"God," Hammer said. "The baby all right?"

"Screaming, seems feverish," West replied.

"How young?" Hammer asked.

She stared through the patrol car window at the suspect, a white man with thinning brown hair and a pudgy, flushed face. She thought he looked rather ill.

"I'd say less than a year old," Budget replied. "Child Protective Services just removed her from the scene, taking her to Chippenham Hospital to make sure she's okay while we try to find next of kin."

"We might have a lead on that," West said. "There was a note in the victim's purse. Possibly written by the mother. Something about the baby's doctor whose office might be on Pump Road. The note refers to a sick baby named 'Loraine.' We're also making arrangements for temporary foster care, which we hope we won't need."

Hammer stared at the red Jeep, noting

the Confederate flag bumper sticker. She noted the BUB-AH vanity plate. She took a closer look at the suspect. He was shirtless and wearing camouflage pants.

"What's the victim's name?" Hammer asked.

Budget flipped back pages of his notepad.

"Ruby Sink," he said. "Seventy-two years old with a Church Hill address."

"Miss Sink?" Hammer interrupted in horror. "Oh my God! She's one of my neighbors. I can't believe it."

"You knew her?" Budget was startled.

"Not well. Dear God! She's on the Hollywood Cemetery board of directors. I just talked to her."

"Christ!" West said, throwing Bubba a killing look.

"Another ATM?" Hammer asked as a terrible darkness settled over her.

"We know she withdrew two hundred dollars at 0802 hours," Budget answered. "We found the receipt. The cash is gone."

Pieces were fitting together, although not without a little forcing. Hammer recalled the fragmented cell phone conversation between two men named Bubba and Smudge. They were planning to rob and murder a woman. The name Loraine and something about pumps were in the mix. Hammer had supposed their intended victim was black. But perhaps she had misunderstood. Hammer stared at the suspect again.

"Tell me about him," she said.

"Butner Fluck the fourth, but goes by Bubba," West replied. "Oddly enough, Brazil and I responded to a B and E at his house just yesterday. A lot of guns allegedly stolen from his workshop."

"Interesting," Hammer said.

"Appears he was parked here at the time the homicide occurred," Budget added.

"Did he see anything?" Hammer asked.

"Says he didn't. I recovered a forty-four Magnum that was concealed under the seat. One of these eight-inch-barrel jobs with a scope. Recently fired, four rounds missing. Plus, I'd stopped him maybe a half hour earlier, pulled him over to the exact spot where his Jeep is now . . ."

"Wait a minute." Hammer held up her hand. "Start over."

"I know it's rather bizarre," West tried to clarify. "But the suspect was driving erratically shortly after seven this morning and Officer Budget pulled him over here, exactly where the Jeep is now. No outstanding warrants, nothing on him. He was charged with reckless driving and released. Less than an hour later, the victim's discovered behind Kmart."

"I heard the call over the radio and responded," Budget explained. "And there's the same Jeep right where I'd seen it last, the suspect hiding on the floor, the gun in plain view."

"So he never moved after you pulled him," Hammer said. "The Jeep was right here when the victim was robbed at the money stop and then murdered behind Kmart."

"That's how it appears," West said.

"What about his demeanor?" Hammer stared at Bubba.

"Extremely agitated, sweating profusely," Budget replied. "He has blood on his tee shirt. We said we'd like to take the shirt to the lab, but he was under no obligation to let us. He was compliant."

"Anything else that might link him to the homicide?" Hammer asked.

"Not so far. Not until we can see if the bullets in the victim were fired from his gun. But it's kind of doubtful, to be honest. The shells we found in the car are nine-millimeter, ejected from a pistol."

"This is all very strange," Hammer said. "And it sounds like all we've really got on him is a class one misdemeanor."

"Yes, ma'am."

Hammer stared again at the fat man in the back seat of the cruiser. He stared back at her with exhausted, miserable eyes.

"Well, it doesn't appear to me that we have probable cause to hold him," Hammer said with extreme disappointment.

"We don't," West agreed. "But we couldn't be sure of that at first."

"It's hard for me to imagine he was sitting here while a woman was robbed and never saw a thing," Hammer angrily remarked as she thought again of Bubba and Smudge and their broken conversation.

"Nobody ever sees a thing," West said.

chapter twenty-eight

Governor Mike Feuer was a tall, lanky man in his early sixties, with piercing eyes that burned with compassion and fierce truth. Republicans often compared him to Abraham Lincoln without a beard. Democrats called him *The Führer.*

"I understand completely. And of course I'm upset, too," he was saying into a secure phone in the back of his bulletproof black limousine as he rode through downtown.

"Governor, have you seen it already yet?" Lelia Ehrhart's voice came over a line that could not be tapped or picked up by cell phones, scanners or CB radios.

"No."

"You must be able to."

He sighed, glancing at his watch. Governor Feuer had ten meetings scheduled today. He was supposed to call at least six legislators who were fighting hard for and against House and Senate bills flowing through a typically turgid General Assembly.

He was supposed to be prepped for an interview with *USA Today,* sign a proclamation, meet with his cabinet, be briefed by the House Finance Subcommittee and hold two press conferences. It was his mother's eighty-sixth birthday and he had yet to get around to sending flowers. His back was acting up again.

"If you could just have time to take to drive through and see it for yourself in person, Governor," said Ehrhart. "I think you'll be shocking, and if you aren't taking a look today, it's a risk because it has eventually to be removed at some point to be restored. It won't do any good at the most if you are looking later, because by then it will be original again."

"Then the damage must not be too extensive," he reasonably replied as plainclothes Executive Protection Unit state police officers rode in unmarked Chevrolet Caprices in front of his limousine and behind it.

"It's the action of it that matters, Governor," she went on in her unique accent.

Governor Feuer imagined her on the floor as a child, laboring over building blocks that she could not quite get in the right order.

"The vile deliberation of it," she was saying.

"Frankly, I'm more concerned with . . ."

"Please take a minutes. And I wasn't intentioned to interrupt."

She did mean to, but the governor let it pass because he was a secure, fair man. He believed in second chances. Lelia Ehrhart was entitled to one more this day before he hung up on her.

"Of course, the cemetery's closed and won't be opening to the public this minutes," Ehrhart said. "But I'll make sure it's unlocked isn't hooked for you to get in."

The governor pressed the intercom button.

"Jed?"

"Yes, sir," Jed replied from the other side of the glass partition, his attentive eyes in the rearview mirror.

"We need to swing over to Hollywood

Cemetery." Governor Feuer glanced at his watch again. "We'll have to make it quick."

"Whatever you say, sir."

"Lelia," the governor said into the phone. "Consider it done."

"Oh, you're so wonderful!"

"I'm not, really," he wearily replied as he thought of his mother's birthday again.

Lelia Ehrhart returned the portable phone to its charger inside her completely equipped gym on the third floor of her brick mansion behind wrought-iron gates on West Cary Street. Her brow was damp, her arms quivering from working latissimus dorsi, rhomboids, trapezius, triceps, deltoids and pectoralis on the incline, chest and shoulder presses, and the lat pulldown, and the low row, just before the governor had returned her phone call.

"When now?" she cheerfully asked her trainer, Lonnie Fort.

"Seated row," he said.

"No most rowing. I simply can never." She sipped Evian and dabbed her face with a towel. "I think we've got to all those muscles, Lonnie. I really don't like working it out this early, anyway. My entire system's in the state of shock. It's like getting out of bed and jumping on the Arctic Ocean. And I'm not a little bit penguin," she said in a cute voice. "Nothing cold-natured with me."

"I'm sorry we had to meet so early, Mrs. Ehrhart."

"Not your fault, not in the smallest. I forgot you had a damn dental appointed."

Lonnie studied the circuit Ehrhart was supposed to complete this morning, recording the number of reps and their weights.

"Thanks for fitting me on," she said. "But it wasn't very nice that Bull to scheduled you at the same time of nine A.M. in the morning when we always do this. Of course, he has so much people working for him. He probably knew nothing to remember about it since others always do for him so he doesn't."

"I'm sure you're right, Mrs. Ehrhart."

The son of a bitch. She thought of her wealthy dentist husband with all his radio ads and strip mall offices and sycophantic employees. He'd had affairs with three dental hygienists that she knew of, and although the number most likely far exceeded that, what difference did it make? Lelia Ehrhart would never forgive him for the first one.

"So tell to me, Lonnie, will Bull go to crown all your teeths like he does all everybody else's?" Ehrhart asked her trainer, who was so beautifully constructed she wanted to trace her fingers and tongue over every inch of him.

"He says he can give me a Hollywood smile," Lonnie answered.

"Ha! He says this always to everyone."

"I don't know. His hygienists sure have pretty smiles. They told me he crowned all their teeth."

Just the word *hygienist* pierced Ehrhart like a foil.

"But I don't know," Lonnie said again.

"Don't do it! No!" Ehrhart told him. "One time it's done there's no to undone it and it's permanently. Bull's grinded up all the teeths in the city, Lonnie."

"Well, he's sure made a good living," said Lonnie.

He attached the short extension cable to the lower pulley of the Trotter MG2100 total fitness machine. He attached the revolving straight bar, his sculpted muscles sliding and bunching beneath smooth, tan skin.

"You'll end up with at the end with all this little nibs, looking like a man-eating cannibals. You'll get TMJ and lisps when you talk and end up with several roots canals," the dentist's wife warned him. "Your teeths are so beauty!"

"I have this space between my two front ones." He showed her.

"They're perfect! Some peoples think space is really sexual."

"You're kidding?" He looked at his teeth in one of the many wall-size mirrors.

"Oh no, I'm never."

She looked intensely at his mouth and was enraged that she'd ever let her husband talk her into crowning all her teeth. She felt ruined. The crowns weren't as natural as the teeth he'd ground away, and she got frequent headaches and had pressure and temperature sensitivity in three molars. Lelia Ehrhart envied natural teeth, even if they weren't perfect. She envied beautiful bodies. She was obsessed with both and would never have either.

"Arm curls." Lonnie got back to business, holding the bar in both hands to demonstrate.

"My arms are shaken," she complained with a flirty porcelain smile. "You need to show me another again one more time. I never can get these one right. I always feel them behind my back and I know that's not supposedly to be."

He moved the pin to one hundred and fifty pounds and demonstrated, his biceps bunching like huge swells in an ocean, a gathered energy capable of great force, a slope for her to climb and conquer.

"Lift just with your arms," he said. "Don't lean back. You use your back, you're cheating."

He lowered the weight to twenty pounds. Ehrhart took the bar and held it shoulder width apart with an underhand grip, palms facing up, elbows close to her sides, just as she had been taught. She eyed her form in mirrors, not sure her blue Nike tights had been a good choice. The red stripes emphasized her wide hips. When all was said and done, black was always best for lower body, bright colors for upper, such as the chartreuse sports bra she had on today.

"Twenty reps," Lonnie told her.

She was energized by her conversation with Governor Führer. How many people could ask to speak to the governor of Virginia and have him on the phone twenty-two minutes later? Not many, she told herself as she strained. Not many at all, and this time it had nothing to do with her husband's power and contributions.

"All of us have our complexions," she said to Lonnie as she struggled for breath. "Our insecure hidden secret places that others can't see. Even I do. I've lost counting." She huffed.

"Sixteen."

"Seventeen, eighteen. Goodness, you're wearing me in!"

"What complexes could you possibly have? How many women your age work out like you do and have their own gym? Not to mention a house like this."

The comment seared Ehrhart's ego and self-worth. She wanted him to say that no other woman on earth looked like her, that age and a wealthy husband had nothing to do with it. She wanted to hear him say she was divine, her face so beautiful it turned all mortals to stone, her body fatal to those who dared look at it. She wanted Lonnie to taste blood when his eyes wandered over her. She wanted him possessive, obsessive, jealous. She wanted him to feel a raging lust that kept him up all night.

"I supposedly my most big complexion is

worrying I don't have enough times for my husband," she lied. "Filling his endlessly needs, which are unsatisfying. I suppose I worry anxiously my rule in state government carries with it such huge responsibles I often neglected family and many, many friends and don't have times for them. I worry anxiously about getting over muscled. I didn't want to be over developing."

Lonnie looked her up and down.

"Oh, you shouldn't worry about that," he reassured her. "You don't have the kind of body that will get overbuilt, Mrs. Ehrhart."

"I suppose I'm much the soft, female typed," she decided.

"Next time we'll measure your body fat again."

"And then the children," she went on with her complexes, which were multiplying the more Lonnie talked. "Last night I was too busy and spend much too little times with thems individually, either one, because of my commission meeting I had to call to order and make it earlier. And I barely had times for that. And why?" She gave him a coquettish smile. "To be here with you an hour earlier than before the usual."

"I admire your dedication," Lonnie said,

glancing at his watch and setting the clipboard on a weight bench. "That's what it takes. No pain, no gain."

"Don't crowns your teeths!" she told him with feeling. "And don't you dare tell Bull I lost away his business." She winked at Lonnie. "When next?"

"Abs," Lonnie said. "And then we're almost done."

"I can't tell if I see any progression." She placed her hands on her abdomen and looked in the mirror. "All that misery for a thing more. I hate abs so much more intensively than others."

He studied her rectus abdominus and Iliopsoas, sweat staining his gray MetRex tank top and buffing his skin.

"Why bother it?" she went on.

"You forget where you were when you started," he said. "You don't see how much you've improved because you look at yourself every day. Your abs are definitely better, Mrs. Ehrhart."

"I am very doubting. You look."

She took his reluctant hands and placed them on her abdomen.

"Well?"

He had no response.

"Maybe when you get to be my older age at this stage of life, it's hopeless and can't be changed. Nature is just won't collaborating and do what you want it to do."

Lonnie didn't move. She slid his hands up a little.

"You're in great shape," he exaggerated.

"Bull's out crowning every tooths in North of America," Ehrhart answered, sliding his hands up more. "You know why he nicked his name Bull? It's not because of the general he thinks he's relations with, Lonnie."

"I thought maybe it had to do with the stock market."

"The reason is because of . . ."

"I've really got to go, Mrs. Ehrhart."

She pressed his large, strong hands against her, finally cupping them over her very small breasts.

"What's the oldest older woman you once ever had before?" she whispered.

"I guess my eighth-grade teacher," he said.

"What was that have been?"

"When I was in the eighth grade."

"My, you must have been bigger for your age then."

"Mrs. Ehrhart, I've gotta go so I'm not late

for my appointment. Your husband's really hard to schedule. Well, I guess I wouldn't get in at all if it wasn't for you."

Lelia Ehrhart removed his hands. She angrily grabbed a towel and wrapped it around her neck.

"So what's the next place where we go from here?" she demanded as all her phobias and insecurities roared at her.

"You haven't done squats," he said.

chapter twenty-nine

Governor Feuer neatly folded the *New York Times, Wall Street Journal, Washington Post, USA Today* and the Richmond paper. He stacked them on the black carpet and stared out the tinted window at pedestrians staring at him.

Everyone knew that a black stretch limousine with 1 on the license plate was not Jimmy Dean or Ralph Sampson. It was not kids going to the prom.

"Sir?" Jed said over the intercom. "I'll just shoot over on Tenth, cut across Broad to avoid all that traffic, then wind around the courthouse onto Leigh and get on Belvidere.

From there it's pretty much a straight shot into the cemetery."

"Ummmm."

"If that suits, sir," added Jed, who was obsessive-compulsive and needy.

"That's fine," said the governor, who had worked his way up from attorney general to lieutenant governor to governor, and therefore had not navigated Richmond's streets alone for more than eight years, but rather had watched his travels throughout his beloved Commonwealth from a back seat through tinted glass, police escorts leading the way and protecting his rear.

"I've got the package," Jed said loudly in his two-way, secure radio. "Going to be turning on Tenth."

"Gotcha covered," the lead car came back.

The altercation between Patty Passman and Officer Rhoad had gone beyond a squabble or fit of pique that might have been reasonably resolved, forgiven or perhaps forgotten.

Cars were double-parked and parked on an angle and within fifteen feet of a fire hydrant and on the wrong side of the street and on the sidewalk along 10th. Drivers and pedestrians had gathered around a fight in progress as police cruisers with sirens screaming and lights flashing raced in from all directions.

Passman had Rhoad on hold. He was running around in circles, screaming "MAY-DAY" into his portable radio while she twisted and squeezed.

"God! God!" Rhoad shrieked as she doggedly followed his every move, on his heels, killing him. "Let go! Please! Please! Ahhhhhhhhh! AHHHHHHHH!"

The crowd was frenzied.

"Go, girlfriend!"

"Yank it hard!"

"Get him!"

"In the nuts! Hooo-a hooo-a hooo-a!"

"Hey! Punch her! Man, fucking poke her eyes out!"

"Yeah! Knock her nose to the back of her head so she can smell her ass!"

"Pull that banana off the tree, girlfriend!"

"Shift him into neutral, baby!"

"Let go, fatso!"

"Untie his balloon!"

"Go, girl!"

The crowd cheered on as a gleaming

black stretch limousine and two unmarked black Caprices with multiple antennas floated across Broad Street. The convoy pulled off to the side of 10th Street, making way for two cruisers with flashing lights and screaming sirens. Other police cars were screeching in from Marshall and Leigh. A fire truck wailed and rumbled along Clay.

Jed was desperate to jump out of the limousine and get involved. The cops must be after a fugitive, someone on the FBI's ten most wanted list, maybe a serial killer. Clearly, the fat lady was a psycho of some sort, and it was obvious that the uniformed officers could not restrain her.

"What's going on?" Governor Feuer inquired over the intercom.

"Some wacko woman, probably high on PCP or crack. Wow, look at her go, like a damn pit bull! She's got half a dozen cops playing Ring Around the Rosie and falling on their butts!"

The governor made his way to the other side of the black leather horseshoe-shaped seat that could comfortably accommodate six. He strained to see over the back of Jed's big head.

Governor Feuer was startled by the obese woman flying after a tall, rather elderly skinny cop. A pair of handcuffs dangled off one of her wrists and her free hand was shoved up the poor fellow's crotch. She was twisting and crushing, cursing, kicking. She was whirling and swinging the loose handcuff like a numchaku, scattering arriving troops.

"Wow!" Jed exclaimed.

"How awful," said the governor. "How perfectly awful."

"We need to do something, sir!"

Governor Feuer agreed, his anger rising. There was nothing funny about this. There was nothing entertaining about violence. He jerked open his car door. Before Jed or EPU police could stop him, the governor popped the trunk and snatched out a fire extinguisher.

He ran into the melee and to the astonishment of all blasted Patty Passman with Halon 1301. Shocked, she released Rhoad. Cops tackled her to the ground. Four EPU police officers quickly escorted Governor Feuer back to his limousine.

"Way to go, sir!" Jed was very proud of his commander-in-chief.

The governor checked his black cashmere pinstripe suit for a Halon residue, but the miracle extinguisher left not a trace. He watched the cuffed, crazed woman as she was stuffed into the back of a patrol car. The poor officer was on his knees in the middle of the street, clutching himself and crying. The media was rolling in, advancing with television cameras and microphones like drawn swords.

"On to Hollywood," Governor Feuer ordered.

"There's really not time, sir," Jed suggested.

"There's never time," the governor said, waving him on.

Weed decided he had stayed long enough in the big hole with broken clay pipes in the bottom of it. Water was leaking from somewhere. A Bob Cat was parked nearby and lots of shovels and hoes were scattered on the ground.

He had begun to worry that the hole was really a grave, even though it wasn't at all shaped like one. Maybe everybody was on an early lunch break or something. Maybe all of a sudden dirt would start falling in and Weed would be buried alive.

He peeked out and didn't see a sign of Brazil or anyone else. He listened hard. Only birds were talking. He climbed out of the hole and made a dash for the cemetery fence. He climbed to the top of it as the Lemans slowly cruised into view. Dog, Beeper and Sick were looking for him so Smoke could shoot Weed and dump him in the river. Weed dropped back inside the cemetery and ran with no particular destination in mind, zigzagging around graves and leaping over monuments.

Brazil too was running fast and could have continued his seven-minute-mile pace for hours, although boots would not have been his footwear of choice and his shins were beginning to hurt. The more frustrated he got, the faster he ran.

He cut over to Riverview, flying past memorials, monuments, plaques, sculptures, vases and tablets. Tiny Confederate flags waved him on. A groundskeeper with extra spools of nylon twine tied on his belt trimmed around stones, the weed-eater popping and buzzing as he maneuvered it with the skill of a surgeon.

"You seen a kid in Chicago Bulls stuff?" Brazil called out as he got close.

"Like the statue?"

"Only smaller," Brazil said, running past.

"Nope," the groundskeeper said as he trimmed.

Brazil wove between a marble lamb and a mausoleum, jumped over an English boxwood and to his amazement landed almost on top of Weed. Brazil grabbed him by the back of his jersey, kicked his feet out from under him and sat on him. He pinned Weed's arms to the ground.

"I changed my mind," Weed yelled. "You can lock me up."

Bubba had lost control and it was obvious to all. He was humiliated and sick to his stomach when Officer Budget opened the back of the patrol car and exclaimed, "*Shit, man.*" Bubba felt sure one more hideous nickname had just been added to the list.

"I'm sorry," Bubba said. "But I told you . . ."

"Man, oh man!" Budget cried.

He was beside himself, almost gagging as he unlocked Bubba's handcuffs while Chief Hammer and West looked on.

"And just who's going to clean this up! Man, oh man! I can't believe it!"

Bubba's shame could not have been deeper. He had been so certain it was his destiny for his path to cross with Hammer's. But not like this. Not half naked, dirty, fat and soiled. He could not look at her.

"Officer Budget," Hammer flatly said, "if you'll just leave me alone with him for a few minutes, please. Major West? I'll meet you behind the Kmart?"

"We'll let you know what the medical examiner says," Budget told Hammer, "in case you don't get there before he leaves."

"*She,*" West corrected him.

Hammer turned her attention to Bubba. He was stunned that she did not seem to notice his unspeakable predicament.

"Chief Hammer?" he stammered. "I, uh . . ." He swallowed hard. "I didn't mean . . ."

She held up a hand to silence him.

"Don't worry about it," she told him.

"How can I not!" he cried. "And all I wanted to do was help!"

"Help who?"

She seemed interested and sincere. Bubba hadn't realized she was so attractive, not in a pretty way, but strong and striking in her pinstripe pants suit. He wondered if she had a gun. Maybe she carried one in her black handbag. His thoughts crazily moiled as the wind shifted to Hammer's disadvantage. She moved several feet to her right.

"Who is it you're trying to help?" she asked. "The woman who just got murdered? Did you see something, Mr. Fluck?"

"Oh my God!" Bubba was shocked. "A lady was just murdered, right here! When?"

"While you were parked here, Mr. Fluck."

Bubba's bowels were irritably gathering again, like dark clouds about to release another lashing, violent storm. He thought of his sweaty tee shirt, covered with blood and on its way to the police labs.

"You sure you didn't see anything?" The chief continued to press.

"My Anaconda was hung," he answered.

She just stared at him.

"I couldn't get it off," he said.

Still, she said nothing.

"So I got down and started tugging on it, you know, manipulating it as best I could.

See, I was afraid it might go off. Then I got a nosebleed."

"This was when?" Hammer asked.

"I guess when the lady got killed. I swear. I was on the floor ever since Officer Budget left me. That's all I was doing until he was knocking on my window. I couldn't have seen anything, because I was on the floor, is what I'm saying, ma'am."

He couldn't tell if she believed him. There was nothing cruel or disrespectful about her demeanor, but she was shrewd and very smart. Bubba was in awe of her. For a moment he forgot his plight until Channel 8's cameraman trotted toward them, heading straight for the chief, then getting a disgusted look on his face. He stared at Bubba's camouflage pants and changed course.

"It appears the victim was robbed right here at the money stop," Hammer spoke to Bubba. "I'm not telling you anything confidential. I'm sure you'll be hearing all about it on the news. You were parked less than fifty feet from the money stop, Mr. Fluck. Are you absolutely certain you didn't hear anything? Maybe voices, arguing, a car or cars?"

Bubba thought hard. Channel 6 headed

toward them and quickly went the other way. Bubba would have done anything to help this brave woman, and it broke his heart that the one time he had a chance, he could do nothing but stink.

"Shit," muttered a WRVA reporter as he stopped and backed up. "Wouldn't go over there if I was you," he said to a crew from Channel 12.

"What's going on?" *Style Magazine* called out to *Richmond Magazine*. "A sewer line break?"

"Hell if I know. Shit, man."

Bubba went on red alert.

" 'Shit man' is right." A *Times-Dispatch* reporter waved his hand in front of his face.

Bubba's blood heated up. He didn't hear a word Chief Hammer was saying to him. Bubba was completely focused on the knot of reporters, cameramen, photographers and technicians gathered by his Jeep. They were restless and angry, talking and bitching loudly amongst themselves and calling him *Shit Man.*

"Anybody seen what's going on back there behind the building?"

"They won't let anybody close."

"You can forget it. The minute you get to the garden center, the cops push you back."

"Yeah, one asshole put his hand over my lens."

"Shit, man."

Bubba's mind whited out the way it always did when he heard the voices and the laughter shrieking from dangerous, painful convolutions in his brain. He saw a legion of little faces distorted by taunts and cruel grins.

"My editor's gonna kill me. Shit, man!"

"Stop it!" Bubba screamed at the press.

His eyes suddenly focused. Hammer was staring at him, rather startled. The media wasn't interested.

"Maybe the body's decomposing," one of them was saying.

"It's back behind the store."

"Could've been here first. Maybe they moved it for some reason."

"That wouldn't make sense."

"Well, they wouldn't want to leave it here right in front of the bank."

"No way it could have been here long enough to decompose without someone spotting it before this morning."

"Oh, so now you're a medical examiner."

"Maybe it was dumped. You know, the victim's been dead for a while, is getting ripe and the killer dumps her."

"It's a her?"

"Maybe."

"Dumps her *here?*"

"I'm just throwing things out."

"Yeah, asshole, 'cause you want the rest of us to write them down and make fools out of ourselves."

"Then what stinks so bad?"

"Chief Hammer?" a reporter raised his voice without getting any closer. "Can I get a statement?"

"Don't talk to them!" Bubba said to her in a panic. "Don't let them do this to me! Please!"

"Truth is, I think our source is him," a reporter broke the news. "Look at his pants. Not all of that's camouflage."

"Shit, man."

"See!" Bubba hissed.

"How can she stand there like that? It's bad enough way back here."

"I've heard she's tough."

"I'm interested in your vanity plate," Hammer said to Bubba.

* * *

Officer Horace Cutchins wasn't interested in anything except his pocket Game Boy Tetris Plus as he drove the detention wagon at a good clip along Leigh Street.

He'd been on duty only three hours and had already transported two subjects to lockup, both of them gypsies caught burglarizing a Tudor-style home in Windsor Farms. Cutchins didn't understand why people didn't learn.

Gypsies passed through the city twice a year on their migrations north and south. Everyone knew it. The press ran frequent stories and columns. Sergeant Rink of *Crime Stoppers* offered impassioned warnings and prevention and self-defense tips on all local television networks and radio stations. "Gypsies Are Back" signs were prominently posted as usual.

Yet wealthy Windsor Farmers, as Cutchins jealously called them, still went out to get the newspaper or worked in their gardens and yards or sat by their pools or chatted with neighbors or frapped around the house with alarm systems off and doors unlocked. So what did they expect?

Cutchins was just turning into Engine Company #5's back parking lot, where he was looking forward to resuming his puzzle game, when the radio raised him.

"Ten-25 unit 112 on Tenth Street to 10-31 a prisoner," the communications officer told him.

"Ten-4," he answered. "Fuck," he said to himself.

He'd heard the mayday earlier and knew that Rhoad Hog was involved in an altercation with a disorderly female. But when it appeared that an arrest had been made, Cutchins just assumed the subject would be transported in a screen unit.

After all, it wasn't likely that a female could kick out the Plexiglas, and even if the partition didn't fit right because the numb nuts with General Services had taken one from a Caprice, for example, and retrofitted it for a Crown Vic, it didn't matter in this case. A female prisoner was not equipped to pee on the officer through gaps and spaces caused by improper installment.

Cutchins made a U turn. He shot back out on Leigh Street, stepping on it, wanting to get the call over with so he could take a break. He swung over to 10th and rolled up on the problem as Detective Gloria De Souza climbed out of her unmarked car.

Rhoad Hog and three other uniformed guys were waiting for Cutchins, their prisoner an ugly fat woman who looked vaguely familiar. She was sitting on the curb, wrists cuffed behind her back, hair wild. She was breathing hard and looked like she might do something unexpected any minute.

"Okay, Miss Passman, I'm going to have to search you," said Detective De Souza. "I need you to stand up."

Miss Passman didn't budge.

"Cooperate, Patty," one of the officers urged her.

She wouldn't.

"Ma'am, you're going to need to stand up. Now don't make this harder than it has to be."

Passman wasn't trying to make things harder. She simply could not rise to the occasion on her own, not with her hands shackled behind her.

"Get up," De Souza sternly said.

"I can't," Passman replied.

"Then we'll have to help you, ma'am."

"Go ahead," Passman said.

De Souza and another officer got Passman under each arm and hoisted her up while Rhoad hung back at a safe distance. Cutchins hopped out of his white Dodge van and went around to the back to open the tailgate. De Souza bent over and briskly slid her hands up Passman's stout legs, over sagging pantyhose with runs, feeling her way up into areas where no woman, other than Passman's gynecologist, had ever gone before. Passman tried to kick De Souza and almost fell.

"Get the flex cuffs!" De Souza demanded as she held Passman's legs still. "You do that again, ma'am, and I'm gonna hogtie you!"

De Souza held on as an officer looped the plastic flex cuff around Passman's ankles, jerking it tight as if she were a tall kitchen bag.

"Ouch!"

"Hold still!"

"That hurts!" Passman screamed.

"Good!" Rhoad cheered.

Detective De Souza resumed her search, running experienced hands over Passman's topography, into its crevices, through its canyons, between its foothills and under and over them while Passman cursed and yelled and called her a diesel dyke and cops helped Passman to her feet.

"Get your fucking hands off me, you queer!" Passman shouted. *"That's right! You sleep with the coach of your fucking queer softball team the Clit Hits and everybody in the entire police department and radio room knows it!"*

Cutchins momentarily forgot his puzzle game. He'd always thought it a waste that a good-looking woman like De Souza was *into same,* not that he minded lesbians, and in fact watched them whenever he had access to pay TV. He simply objected to discrimination. De Souza did not share herself with men, and Cutchins didn't think that was fair.

"Nothing on her but an attitude," De Souza said.

Unfortunately, Cutchins had parked on the other side of 10th and it was shift change at the Medical College of Virginia hospital. Instantly, traffic was heavy, sidewalks and streets congested with nurses, dietitians, orderlies, custodians, security guards, administrators, resident doctors and chaplains, all of them worn out, underpaid and cranky. Cars stopped to let the tied-up lady and the cops cross to the awaiting wagon. Pedestrians slowed their impatient get-out-of-my-way steps as Passman awkwardly hopped ahead.

"Fuckheads! What are you staring at!" she yelled to all.

"Go jump!" a secretary yelled back.

"Jumpin' Jack Flash! Jumpin' Jack Flash! Jumpin' Jack Flash!" chanted a group of sleep-deprived residents.

"Hop-a-long!"

"Motherfuckers!" screamed Passman, whose blood sugar was as low as it had ever been while she was conscious.

"Jumpin' bean!" cried a records clerk.

Passman struggled, writhing like a python, hissing and baring her teeth at her detractors. Officers did their best to move her along while bystanders and drivers got more worked up and Rhoad tagged along out of range.

Pigeon had gotten bored with the cemetery and was rooting through a trash can, where so far he had salvaged part of a 7-Eleven breakfast burrito and a twenty-two-ounce cup of coffee that was half full.

He watched the heartless parade pass by,

some woman hopping along as if she were in a sack race. He suddenly felt self-conscious of his stump and was angered by the crowd.

"Don't pay any attention to them," he counseled the fat lady as she hopped past and he took a bite of the burrito. "People are so rude these days."

"Shut up, you crippled garbage-picker!" the woman yelled at him.

Pigeon was sorrowed by yet another rotten example of human nature. He continued his treasure hunting, always drawn by crowds that might throw things away.

De Souza gripped Passman's arm like a vise. "He started it!" Passman twisted around to glare at Rhoad. "Why don't you lock his ass up!"

Cops shoved her inside the wagon and slammed the tailgate shut.

It was Chief Hammer's NIJ mission to implement the New York City Crime Control Model in the Richmond Police Department, as she had in Charlotte and would do in other cities should health, energy and grant money allow. Understandably, this created a bit of a dilemma for her.

She was losing stamina and professionalism as she stood close to Bubba and listened to him talk. She wanted out but simply could not and would never pass the buck, look the other way, walk off and make this a problem for someone else. Hammer was here, and that was that. When a cop asks a suspect a question, the cop must listen to the answer, no matter how long and drawn-out it is.

Bubba was telling her about his vanity plate, recalling his trip to the DMV on Johnston Willis Drive, between Whitten Brothers Jeep and Dick Straus Ford, where he had waited in line at customer service for fifty-seven minutes only to learn that *BUBBA* was taken, as were *BUBA, BUBBBA, BU-UBBBA, BUBEH, BUBBEH, BUBBBEH, BG-BUBA, BHUBBA* and *BHUBA*. Bubba had been crushed and exhausted. He could think of nothing else that didn't exceed seven letters. Despondent and emotionally drained, he had accepted that the vanity plate was not meant to be.

"Then," he seemed momentarily energized by the tireless account, "the lady at the
counter said *Bubah* would work, and I asked
if I could hyphenate it and she didn't care
because a hyphen doesn't count as a letter
and that was good because I thought it
would be easier to pronounce *Bubah* with a
hyphen."

Hammer believed that Bubba had an ac-
complice named Smudge, and a graphic
and believable scenario was materializing in
her mind even as Bubba droned on and reporters continued to keep their distance.
Bubba and Smudge somehow knew that
Ruby Sink and Loraine were headed to the
First Union money stop near the Kmart.

Possibly the men had been lying in wait
for the wealthy Miss Sink, headlights and
engines off, and when she left her resi-
dence, Smudge and Bubba tailed her, weav-
ing in and out of traffic, keeping tabs on
each other over cell phones and CBs.

It was at this point that Hammer's recreation of the crime became less well defined. Frankly, she couldn't figure out what
might have happened next and was not the
sort to make things up. Yet she simply could

not, would not walk away with no accountability and tell her troops the murder was
their problem.

Somehow, Hammer had to get Bubba to
answer the question of Smudge without
Bubba thinking she had asked.

chapter thirty

Governor Mike Feuer had been on the car phone for the past fifteen minutes, and this was fortunate for Jed, who had made five wrong turns and sped through an alleyway, losing both unmarked Caprices, before finding Cherry Street and driving past Hollywood Cemetery and ending up at Oregon Hill Park, where he had turned around and gone the wrong way on Spring Street, ending up on Pine Street at Mamma'Zu, reputed to be the best Italian restaurant this side of Washington, D.C.

"Jed?" The governor's voice sounded over the intercom. "Isn't that Mamma'Zu?"

"I believe so, sir."

"I thought you said it closed down."

"No, sir. I think I said it *was closed* when you wanted to take your wife there for her birthday," Jed fibbed, for it was his modus operandi to say a business had closed or moved or gone under if the governor wanted to go there and Jed did not know how to find it.

"Well, make a note of it," the governor's voice came back. "Ginny will be thrilled."

"Will do, sir."

Ginny was the first lady, and Jed was scared of her. She knew Richmond streets far better than Jed was comfortable with, and he feared her reaction if she learned that Mamma'Zu had not closed or moved or changed its name. Ginny Feuer was a Yale graduate. She was fluent in eight languages, although Jed wasn't certain if that included English or was in addition to English.

The first lady had quizzed Jed repeatedly about his creative, time-killing routes. She was on to him and could get him reassigned, demoted, kicked off the EPU or even fired from the state police with a gesture, a word, a question in pretty much any language.

"Jed, shouldn't we be there by now?" the governor's voice sounded again.

Jed eyed his boss in the rearview mirror. Governor Feuer was looking out the windows. He was looking at his watch.

"In about two minutes, sir," Jed replied as his chest got tight.

He picked up speed, following Pine the wrong way. He took a hard right on Oregon Hill Parkway which ran him into Cherry Street where the ivy-draped cemetery fence on the left embraced and welcomed him like the Statue of Liberty.

Jed followed the fence, passing the hole in it and the Victory Rug Cleaning sign. He drove through the cemetery's massive wrought-iron front gates that Lelia Ehrhart had made sure would be unlocked for them. He passed the caretaker's house and business office, following Hollywood Avenue. Jed would have rolled up on the statue in a matter of moments had he not turned onto Confederate Avenue instead of Eastvale.

It was clear to Brazil why the media, the unimaginative, the insensitive, the resentful, and those citizens not indigenous to Richmond often trivialized Hollywood Cemetery by referring to it as the City of the Dead.

As Brazil and Weed walked deeper into having-no-idea-where-they-were, Brazil's respect for history and its dead was greatly diluted by fatigue and frustration. The famous cemetery became nothing more than a heartless, unhelpful metropolis of ancient carriage paths, now paved and named, that had been laid out by first families who already knew where they were going.

It wasn't possible to find sections or lot owners or the way out unless one had a map or an *a priori* knowledge or was lucky as hell. Brazil, sad to say, was heading west instead of east.

"Is it hurting?" Brazil asked his prisoner.

Weed had cut his chin when Brazil tackled him. Weed was bleeding and Brazil's day had just gotten worse, if that was possible. The sheriff's department would not accept a juvenile who was visibly injured. Weed would have to get a medical release, meaning Brazil would have no choice but to take Weed to an emergency room where the two of them would probably sit all day.

"I don't feel nothing." Weed shrugged,

holding one of Brazil's socks against his chin for lack of any other bandage.

"Well, I'm really sorry," Brazil apologized again.

They were walking along Waterview to New Avenue where Weed stopped to gawk at tobacco mogul Lewis Ginter's granite and marble tomb. He couldn't believe the heavy bronze doors, Corinthian columns and Tiffany windows.

"It's like a church," Weed marveled. "I wish Twister could have something like that."

They walked in silence for a moment. Brazil remembered to turn his radio back on.

"You ever had anybody die on you?" Weed asked.

"My father."

"Wish mine was dead."

"You don't really mean that," Brazil said.

"What happened to yours?" Weed looked up at him.

"He was a cop. Got killed on duty."

Brazil thought of his father's small, plain grave in the college town of Davidson. The memories of that spring Sunday morning when he was ten and the phone rang in his simple frame house on Main Street were still

vivid. He could still hear his mother screaming and kicking cabinets, wailing and throwing things while he hid in his room, knowing
without being told.

Again and again the television showed his
father's bloody sheet-covered body being
loaded into an ambulance. An endless motorcade of police cars and motorcycles with
headlights on rumbled through Brazil's
head, and he envisioned dress uniforms and
badges striped with black tape.

"You ain't listening to me," Weed insisted.

Brazil came to, shaken and unnerved.
The cemetery began closing in, suffocat-
ing him with its pungent smells and restless sounds. The radio reminded him that
he should call again for a 10-25, but he
wasn't going to do it. Brazil was not going
to let the entire police department, including West, know he was lost inside Hollywood Cemetery with a fourteen-year-old
graffiti artist.

They headed out again on New Avenue. It
eventually curved around the western edge
of the cemetery and turned into Midvale,
where in the distance they could see what
appeared to be a long black hearse traveling
toward them at a high rate of speed.

* * *

Cemetery monuments and markers and holly trees streamed past Governor Feuer's tinted windows as he ended another phone call, having by now lost all patience and willingness to give second chances.

Jed was driving too fast. It was taking longer to find Jefferson Davis's statue than it had probably taken to paint it. The unmarked Caprices and their EPU drivers were nowhere to be seen.

"Jed." This time Governor Feuer hummed down the glass partition first. "What happened to our backups?"

"They went on, sir."

"Went on where?"

"Back to the mansion, I believe, sir. I'm not sure, but I think Mrs. Feuer needed to run an errand or something."

"Mrs. Feuer is on her way to the Homestead."

"I hear that's quite a resort, up there in the mountains with spas, unbelievable food and skiing and everything. I'm glad she's going to relax a little," Jed nervously prattled on.

"Where the hell are we, Jed?" Governor Feuer restrained himself from raising his voice.

"There's a lot of detours, sir," Jed replied. "From funerals, I guess."

"I don't see any funerals or any sign of them."

"Not on this street, no sir."

"In fact, I haven't seen another car," the governor testily said.

"This is for through traffic, sir."

"Through traffic? *Through* to where? There is no *through.* There's only one way in and out of the cemetery. If you went *through,* you'd end up in the James River."

"What I meant, sir, was that this isn't a funeral route," Jed explained, slowing down a bit.

"For God's sake, Jed." The governor lost his cool. "There's no such thing as a funeral route in a cemetery. The cars go where the person's being buried. You don't bury people along routes. We're lost."

"Not at all, sir."

"Turn around. Let's go back," Governor Feuer said as a cop and a little kid suddenly flowed past his right window.

Governor Feuer turned around in his seat, staring out the back window at a uniformed officer and a boy dressed like the Bulls. They were walking slowly and unsteadily, as if their legs would go out from under them any minute.

"Stop the car!" Governor Feuer ordered.

Jed slammed on the brakes, sending newspapers sliding across the carpeted floor.

The scene behind Kmart was slowing down and thinning out. The medical examiner's van was en route to the morgue where Ruby Sink would be autopsied later this day, and uniformed officers had begun to scatter, returning to the streets.

Detectives sought out witnesses and Miss Sink's next of kin while the media tried to get there first. The fire department was long gone, leaving West and two crime-scene technicians to finish up.

So far, dozens of latent prints in addition to the three nine-millimeter cartridge cases had been recovered from inside the car, which soon would be carried off in a flatbed truck for further processing by forensic scientists in the shelter of a bay. Eventually, firing pin impressions would be scanned into ATF's computer system to determine if they matched those recovered from other crimes.

Prints would be run through the Automated Fingerprint Identification System known as AFIS. Hairs, blood and fibers would go to DNA and the trace evidence labs.

"We need to get this out of the sun, or the blood and any other biological evidence are going to start decomposing really fast," West said to crime-scene technician Alice Bates, who was taking photographs of the inside of the Chevy Celebrity.

"We've got it covered," Bates said.

A second technician named Bonita Wills was focusing on the scattered contents of the victim's pocketbook that were strewn on the floor of the passenger's side. West leaned inside the open driver's door to look, her suit jacket brushing against the frame.

"Oh great," she muttered as she tried to brush black fingerprint powder off her jacket.

West studied blood spatter on the rearview mirror, on the roof near it, the drips on the steering wheel and the pool of coagulating blood on the passenger's seat. When she had first arrived at the scene, Miss Sink had been slumped over on her right side, her head on the passenger's seat. There were blood spatters on her forearms and elbows and the roof above the driver's seat, and all this gave West a depressing picture.

It appeared that Ruby Sink had been sitting behind the wheel, elbows raised, hands under something, perhaps her face, when she had been shot execution style. Then the killer had climbed out of the car, and Miss Sink's body had slumped over on the passenger's seat where she had bled very briefly before dying.

"The bastard," West said. "Doing that in front of a baby. For two hundred fucking bucks. Goddamn son of a bitch."

"Don't touch anything," Wills warned her, as if West had sat behind a desk all her life.

West checked her temper. She was tired of being treated like an interloper, like an idiot, when it hadn't been so long ago that she was regarded with respect and even friendliness by a department a lot bigger and better than this one.

She stepped back from the car, looking around, hot and impatient in her smudged suit. The perimeter behind Kmart was secured by yellow crime-scene tape and West had no intention of letting anyone in anytime soon, and this included drivers making deliveries to the department store.

"Where's the truck?" West was all business. "I don't like this. Everybody's flown the coop and other than the body, the car is the most important piece of evidence."

"I wouldn't sweat it too much," Wills said. "This thing's a pigpen of prints. They could be anybody's, depending on how many people have been inside it, outside it, whatever. Most will probably be hers."

"Some will be his," West said. "This guy doesn't wear gloves. He doesn't care if he leaves spit, hairs, blood, seminal fluid because he's probably some fucking piece of shit who's just got out of some juvenile training school and all his records have been destroyed to protect his precious confidentiality."

"Hey, Bates," Wills called to her partner, "make sure you get the trunk good around the lock. In case he went in there."

"I'm way ahead of ya."

West got on her radio and requested an officer to guard the crime scene. She got back in her car and drove around to the front of Kmart. The parking lot was full of shoppers looking for a deal. A few of them were standing in front of the store, staring at First Union Bank and speculating in hushed, excited voices. Most were inside, probably pushing carts up and down aisles, oblivious.

West pulled up to the bank and was surprised to see that Hammer was still talking to Bubba, both of them standing in the bright sun. West got out and walked toward them. She slowed her pace when the stench reached her. She stared at Bubba's camouflage.

"Certainly I think it's a good idea for citizens to get involved," Hammer was saying to Bubba. "But within limits. I don't want our volunteer police carrying guns, Mr. Fluck."

"Then a lot of us won't do it," he let her know.

"There are other ways to help."

"What about pepper spray or tactical batons? Could they carry those?"

"No," Hammer replied.

West knew exactly what her boss was doing. Chief Hammer was an expert at playing people, dribbling the conversation in many directions, faking and passing until she saw an opening to score. West went along with it.

"Well, Chesterfield's auxiliary police carry guns," Bubba pointed out, swatting at flies. "I know a bunch of the guys. They work hard and really like it."

Hammer noticed West's suit. She stared at the black fingerprint powder on the jacket.

"How'd you get smudge on . . . " Hammer said without finishing, laying the trap.

"I didn't," Bubba replied. "Actually he's been trying to get me on, but I'd have to move to Chesterfield."

Hammer gave him a feigned puzzled look. "Excuse me?"

"My buddy Smudge." Then Bubba looked puzzled, too. "How'd you know about him?"

"Sorry for your inconvenience, Mr. Fluck," Hammer said. "Why don't you go on home and freshen up. Deputy Chief West? A word with you."

The two women walked away from Bubba.

"That was pretty clever," West marveled. "I guess you were referring to my jacket but made it sound like you knew about Smudge."

"I was lucky," Hammer said as a car pulled into the parking lot and sped toward them. "And I want him under surveillance. *Now.*"

Roop jumped out in such a hurry he didn't bother turning off the engine or shutting the door.

"Chief Hammer!" he excitedly said. "I got another phone call. Same guy."

"You sure?" Hammer asked.

"Yes!" Roop exclaimed. "The Pikes are claiming responsibility for the ATM homicide!"

chapter thirty-one

Brazil had never met Governor Feuer and it did not register that this indeed was the man walking briskly toward him and Weed on Midvale Avenue.

The man was tall and distinguished in a dark pinstripe suit. He was in a hurry and seemed very anxious about something. Brazil wiped sweat out of his eyes, his mouth so parched he could barely speak.

"Is everything all right?" Brazil asked.

"I was about to ask you that, son," the man said.

Brazil paused as he processed the familiar voice and fit it with the face.

"Oh," was all Brazil said.

"I seen your picture all over the place!" exclaimed Weed.

"Looks like you two have been through it," the governor said. "What did you do to your chin?" he asked Weed.

"Cut myself shaving."

The governor seemed to accept this.

"How on earth did you end up out here? Are you hurt? No backup? Doesn't your radio work?" Governor Feuer asked Brazil.

"It works, sir."

Brazil's words were sticky, as if he had communion wafers in his mouth. His tongue got caught on every syllable. He sounded a little drunk and wondered if he was delirious. Maybe none of this was happening.

"Let's get both of you some water and out of the sun," the governor was saying.

Brazil was too exhausted and dehydrated to have much of an emotional reaction.

"You should know I've got a prisoner," Brazil mumbled to the governor.

"I'm not worried unless you are," Governor Feuer said. "My driver's state police."

Jed smiled as he stood attentively by the limousine. He opened a back door and the governor got in. Jed nodded at Brazil and Weed to do the same.

"Jed, you've got water, don't you?" Governor Feuer said.

"Oh yes sir. Chilled or unchilled?"

"Doesn't matter," Brazil said.

"Chilled would be good," Weed answered.

Brazil was overwhelmed by air conditioning and an expanse of clean, soft gray leather. He sat on the carpeted floor and nodded for Weed to do the same. The governor gave them an odd look.

"What are you doing?" he asked Brazil.

"We're pretty sweaty," Brazil apologized. "Wouldn't want to mess up your upholstery."

"Nonsense. Have a seat."

Air conditioning blasted their drenched clothes. Jed slid open the glass partition and handed back a six-pack of chilled Evian. Brazil drained two bottles, barely breathing between swallows. A stabbing sensation ran up his sinuses to the top of his head. He bent over in agony and rubbed his forehead.

"What is it?" the governor asked, alarmed.

"Ice cream headache. I'll be fine."

"Those are miserable. Nothing worse."

"Uhhh."

"I get 'em when I drink Pepsi too fast," Weed commiserated.

Jed's voice came over the intercom. "Where to, sir?"

"Where can we take you?" the governor asked Brazil. "Home? Back to headquarters? The jail?"

Brazil rubbed his forehead. He poured water on a napkin and gently cleaned Weed's cut and wiped dried blood off his neck.

"What will it be?" the governor asked.

"Honestly, Governor, you don't have to do that. I can't let you go to the trouble," Brazil said.

Governor Feuer smiled. "What's your name, son?"

"Andy Brazil."

"As in the NIJ fellow who wrote the op-ed on juvenile crime?"

"Yes, that's me."

The governor was favorably impressed.

"And you?" he asked Weed.

"Weed."

"That's your real name, son?"

"How come everybody always asks me that?" Weed was tired of it.

"I guess headquarters would be good, sir," Brazil said.

"Swing by headquarters," the governor told Jed. "I guess you'd better call my scheduler and tell him I won't make it to whatever."

Time had stopped for Patty Passman as she sat in the urine-sticky dark on the cold metal floor of the wagon, arms wrenched behind her, ankles immobilized. Her hands and feet were numb. She was chilled to the core. She envisioned gangrene and amputations and lawsuits.

The scales of her unfortunate chemistry were back in balance. Although weak and somewhat banged up, she was thinking with clarity and premeditation. She knew exactly what Rhoad was doing. The wagon could not carry her to lockup for processing until he filled out at least one arrest sheet. The son of a bitch was trumping up every charge imaginable, filling out the paperwork on every single one because the longer he took, the longer she sat, trussed up like a turkey inside an icebox.

Passman wriggled backward across unforgiving metal, finally finding a side of the van to lean against. She shifted positions every few seconds to relieve the bite of the handcuffs and the ache in her shoulders.

"Oh please hurry," she begged in the dark as the tears came. "I'm so cold. Oh God, I hurt! Please! You're so mean to me!" She burst into sobs that no one heard or would have been moved by were she standing in the middle of a packed coliseum.

No one cared. No one ever had.

Patty Passman's first mistake in life was being born a girl to parents who already had six girls and were devastated when they had yet one more on their last try. Passman spent her childhood trying to make it up to them.

She pounded on her sisters and told them they were ugly, stupid and flat-chested. She broke toys, dismembered dolls, drew obscene pictures, passed gas, belched, spat, didn't flush the toilet, was insensitive, hoarded candy, kept quarters meant for the Sunday school offering, lost her temper, teased the dog, played Army, played doctor with other girls in the neighborhood and refused to play the piano. She did all she could to act like a boy.

She toned it down as years passed, only

to find she had been gender contraire for so long she had fallen too far behind in the female race to ever catch up or even come in last. She was disqualified and defaulted by all except Moses Pharaoh, who nominated her for the wrestling homecoming court because, he told her as he escorted her across the spotlit basketball court that illustrious night, he was turned on by fat women with small teeth.

Afterward, the two of them ate lasagne, garlic bread, salad and cheesecake at Joe's Inn. On the way home in his '69 high-performance Chevelle, with its 425 horsepower and 475 pounds of torque, Moses drove her up to the observation point at the end of East Grace Street.

What Passman knew about kissing she had learned from movies. She was not prepared for the huge garlic-tasting thick tongue thrust down her throat. She was shocked when Moses shoved his hands down her chiffon neckline, groping for the Promised Land. He parted her, crossed her, broke all ten commandments, or seemed to, on that awful night when her long pink satin dress was pushed up and crushed, all because she had not been born a boy.

She was shivering and feeling crazed again when the wagon rumbled awake. It pulled ahead. With each turn it took she rolled on her side like a log in the tide. Minutes seemed forever. The van finally halted.

"Sally Port One, put the gate up," a male voice announced.

Passman heard what sounded like a grate lurch and begin slowly roll-ing up. The van drove ahead and stopped again. The grate screeched back down. The van's tailgate swung open, a cop standing there, chewing gum.

He was disheveled, his waist drooping over his duty belt like excess pizza dough hanging off the pan. One eye was hazel, the other brown, his graying hair slicked back, ears and nostrils bristly like stiff paintbrushes. Wagon drivers were the flatworms of law enforcement, a throwback to a spineless, lazy, lower order of life Passman had grown to despise.

"O-kie do-kie," he said to her. "Let's head 'em up and move 'em out."

Passman squinted at him from her supine position on the floor.

"I can't," she said.

He clicked her a *giddy-up* out of the side of his mouth.

"I'm not going anywhere until you at least undo my ankles." She meant it.

Her dress was pushed up to her padded hips and she could do nothing about it. He was staring. She knew if she lost her temper again, it would only ensure further bondage.

"Please undo my ankles so I can get out," she said again.

"Pretty please with sugar on top?"

She thought she recognized his voice, then was certain.

"You're unit 452," she said.

"Guess I'm famous. Now I'm gonna cut off these flex cuffs, but you so much as twitch and I'm gonna keep you busy."

She did not know his name, but one thing Passman did know was voices. She had total recall when it came to words uttered on the air by hundreds of units she never saw. Unit 452 cut off the flex cuffs with a pocketknife and the feeling rushed back to her feet in swarms of tiny pins. She worked her way to the open rear of the van, her skirt hiking higher, far above the brown tops of her panty hose, up to the waistband. He stared, chomping gum. She inch-wormed her way to the ground.

Unit 452 pushed a button on the wall to

open the door to lockup, and on his way in used a key from his snap holder to secure his pistol inside the gun safe. He got out another key, this one tiny, and unlocked her handcuffs.

"Unit 452," Passman mimicked him. *"Go ahead, 452. I'm 10-7 2600 block of Park. Ten-4, 452. That'd be the Robin Inn, for a meal. Uh, 10-4 . . ."*

"You!" Unit 452 was shocked and deeply offended. "You're the one! That bitch in the radio room!"

"You're that dumb shit who's always hiding out at Engine Company Number Nine playing your fucking nutless puzzle games. Tetris Plus, Q*Bert, Pac Man, Boggle!" Passman accused.

"What, what?" Unit 452 stammered.

Passman had him.

"Everyone knows," she went on as Deputy Sheriff Reflogle took the arrest sheets from unit 452 and began to search Passman.

"Looks like you're getting the book thrown at you, girl," Reflogle said. "Must've been a bad time at home to act out like this."

Passman wasn't listening.

"You're a joke in the radio room!" she railed on to Unit 452. *"B is boy, not bravo,* and *H* is *Henry,* not *hotel,* you shit dick! What do you think you are, an airplane pilot?"

"Now you quiet down," Deputy Reflogle said to her as he fished eight quarters out of her skirt pockets.

He rolled Passman's fingers on an ink pad and transferred her loops and whirls to a ten-print card. He took mug shots. He asked her about aliases. He asked about a.k.a's in case she didn't know what aliases were. He locked her inside a holding cell. It was not much bigger than a locker, a hard bench to sit on, a small square screen to see through. She ate cherry Jell-O, cottage cheese and fish sticks for lunch.

The magistrate's office for the city of Richmond was on the first floor of the police department, past the information desk and in close proximity to lockup and Sally Port 1.

It was not quite four o'clock in the afternoon. Vince Tittle wasn't feeling good about his job or life. It wasn't hard to look back and see where he had cracked the glass, chipped the china, scorched the sweet milk in the pot. He had succumbed to a favor. He had sold his soul for an office that looked very much like a tollbooth.

Tittle had not always thought the worst about himself. Until four years ago he had enjoyed a fulfilling career as a photographer at the morgue. He had been proud of taking pictures perfectly to scale. He had been a magician with lighting and shutter speeds. His art went to court. It was viewed by prosecutors, defense attorneys, judges and juries.

The chief medical examiner adored him. Her deputy chiefs and the forensic scientists did, too. Defendants hated him. Tittle's lust for justice was what got him into trouble. His road to hell began when Tittle joined the Gentleman's Bartering Club, which included hundreds of people with training, skills and talents that Tittle couldn't always afford. He took family portraits, and photos for Christmas cards, calendars, graduations and debutante balls, swapping his skills for virtual cash minus a ten percent commission that went to the club.

Tittle rarely shopped in reality after that. He could take wedding pictures, for example, and earn a thousand virtual dollars, which in turn he might virtually spend on roof repair. Tittle was addicted to his camera. Soon he became virtually wealthy, which is how he met Circuit Court Judge Nicholas Endo, who was at war with his wife and losing.

Judge Endo believed Mrs. Endo was having an affair with her dentist, Bull Ehrhart, and wanted to catch her in the act. Tittle would never forget what Judge Endo said to him one night when they were drinking bourbon in the clubhouse.

"Vince, you've got virtually everything a man could want," said the judge as he paid five virtual dollars for a drink that was real. "But there's got to be one thing in this club you can't buy, and I bet I damn well know what it is."

"What?" Tittle said.

"You love court. You love the law," said the judge. "Taking photographs of stiffs is getting boring. Has to be. Should always have been, Vince."

Tittle slowly swirled ice in his Maker's Mark. The truth pained him deeply.

"Come on. Come on." The judge leaned across the table and said in the tone that reminded Tittle of *come here, kitty, kitty, kitty,* "I mean, Vince, how goddamn challenging can it be to shoot a liver on a scale, a brain on a cutting board, stomach contents, little cups of urine and bile, bite marks, axes in the back of people's heads?"

"You're right," Tittle muttered, motioning for Seunghoon the cocktail waitress. "This round's on me."

"What will it be, sugar?" Seunghoon asked.

"Another round. You got Booker's?"

"Shoot. I don't think so, cutie. But you know what? I believe Mr. Mack carries it in his restaurant. He has quite a bar."

"We ought to get that in." Judge Endo rendered his verdict. "Best damn bourbon known to man. Hundred twenty proof, knock you back to China. Maybe next time a movie comes to town, Vince, you could take a couple shots of Mack with a celebrity or two? He can hang them in his restaurant. Charge him two hundred virtual dollars, turn around and buy the Booker's with it."

"Okay," Tittle agreed.

Their conversation went on for quite a while before the judge got into the substance of his case.

"I think you'd make a damn good magistrate, Vince," he said, puffing on an illegal

Cuban cigar. "I've always thought so." He blew a smoke ring.

"It would be an honor," Tittle said. "I would like a chance to punish bad people. I've always wanted that."

"How 'bout we make a trade?"

"I'm always doing it," Tittle said.

Judge Endo went on to say that he wanted explicit photographs of Mrs. Endo's adultery. He didn't care if they were doctored. He didn't care how Tittle did it. Judge Endo just wanted to keep his house, his car and his dog, and have his grown children take his side.

"It won't be easy," the judge said, jaw muscles clenching. "I know, I've tried everything I can think of. But you pull it off, I'll take care of you."

The next day, Tittle went to work. He discovered soon enough that Mrs. Endo's MO was so simple it was complicated. Bull Ehrhart had forty-three strip mall offices throughout the greater Richmond area, and twenty-two additional ones as far away as Norfolk, Petersburg, Charlottesville, Fredericksburg and Bristol, Tennessee.

Twice a week, Mrs. Endo used a different alias to make a late-day appointment at a different office. When she'd done the circuit, she'd start again. She'd change her accent, hair color and style, experimenting with makeup, glasses and designer clothes.

For weeks, Tittle failed. The adulterous couple was too careful and clever. Just when Tittle was about to give up, he found a crow that had flown into his kitchen window because it didn't see the glass and died of a head injury, Tittle could only suppose. Tittle got an idea. He put the dead crow in the freezer. He painted a camera and tripod yellow.

Late that afternoon he followed Mrs. Endo to dental office number 17 on Staples Mill Road, near Ukrops, and set up his faux surveyor's equipment in the parking lot. It was five-thirty P.M. The only office lit up was a corner one, the windows covered by shut Venetian blinds. Tittle gave Mrs. Endo and Dr. Ehrhart fifteen minutes to get into it as Tittle pointed the twelve-hundred-millimeter telephoto lens and attached the cable release.

He pulled the frozen crow out of a pocket of his coat and hurled it at the window, where it hit with a sickening thud, shaking the glass. The blinds suddenly flashed open.

The naked dentist looked out and around and down at the ground, discovering the poor bird that had flown into the glass. The naked Mrs. Endo put a hand over her mouth, shaking her head in pity.

They paid no attention to the surveyor walking off the job with his bright yellow equipment. The divorce turned out favorably for Judge Endo. In return, he gave Tittle the appointment, as promised in their bartering agreement.

Magistrate Tittle's guilt grew with the years. He became increasingly depressed and intimidated when Judge Endo called from time to time to remind him of the favor and the necessity of going to the grave, in this case Hollywood Cemetery, with the secret swap that had brought about Tittle's dream-come-true. Magistrate Tittle never told a soul.

He confessed his sin to God and swore to make restitution. Tittle took photographs no more. He resigned from the barter club. He reported its members to the IRS. He turned in the neighbor who illegally hooked up cable. Tittle exposed the lady in the grocery store who was trying to pass expired manufacturers' coupons. He admitted when something was his fault. He was humble and hardworking.

Magistrate Tittle became known for his zero tolerance of felons, fools, rotten kids and stupid cops. He was admired for his fairness and truth if one was unjustly accused. This was both good and bad for Officer Rhoad, who had not made an arrest in over twenty years. When Rhoad had flipped through the Virginia code, looking for charges to bring against Patty Passman, he had been certain Magistrate Tittle would empathize and go with life imprisonment with no TV or chances for appeals and lawsuits.

Tittle was reaching back to the coffeemaker to pour another cup, his grim gray suit jacket draped over a chair, when Officer Rhoad appeared at his window.

"I need to get some warrants," Rhoad said.

"What makes you think I can see you right this minute," said Tittle.

"Because you don't look busy, I guess."

"Well, I am," he said through the small opening in the bulletproof glass. "I should make you sit over there for an hour or two, but I'm about to go home. So let's get this over with."

Tittle shoved out a metal drawer. Rhoad placed his thick stack of arrest sheets in it. Tittle pulled them in and started looking through them. Tittle was silent for a long time while Rhoad watched through the glass.

"Officer?" Tittle finally spoke. "You ever heard of piling on charges?"

"Certainly," said Rhoad, who was used to quotas and assumed the magistrate was paying him a compliment.

"Use of police radio during commission of a crime," Tittle started going through the charges.

"Obstructing justice. Subject did knowingly attempt to impede this officer from engaging in his duties."

Tittle went to the next one. "Using abusive language."

"You should have heard her," Rhoad indignantly said.

"Disorderly conduct in public places. Resisting or obstructing execution of legal process." Tittle peered up over his reading glasses. "Crimes against nature?"

"She grabbed me." Rhoad's face got hot.

"She carnally knew you by anus?"

"No, sir."

"What about by mouth."

"Just the things she said."

"This isn't about *things said,* officer. What about bestiality?"

"Yes! She was a beast! She was awful!"

"Officer Rhoad," Tittle said in a hard tone. "Bestiality means screwing animals. No probable cause." He tossed the arrest sheet in a to-be-shredded basket. "Let's see." He continued. "Keeping, residing in or frequenting a *body* place."

"She wouldn't let go," Rhoad said, the memory clearly smarting.

"B-A-W-D-Y, not B-O-D-Y," Tittle said slowly and deliberately as he tossed the report in the basket. "Entering property of another for purpose of damaging it."

"Same thing. She touched my property, sir."

"What property, Officer Rhoad?"

"Well, my privates. She tried to damage my privates."

That report went into the basket with the others.

"Trespass after having been forbidden to do so," Tittle read.

"I told her to stop."

"Aggravated sexual assault. How did you arrive upon that one?"

"Because it was my privates she went after," Rhoad reminded him.

"I suppose *attempted rape* is for the same reason."

"What if it were you?"

"Sexual battery, rape. No probable cause," Tittle said, strained. "And oh. Here we have *threatening the governor or his immediate family?*"

"She said, 'I'm going to find the governor or his wife or children or relatives. And then you'll be sorry!' "

Rhoad averted his eyes. He wasn't really sure of this one. So much was a blur now. Tittle balled up the arrest sheet and tossed it on the floor.

"Oral threats. Bodily injuries caused by prisoners. Assault and battery. Malicious bodily injury. Aggravated malicious wounding."

Tittle balled up each sheet, pummeling them at the trash basket.

"Shooting, stabbing with intent to maim, kill. Failure to obey order of conservator of the peace. Treason. *Treason?*"

"Subject did resist the execution of the laws under color of its authority," Rhoad cited. "She levied war against the Common-wealth when she attacked me."

"You need a therapist."

"I'm a citizen of the Commonwealth, aren't I?" Rhoad argued.

"Why did this woman grab your genitals, Officer Rhoad?" Tittle had never met such an idiot in his life. "Did she swoop in out of nowhere? Was she provoked? A spurned lover?"

"She tried to stop me from putting a parking ticket on her car," Rhoad explained.

"I don't buy it."

"Well," Rhoad said, "I'd done it a few times before."

Brazil was wise enough to ask Governor Feuer to drop off his guest passengers a block from the police department, thus avoiding a scene that would be difficult, if not impossible, to explain.

"I'm going to take you to MCV," Brazil said to Weed as they walked along the sidewalk. "Then let's get your mother to come for you. You don't want to be locked up all night."

"Yes I do," Weed told him.

Brazil noticed Weed was very agitated, looking all around as if afraid someone was following them.

"You're not making any sense to me," Brazil went on. "And you know why?" He opened double glass doors on the lower lot of headquarters. "Because you're not telling me everything, Weed. You're holding back."

Weed had nothing to say. Brazil checked out a car and let the radio room know where he was going. He and Weed sat in MCV's emergency room, where Weed could not be treated without one of his parents being present. Weed's mother didn't answer the phone and she wasn't at work. Weed's father was out cutting grass somewhere and didn't return Brazil's call. Brazil's radio would not transmit from inside the hospital. He felt cut off from the world, angry, helpless and miserable.

Brazil finally had to get a judge to grant permission for treatment, which would have resolved the matter had there not been a school-bus accident midafternoon. The E.R. could not get to Weed until almost eleven P.M., when a nurse cleaned Weed's cut and put a butterfly bandage over it.

"I don't get it," Brazil was saying to Weed

as they drove back to headquarters. "Are you sure you have a mother?"

The remark hurt Weed. Brazil could tell.

"She don't answer the phone very much, especially when she's sleeping, and she sleeps a lot in the day."

"Why wouldn't she answer the phone otherwise?"

"'Cause Daddy's always calling. He says real mean things to her. I don't know why, and he has to have the number 'cause I stay with him sometimes."

They parked in the back lot and Brazil escorted Weed inside the police department. They walked past the information desk and Weed didn't seem to care where he was being taken. His mood continued to sink.

"You know something," Brazil told him. "You know something big. Something so big you're scared, real scared."

"I ain't scared of nothing," Weed told him.

"We're all scared of something," Brazil replied.

Handcuffed prisoners drifted in and out, heading to lockup, muttering, staggering and swaggering, some wearing sunglasses and cool clothes, many of them high or drunk. The air smelled of body odor, alcohol and marijuana. Brazil turned right, passing through another set of double doors. He opened one leading into a small drab room with desks built into the walls, and plastic chairs, and ugly green upholstered benches stained with unpleasant, recalcitrant life.

Brazil went to a phone and dialed the pager number of the intake officer on call. There was an old radio on a table and Brazil tuned it in to 98.1. He sat on top of a desk and looked at Weed.

"Talk to me," Brazil said.

"Got nothing to say." Weed sat on a bench.

"Why did you decide to paint the statue?"

"Felt like it."

"Did someone tell you to do it? One of the Pikes?"

"I don't know nothing about Pikes."

"Bullshit," Brazil said. "Where'd you get that number tattooed on your finger?"

A radio announcer was going on and on about the ATM homicide, and at first the news and the name of the victim did not penetrate Brazil's fatigue and frustration. Then he caught it.

". . . confirmed her identity as a seventy-one-year-old Church Hill woman named Ruby Sink . . ."

"Wait a minute!" Brazil turned up the volume.

". . . made a withdrawal at the ATM, was abducted and shot to death in her own car. A gang known as the Pikes has claimed responsibility. This is the same gang that claimed responsibility for the vandalism of Jefferson Davis's statue in Hollywood Cemetery . . ."

Brazil was beside himself. He paced furiously, his fists clenched. He was confused and disbelieving as he envisioned Ruby Sink and remembered when she had called him last.

"No!" he exclaimed. *"No!"*

Brazil pounded the wall and kicked the trash can. It clanged across the floor, paper, fried chicken boxes and fast food wrappers spilling.

"How could someone do that to a helpless old woman!"

His last conversation with her sounded in his mind. He could hear her voice. He had used her to make West jealous. Brazil clenched his fists so hard his nails dug into his palms. He grabbed Weed by the shoulders.

"You know them, I know you do!" he said in

fury. *"They just murdered someone, Weed!*
Someone I knew! Someone who never did
anything to anybody! A human being with a
name and a family and now people who
loved her have to deal with what happened
just like you do with Twister!"

Weed stared at him in shock.

"You're going to protect monsters like that?"

Brazil let go of Weed and walked across
the room. Brazil tried to control himself. He
was trembling, his heart pounding so hard
he could feel it in his neck.

"I tried to tell you on the computer," Weed
sadly said.

"Tell me? Tell me what?"

"The fish map."

Brazil's mind had an electrical outage.

"On AOL. A map with pikes on it," Weed
explained.

"Pikes as in fish?" Brazil came back.

"Uh huh. I did a papier-mâché pike in Mrs.
Grannis's class. Trying to tell somebody
where they are."

"Wait a minute." Brazil pulled up a chair
and sat down. "The fish on the map. That's
where the Pikes have their clubhouse?"

Weed nodded. "In the back of Southside
Motel. Behind a big piece of wood."

"You've been there?"

"I didn't wanna be. I swear. But Smoke made me go and he hit me, too." Weed wouldn't look up.

"Who is Smoke?" Brazil said.

"He broke in the garage and took all them guns. He made me go along and I held pillowcases for him. So I guess I get locked up for that and everything and I don't care 'cause if I go out, Officer Brazil, Smoke gonna kill me. I know it. He's looking for me now. That's why I told you to lock me up."

"Do you know Smoke's real name?"

"He's just Smoke. Never heard no other name."

"He go to school with you?"

"Uh huh."

"And you don't know his real name?"

"He's a senior and I don't know no seniors except the ones in art class, and Smoke never been in one of my art classes. Not the band, either."

"He get in a lot of trouble in school?" Brazil asked.

"I never even noticed him until he come looking for me and found me after school in the band room. He asked if I wanted a ride to school in the morning and something told me not to tell him no. And next thing he's talking about guns and the Pikes and how nobody in the school deserved to be a Pike except the ones he picked. He said he had special things to do."

"Did he tell you what these special things were?"

"All he kept saying was everybody was going to know him. He'd be more famous than Twister ever was, 'cause there's still pictures of Twister and trophies in the glass cases so I guess that's how Smoke heard about him."

"Think hard, Weed." Brazil put his hands on Weed's shoulders. "Was Smoke planning something that might make him famous? Maybe something bad?"

"I think he wants to shoot people," Weed said.

chapter thirty-two

Brazil tried to figure out what to do. If Smoke was planning to show up at school with semiautomatics and take out as many people as he could, Brazil had to do something fast. He grabbed the phone and called West, waking her up.

"Get down here right away," Brazil said. "Don't ask why, just come."

"Where's *here?*" she groggily asked.

"HQ. We need to get as many cops as we can at Godwin tomorrow to make sure Smoke doesn't show up, and we need to get that going now."

West tried to wake up. Brazil could hear her moving around.

"I'll meet you in the detective division in maybe two hours," Brazil said.

"Yeah," she said.

Weed was getting increasingly frightened. He picked at his jersey and kept sighing as if he was having a hard time breathing.

"He made me do things. He put a gun to my head and said he'd shoot me if I didn't. Then a couple weeks ago he stopped showing up at school."

"So he didn't give you rides anymore." Brazil was taking copious notes.

"He'd drop me off and leave. Then he started making me late, started dragging me around, making me miss band practice. And I was supposed to play in the Azalea Parade on Saturday." The light went out of his eyes. "I been practicing all year. And now I guess I can't."

The phone rang, startling both of them. Brazil answered it. He was wired and somewhat impatient as he explained Weed's transgressions to Intake Officer Charlie Yates.

Brazil charged Weed with violating Code 18.2-125, *Trespass at night upon any ceme-*

tery, a class 4 misdemeanor, and 18.2-127, *Injuries to churches, church property, cemeteries, burial grounds, etc.,* class 1 misdemeanor, and 182.2-138.1, *Willful and malicious damage to or defacement of public or private facilities,* a class 1 misdemeanor or a felony, depending on how much damage was done.

"So which is it?" Yates wanted to know.

"Misdemeanor, class one," Brazil said. "We don't know how much cleaning up the statue's going to cost. If it's more than a thousand dollars, we'll deal with it at the trial."

Weed was staring wide-eyed at Brazil. It was obvious Weed did not understand. He was terrified.

"Hearing's set for Friday," Yates went on. "He got someone . . . ?"

"I want the hearing in the morning," Brazil interrupted. "It's really important, Charlie."

"Hey, no big deal." It made no difference to Yates.

It did to Brazil. He knew from this month's court calendar that Judge Maggie Davis was on the bench. She had a policy that her courtroom was not open to the public unless the juvenile had committed a felony, and the last thing Brazil wanted was Weed's hearing open to the public. He didn't want some reporter making the rounds and walking in. He didn't want anyone except the attorneys and judge to hear what he and Weed might have to say.

"He got someone to pick him up tonight and take him home?" Yates was asking.

"We haven't been able to locate his mother."

She was in the operating room and could not be disturbed, not that Brazil had tried very hard. Weed didn't want to go home and Brazil didn't want him to, either.

"There's no beds in detention. I just checked," Yates said.

"Never are," Brazil replied.

"So if he can't go home, he's going to end up in a holding cell until the morning."

"That's fine," Brazil said, not taking his eyes off Weed. "As soon as you can get here, I'll sign the petition and take him on over. And try to make it fast, Charlie. There's a lot going on."

Weed had an intake room without much of a view, a cell no bigger than a closet, everything stainless steel, including the bed. He could not sleep. He stared out a small grate and watched other kids brought in who reminded him of Sick, Beeper, Divinity and Dog. No one reminded him of Smoke. Smoke didn't look like what he was.

It was dark when Officer Brazil had transported Weed to this place. They called it the Juvenile Detention Home, but it wasn't like any home Weed had ever been in. He couldn't see what the outside of it was like but he knew it was in a bad part of town, because right before he'd gotten here they'd driven past the jail. It was all lit up, rolls of razor wire shining like knife blades waiting to cut someone. Weed's stomach got hollow and he had a cold feeling in his heart.

Weed was still mad they had made him take off all his clothes and go into the shower. When he came out they had a uniform for him to wear. It was nothing to make Weed proud. He was reminded of what his daddy wore cleaning out gutters and clipping hedges when he wasn't gambling away what he earned.

"Hey!" Weed banged on the door.

Someone was cussing and a deputy was telling a cocky badass boy everything he had done wrong and why he was going to pay for it.

"Hey!" Weed pounded the metal door with his fist, standing on his tiptoes to see through the grate.

Suddenly a deputy was in his face, nothing but a crisscross of metal between them. Weed could smell cigarettes and onions on his breath.

"You got a problem?" the deputy asked.

"I wanna see my police officer," Weed told him.

"Yo!" the deputy called out. "He wants to see *his po-lice officer!*"

Laughter and bad-mouthing followed.

"What, you got your own personal po-lice officer?" the deputy smarted off to Weed. "Now ain't that something."

"He's the one who brought me in," Weed said. "Tell him I got to talk to him."

"You can tell him in court."

"When's that?"

"Nine in the morning."

"I need to find out if he called my mama!" Weed exclaimed.

"Maybe you should've thought about your mama before you broke the law," the deputy said.

chapter thirty-three

At shortly after three A.M. a SWAT team raided the Pikes' clubhouse at the Southside Motel and found the room abandoned. Police recovered no guns or ammunition. They found nothing but liquor and trash and filthy mattresses.

Brazil was on one phone, West on another, each of them in a cubicle inside the detective division. Brazil had called Godwin's principal, Mrs. Lilly, at home, and when she realized what it was about, she met the registrar at the high school and they started going through records.

Eventually they figured out that Smoke's

real name was Alex Bailey, but the address listed in his school records didn't exist, the phone number didn't work, and there was no photograph of him on file. Although the yearbook wasn't out yet, a check of those who had gotten their pictures taken for it did not include him. All anyone really knew was the classes he had been in and that last summer he had moved here from Durham, North Carolina, where the obscure private high school he supposedly had transferred from didn't exist.

Brazil called every Bailey in the city directory, waking people up. No one seemed to have a family member named Alex who went to Godwin High School.

"How the hell did he get away with it?" Brazil said to West. "He uses a bogus address, phone number, name of his former high school and who knows what else."

West was smoking a Carlton. She'd sort of quit months ago, but at times like this she needed a friend.

"Who's going to check?" she said. "You ever had your high school call you at home or come see you?"

"I don't remember."

"Well, I sure as hell didn't. Most people

don't unless they get in trouble. And it sounds like he was just your average kind of keep-to-yourself nobody until a couple weeks ago. Then he cuts classes or doesn't show up at all. Maybe the school starts calling. But guess what? By then it's too late."

"I wonder what his parents know." Brazil reached for his Styrofoam cup of what once was drinkable coffee.

"Denial. Maybe protecting him. Don't want to face it and never have. No question in my mind this kid's not new to the system. No pictures of him anywhere, including the yearbook, just like all these other little felons, so we don't know what they look like. I bet you anything he's got a record in North Carolina, probably transferred from *Dillon High School*." She sarcastically referred to the juvenile training school in Butner, North Carolina. "His fucking family probably moved him here when he turned sixteen and all his records were expunged. So the asshole gets to start all over again, clean as a Boy Scout."

Brazil swirled the coffee in his cup. He took a deep breath and let it out slowly.

"So. You going to bother going to bed tonight?" West said.

"There's no night left," Brazil said.

"You want to come over, maybe scramble up a few eggs or something?"

Sadness walked through Brazil's eyes.

"As long as we stop at my house first," he said. "There's something I've got to get."

The Azalea Motel on Northside's Chamberlayne Avenue was not where the police would have expected to find Smoke. He also liked the irony of the name, since the Azalea Parade was the day after tomorrow. Smoke had big plans.

He sat on his single bed in his single room and thought where he was staying wasn't much better than the clubhouse. The Azalea Motel was the sort of place where people did drugs and got murdered and nobody cared. Smoke got room 7 for twenty-eight dollars a night. He stared blankly at the TV and drank vodka from a plastic cup. Smoke had been monitoring the news. At five after six A.M., his phone rang.

"What," he answered.

It was Divinity.

"Baby, they raided our place just like you

said they would," she told him in an excited voice.

Smoke smiled as he stared at the trash bags full of guns and ammunition in the corner.

"Sick and me parked the car at the dirty bookstore and we was in the woods watching, you know, baby. It was all we could do not to laugh. Them busting in there with all their stuff on and big guns and all. You sure was right about getting out when we did, sugar. But I wanna know when I'm gonna see you, huh?"

"Not now," Smoke told her without much interest as he spun around the cylinder of a Colt .357.

"I sure could do with a little more *I miss you* enthusiasm." Divinity's voice was hurt on the way to being mad.

Smoke wasn't listening. His mind wandered back to the old woman and her fear. Smoke had never scared anybody that much. He was awed by his power and as drunk from it as he was from vodka. He loved the way it felt to squeeze the trigger. He had been so high he barely heard the explosions when he blew apart her head. He threw back another swallow of vodka.

"What'cha gonna tell the others?" Divinity was asking.

Smoke came to.

"About what?" he said.

"You ain't even listening." Her voice was getting sharp.

One thing Smoke avoided was fighting with Divinity. She could make a scene, and that was what he didn't need right now.

"I'm just so tired," he said, sighing. "And I miss you and it makes me crazy I can't see you until Saturday night. That's when we'll be free and clear."

"How?"

"You'll see."

"What about Dog and the rest of them?"

"I don't want them anywhere near me," Smoke said. "None of you come anywhere near the Azalea Parade."

"I don't understand this big shit about some little parade named after a bush." Divinity hadn't softened much.

"Baby, I'm gonna be the king of it," Smoke said.

"What'cha gonna do, ride on a float?"

He couldn't stand it when she got sarcastic. He slammed down the vodka bottle and snapped the revolver's empty cylinder in place. He dry-fired at the TV.

"Shut up!" he said in his voice from hell, that tone he got when the change came over him. "You just do what I say, bitch."

"I always do." Divinity backed down.

"Don't you call anymore. Don't you come around, and the others don't know where I am, right?"

"I ain't told 'em nothing. So you dumping me?"

"For two days."

"Then we're good?"

"As good as it gets," he said.

Brazil ran into his house for only a moment and when he returned to West's car, he was carrying a grocery bag with something in it. He had a strange look on his face.

"What's that?" West asked.

"You'll see," he said. "I don't want to talk about it right now."

"You got a body part in there or something?"

"In a way," Brazil morbidly said.

West knew about Ruby Sink. The word

had traveled like electricity. Everyone in the police department found out Miss Sink was Brazil's landlady, and when West heard the truth, she felt sick with guilt. She felt stupid and ignorant. Brazil's so-called girlfriend had been a seventy-one-year-old woman who rented a row house to him. West felt absolutely terrible and for hours had been trying to think of what to say.

She drove through the Fan. Nothing was open, not even the Robin Inn. She parked in front of her town house and turned off the engine but didn't get out. She looked at Brazil in the dark. Her heart stirred as she stared at his face sharply defined by shadows from the streetlight.

"I know," she said.

He was quiet.

"I know about Ruby Sink. That she was your landlady. The landlady I heard you were seeing."

Brazil turned to her, baffled.

"Seeing?" he said. "Where the hell did you hear something like that?"

"The talk was all around the department from day one," West replied. "People told me you had a thing going with your landlady. Then I heard you on the phone with her and . . . well, it sounded like it was true, in a way."

"Why? Because I was nice to her when she paged me?" Brazil said with emotion. "Because she was lonely and always bringing me cookies, cakes and things?" His voice wavered. "Leaving them on my doorstep because I was never fucking home and never gave her the fucking time of day!"

"I'm sorry, Andy," West gently said.

"It's like my mother." He dissolved. "I don't call her. She's so fucking drunk all the time and I can't stand it and won't listen to the awful things she says. I don't know. I don't know."

West moved over and put her arms around him. She held him close to calm him. Her blood got hot and her chemistry woke up.

"It's all right, Andy," she said. "It's going to be all right."

She wanted to hold him forever, but suddenly the awkwardness of it overtook the magic. She thought of her age. She thought of his talent, of everything that made him so unusual and special. He was probably hugging her back because he was terribly upset, no other reason. His heart probably wasn't pounding like hers. He probably wasn't as aware of their bodies touching as she was. She abruptly pulled away.

"I guess we should go in," she said.

Niles heard them long before they gave a thought to him. He was waiting by the front door when his owner and Piano Man walked in.

Piano Man took a moment to pet Niles, while Niles's owner couldn't be bothered. Niles stayed where he was, tail switching. He watched with crossed eyes and plotted as they went into the kitchen.

When they were out of view, Niles jumped up on the table in the foyer. He hooked a claw into the florist's card. He jumped down, landing silently on three legs.

West did not think she could eat the sweet potato pie. She stared at the slice Brazil set before her. The idea that Ruby Sink had made it before her cold-blooded murder was too much for West to process.

"I can't throw it away." Brazil sat across from West at the kitchen table. "It would be heartless to throw it away. I just can't. You couldn't either, Virginia. She would want us to eat it."

"This is kind of sick," West said, blinking, focusing, looking at him. "I don't think I can."

Brazil picked up his fork. He flinched as he cut off the point of his slice. He raised it. He took a deep breath and put it in his mouth. West watched him chew once or twice and swallow. It surprised her that he looked enormously relieved. Tension left his face. His eyes brightened and got that fierce blue flame in them that she had learned to recognize and take very seriously.

"It's okay," he told her in a strong voice. "Trust me." He nodded for her to eat.

West had never backed down from a challenge, especially in front of him. It was one of the hardest things she'd ever done when she took a bite of that pie. It surprised her that it didn't taste weird or dead or who knows what. She had no idea what she had expected.

"Brown sugar, coconut milk, cinnamon," said Brazil, who spent more time in the kitchen than West did.

He took another bite, this time without hesitation. West matched him.

"Raisins, vanilla extract." Brazil concentrated on his tongue as if he were tasting fine wine. "Ah. Ginger. A hint of it. And a breath of nutmeg."

"Breath of nutmeg?" West said. "Where the hell does that shit come from?"

Brazil took another bite. So did she. She might just eat another slice to spite him.

Neither of them heard Niles, not that they ever did. He walked in holding up a paw, a white square of paper caught on one of his claws.

"Baby?" West said in alarm, certain he was injured. "Oh sweetie, what did you do to yourself?"

She didn't realize what was on his claw until Niles was in Brazil's lap and the florist's card from the hallway table was in plain view. Brazil got a confused expression on his face.

"Schwan's Flowers and Gifts? Charlotte?" he read aloud what was on the envelope as he pulled out the card. " 'Thinking of you, Andy,' " his voice trailed off.

West tried to act nonchalant and failed. She hated Niles and would pay him back for this.

"How did this end up on your hallway table?" Brazil wanted to know.

"How do you know it was on the table?" she said coolly as she imagined leaving Niles out in a hailstorm.

"I saw it there when we were here working on the computer!"

"Why were you looking at anything on any table!" Old anger and hurt jumped off the shelf where she had been storing them for months.

"Because you put it there so I would see it," he exclaimed.

"How arrogant of you!"

"Then why?" he said. "And don't tell me Niles did it."

West pushed away her plate and stared past him. She tried to think how to say it. Confessing feelings was as dangerous as counting money when you walked down a dark street in a bad part of town.

"Because you didn't care about me anymore." She was out with it.

"That's because you didn't care about me first," he argued.

"And that's because I thought you dumped me the minute we got to town and started seeing someone else without even having the courtesy to tell me."

"Virginia, I haven't seen anybody," Brazil said in a softer tone.

He reached out and took her hand. She had a hard time swallowing.

"And I didn't dump you," he said.

He moved his chair next to hers and kissed her. In the bedroom he discovered the wineglasses of Mountain Dew.

Hammer wanted to dump the entire NIJ project. Her mind was a riotous crowd of dissenting, unhappy people who would not let her sleep. She thought about Bubba and how badly she had maligned him. She obsessed over how badly she had handled Lelia Ehrhart and those like her.

Part of Hammer's mission was to enlighten people. She saw no evidence that she had. Part of her plan was to modernize the police department. And what happened? The entire COMSTAT telecommunications network crashed. The ATM robberies escalated to murder. There were gangs. There was Smoke.

Hammer didn't think she could ever again

endure seeing Ruby Sink's house or even the block Miss Sink had lived on. Miss Sink, in her pink robe and slippers, had shuffled through Hammer's mind all night. Hammer could not get away from their last conversation on Miss Sink's sidewalk. Hammer could see the old woman in such detail it hurt her heart and pierced her with guilt.

"I'm a failure," Hammer said to Popeye.

Popeye was under the covers, between Hammer's feet.

"I've caused harm. I should never have come here. I bet you wish you still lived in Charlotte where you had a yard, don't you?"

Her eyes filled with tears. Popeye burrowed up to her and licked her face. Hammer couldn't remember the last time she had cried. She had been so stoical when Seth had died because she believed she had to be. She had been rational about the reasons her sons did not seem to want to see her. Hammer had been courageous, innovative, community-minded. All of it so she would be too busy to be lonely, and it hadn't worked. She got up and dressed.

* * *

There was no answer at Brazil's house when Hammer called from her car phone. She tried West next and was relieved that he and West were there.

"I've got something important to say to both of you," Hammer said over the line.

Parking in the Fan wasn't as much of a problem at this early hour, and she managed to squeeze into a space on the curb right across the street from West's town house. Hammer was numb. She did not feel present, nor did she want to be when Brazil opened the front door.

"Thank you for seeing me," Hammer said to Brazil as they walked into the living room.

"Thank *you*," he replied. "It's kind of messy."

Hammer didn't care. She didn't even notice her surroundings, messy or not. She sat in a straight-back chair while West and Brazil sat across from her on the couch.

"Virginia, Andy," she began, "I'm going to resign."

"Oh God," West said, shocked.

"You can't," Brazil said, sick.

"Basically," Hammer went on, "I've pretty much screwed up everything here. I used to be a good police officer, a good chief. Every-body hates us."

"Not *everybody*," Brazil said.

"Most of them," said West. "I mean, let's be honest about it."

"Well, I guess the Charlotte connection doesn't help," Brazil supposed.

"Or our locking up the COMSTAT network pretty much around the globe," Hammer said.

"Or our failure to crack the ATM cases be-fore they progressed to a horrible murder. Or a communications officer getting in a fight with a traffic cop, both of whom had just re-ceived commendations several days before." West helped her out with the list.

Hammer folded her hands in her lap and kept them still. She did not interrupt. She did not get up and pace.

"Judy," West said. "Where are you going to go? Back to Charlotte?"

Hammer shook her head.

"Nowhere," she answered. "If I can't han-dle Richmond, I'm not going to be able to handle someplace else. When the horse dies, get off. I'm retiring from police work. I don't know where I'll live. It doesn't matter."

"That reminds me," West said. "We need to talk about the Azalea Parade."

"How did what she just said remind you of that?" Brazil asked.

"The horse comment. We've got mounted cops in the parade," West said. "And"— she looked at Hammer—"Andy and I are supposed to ride in your convertible."

"What kind of convertible is it?" Hammer looked distracted.

"Dark blue Sebring," Brazil said. "Modest, not showy, although one of the big guys at Philip Morris wanted to drive you in his red Mercedes V12 convertible."

"Not a good idea," Hammer muttered.

"I don't think you should be in the parade at all," West said with conviction. "The parade could be a possible target for Smoke. And I hate for you to be riding slow in a convertible anyway. There're a lot of kooks out there."

Hammer got up. She really didn't care what happened to her.

"It's important," she dully said. "Every little thing we do to reach the community is helpful. I won't back out of a promise."

"Well, we're going to have fifty off-duty cops there in addition to the regular shifts,"

West told her. "To the public, it will appear we're there mainly for traffic control. And we're mobilizing about twenty plainclothes guys to mingle, just in case Smoke shows up or someone else decides to cause a problem."

Bubba was thinking the same thing. He believed Chief Hammer should not be riding in an open car in the Azalea Parade, and worse, it had been in the newspaper so everybody knew it. It was pos-sible this was where all roads met. Bubba had been called to save her from a terrible danger. Bubba also figured the Pikes somehow factored in.

At eight o'clock this morning, he was already parking in front of Green Top Sporting Goods on U.S. Route 1, some twenty minutes outside of Richmond. There was no place Bubba would rather be. The minute he walked through the door and was greeted by thousands of fishing rods and all that went with them, his pulse quickened. When he turned to the right and saw hundreds of rifles, shotguns, pistols and revolvers, he got flushed. He felt lust in a way he had never experienced with Honey.

"Hey, what'cha know." He was enthusiastically greeted by Fig Winnick, the assistant manager.

By Virginia law, a citizen could buy one handgun every thirty days and no more. This had given rise to the tongue-in-cheek Gun-of-the-Month Club. It was a small but clever group of one hundred and eighty-nine men and sixty-two women who sent each other reminders when their thirty days, loosely interpreted as a month, were up. It was April 2.

"If only I'd come in two days ago, I could have bought a gun then and another one today," Bubba misinterpreted, as usual.

"Wishful thinking," Winnick told him again. "Doesn't work that way, Bubba. And it sure as hell is too damn bad."

"So you're saying it's not once a month," Bubba challenged what he refused to believe.

"Not literally. But sort of. If you start with the first day of each month."

"You know, someone stole all my guns." Bubba browsed.

"The guys were talking about it," Winnick sympathized.

"So all I got left's the Anaconda and I

need something I can pack easier," Bubba spoke the language.

"I got just the thing."

Winnick lovingly opened a showcase and gently pulled out a Browning 40 S&W Hi-Power Mark III pistol. He handed the beauty to Bubba.

"Oh God," Bubba muttered as he fondled the silver chrome pistol. "Oh, oh, oh."

"Molded polyamide grips with thumb rest," Winnick said. "Weighs thirty-five ounces, four and three-quarters barrel. Feels great to the hand, huh?"

"Boy. No kidding."

Bubba pulled back the slide and snapped it forward. There was just no better sound than that.

"Low profile front sight blade, drift-adjustable rear sight," Winnick went on. "Ambidextrous safety, ten-round magazine."

"Imported from Belgium." Bubba wasn't going to be fooled. "The genuine thing."

"Nothing but."

"What about a matte blue finish?" Bubba inquired. "It doesn't show up as much."

"Sorry," Winnick apologized. "Damn. If only you had come in yesterday. We had about eleven left."

"Well, I guess this one will have to do," Bubba said.

Patty Passman also was thinking ahead. She hadn't missed an Azalea Parade in twelve years and she didn't intend to miss this one. Although Rhoad had unfairly charged her with many things, it was only *assault on a police officer* that had stuck. She wished bail bondsman Willy "Lucky" Loving would show up to get her the hell out of here.

Lockup was just a holding area and inmates wore their own clothes, giving up only their belts to make it trickier to commit suicide. Passman was sticky, her panty hose so torn up she'd had no choice but to take them off right in front of her cellmate, Tinky Meaney, a truck driver for Dixie Motorfreight, who had gotten picked up for getting into a scuffle in the parking lot of the Power Clean Grill on Hull Street. Passman didn't know the details, but of one thing she was certain, Tinky Meaney wasn't on the list of those Passman might have invited to a slumber party.

"I sure wish he'd hurry up," Passman said from her narrow steel pull-down bed.

She said this often to make certain Meaney didn't think that Passman enjoyed Meaney's company and was in no hurry to leave it. Meaney was a big woman. She was the sort who always said they weren't fat, just big-boned and solid. This was nonsense.

Meaney's thighs were thicker than the biggest Smithfield hams Passman had ever seen, and every time Meaney stalked about the tiny cell, her jeans swished as her upper legs rubbed together. Her hands were thick with stubby fingers and big knuckles that were scraped and bruised from the fistfight that had landed her here. She had no neck. As she sat on the edge of her bed staring at Passman, Meaney's breasts sagged over her empty belt loops. Unshaved pale legs showed between the hem of her jeans and the top of her hand-tooled black and red cowboy boots.

"What the hell are you staring at?" Meaney caught Passman looking.

"Nothing," Passman lied.

Meaney stretched out on her side and propped up on an elbow, chin in hand. She stared without blinking, a look in her tiny dark eyes that Passman recognized instantly. At the same time Passman realized in amazement that Meaney's breasts were even bigger than Passman had thought. One was hanging over the side of the bed, almost touching the floor, and brought to mind a sandbag. Passman realized Meaney wasn't wearing a bra under her Motor Mile Towing & Flatbed Service sweatshirt.

Passman was painfully reminded of yet one more lousy card she'd been dealt in life. No matter how much weight she had put on over the years, her breasts were elusive. Their fat cells dodged any opportunity for growth and development and always had. She suspected that when, as a young girl, she had tried to be a boy, that part of the programming never got deleted when she later returned to her proper gender.

It was unbearably humiliating in eighth-grade health class to watch the films on menstruation, the female outline on the screen developing right before Passman's eyes, the breasts rounding, the pear-shaped muscular uterus discharging its menses in little hatch-marks flowing through the mature female outline, then out of it, on the screen.

All the other girls could relate. Passman

could not. She could have gotten by in life without a bra, had she been honest about it. Her periods were more like commas, brief pauses each month that exacerbated her hypoglycemia and made her very cranky.

Passman was still staring, lost in tortured memories of puberty. Meaney smiled like a jack-o'-lantern and stretched provocatively. Passman came to. She quickly averted her gaze.

"I sure wish he'd hurry up," Passman said again, this time with more emphasis.

"It ain't so bad in here," Meaney said in her twangy drawl. "I recognize your voice. Hear you all the time when I'm in the vincinity, riding through. Channels one, two and three, know 'em by heart. Four-sixty point one hundred megs, 460.200, 460.325. I always thought you had a nice voice."

"Thank you," Passman said.

"So, what'd you do?"

Passman thought it wise to send out a warning.

"Beat the shit out of some guy," she answered. "I lost control and should've held back a little more than I did. Huge son of a bitch. Had it coming."

Meaney nodded. "Mine had it coming, too,

fucking son of a bitch. I'm sitting in the bar minding my own business, you know, after a long day on the road, I mean long. He comes over to my table, this big ole trashy fucker in a cowboy hat. I recognized him." She nodded. "And he recognized me." She nodded again. "He was in his personal car this night. Nineteen ninety-two Chevy Dually, lowered, loaded, four-fifty-four, aluminum wheels, tinted windows, air ride, all the hitches.

"It was in the lot and he asked if I liked it. I said I did. He asked what I drove. I told him a Mack. He asked if I'd ever drove a Peterbilt. I said I'd driven all there was. He asked if I'd ever had a blowout in a Peterbilt. I said I hadn't. He asked if I wanted to. I said, *Why would I?* And he yanked down his zipper, so I threw him up against his Chevy Dually.

"Then I musta really gone at him because he looked like hamburger, a bunch of broke bones, teeth everywhere but in his mouth, most of his hair yanked out, ear tore off. What I hate about someone pissing me off like that is later on I can't remember a thing. I guess I must have a spell of some sort, like an epilepick."

"I'm the same way," Passman said.

"So, you live around here?"

"We're over near Regency Mall."

"Who's *we?*" Meaney's eyes got smaller and darker.

"Me and my boyfriend." Passman lied out of self-defense.

"I had one once," Meaney reminisced. "Then I was in lockup one day. I forget what for. And there was another girl in there with me." Meaney nodded and lay on her back, hands behind her head, body spilling everywhere.

Passman was beginning to panic. She was going to kill the bondsman Lucky Loving if he didn't hurry up. She didn't want to encourage Meaney, not in the least, but she had to know the rest of the story. She needed to get as much information as she could. Forewarned is forearmed, her mother always used to say.

"What happened?" Passman asked after a long, intense silence.

"The things we did. Ha!" Meaney grinned, enjoying the memory. "Let me tell you something, honey. There ain't a thing a man's got that you can't find under your own hood, if you know what I mean."

chapter thirty-four

The Oliver Hill Courts Building was modern and full of light and Ayokunle Odeleye mahogany carvings. Brazil had never seen a court building that looked less like one, and it made him feel a little more optimistic when he walked in, Weed's case file under his arm. It was five minutes before nine, and unlike other juvenile systems, this one had an exact time schedule docket.

If the arraignment was at nine, it would begin at nine, and that's exactly what time it was when the intercom announced, "Weed Gardener, report to courtroom number two, please."

Judge Maggie Davis was already on the bench, formidable and distinguished in her black robe. She was young to be a judge, and when the General Assembly had appointed her, she had charged in and made changes. Although she protected the confidentiality of juveniles who committed lesser crimes, she did not coddle or shield violent offenders.

"Good morning, Officer Brazil," Judge Davis said as Brazil seated himself on the first row and the clerk handed the judge Weed's file.

"Good morning, Your Honor," said Brazil.

A deputy escorted Weed in from the back and positioned him in front of the judge, where he seemed even smaller in his ill-fitting blue jumpsuit and detention-issue black Spalding hightops. But Weed held his head up. He didn't seem dejected or ashamed and in fact seemed to be looking forward to the arraignment, unlike Commonwealth's Attorney Jay Michael or Sue Cheddar, the public defender on his heels, or Mrs. Gardener, who was at the door explaining to a deputy who she was.

". . . yes, yes, my son," Brazil heard Mrs. Gardener say.

"Mrs. Gardener?" Judge Davis inquired.

"Yes," Mrs. Gardener whispered.

Weed's mother had put on a crisp blue dress and matching shoes, but her face belied her neat facade. Her eyes were puffy and exhausted, as if she had been crying all night. Her hands shook. She had burst into tears and called herself a failure as a mother when Brazil had finally gotten her on the phone to tell her about Weed. She had told Brazil that she'd quit feeling or facing anything after Twister died.

"You can come up here," the judge kindly said to Mrs. Gardener.

Mrs. Gardener came to the front of the courtroom and quietly sat in a corner of the first row, as far from Brazil as she could get. Weed did not turn around.

"Are you expecting any other family?" the judge asked Mrs. Gardener.

"No ma'am," she barely said.

"All right," Judge Davis said to Weed, "I'm going to tell you your rights."

"Okay," he said.

"You have the right to counsel, to a public hearing, to the privilege against self-incrimi-

nation, to confront and cross-examine witnesses, to present evidence, and the right to
appeal a final decision of the court."

"Thank you," Weed said.

"Do you understand them?"

"No."

"What this means, Weed, is you have a
right to an attorney and you don't have to
say anything this morning that might incrimi-
nate you. Those other rights don't apply unless you go to trial. Does that make sense,
do you understand?"

"What does incriminalate mean?"

"For example, saying something that will
be used against you."

"How do I know what that is?" Weed
asked.

"I'll stop you if you start doing it, how's
that?"

"What if you don't stop me quick enough?"

"I will, don't worry."

"You promise?"

"Yes," Judge Davis answered. "Now." She
looked at Weed. "The purpose of this arraignment is to determine whether I should
keep you locked up in detention before your
trial date or let you go."

"I wanna stay locked up," Weed said.

"We'll talk about that as we proceed," said the judge.

She looked at the petition Brazil had signed.

"Weed, you've been charged with 18.2-125 of the Virginia code, *Trespass at night upon any cemetery*, and 18.2-127, *Injuries to churches, church property, cemeteries, burial grounds, etc.*, and 182.2-138.1, *Willful and malicious damage to or defacement of public or private facilities.*" She leaned forward. "Do you understand the seriousness of these charges?"

"I only know what I did or didn't do," Weed said.

"Do you believe you're guilty or not guilty?"

"Depends on what happens if I say one or another," Weed said.

"Weed, it doesn't work that way."

"I just wanna have my say."

"Then plead not guilty and you can have your say at the trial," she told him.

"When's that?"

"We'd have to set a date."

"Could we do it tomorrow?"

"Twenty-one days from now."

Weed looked crushed.

"But the Azalea Parade's Saturday," he explained. "Can't I have my say now so I can march in it and play the cymbals?"

Judge Davis seemed to find this juvenile a little more interesting than most. Commonwealth's Attorney Michael was befuddled. Public Defender Cheddar had a blank expression on her face.

"If you want to have your say, Weed, then plead not guilty." The judge tried to make him get the drift.

"Not unless I get to be in the parade," he stubbornly told her.

"If you don't plead not guilty, the alternative is guilty. Do you understand what a guilty plea means?" Judge Davis asked with surprising patience.

"Means I done it."

"It means I have to sentence you, Weed. Maybe I'll put you on probation, maybe I won't. You may lose your freedom, go back to detention, in other words, and if that's the case, there's absolutely no chance of your being in any parade anytime soon."

"You sure?" Weed asked.

"Sure as I'm sitting here."

"Not guilty," he said, "even if I am."

Judge Davis looked at Mrs. Gardener. "Do you have an attorney?"

"No, ma'am," Mrs. Gardener replied.

"Can you afford to hire one?"

"How much would it cost?"

"It could be expensive," said the judge.

"I don't want an attorney," Weed piped up.

"I'm not talking to you," the judge warned.

"Don't hire one, Mama!" he said.

"Weed!" the judge sternly said.

"I'm gonna defend myself." Weed wouldn't stop.

"No, you're not," Judge Davis replied.

She appointed Sue Cheddar to defend Weed, and Cheddar moved to Weed's side and smiled at him. She wore a lot of makeup, her mascara so thick it reminded Weed of asphalt right after they put it down. Little gold stars had been painted on red nails so long her fingers never touched anything first. Weed wasn't impressed.

"I don't want her," he said. "I don't need nobody to talk for me."

"I've decided you do," said the judge. "Mr. Michael, please present evidence to the state for continued custody," she said to the commonwealth's attorney, who looked over at Brazil and passed the baton.

"Your Honor, I think the arresting officer is better able to do that at this time," Michael said. "I haven't really looked at anything yet."

Weed didn't like the way Sue Cheddar was handling things. Every time he tried to say what was what, Cheddar told him to hush. He didn't understand how the truth ever got out if people weren't allowed to tell it because they might get in trouble when they ought to be in trouble anyway.

After a while, when Brazil was leading up to the crime, Weed got tired of Cheddar basically telling him to shut up. He was insulted and indignant. She didn't seem to object to anything except Weed, and she was supposed to be on his side. So he took over. He decided that if Officer Brazil was going to tell Weed's story, Weed would object for himself all he wanted, even if he agreed with Brazil.

"About two o'clock Tuesday morning, Weed climbed over the Hollywood Cemetery fence, trespassing on private property," Brazil was standing before the judge and summarizing.

"We didn't even get there until after three," Weed corrected him again.

"That's immaterial," Judge Davis said as she had numerous times before.

"Shhhhh . . ." Cheddar hissed.

"Apparently he was with a gang and was coerced . . ." Brazil went on.

"No, I wasn't," Weed objected. "I was just with Smoke and Divinity. Dog, Sick and Beeper wasn't there."

"Immaterial," said the judge.

"Point is," Brazil went on, "Weed carried paints into the cemetery with the intention of defacing Jefferson Davis's statue."

"I didn't know who it was," Weed cut in. "And I didn't de-face him. He still has a face. You go look."

"Your Honor." Public Defender Cheddar's voice was tight and high. "I don't think my client understands the bit about self-incrimination."

"He said he did," Judge Davis replied.

"Yeah," Weed told Cheddar.

"Please continue, Officer Brazil," said the judge.

"Weed painted a Spiders basketball uniform on the statue and at or around five A.M.

left the cemetery by climbing over the fence again."

"It wasn't that early," Weed protested. "I know, 'cause the sun was starting to show up and that always happens after six 'cause that's when I get up, too, 'cause I gotta make my own toast and jelly before I go to school 'cause my mama works too late to get outta bed that early."

Mrs. Gardener bent her head. She hid her face, wiping tears.

"Immaterial," said Judge Davis.

"And besides," Weed declared, "it's just poster paint. You go look. A hose will get it off, but they been so busy studying what to do about it they never even wet their finger and touched it to see if it would stick. First rain's gonna ruin it," he concluded with a trace of disappointment.

No one spoke for a moment.

Papers shuffled.

The C.A. was staring off, not present.

Brazil was amazed.

It took several synapses before Cheddar got it.

"Then it's not really defaced," Cheddar announced as if her voice was a gavel.

"How do you know?" Weed objected to his attorney. "Anybody looked at it today?"

Nobody had.

"Then don't be telling . . ." he started to say before Cheddar clamped her hand over his mouth.

"How many times I gotta tell you to keep your mouth shut so I can do my job!" Cheddar exclaimed.

Weed bit her.

"Lord in heaven!" Cheddar exclaimed. "He bit me!"

"Not hard," Weed said. "But she started it. What if she cut me with those nails? You seen them things up close?" He rubbed his mouth with his sleeve.

"Order!" Judge Davis declared.

"What if I clean up the statue?" Weed said. "If you want me to, I will." It was a big sacrifice for Weed to make, but he knew Twister's monument couldn't last forever. "All I want is to be locked up except for Saturday when the Azalea Parade is."

"We're not there yet, Weed," Judge Davis firmly told him. "I can't decide anything until I've heard the evidence. And please refrain from biting your counsel again."

"What if I promise to fix the police computer? Would you let me play my cymbals in the parade?" Weed went on.

"He's referring to what the press has been calling 'Fishsteria,' " Brazil told her.

Cheddar was visibly alarmed. "He has that?" she asked, her face stricken.

"He caused it," Brazil said.

"Your Honor, may I approach the bench?" Cheddar panicked.

She lunged forward and grabbed the edge of the bench, standing on her tiptoes, leaning as close to the judge as she could.

"Your Honor," she whispered excitedly, but everyone could hear. "If what's being said here is my client's the one spreading that fish sickness, then I need to know if others are in danger of catching it!"

Cheddar shot Weed a menacing look.

"Others meaning me," Cheddar went on. "He bit my hand, Your Honor."

"I don't think we're talking about that sort of disease," Judge Davis told her with a glint of irritation.

"Your Honor," Cheddar said in a more demanding tone, her nails flashing as she gestured. "How do I know for an absolute true fact that he doesn't have some sort of bug of some type that all of us should be concerned about! Especially me because his teeth made contact with my skin!"

She held up her hand like the Statue of Liberty.

"Doesn't look like he broke the skin," the judge observed.

"Then you're saying you're not going to send him to mental health or someplace where they can do tests?" Cheddar's voice rose to a shriek.

"That's what I'm saying," Judge Davis said.

"Then I quit!" Cheddar threw her hands up, red and gold flashing.

"No you don't 'cause I fired you first!" Weed called out as Cheddar grabbed her falling-apart briefcase, papers spilling, and rushed out of the courtroom.

"Your Honor," Brazil spoke up. "The truth is, we really need our COMSTAT telecommunications system up and running again." He was out of line, but didn't care. "The network's down all over the world because of the fish thing."

"Officer Brazil, that is irrelevant to this case."

"Of course," Brazil mumbled a deliberate

challenge to Weed, "he probably couldn't fix it anyway."

"Can too," Weed said.

"Oh yeah?" Brazil taunted. "Then how?"

"Just take out the program I did when I punted and messed up the HTML interpreter in AOL."

Judge Davis couldn't help herself because like all else in the world, she used AOL and lived in fear of color bombs, IM bombs, HTML Freeze/Lag, HTMO errors, a combination of the above, or possibly the less innocuous but more annoying Blank IM bombs.

"What's *punting?*" she asked Weed.

"The bug's in autowrap in the text handler," he informed her as if his explanation was as obvious as colors. "See, if you use VBMSG subclassing, you know? To hold the window open and do some other things I told it to do, you know? 'Cause, see, like I said, there's this bug. So I told it to put my map on there and hold it. And the Anti-Punt program won't work, either, because I made my program hit Reply on the IM."

Amazement stilled the room. Brazil was writing everything down. The C.A.'s mouth was open in disbelief.

"But I never meant for my fish screen to go everywhere," Weed added. "Someone must've stuck all these addresses together, and it ain't me who did."

"Does anybody understand what he just said?" the judge asked.

"I sort of do," Brazil said. "And he's right about the addresses."

"It won't take me but a minute to show him how to fix it, then you can lock me up," Weed said. "And I can do the parade and get locked up again."

He looked up at her, fear shining in his eyes. He could tell Judge Davis understood something bad would happen if she let him go home. He turned around and looked at his mother.

"It's okay, Mama," he said. "It ain't got nothing to do with you."

Tears filled her eyes, and his got a little swimmy, too.

The C.A., whose job it was to punish to the fullest extent of the law, finally argued the case.

"The release of him is an unreasonable danger to the property of others." He quoted the code. "I think there is clear and convincing evidence *not* to release him."

The judge leaned forward and looked at Weed. She had made up her mind. Weed's heart jumped.

"I find there is probable cause for the state," the judge let everybody know, "and an adjudicatory hearing will be held twenty-one days from today. The state may summon witnesses, and the juvenile will remain in detention. But I order that the juvenile be released into the custody of Officer Brazil this Saturday." She looked at Weed. "What time is the parade?"

"Ten-thirty," Weed said. "But I gotta be there earlier than that."

"When does it end?"

"Eleven-thirty," Weed said. "But I gotta stay longer than that."

"Nine A.M. to one P.M.," the judge said to Brazil. "Then back in detention pending the court date."

chapter thirty-five

The morning of the Azalea Parade Weed's soul was as light as light itself. He wished he could paint the way he felt and the way the morning looked as Officer Brazil drove him to George Wythe High School, where the Godwin marching band was waiting and warming up.

Weed was proud and sweating in his polyester and wool blend red-and-white uniform with its many silver buttons and its stripes down the legs. His rolled-heel black shoes looked like new, the Sabian cymbals polished and safely in their black case in the back seat.

"Too bad you haven't had more time to practice," Brazil said.

Weed knew that out of the 152 members of the band, he was probably the only one who had missed a week of practice. He hadn't had a chance to look at his drill charts or work on forward march, pull mark time, pull halt, high mark, backward march, his favorite freeze-spin and especially the crab step, which was unique to the percussion section of Godwin's finely tuned precision marching band.

"I'll be all right," Weed said, staring out the window, his heart thrilled.

Already crowds were gathering. It was predicted this might be the biggest turnout in the history of the parade. The weather was perfect, in the seventies, a light breeze, not a cloud. People were spreading out blankets, setting up lawn chairs, parking strollers and wheelchairs, and those who lived along the parade route had decided it was a good day for a yard sale. Cops were everywhere in reflective vests and Weed had never seen so many traffic cones.

* * *

Brazil was worried. Thousands of people were gathering and those participating in the parade filled the George Wythe High School parking lot. If Smoke had a plan, Brazil didn't see how it was possible to pluck one teenager out of such congestion, especially if no one, except Weed, seemed to know what Smoke really looked like.

"Weed, I want you to make a promise, okay?" Brazil said as Weed collected his cymbal case from the car. "You'd recognize Smoke or any of his gang."

"So."

Weed was in a hurry, anxiously staring off at his marching band, which from this vantage was a patch of bright red and white somewhat lost in a swarm of colorful uniforms and flashing instruments and swords and twinkling batons and twirling flags. Floats hovered restlessly in an endless line. Masons were dressed like clowns. Mounted police were letting kids pet the horses. Antique cars rattled.

"We're better than that," Weed said, watching the Navy League Cadet Corps practice marching. "Look at that bus! That band came all the way from Chicago! And there's one from New York!"

"Weed, did you hear what I said?" Brazil asked out his open window.

Sergeant Santa worked the crowd. One of the Florettes lost track of her baton and it bounced several times on the road. People dressed for the Old West were showing off miniature horses that had azalea blossoms in their manes. The Independence Wheelchair Athletic Association was ready to go. Weed was dazzled.

"Weed!" Brazil was about to get out of the car.

"Don't you worry, Officer Brazil," Weed said. "I'll let you know."

"How?" Brazil wasn't going to take any bullshit.

"I'll do a real long crash and flash my cymbals good when I'm not supposed to," Weed said.

"No way, Weed. How am I going to notice that with everything else going on?" Brazil countered.

Weed thought. His face got tense, his shoulders slumped and he looked heart-broken when he said, "Then I'll cut one loose. You can't miss that. Course you'll have to explain later why I did or I won't be playing cymbals in the band no more."

"Cut one loose?" Brazil was lost.

"Let go of the strap. You ever seen an eighteen-inch cymbal roll down the road?"

"No," Brazil confessed.

"Well, you see one," Weed told him, "then you know I'm telling you trouble's about to start."

Lelia Ehrhart was already having trouble. She was closely inspecting the Blue Ribbon Crime Commission's red Cadillac convertible, with its streamers of blue ribbons that would float and flutter beautifully once the car was rolling along the parade route. She realized with horror that there wasn't a single azalea blossom, not even one.

"We must carry on to the theme and message of the parade," she told Commissioner Ed Blackstone.

"I thought the blue ribbons did that," replied Blackstone, who was eighty-two but maintained that age didn't matter. "I thought it was called the Azalea Parade because of azaleas, which are everywhere, and it wasn't expected that we fill the car with them, especially since we don't have many seats anyway."

Ehrhart could not be persuaded, and she directed that the white leather front passenger's side and most of the back were to be lush and dense with pink and white azalea bushes. This reduced the number of waving and smiling commissioners from three to one.

"I guess I'll have to ride alone by myself," Ehrhart said.

"Well, I'm going to tell you something, Lelia," said Blackstone as he leaned against his walker, straining to see through the huge glasses he'd been wearing since his last cataract surgery. "You're going to have bees. That many blossoms, and bees will show up, mark my words. And don't say I didn't warn you about making those streamers so long. Twenty feet." Blackstone was severe on this point. "Anybody gets close to your rear with all those streamers of blue ribbons endlessly flying, something's going to get tangled up."

"Where's Jed?" Ehrhart frowned.

"Over there." Blackstone pointed at a tree.

Ehrhart searched the masses and spotted Jed hanging around an antique fire truck, talking to Muskrat, who had fixed her car a time or two. She didn't like to be reminded that

Governor Feuer had declined to participate in the parade, even after Ehrhart had offered to ride with him. At least he had volunteered Jed to drive the commission's car, which was on loan from one of Bull Ehrhart's patients.

"Tell to him it's times to come now," Lelia Ehrhart ordered Blackstone.

Blackstone motioned at the tree to hurry along.

Neither Brazil nor West liked crowds, but Chief Hammer refused to bask in the limelight alone, especially since she hated parades and other public celebrations more than West and Brazil did.

"I can't believe you're doing this," West complained from the backseat of the dark blue Sebring. "You got this psycho kid out there waiting to make himself a legend by doing something really, really bad, and what do you decide?" She slid into the driver's seat and began adjusting mirrors. "You decide to ride in an open convertible."

"I don't like it, either," said Brazil as he climbed in back, next to Hammer. "You sure you don't want me to drive?" he asked West.

"Forget it," she replied.

Brazil got out paperwork.

"We need to find the Mustang Club," he said, "because we're in front of them. And"—he traced his finger down a list—"right behind Miss Richmond."

"Yuck," West said.

Pigeon and a fat man were within two feet of each other at Westover Hills and Bassett, across from Brentwood South.

The fat man seemed ready for action as he clandestinely searched the crowd through a pair of Leica binoculars. Pigeon was rooting for half a hot dog with mustard and relish that a little kid had just tossed into a trash can, as if hot dogs grew on trees.

Pigeon never missed the Azalea Parade. People were so wasteful. Not one kid this day and age knew the value of a dollar, not even those folks on food stamps. He fished out an almost entire bag of potato chips that some little brat couldn't toss without violently squeezing, crushing and pulverizing first.

"What we need is another good war," he said to the fat man, although they were not acquainted.

"I've been saying that for years." The fat

man couldn't have agreed more. "No one understands what it's like."

"How could they?" Pigeon said, peering inside the bag, unable to find a chip bigger than a dime.

"My name's Bubba," Bubba said as he continued his sweep with the binoculars.

"I'm Pigeon."

"Nice to meet you."

Pigeon homed in on another kid who dropped his bubble gum on the sidewalk after three chews, when there was still plenty of flavor left. A woman in jogging clothes stepped on it.

"Thanks a lot!" she called out to the kid as he popped open a can of Orange Crush and walked off.

She lifted her foot and stared at strings of pink gum leading to a blob fixed to the tread of her right Saucony running shoe.

"I hate you!" she screamed at the kid as people walked around her, looking for a spot with a decent view. "I hate all children! I hate people!"

"That would piss me off, too," Pigeon said. "Nobody cares anymore."

* * *

Bubba focused on Smudge and his wife opening lawn chairs in a yard no more than fifty feet to Bubba's right.

"He probably doesn't even know those people," Bubba mumbled with fresh fury. "Just helps himself like he does with everything in life."

"All the world's like that now," Pigeon said.

"He knows I'm here, too," Bubba said. "The son of a bitch knows he owes me a thousand dollars. Says he has amnesia, doesn't remember the bet, so it doesn't count."

"I don't know what happened to honesty," Pigeon said.

Bubba watched Smudge open a checkered tablecloth and spread it out in the grass. He set down a blue ice chest, opened the lid and rummaged.

Pigeon searched in vain for a cigarette butt. He could tell the price had shot way up. People were smoking closer to the filter, leaving nothing for him.

He was shocked yesterday morning when he was picking his way along Main Street, downtown, and observed on the Dow Jones electronic message board outside Scott & Stringfellow brokers that the price per pack had increased another two dollars and eleven cents. If only Pigeon had bought more when he had the money from the pawn shop. He could have done some quick trading. He'd probably be rich.

Even as Pigeon was thinking that, Bubba reached into his shirt pocket for a pack. He shook out a cigarette without lowering the binoculars.

"Those Merit Ultimas any good?" Pigeon asked as Bubba lit up. "That's one I haven't tried yet."

"Oh yeah," Bubba said. "Anything Philip Morris makes is the best."

"I've always thought so. How are those different from regular Merits?" Pigeon slyly asked.

"Want to try one?"

"That would be nice," Pigeon said as Bubba passed him the pack. "Why, thank you very much."

Wailing police sirens and the thunder of cops on motorcycles sounded in the distance, signaling that the parade was starting. Weed was so excited his knees were shaking.

He was positioned to the right of Lou Jameson on the snare drum, who was wearing sunglasses like all the drummers did. He had never been very friendly to Weed and more than once had commented that anybody could play cymbals and he'd seen girls doing it in other bands.

Western Guilford High School in white and black was directly in front of Godwin. Lakeview Junior High in gold and green was to the rear. Bright, brave uniforms of all colors and designs must have stretched for a mile, Weed calculated. The parade was starting to move. The lead band out of New Jersey exploded into "God Bless America," which wasn't very original and the trumpets were a little off.

Weed stood tall and proud. He did a few toe lifts to loosen up.

"Left foot out and point flex and point flex and really stretch it," he recited.

Jameson looked at him with disdain.

"Left heel two inches off ground while ball and toe remain touching the ground." Weed practiced a *low mark time* with a quick, snappy motion. "Ankle touches knee on end of each beat, toe pointed straight down the leg, feet flat." He executed a perfect *high mark.* "Push down on beat on left foot, then *mark time.*"

"Hey, cut it out," Jameson said.

"No," Weed retorted.

He used to be intimidated by Jameson. But after being arrested, getting locked up in detention, mouthing off to a defense attorney and striking a deal with a judge, Weed wasn't scared of anyone.

"Three, four, halt. To left, right, foot crosses over, mark time hut, and one, two, three, four, weight on toes." His crab step was flawless.

"I told you to fucking cut it out," Jameson whispered.

"Make me."

"I'll beat your ass."

"Hope you beat it better than you do that drum," Weed said.

"TO THE READY!" the drum major shouted from the front.

Weed came to attention. One thing about his cymbals, they sure got heavy.

"BAND, TEN-HUT!"

He strained to see what the color guard was doing way ahead. When the woodwinds started forward marching, he knew he was next.

There was nothing random about Smoke's decision to steal the black nylon Stanley tool belt when he broke into Bubba's workshop. Its extra deep pockets were perfect and he had known it at the time, because Smoke had been planning for a while.

He was dressed in worn-out, soiled jeans, a filthy tee shirt and dirty scuffed Red Wing boots. A paint-spattered baseball cap was low over his eyes. He wore Oakleys and hadn't shaved in days. No one paid any attention to him as he walked across yards, trying to see the parade like everybody else.

Smoke had conducted a thorough surveillance in the George Wythe parking lot while the parade was lining up. He knew where everyone was. He had spotted Weed. Smoke had walked right past the police chief and the two cops who had spoken in Godwin's auditorium. It was hilarious. Smoke's nerves were humming. He was pumping adrenaline and almost manic.

Concealed inside the pouches around his waist were the stolen Beretta and four ten-round clips and two fifteen-round clips and his Glock with three seventeen-round clips. That made a grand total of one hundred and twenty-one Winchester 115 grain Silvertip high-power cartridges.

He watched antique Jaguars and Chryslers cruise by, then the Corvette Club. People were waving and clapping, the weather great, everybody in a good mood. He spotted a sloping lawn that was a little higher above the street than those around it. Some jerk and a mousy woman were having a picnic on a red-checked tablecloth. Smoke had found the perfect spot. He walked right up to them, crossed his arms and looked out as the Veterans of Foreign Wars and the Red Cross rolled by.

Bubba recognized the Stanley tool belt immediately. Some construction guy was wearing it. The big black belt with its deep pouches was exactly like the one missing from Bubba's garage. Bubba focused the binoculars a little more, zooming in on the guy's face.

He looked about fifteen or sixteen, kind of puny and pale. The pouches were bulging

and looked heavy. He had the padded yellow belt pulled as tight as it would go, the
entire rig huge on him because it was an
extra-large and the kid couldn't weigh more
than a hundred and twenty pounds. Bubba
didn't see a single tool, no tape measure, no
nails, nothing in the hammer holder, not so
much as a handle protruding.

"That's my belt," Bubba said as his heart
picked up speed. "I know it is!"

Pigeon looked where Bubba was looking,
squinting as he smoked another Merit Ultima that Bubba had been pleased to give
him.

"How do you know?" Pigeon inquired.

"I see a little white mark on the quick-re-
lease belt buckle. It might be my initials. I
paint my initials in white on all my tools, on
everything, to make sure when Smudge bor-
rows something he can't turn around and
say it's his!"

"Who's Smudge?" Pigeon asked, tapping
an ash.

The last of some band in black and white
was marching by, playing "Take the 'A' Train."
The drum major of the Godwin band was
right behind it. Bubba stared through the
binoculars, blood rushing to his head, his

heart beating faster than a snare drum as he focused on the dark blue convertible carrying Hammer, West and Brazil. They were one band behind Godwin.

The guy wearing Bubba's tool belt seemed tense. His right hand was twitching. He seemed to be waiting for something or someone. He was searching the ranks of the Godwin band, then looking straight at Chief Hammer. Bubba was sure of it.

Godwin started in on the theme from *Titanic*. The construction guy looked left and right and slipped his right hand into a pouch and kept it there. Bubba's stolen guns flashed in his head. He ran out into the street as the woodwinds were going by. He wanted to pull out his new Browning but thought better of it.

"Stop him!" he yelled at the top of his lungs.

The fat man Smoke had met at Muskrat's Auto Rescue and soon after burglarized was pointing right at Smoke and yelling. Smoke was cool. He looked around and shrugged.

"What a wacko," he said to the man and woman picnicking next to him.

Cops were running out. One galloped up on a horse. They were trying to calm the fat man and get him out of the street. Smoke smiled. This was going to be better than he thought. He zoomed in on Weed. The little retard was crashing and flashing his cymbals, the dude to the left trying to outdo him on the snare drum. Smoke took his time. He didn't want to slip his hand into the pouch again until the fat man quit pointing at him.

"Somebody do something!" the fat man was screaming as two cops grabbed his arms. *"Get him, not me! The kid up there in the Stanley tool belt!"*

Pigeon was concerned. He walked out on the street as Bubba struggled with the cops and continued to yell.

"Look, he's with me," Pigeon told the cop on the horse.

"Stand back!" the cop yelled at Pigeon.

"It's his tool belt. You can see the white initials on the buckle. I mean with binoculars you can." Pigeon wasn't to be deterred. "The kid stole it."

Bubba's binoculars flew off. A pistol fell out of somewhere and clattered to the street. This seemed to upset the cops quite a lot. All of them snatched handcuffs and red pepper spray off their belts. The Godwin band quit playing and froze as some little kid suddenly broke out of formation and rolled his cymbal down the street. Pigeon realized it was Weed.

Chief Hammer had no idea what was going on. The parade halted as what sounded like a huge bronze hubcap rolled toward her car.

"What's happening?" Hammer asked, standing up in the back seat, trying to see.

West stopped the car.

"GET DOWN!" Brazil yelled as he pushed Hammer to the floor and band members jumped out of the way and the cymbal hit a little dip in the road and picked up speed, loudly flying past, scattering the Mason clowns, sending Sergeant Santa scurrying, almost running the mayor's car into the crowd. The Florettes dropped their batons.

Jed saw the cymbal coming before Lelia Ehrhart did, and he suddenly threw the red Cadillac into reverse. Azalea bushes jumped off the back seat, clay pots breaking, bees darting out of harm's way, dirt flying everywhere as streamers of blue ribbons changed direction and flew in Ehrhart's face.

The blond cop Jed had picked up in the cemetery the other day had just leaped out of Chief Hammer's car and was running like hell. Jed slammed on the brakes. A pink azalea bush sailed over the back of the front seat and Ehrhart shrieked. The cymbal went screaming past, flashing in the sun like a runaway gold chariot wheel.

Jed jumped out of the Cadillac without opening the door, neglecting to put the car in park. It began moving forward on its own as Ehrhart fought with streamers of blue ribbons, getting more entangled, and Patty Passman, nearby in the rioting crowd, threw down her Death by Chocolate ice cream cone and pushed people out of the way.

"MOVE, FUCKHEADS!" She shoved and punched, sugar-charged and unstoppable.

She chased the red Cadillac and hurled her fat body over the driver's door, landing with her feet in the air, grabbing the gear shift and jamming it into park.

* * *

Smoke was momentarily confused by the commotion. The plan in his head turned to page three and stopped. He looked around and backed up a little, almost slipping on the grass. At first it didn't register that the blond cop he had heard at school, and Weed and a street person were running toward him at top speed.

"EVERYBODY GET DOWN!" the blond cop was yelling.

The crowd started panicking. The cops lost interest in the fat man. They charged toward Smoke, too, the blond cop running the fastest.

"YOU SON OF A BITCH!" the fat man screamed at Smoke.

The picnicking couple dove out of the way as the fat man ran across their red-and-white-checkered tablecloth. Smoke panicked and pulled out the Beretta. In his confusion he forgot how to take the safety off.

People were thundering toward Smoke from all directions, with Weed in the lead, the plume on his black hat straight back as he ran at incredible speed. Smoke dropped the Beretta and groped for his Glock as Weed leaped five feet in the air and punched Smoke in the nose and grabbed his hair, knocking Smoke to the ground. They struggled over the Glock. Smoke let go of it when Weed bit his wrist hard.

"I'M GOING TO KILL YOU, YOU PIECE OF SHIT!" Weed kept yelling as he pummeled Smoke with his fists.

Brazil struggled to handcuff Smoke, who was rolling in the grass and yelling, clips of ammunition falling out of the stolen tool belt around his waist. At this point, community involvement was making matters worse.

Bubba was poised, taking jabs at Smoke whenever Weed left an opening. Pigeon was on the ground, trying to hold Smoke's ankles. Other cops were grabbing at Smoke and getting in Brazil's way. Unfortunately, one of them started squirting pepper spray. Then everyone was rolling on the ground, hands over their eyes, yelling in pain.

Smoke kicked straight up and caught one of the cops in the groin and grabbed the Sig Sauer pistol out of the other cop's holster. Smoke was bloody and breathing hard as he gripped the pistol in both shaking hands, his eyes watering and crazed with rage. He didn't see the two women cutting through the space between the two houses behind him.

* * *

Hammer and West had their pistols out and were moving in fast. It seemed Smoke was trying to figure out who to shoot. He wildly pointed the gun at a fat man Hammer recognized as Bubba. Then the gun was pointed at Brazil and the other cops on the ground, then out at the fleeing crowd and participants in the parade.

Hammer didn't have a clear shot because a street person and a little kid in a band uniform were in the way. Drifting pepper spray irritated Hammer's eyes and lungs. She and West split up as Smoke wheeled around, apparently hearing the sound of approaching feet. The barrel of his pistol seemed huge and unreal as he pointed it straight at Hammer's face. She couldn't shoot first. There were too many people in the way.

Hammer hadn't been in a good fight in a while but she hadn't forgotten her training. She hurled her pistol at Smoke as hard as she could, and it sailed and spun like a boomerang, and Smoke involuntarily raised his arms to ward it off, giving Hammer an opportunity to dive at his feet, knocking him down. They struggled over his gun.

"GIVE IT UP!" Hammer demanded.

He tried to point the gun into her ribs and she managed to get a good purchase on one of his thumbs. She bent it straight back, an old and reliable police trick. He howled in pain. She wrested the gun away from him and shoved it hard under his chin.

"MOVE I'LL BLOW YOUR MOTHER-FUCKING HEAD OFF!" she yelled at him.

Her finger was on the trigger. She wanted him to give her an excuse.

"You goddamn little bastard," she said in his face. *"That helpless old woman you murdered was my neighbor."*

Brazil had recovered enough to help West handcuff Smoke and haul him away. Bubba sat up, tears streaming down his cheeks. Pigeon was facedown, still covering his eyes. The sock had come off his stump. Weed was unsteady as he got to his feet. He looked at Chief Hammer with red, watering eyes. She was standing very still, a gun at her side, pointed at the grass.

"Thanks," Weed said to her. "I sure am glad you're here."

chapter thirty-six

That night it rained. Water spilled from the sky in waves that reminded Weed of pictures he had seen of oceans. Next, hail was bouncing off streets, the wind pushing so strong, Weed bet it could ring doorbells.

"Who is it?" he whispered in the dark, messing with the powers that be. "Come in," he talked to himself. "Oh 'cuse me, I guess I forgot how to unlock the door."

Tears filled his eyes, his attempts at being funny not amusing anyone else since no one else was there. Lightning flashed in his barred window and snapped and cracked like popping bubble wrap. Weed imagined a tornado and thought of Twister. Weed had heard he wasn't supposed to walk around with a golf club, play the cymbals or talk on the phone when lightning was flying everywhere, and here he was sitting on a stainless steel bed.

Oh well. Who cared if he was dead.

Somewhere in a different part of the detention home, in what was called a pod, Smoke was locked up, too. The thought of that made Weed feel little bugs all over his skin. He scratched and brushed himself off, his heart bouncing everywhere. He was having difficulty breathing and couldn't seem to get warm. He pulled the covers more tightly around him and thought of his steel bed again when lightning flamed like a big gun.

Chief Hammer hated lightning and usually stayed away from windows and objects that conducted electricity. But she couldn't sit still. She was pacing in her living room before windows and near lamps and iron fireplace tools and beneath the brass chandelier while Brazil and West restlessly sat on her couch, relentlessly replaying the day's events.

"I don't care what anyone says," Brazil repeated his biggest concern as the power went out. "Weed shouldn't be in the same facility Smoke's in. Different pods or not. Smoke's already proven how clever, how diabolical he is."

"Didn't prove it enough to stay out of lockup," West reminded them. "But I don't like the situation either."

"I'm going to tell you right now," Brazil went on. "If Smoke wants to do something, he will."

"Yes, yes, yes," Hammer said as she moved this way and that while Popeye snored from a wing chair and thunder boomed.

Brazil was worried to the point of taking drastic action, although he wasn't sure what that was. Apparently, Smoke hadn't wanted Divinity, Beeper, Dog and Sick running loose while he was locked up. He had told the police how to find every one of them, and now all of the Pikes were supposedly in different pods in detention, maybe one or two corridors away from where Weed was being held in his single room with its steel toilet and fold-down bed.

"We're going to need Weed to testify against all of them," Brazil went on.

"Don't care who's sleeping where," West added, "Weed could end up in recreation with Smoke or any of the guys. And Miss Divinity's a snake, too."

"Andy, Virginia, both of you are absolutely right." Hammer stopped pacing long enough to light several candles. "We need to get him out tonight."

This required an unusual, unorthodox plan, and Hammer had one. At quarter past eight, she called Judge Maggie Davis at home.

"I'm glad you're there," Hammer quickly said.

"Wouldn't want to be anywhere else on a night like this," said the judge. "I'm sorry I missed the parade. Good God. Way to go, Judy. Wish I'd been there to see you take out the little shit."

"I didn't do much." Hammer dismissed the compliment. "We've got to get Weed Gardener out of detention as soon as possible."

"I thought he wanted to be in detention."

"That was then," Hammer said. "Now

you've got Smoke and his gang in there. That's not good, Maggie. Not good at all."

The judge deliberated for a moment.

"What do you propose?" she finally asked the chief.

Hammer was well aware that what she was about to suggest could not happen. But most of what she had accomplished in life could not happen, according to those who stood around and watched.

"Can you get hold of the commonwealth's attorney and the public defender?" Hammer asked.

"Of course," Judge Davis replied.

"I'll make sure the gates are unlocked."

"What gates?" Judge Davis asked.

At nine o'clock, the six of them pulled up in four cars at the front iron gates of Hollywood Cemetery. Rain lashed ancient boxwoods and trees, and headstones and monuments were wet and eerie as headlights swept over them.

The chief, Brazil and West were in the lead car. Behind them was Judge Davis in her Volvo and Commonwealth's Attorney Michael in his Honda Accord. Trailing from a bit of a distance was an old Mercury Cougar carrying Sue Cheddar, who had quit and then been fired by Weed and was now ordered by Judge Davis to stay on the case.

"I sure as hell hope he was telling the truth," West said to Hammer and Brazil.

Wipers beat and the rain beat back. Hammer was driving very slowly, leaning over the steering wheel and squinting to read street signs.

"He was," Hammer said as if she knew Weed very well.

They splashed along Waterview Avenue, tree branches whipping and violently grabbing at them. Silhouettes of angels watched them pass. Dark tombs drew Hammer's imagination through windows of stained and leaded glass, and she remembered childhood fears. She was ten when her next-door neighbor, Mrs. Wheat, was buried in the Baptist church cemetery a block away, her gray granite headstone in plain view from the street. Every morning on Hammer's way to school, she would run past the cemetery as fast as she could because she had never liked Mrs. Wheat and was certain Mrs. Wheat knew it now that she was in heaven.

Hammer still hated cemeteries. She did

not like anything about them. She was afraid of their pungent smells and insect sounds and subtle mounds. She was afraid of death. She was afraid of what she felt about Seth's. She was afraid of being alone. She was afraid of failure. She was afraid of fear. All of her many fears took energy, and frankly, at this moment, she was fucking fed up.

"This is ridiculous," she said to West and Brazil. "I'm not going to quit, retire, do nothing, whatever."

"Well, if you do, I'm not hanging around here," West retorted.

"I'm history, too," Brazil let his boss know as they neared Davis Circle.

"Are they still behind us?" Hammer peered in the rearview mirror.

"You absolutely shouldn't quit, Chief Hammer," Brazil advised her. "Especially now. I think the more people pick on you, the more you should offend them with your presence."

"That's very astute." Hammer considered Brazil's words. "I rather like that thought."

Not everyone had praised Hammer for tackling Smoke and putting a gun to his head while yelling obscenities. The mayor told all TV networks in time for the six o'-clock news that the incident should never have happened to begin with and he had gone on to label Hammer's heroics a self-serving publicity stunt. Lelia Ehrhart told Q94 that Hammer was a "Jack Footed Thung" who didn't give a "hoo" about prevention. The city manager had called for a thorough investigation by internal affairs.

"Don't be discouraged by today." Brazil seemed to know what she was thinking. "Don't forget, Governor Feuer was impressed. He called to congratulate you. He ought to count more than the other ones do."

"Aren't we supposed to turn somewhere?" Hammer couldn't see a damn thing.

Brazil saw Jefferson Davis first.

"I'm melting! I'm melting!" Brazil mimicked the Wicked Witch in *The Wizard of Oz*.

"Well, I'll be damned," West said as the statue was fully exposed by Hammer's high beams.

She stopped her Crown Victoria and turned the police spotlight on the statue.

"Hot dog!" Brazil exclaimed. "Shit, I wish Weed could be here to see this."

"I don't know," Hammer thoughtfully said. "He'd probably be disappointed."

"Yeah." Brazil sadly reconsidered. "I guess you're right. Twister's moved on."

Jeff Davis was fast losing his newly acquired race and position on the University of Richmond Spiders basketball team. His face was streaked black, his red-and-white uniform in pools around his no-longer-Nike footwear and the orange-smeared marble base that supported him. The basketball he held in his left hand had turned back into a hat.

Car doors were opening and shutting, lights scattered with rain. Feet sloshed and sounded wetly over stone. Judge Davis was a native of New York. She walked up to the statue and looked it over carefully. She bent down and plucked a tiny Southern Cross out of the sod. She waved it from its slender stick as if trying to see how it worked or what the big fuss was all about.

"I think it's clear this isn't vandalism anymore," Hammer announced. "Nor was it ever. We just thought it was."

Sue Cheddar was under a bright pink parasol and only her long, animated nails were visible as she spoke.

"See," she said as red claws flashed at Commonwealth's Attorney Michael.

He was getting soaked and looked like a defeated Confederate soldier in his ill-fitting gray suit and skinny dark tie. His hair was plastered to his head, rain running down his tired face as he watched the president of the Confederacy lose his glory once more.

"Point is, Weed meant to do damage," Michael said with no conviction. "Goddamn, will this rain ever stop? You ought to see my yard. The road in front, too, since the city doesn't do a damn thing to maintain it. Water must be six inches deep."

"Do we have any further arguments?" Judge Davis faced all of them as rain turned back into hail and began to click and clatter.

"Not me," West said.

"Of course not," said Hammer.

"Nope," Brazil agreed with everyone.

"Then I rule that the charge against Weed Gardener be dismissed," Judge Davis decided as a marble woman with an open Bible and an angel looked on. "Officer Brazil." She nodded at him. "Let's get the paperwork. I want him released immediately."

"Right this minute," Hammer agreed. "Virginia, Andy? Straight to detention. We're taking Weed home."

Brazil cheered and put his arm around

West. Chief Hammer began to clap. West did, too. Cheddar joined in, although it wasn't possible for her hands to touch. Commonwealth's Attorney Michael shrugged. Paperwork was completed and the six of them returned to their cars. Jefferson Davis receded into the night as the small motorcade followed Waterview through rain that no longer seemed so harsh, past monuments that did not seem quite so sad.